PONY

ALSO BY R. J. PALACIO

Wonder
365 Days of Wonder
Auggie & Me
We're All Wonders
White Bird

R. J. PALACIO

ALFRED A. KNOPF NEW YORK

THIS IS A BORZOI BOOK PUBLISHED BY ALFRED A. KNOPF

This is a work of fiction. All incidents and dialogue, and all characters with the exception of some well-known historical and public figures, are products of the author's imagination and are not to be construed as real. Where real-life historical or public figures appear, the situations, incidents, and dialogues concerning those persons are fictional and are not intended to depict actual events or to change the fictional nature of the work. In all other respects, any resemblance to persons living or dead is entirely coincidental.

Jacket images (horse, scenery) used under license from Shutterstock.com
Jacket back panel image (boy) courtesy of the author
Jacket design by 1000Jars
Interior image (horse) used under license from Shutterstock.com
Interior image (moon) The Moon, 1857 copyright © by Getty Images
All other interior images courtesy of the author

 Published in the United States by Alfred A. Knopf, an imprint of Random House Children's Books, a division of Penguin Random House LLC, New York.

Knopf, Borzoi Books, and the colophon are registered trademarks of Penguin Random House LLC.

Visit us on the Web! rhcbooks.com

Educators and librarians, for a variety of teaching tools, visit us at RHTeachersLibrarians.com

Library of Congress Control Number: 2021941721
ISBN 978-0-553-50811-6 (trade) — ISBN 978-0-553-50812-3 (lib. bdg.) —
ISBN 978-0-553-50813-0 (ebook)

The text of this book is set in 12.25-point Atma Serif Offc Pro.
Interior design by R. J. Palacio

Printed in the United States of America
September 2021
10 9 8 7 6 5 4 3 2 1

First Edition

For my mother

PONY

Our natures can't be spoken . . .

—Margot Livesey
Eva Moves the Furniture

Fare thee well, I must be gone
And leave you for a while.
But wherever I go, I will return,
If I go ten thousand miles.

Ten thousand miles, my own true love,
Ten thousand miles or more.
And the rocks may melt and the seas may burn,
If I no more return.

Oh, come back, my own true love,
And stay a while with me.
For if I had a friend all on this earth,
You've been a friend to me.

—Anonymous
"Fare Thee Well"

ONE

I have left Ithaca to seek him.

—François Fénelon
The Adventures of Telemachus, 1699

From the *Boneville Courier,* April 27, 1858:

A country boy of ten living near Boneville was, recently, walking to his house in the vicinity of a large oak tree, when a violent storm arose. The boy took refuge beneath the tree scant moments before it was struck by lightning, sending the boy tumbling to the earth, as if lifeless, his clothes smoked to cinders. Fortune smiled upon the child that day, however, for his quick-witted father, having witnessed the event, was able to revive him by means of a fireplace bellows. The child remained unaltered by the experience afterward but for one peculiar souvenir—an image of the tree had become emblazoned upon his back! This "daguerreotype by lightning" is one of several documented in recent years, making it yet another wondrous curiosity of science.

1

IT WAS MY BOUT WITH LIGHTNING that inspired Pa to become immersed in the photographic sciences, which is how this all began.

Pa had always had a natural curiosity about photography, having come from Scotland, where such arts flourish. He dabbled in daguerreotypes for a short while after settling in Ohio, a region naturally full of salt springs (from which comes the agent bromine, an essential component of the developing process). But daguerreotypes were an expensive enterprise that turned very little profit, and Pa did not have the means to pursue it. *People haven't the money for delicate souvenirs,* he reasoned. Which is why he became a boot-maker. *People always have a need for boots,* he said. Pa's specialty was the calf-high Wellington in grain leather, to which he added a secret compartment in the heel for the storing of tobacco or a pocketknife. This convenience was greatly desired by customers, so we got by pretty well on those boot orders. Pa worked in the shed next to the barn, and once a month traveled to Boneville with a cartful of boots pulled by Mule, our mule.

But after lightning imprinted my back with the image of the oak tree, Pa once again turned his attention to the science of photography. It was his belief that the image on my skin had come there as a consequence of the same chemical reactions at play in photography. *The human body,* he told me as I watched him mixing chemicals that smelled of rotten eggs and cider vinegar, *is a vessel full of the same mysterious substances, subject to the same physical laws, as everything else in the universe. If an image can be preserved by the action of light upon your body, it can be preserved by the same action upon paper.* That is why it was not daguerreotypes that drew his interest anymore, but a new form of photography involving paper soaked in a solution of iron and salt, to which is transferred, by means of sunlight, a positive image from a glass negative.

Pa quickly mastered the new science, and became a highly regarded practitioner of the *collodion process,* as it was called, an art form hardly seen in these parts. It was a bold field, requiring great experimentation, and resulting in pictures most astounding in their beauty. Pa's *irontypes,* as he called them, had none of the exactitude of daguerreotypes, but were imbued with subtle shadings that made them look like charcoal art. He used his own proprietary formula for the sensitizer, which is where the bromine came in, and applied for a patent before opening a studio in Boneville, down the road from the courthouse. In no time at all, his iron-dusted paper portraits became quite the rage around here, for not only were they infinitely cheaper than daguerreotypes, but they could be reproduced over and over again from a single negative. Adding even more to their allure, and for an extra charge, Pa would tint them with a mix of egg wash and colored pigment, which gave them a lifelike semblance most extraordinary to behold. People traveled from all over to have their portraits taken. One fancy lady came all the way from Akron for a sitting. I assisted in Pa's studio, adjusting the skylight and cleaning the focusing plates. A few times Pa even let me polish the new brass portrait lens, which had been a major investment in the business and required delicacy in its handling. Such had our circumstances turned, Pa's and mine, that he was contemplating selling his boot-making enterprise altogether, for he said he much preferred *the smell of mixing potions to the stink of people's feet.*

It was at this time that our lives were forever changed by the predawn visitation of three riders and a bald-faced pony.

2

MITTENWOOL WAS THE ONE WHO roused me from my deep slumber that night.

"Silas, awake now. There are riders coming this way," he said.

I would be lying if I said I was jolted up right away, to my feet, by the urgency of his call. But I did no such thing. I simply mumbled something and turned in my bed. He nudged me hard then, which is not a simple feat for him. Ghosts do not easily maneuver in the material world.

"Let me sleep," I answered grumpily.

It was then that I heard Argos howling like a banshee

downstairs, and Pa cock his rifle. I looked out the tiny window next to my bed, but it was a black-as-ink night and I could see nothing.

"There are three of them," said Mittenwool, squinting over my shoulder through the same window.

"Pa?" I called out, jumping down from the loft. He was ready, boots on, peering through the front window.

"Stay down, Silas," he cautioned.

"Should I light the lamp?"

"No. Did you see them from your window? How many are there?" he asked.

"I didn't see them myself, but Mittenwool says there are three of them."

"Guns drawn," Mittenwool added.

"They have their guns drawn," I said. "What do they want, Pa?"

Pa didn't answer. We could hear the galloping coming toward us now. Pa cracked the front door open, rifle at the ready. He threw on his coat and turned to look at me.

"You don't come out, Silas. No matter what," he said, his voice stern. "If there's trouble, you run over to Havelock's house. Out the back through the fields. You hear me?"

"You're not going out there, are you?"

"Get ahold of Argos," he answered. "Don't let him out."

I collared Argos. "You're not going out there, are you?" I asked again, frightened.

He did not stop to answer me but opened the door and ventured out to the porch, aiming his rifle toward the approaching riders. He was a brave man, my pa.

I pulled Argos close to me and then crept over to the front window and peeked out. I saw the men advance. Three riders, just like Mittenwool had said. Behind one of them trailed a fourth horse, a giant black charger, and next to it, the pony with a bone-white face.

The horsemen slowed down as they approached the house, in deference to Pa's rifle. The leader of the three, a man in a yellow duster on a spotted horse, put his arms up in the air in a peaceful gesture as he brought his steed to a full stop.

"Ho there," he said to Pa, not forty feet from the porch. "You can put down your weapon, mister. I come in peace."

"Put yours down first," Pa answered, his rifle shouldered.

"Mine?" The man looked theatrically at his own empty hands, and then left and right, making a show of only now noting his companions' drawn weapons. "Put those down, boys! You're making a bad impression." He turned back to Pa. "Sorry about that. They mean no harm. Just force of habit."

"Who are you?" Pa said.

"Are you Mac Boat?"

Pa shook his head. "Who are you? Come storming here in the middle of the night."

The yellow-duster man did not seem afraid of Pa's rifle in the least. I could not see him well in the dark, but I judged him to be smaller than Pa (Pa being one of the tallest men in Boneville). Younger, too. He wore a derby hat like gentlemen do, but he wasn't one, as far as I could see. He looked a ruffian. Pointy-bearded.

"Now, now, don't get riled," he said, his voice light. "My boys and I meant to arrive at sunup, but we made better time than we thought. I'm Rufe Jones, and these here are Seb and Eben Morton. Don't bother trying to tell them apart, it's impossible." It was only then that I noted the two hulking men were exact duplicates of each other, wearing identical melon hats with wide bands down low over their moon-round faces. "We've come here with an interesting proposition from our boss, Roscoe Ollerenshaw. You heard of him, I'm sure?"

Pa made no response to that.

"Well, Mr. Ollerenshaw knows of you, Mac Boat," Rufe Jones continued.

"Who is Mac Boat?" Mittenwool whispered to me.

"I don't know any Mac Boat," Pa said from behind his rifle. "I am Martin Bird."

"Of course," Rufe Jones answered quickly, nodding. "Martin Bird, the photographer. Mr. Ollerenshaw's very familiar with your work! That's why we're here, you see. He has a business proposition he'd like to discuss with you. We've come a long way to talk with you. Might we come inside for a bit? We've been riding all night. My bones are chilled." He raised the collar on his duster to illustrate the point.

"If you want to talk business, you come to my studio in the daylight hours like any civilized man would," Pa said.

"Now, why would you adopt that tone with me?" Rufe Jones asked, as if perplexed. "The nature of our business requires some privacy, is all. We mean you no harm, not you or your boy, Silas. That's him hovering by the window behind you, right?"

I swallowed hard, I'm not going to lie, and pulled my head back from the window. Mittenwool, who was behind me, nudged me to crouch down farther.

"You have five seconds to get off my property," Pa warned, and I could tell from his voice he meant it.

But Rufe Jones must not have heard the threatening tone in Pa's words, for he laughed. "Now, now, don't get vexed. I'm just the messenger here!" he replied calmly. "Mr. Ollerenshaw sent us to come get you, and that's what we're doing. Like I said, he means you no harm. In fact, he wants to help you. He wanted me to tell you there's a lot of money in it for you. *A small fortune* were his exact words. For very little inconvenience on your part. Just a week's work and you'll be a rich man. We even brought you horses to ride! A nice big one for you, and a fetching little one for your boy. Mr. Ollerenshaw is something of a horse collector, so you should consider it an honor that he's letting you ride his fine steeds."

"I'm not interested. You now have three seconds to leave," answered Pa. "Two . . ."

"All right, all right!" said Rufe Jones, waving his hands in the air. "We'll leave. Don't you worry! Come on, fellas."

He pulled on his horse's reins and circled around, as did the brothers, wheeling the two riderless horses behind them. They started slow-walking into the night away from the house. But after a few steps, Rufe Jones stopped. He held his arms out to his sides, crucifixion-like, to show he was still unarmed. Then he looked over his shoulder at Pa.

"But we'll only come back tomorrow," he said, "with a lot more men. Mr. Ollerenshaw is not one to give up easily, truth be told. I came in peace tonight, but I can't promise it'll be the same tomorrow. Mr. Ollerenshaw, well, he wants what he wants."

"I'll get the sheriff involved," threatened Pa.

"Will you, Mr. *Boat*?" said Rufe Jones. His voice sounded more menacing now. It had none of the previous lightness.

"The name is Bird," answered Pa.

"Right. Martin Bird, the photographer of Boneville, who lives way out in the middle of nowhere with his son, Silas *Bird*."

"You best get," rasped Pa.

"All right," answered Rufe Jones. But he didn't spur his horse.

I was watching all this breathless, Mittenwool right next to me. A few seconds passed. No one moved or said a word.

3

"HERE'S THE PROBLEM," SAID RUFE JONES, his arms still out at his sides. The singsong lilt returned to his voice. "It's a bother, our going all the way back across these fields, through the Woods, only to come back tomorrow with a dozen more of us, armed to the teeth. Lord knows what can happen with all those guns pointing every which way. You know how it goes. Tragedies can befall. But if you come with us tonight, Mr. Boat, we can avoid all that nasty business."

He flipped his hands over, so the palms faced up now.

"Let's not draw this out," he continued. "You and your boy will have a nice jolly ride with us on those fine horses. And we'll have you both back here in a week. That's a solemn promise from the big man himself. He told me to tell you that exactly, by the way. To use the word *solemn.* Come on, this is a good business proposition for you, Mac Boat! What do you say?"

I saw Pa, his rifle still trained on the man, his finger still on the trigger, clench his jaw. His expression was foreign to me at that moment. I did not recognize the taut angles of his body.

"I am not Mac Boat," he said slowly. "I am Martin Bird."

"Yes, of course, Mr. *Bird*! My apologies," replied Rufe Jones, grinning. "Whatever your name is, what do you say? Let's avoid any nastiness. Put your rifle down and come with us. It's only a week. And you'll return a rich man."

Pa hesitated for another long second. It felt to me like all of time was contained inside that moment. And it was, in a way, for it was inside that moment that my life was forever altered. Pa lowered his gun.

"What's he doing?" I whispered to Mittenwool. I was suddenly more scared than I recall ever being before. It was as if my heart had stopped. Like the world had ceased its breathing.

"All right, I'll go with you," Pa said quietly, breaking the stillness of the night like a thunderclap, "but only if you leave my boy out of it. He stays right here, safe and sound. He won't breathe a word of this to anybody. Nobody comes around here anyway. And I'm back here in a week. You said I have Ollerenshaw's solemn word. Not a day longer."

"Hmm, I don't know," Rufe Jones grumbled, shaking his head. "Mr. Ollerenshaw said to bring the two of you back with us. He was very specific about that."

"Like I said," answered Pa, his voice resolute, "it's the only way I'll go with you peacefully tonight. Otherwise, it *will* become nasty business, whether it's here and now or whenever you turn up again. I'm a good shot. Don't test me."

Rufe Jones took his derby off and rubbed his forehead. He looked at his two companions, but they said nothing, or perhaps they shrugged. It was hard to see anything in the darkness but their flat pale faces.

"Fine, fine, we'll keep it peaceful, then," Rufe Jones agreed. "Just you it is. But it's got to be now. Toss your gun over here. Let's be done with this."

"You can have it when we get to the Woods, not before."

"All right, but let's go."

Pa nodded. "I'll get my things," he said.

"Oh no! I'm not in the mood for any trickeries," Rufe Jones answered quickly. "We're riding now! You get on this horse here and we leave *now,* or else the deal is off."

"No, Pa!" I cried, rushing to the door.

Pa turned to me with that expression, which, like I said, was unfamiliar. Like he'd seen the holy devil. It scared me, his face. His eyes narrowed into slits.

"You stay inside, Silas," he ordered, pointing his finger at me. He sounded so harsh, I stopped in my tracks in the doorway. Never in my life had he spoken to me like that. "I'll be fine. But you're not to leave this house. Not for anything. I'll be back in a week. There's enough food for you until then. You'll be fine. Do you hear me?"

I said nothing. I couldn't have said anything even if I'd tried.

"Do you hear me, Silas?" he said louder.

"But, Pa," I pleaded, my voice trembling.

"This is how it has to be," he replied. "You'll be safe here. I will see you in a week. Not a day later. Now get back inside, quick."

I did as he said.

He walked over to the giant black horse, swung up on him, and without so much as another look my way, turned the horse and galloped away. Within moments, he and the other horsemen vanished into the vast night.

This is how my pa entered into the services of a notorious counterfeiting ring, although I did not know it at the time.

4

I COULD NOT SAY HOW LONG I stood by the door watching the ridge over which Pa had disappeared. Enough to see the sky begin to lighten.

"You come sit down, Silas," Mittenwool said gently.

I shook my head. I was afraid to look away from that spot in the distance into which Pa had gone, for fear that, if I lost sight of it, I'd have no way of finding it again. The fields around our house are flat in every direction save the ridge, which rises slowly eastward and then slopes down into the Woods, a tangle of ancient trees encircled by dense ironwoods through which even the smallest wagons could not pass. That's what they say, at least.

"Come sit down, Silas," Mittenwool repeated. "There's nothing we can do now. We just have to wait. He'll be back in a week."

"But what if he isn't?" I whispered, tears rolling down my cheeks.

"He will be, Silas. Pa knows what he's doing."

"What do they want from him? Who is Mr. Oscar Ren-whatever? Who is this Mac Boat person? I don't understand what just happened."

"I'm sure Pa'll explain it all when he comes back. You just have to wait it out."

"A whole week!" By now the tears had blurred my vision so much that I lost sight of the spot into which Pa had disappeared. "A whole week!"

I turned to Mittenwool. He was sitting next to the table, leaning forward, elbows on his knees. He looked forlorn, for all he tried not to show it.

"You'll be fine, Silas," he said assuredly. "I'll be here with you. And Argos. We'll keep you company. You'll be fine. And before you know it, Pa will be back."

I glanced down at Argos, who had curled up inside the broken dough box he used for a bed. He was a scrappy hound, one-eared and wobble-legged.

And then I looked back at Mittenwool, his eyebrows raised,

trying to instill confidence in me. I have already mentioned that Mittenwool is a ghost, but I'm not entirely sure that's the right word for him. Spirit. Apparition. Fact is, I don't know what the right word for him is, exactly. Pa thinks he is an imaginary friend or some such thing, but I know that's not what he is. Mittenwool is as real as the chair he sits on, and the house we live in, and the dog. That no one but me can see him, or hear him, doesn't mean he's not real. Anyway, if you could see or hear him, you'd say he was a boy of about sixteen or so, tall and thin and shiny-eyed, with a shock of dark, unruly hair, and a hearty laugh. He has been my companion for as long as I can remember.

"What am I going to do?" I said, breathless.

"You're going to come sit down," he answered, patting the chair near the table. "You're going to make yourself some breakfast. Get some hot coffee in your stomach. Then, when you're ready, we're going to take stock of the situation. We'll check the cupboards, see what food you have, and set enough aside for seven days so you don't run out of anything. Then we'll go milk Moo and bring in the eggs and turn some hay for Mule, just like we do every morning. *That's* what we're going to do, Silas."

I sat down at the table across from him while he talked. He leaned over.

"It's going to be fine," he said, smiling at me reassuringly. "You'll see."

I nodded because he was trying so hard to console me and I did not want to disappoint him, but I did not think in my heart that everything was going to be fine. And it turns out I was right. For after I had milked Moo and seen to the chickens and turned some hay for Mule and gotten some water from the well, and after we had emptied the pantry to tally the food, setting aside a portion for every day of the coming week, and swept the floors and cut the firewood into tinder bits, and then made hotcakes that I would not end up eating for I had no hunger at all but a queasiness in my stomach from the swallowing of tears, I looked up through the window and saw the bald-faced pony standing in front of the house.

5

HE WAS NOT AS SMALL IN THE daylight as he had seemed in the dark. Maybe the other horses around him had been especially big, I don't know. But now, grazing by the charred oak, the pony seemed of average height for a horse. His coat gleamed black in the sunlight, and his neck was arched and muscular, topped by that bright white head, which made for a most peculiar spectacle.

I went outside and looked all around. There was no sign of Pa or any of the men who had ridden off with him. The distant fields were silent, as they always were. It had rained a bit in the late morning, but the sky was clear now save for a few long clouds stretched thin as smoke.

Mittenwool followed me as I walked toward the pony. Animals usually get riled around Mittenwool, but this one just eyed him curiously as we approached. He had long black lashes and a small muzzle. Pale blue eyes, set wide like a deer's.

"Hello there, fella," I said softly, cautiously reaching up to pat him on the neck. "What are you doing back here?"

"I'm guessing he couldn't keep up with the big horses," Mittenwool suggested.

"Is that what happened to you?" I asked the pony, who turned his head to look at me. "Did you get left behind? Or did they cut you loose?"

"He's a strange-looking creature."

There was something about the way the pony was regarding me, so directly, that warmed me somehow. "I think he's beautiful," I said.

"Face like a skull."

"Do you think they sent him back for me?" I said. "Remember they'd wanted me to go with Pa, too. Maybe they changed their mind about my staying behind."

"How would the pony have known to come here?"

"I'm just speculating," I answered, shrugging.

"See if there's something in the saddlebag."

I gingerly reached over to check inside, afraid to startle the pony. But he continued to observe me coolly, taking me in without fear or timidity.

The saddlebag was empty.

"Maybe Rufe Jones sent one of the brothers back for me," I said. "And he brought the pony for me to ride, but then something happened to him, he got thrown from his horse or something? And the pony just went on without him?"

"I guess that's possible, but it still doesn't explain how he would have known to come back to the house."

"He probably just followed the same path he took last night," I reasoned, but before I even finished my words, something new occurred to me. "Or maybe it was Pa!" I gasped. "Mittenwool! Maybe Pa got away from those men, and was riding back home to me on that big black horse, but he got thrown—and the pony kept going!"

"No, that one doesn't make sense."

"Why not? It could be! Pa could be lying in the Woods somewhere! I have to go find him!" I started putting my foot, bare as it was, into the stirrup. But Mittenwool got in front of me.

"Hold on, slow down. Let's think this through rationally, all right?" he said soundly. "If your pa had gotten away from those men, he wouldn't have dragged this pony back with him. He would have taken off at full speed so he could get home as fast as possible. So what you're saying just doesn't make a lot of sense, you see. What *does* make sense is that the pony somehow got lost in the Woods, then wandered back here. So I say, let's get him some water, because he must be all tuckered out, and then go back inside the house."

"Mittenwool," I said, shaking my head, for many things had occurred to me while he was talking. And these thoughts had become a call to action in my mind. "Please hear me out. I think this pony being here . . . it's a sign. I think he came back for me. I don't know if Pa sent him, or the good Lord himself, but it's a sign. I need to go look for Pa."

"Come on, Silas. A sign?"

"Yes, a sign."

"Pshaw," he answered dismissively.

"Believe what you will." I raised my foot back up to the stirrup.

"Pa told you to wait for him! *You're not to leave this house. Not for anything.* That's what he said. And that's what you have to do. He'll be back in a week. You just got to be patient."

For a moment, my resolve weakened. It had been so clear a second before, but Mittenwool did that to me sometimes. He could talk me out of things, cast doubt on my perceptions.

"Besides, you don't even know how to ride a horse," he added.

"Of course I do! I ride Mule all the time."

"Mule is more donkey than horse, let's face it. And you're being a bit of a donkey now, too. Come on inside."

"You're the donkey."

"Come on, Silas. Let's go back in the house."

His prodding almost convinced me to abandon my intentions. Truth be told, I'd only ever ridden a horse a couple of times in my life, and both times when I was still so small that Pa had lifted me up onto the saddle.

But then the pony snorted, nostrils flared wide, and I somehow took this as an invitation to ride. With my bare foot still half inside the stirrup, I quickly heaved myself up to the saddle. But as I tried to round my other leg over the side, my foot slipped out of the leather tread and I fell backward into the mud. The pony gave a short neigh and swished his tail.

"Dangit!" I yelled, slapping my hands in the slosh. "Dangit! Dangit!"

"Silas," Mittenwool said softly.

"Why did he leave me?" I cried out. "Why did he leave me all alone?"

Mittenwool crouched down next to me. "You're not all alone, Silas."

"I am!" I answered, feeling a big tear suddenly, unexpectedly, roll down my left cheek. "He left me alone here, and I don't know what to do!"

"Listen to me, Silas. You're not alone. All right? I'm here. You know that." He was looking right into my eyes when he said this.

"I know, but . . ." I hesitated, wiping my tears with the back of my sleeve. I was having trouble finding the right words. "But, Mittenwool, I can't stay here. I can't. Something is telling me to go out and look for Pa. I feel it in my bones. I need to go find him. The pony came for me. Don't you see that? He came for me."

Mittenwool sighed and looked down, shaking his head.

"I know it sounds crazy," I added. "Gosh, maybe I *am* crazy. I'm out here in the mud arguing with a ghost about a pony that came out of nowhere. Sure sounds crazy!"

Mittenwool winced a little. I knew he disliked that word, *ghost*.

"You're not crazy," he said quietly.

I looked at him, eyes pleaful. "I'd only go to the edge of the Woods. I promise, I wouldn't go any farther than that. If I leave now, I can get there and back by nightfall. It's no more than a two-hour ride, right?"

Mittenwool gazed out over the ridge. I knew what he was thinking. Maybe I was thinking it myself. I'd been terrified of those Woods for years. Pa tried to take me hunting there once, when I was about eight, and I literally fainted from fear. I have always seen in trees all kinds of malevolent forms. It is no coincidence, I think, that I was struck by lightning standing near an oak.

"And what are you going to do when you get to the Woods?" Mittenwool argued. "You're just going to peek inside and say too-ra-loo and come back? What good will that do?"

"At least I'll know that Pa's not somewhere close enough that I could've helped him. I'll know he's not lying in a ditch somewhere nearby, in trouble or hurt, or . . ." My voice cut off. I looked at him. "Please, Mittenwool. I have to go."

He turned his face away from me and stood up, nibbling on his lower lip. He always did this when he was thinking hard on something.

"Fine," he finally said, regretful. "You win. No use arguing with a person when they feel something in their bones."

I was about to say something.

"But you're not riding out barefoot!" he continued. "Or without a coat. And this pony needs water. So, first things first, let's bring him to the trough, feed him some oats, and then go pack you some provisions. After that, sure thing, we'll go to the edge of the Woods to look for Pa. Sound good?"

I could feel my heart beating in my ears.

"Does that mean you're coming with me?" I said. I had not dared to ask.

He raised his eyebrows and smiled. "Of course I'm coming with you, you chucklehead."

TWO

The story of I love you,
It has no end.

—Anonymous
"The Riddle Song"

1

I KNOW THIS WILL SEEM UNLIKELY, but I remember the day my mother died. I was in her stomach for most of it, and I could hear her heart beating like a wild little bird as she labored. And when I finally came into Being, Pa put me in her arms and I squirmed and she smiled, but the wild bird in her was fixing to fly by then, so she handed me back to Pa just before her soul left her body. I saw it with my baby eyes, and I remember it now, clear as day, how her soul rose like smoke from a blaze.

I know, upon hearing this, you may be tempted to think that Mittenwool somehow painted the picture of my nativity in my own recollections, but that is not the case. I remember it piercingly well. Mama's eyes and her smile, tired as she was, aggrieved that she could not pass more time with me in this world.

I don't know why I was thinking about the circumstances of my birth as I rode away from my house. It is strange, the places one's mind goes to in unruly times. I must have been thinking about Mama even before I left the house, for why else would I have taken her Bavarian violin with me, on what I thought would be only minor travels? There it was, hanging in its case on a hook near the door, where it had hung for twelve years, never opened, always treasured, and without rhyme or reason, I snatched it from the hook and took it with me as I left. My hands, mind you, were already carrying a coil of rope and a knife and a canteen of water and a sack filled with bread and salted meat, which all made sense for me to take on my journey. But a violin? That made no sense. All I can think is that maybe life knows where it's going before you do sometimes, and somewhere deep inside me, in the rooms of my heart, I knew that I would not be coming home again.

2

THE PONY AMBLED SLOW ENOUGH through the tall grassy fields that Mittenwool could walk at an unhurried pace right next to us, but Argos was not interested in keeping up. No matter how much I pleaded for him to hurry, nor how many times I clicked my tongue for him to come, my one-eared dog followed us indifferently in that droopy-legged way of his. Finally, by the time we reached the top of the ridge, he looked at me as if to say, *I am going back now, Silas. Good-bye!* And then he turned around and hobbled away without a shred of sentimentality.

"Argos!" I called out, my voice thick in the damp air. I started turning Pony around to fetch him.

"Leave him be," said Mittenwool. "He'll make it home fine."

"I can't let him go back alone."

"That dog can fend for himself just dandy, Silas. If he gets hungry, he'll go to old Havelock's house like he always does. Besides, you'll be home by nightfall. Right? That's what you promised."

I nodded, for this was truly my intent at the time. "Yes."

"So let him go back home. Anyway, we can go a little faster now, without having to wait for that slowpoke to catch up."

Mittenwool started running down the other side of the ridge, which was covered in short buffalo grass and tufts of poison buttonbush sprouting in between long stretches of sandstone. This is what makes this particular tract of land so inhospitable for farming, and why these environs are so desolate, why you could walk for hours and not see another soul. No farmers would touch it. No ranchers would go near it. Godforsaken Plains, it should be called on a map.

I took a deep breath, and lightly nudged the pony with my heels to get him to go faster to catch up to Mittenwool. I was scared the creature would pitch a fit and throw me, or break into a wild run. Instead, he broke into the gentlest of trots. It felt like he was floating a few feet above the earth as we overtook Mittenwool.

"Look at you on your winged steed," he said admiringly.

I pulled on the reins to slow the pony. "Do you see how he glides? His feet barely touch the ground."

Mittenwool smiled. "He's a fine horse," he acknowledged.

"Oh, he's better than fine," I replied, leaning forward and patting the pony's neck. "Isn't that right, Pony? You're better than fine, aren't you? You're a splendid horse, is what you are."

"Is that what you're calling him? Pony?"

"No. I don't know what to call him yet. Maybe Bucephalus? That was Alexander the Great's—"

"I know who Bucephalus was!" he interrupted indignantly. "And that's far too grand a name for him. Pony is much better. Suits him more."

"Not from where I'm sitting. I'm telling you, there's something very special about this horse."

"I don't disagree. But I still think Pony's the right name for him."

"Something better will hit me, you'll see. Want to ride him with me?"

"Oh, I'm fine walking." He kicked at the knobby shrubs with his bare feet. For as long as I've known him, Mittenwool has never worn shoes. A white shirt, black trousers, suspenders. The occasional hat. But never shoes. "Though I have to admit, this ground feels very strange underfoot."

"This must be the salt licks," I said, looking around. "Pa digs for the bromine here."

"Like walking on a dried-up pond."

"Remember him saying it was all ocean here once, millions of years ago."

"I don't remember it feeling this crunchy last time we came here."

"Dangit, Mittenwool, I should've gone with him."

"What are you going on about? You know he wouldn't let you."

"I don't mean last night. I mean all those times he'd go

digging for salt here. All those times he went hunting in the Woods. I should've gone with him."

"Hunting's not for everybody."

"If I hadn't been such a crybaby . . ."

"Who wouldn't get scared of a bear? Come on now, that was a long time ago."

I shook my head. "I should've gone when I got older. That's the truth of it."

He kicked at the ground again. "Well, you're here now, that's all that matters. And you know something? I think Pa's going to be quite taken by your doing this, Silas. Not at first, mind you! He's going to be livid that you didn't listen to him—and don't say I didn't warn you! But after a spell he's going to be proud that you did this, that you had the gumption to get on this strange-looking beast to go searching for him all by yourself."

I half smiled despite my mood. "He's not a strange-looking beast."

"You know he is."

"*You're* the strange-looking beast."

"Boo-hoo to you."

"And I'm not by myself."

"Well, he'd think so."

"Tell me honestly. Do you think this is a fool's quest?"

He looked up at the ridge ahead of us, which was jagged, like broken glass.

"I sure hope it is," he said truthfully. "Look, Silas. Pa is a brilliant man. He wouldn't have gone with them if he didn't think it was the best thing to do."

"He *is* a brilliant man," I concurred softly. Then, "Do you think that's why they took him? Maybe it had something to do with the patent?"

"I don't know. Maybe."

"I bet Mr. Oscar Rens, *whatever-his-name-is,* probably heard about this genius living in Boneville. That's why he sent Rufe Jones with this business proposition. Don't you think so?"

He nodded in agreement. "It makes sense."

"I mean, everyone in these parts knows Pa's a genius. It's not just me saying it."

"You're telling me like I don't know that."

"I know you know."

Of course he knew. From the time I was little, we both knew that about Pa. That there wasn't a subject on this great big earth that Pa didn't comprehend. There wasn't a question he couldn't answer. He had only to read a book once to memorize its entire contents—I've seen him do it! It's how his mind works. And there are so many books, so many scientific journals, stored in that mighty mind of his. By all rights, Pa should have been the Isaac Newton of these times. The Galileo. The Archimedes! But when you are born poor and left alone by the time you're ten, the world can close in on you. That's what happened to Pa, as far as I can tell, from the tidbits he's told me over the years. The truth is, Pa doesn't talk about himself much. His life is like a jigsaw into which I try to fit all the tiny pieces of what I know.

But that he's a bona fide genius, that's just something everybody in Boneville knows. The boots with the little drawer in the heel. The color-tinted irontypes. *Your pa's a genius!* I've been told that so many times over the years by his happy customers, I've lost count. People recognize wondrous things when they see them. And with Pa, they don't even know the half of it! If they had an inkling of the other wonders in our home Pa had invented? The mechanical ice machine? The hot-air furnace? The glass bulb that lights the air? There'd be a stampede of people wanting all those things for their houses, too! Pa could be the richest man in town if he chose to be, just from the sale of those inventions. But Pa didn't care about any of that. It was for Mama he'd made these marvels. It was for her he'd built our house and filled it with all the lovely workings of his mind. She'd left everything behind to come live with him, and he'd wanted her to have every creature comfort possible out here in the wilderness. Which she did, for a while.

"Who do you think this Mac Boat is, anyway?"

I had fallen into a bit of a sleep atop Pony.

"What? Oh, I don't know."

"Sorry, didn't know you were napping."

"Not napping. Just resting my eyes. Pony knows where we're going anyway. Look, I'm not even holding the reins." I raised my hands so he could see.

"You just called him Pony."

"Until I can think of a good name for him. Hey, why'd you ask that?"

"Ask what?"

"About Mac Boat. Why do you care who he is?"

"I don't. I guess I'm a bit curious, is all."

"Curious about what?"

"Nothing. I don't know. Don't go reading into it now."

"I'm not reading into anything! Except I don't know why you would ask something unless you were thinking something. And if you're thinking something, I wish you would just go ahead and say it."

Mittenwool shook his head.

"I'm not thinking anything you're not thinking," he answered sullenly, and then he pulled his hat out of his back pocket, put it on, and walked ahead of me.

Pa once asked me, for he was ever curious about my companion, if Mittenwool casts a shadow. The answer is, he does. Right now, as the sun was low on the shining fields behind us, Mittenwool's shadow was like a long dark arrow pointing ahead to the edge of nothing.

3

WE REACHED THE WOODS LATER THAN I thought we would, and stood at the tree line looking in. There was no slow entry into it from here, no spattering of small trees until you got to the dense part inside. It was like a fortress made of giant logs looming behind a hedge of tall spiky shrubs.

"Pa!" I screamed into the wall of trees. I thought there would be an echo, but it was just the opposite. It was like my voice was muffled by an invisible blanket. Like I was making the tiniest sound in the universe. "Paaaaaaaaaa!"

Pony shuffled backward a few steps, as if he were making room for a reply. But none came. All I heard was the cawing of dusk birds and the mighty chorus of insects coming from within.

"Do you see any sign of him?" I asked.

Mittenwool was crouching a little ahead of me, trying to peer through the bramble. "No."

"What about footprints, or horseshoe tracks? Maybe we can see where they entered," I pressed, looking around for any telltale signs of where they might have gone in. I dismounted and walked toward Mittenwool, leaving Pony grazing on some of the dandelions that sprouted between bald patches of rock.

"The rain washed everything clean," said Mittenwool.

"Keep looking."

"Call him again."

"Paaaaaaaaaaaa!" I hollered, cupping my palms over my mouth to see if my voice could penetrate the wall of trees this time.

We waited, alert for an answer. Nothing came.

"Well, he's not here," said Mittenwool. "That's a relief, right? You were afraid you'd find him in a ditch somewhere, and he's obviously not. So that's good. I hope you feel better now."

I shrugged and nodded at the same time, glancing back at the lavender sky behind me. The edges of the dark clouds were starting to glow like embers. Mittenwool followed my gaze.

"We only have about an hour of daylight left. We should start heading back."

"I know," I answered. But I didn't move.

Instead, I looked back into the Woods, trying to remember what Pa had told me about them, the last time we came here together. *This is an ancient forest, Silas. People hunted here for thousands of years. You can still find the trails they left behind, if you know how to look.*

But I did not know how to look. I had never learned, because I had always been too chicken-livered to come back with him again.

"I should have come with him," I mumbled to myself.

"Let it rest, Silas."

I didn't respond, but paced left and right in front of the forest wall, looking for an obvious entry point, a wedge through which I could squeeze myself. The shaggy barks of the first line of trees were dark gray, almost black now, even where the low sun beamed upon them. And beyond them, it looked like night had already descended inside the forest.

I started kicking through the bramble toward the ironwoods.

"What are you doing?" Mittenwool asked.

I ignored him. I just kept looking for a way in.

"Silas, come on now. You promised. It's time to go back."

"I told you I wanted to peek inside."

"Are you forgetting what happened last time?"

"Of course not! Like you have to remind me!"

"Stop yelling!"

"Well, stop arguing with me."

It angered me that he thought he had to remind me. Like I would ever forget that time before. Me going in with Pa, holding his hand. I'd been looking forward to hunting with him in the Woods for weeks. But almost from the moment we walked inside, I started feeling peculiar. My head began to hurt. It was daytime and springtime and the trees were flowering, but I felt the shudder of winter inside me. It came very quickly, like a chill sweeping over my body.

Pa, I don't like it here. Maybe we should go home.

You'll be fine, son. Just hold my hand.

He had no way of knowing the terror taking hold of me.

What's that sound?

It's just birds, Silas. Calling to each other. Just birds.

But they did not sound like birds to me. They sounded like something strange and sad, like wails or shrieks, and the farther into the Woods we walked, the louder they got. Then, all of a sudden, the trees seemed to come alive all around me, human-formed and unquiet, branches shaking. I started to cry, and closed my eyes and covered my ears.

Pa, take me out of here! There's something coming through the trees!

I don't even know what I saw, or thought I saw, because no sooner had I screamed than I fell to the ground. Passed out cold. Mittenwool told me later that my eyes had rolled to the back of my head. I have no recollection of Pa carrying me out of the Woods. All I remember is coming to in the wagon, Pa leaning over me, pouring water on my forehead, stroking my hair, which was matted to my face. I was shivering in his arms.

I saw something, Pa! I saw something in the trees.

You have a fever, Silas, he told me.

What was in the trees, Pa?

Later on, after I was feeling better and we started talking about what had happened, it was Pa who put the notion in my head that it might have been a bear that I had seen. He even suggested that my eagle eyes probably saved our lives, though I knew he was just saying that to make me feel better. Was it a bear I had seen? Maybe it was a bear.

"There has to be a trail inside somewhere," I said, frustrated that we were here, in front of the Woods, and I could not find a way in. "Don't you remember how we got in last time?"

Mittenwool, his arms crossed in front of him, cocked his head. "I can't believe you're not keeping your promise, Silas."

"I told you I wanted to take a peek inside! I won't go in far, obviously. I know better than that. Come on, you must remember the way in."

He looked up. "I honestly don't, Silas. All these trees are the same to me."

I did not believe him. "Dangit!"

"How about we go home now, and come back tomorrow morning?"

"No! Pa passed through here not twelve hours ago! There has to be some trace of where he went! Come on, Mittenwool, please help me. All I want to do is go inside and look around a bit, that's all."

"But look around for what? What exactly do you think you're going to find?"

"I don't know!" I cried.

"You're not thinking straight, Silas."

The calmness with which he said this infuriated me.

"Fine, don't help me," I muttered, unsheathing my knife. "Not like you can help me anyway, you and your long empty arms."

I started hacking through the thicket in front of me, stabbing at it left and right, pushing at the thorny branches, but after a minute or so, I saw the fruitlessness of my labors. It was like trying to cut into ropes of iron.

"Dangit dangit dangit!" I screamed. I threw the knife down and sat cross-legged, elbows on my knees, my face in my bloodied hands, which had been shredded.

"Silas." He had come up behind me.

"Stop!" I said. "I know! *I'm not thinking straight!*"

"Look at Pony over there. Turn around."

It took a second for his words to reach me, for I was too engulfed in my own sadness to hear them. But when I realized what he was saying, I looked over at Pony. He was not where I had left him. He had drifted a couple of hundred feet upwind of us and was now standing in the middle of a large patch of shrubs, head up, ears alert, black tail swishing. Looking into the Woods.

4

I WALKED OVER SLOWLY, CAREFUL not to startle him. I did not want to divert his attention from whatever he was looking at. He didn't so much as flinch as I approached.

I followed his gaze and saw, between two of the meanest-looking ironwoods you've ever seen, a narrow opening in the thicket. It was shaped like a man-sized crack in a wall.

"Well, look at that!" I cried to Mittenwool. "You see? Pony *did* lead me to the trail, just like I thought he would!"

He sighed. "Well, what do me and my *long empty arms* know about anything, anyway?"

"Oh, come on, I didn't mean anything by that."

He hunched his shoulders, tucked both his hands into his coat pockets, and sulked away.

"Fine, be a sorehead!" I called out after him. "Fact is, I was right. He brought me here like I said he would. Isn't that right, Pony?"

I was standing in front of Pony when I said this, my face more or less level with his, and out of the blue, he pushed his muzzle ever so gently into the crook of my neck. Again, I was unfamiliar with horses, or their ways and habits, so I had not expected this gesture of affection. If Mule had pushed his nose into me, it would have been to nip me, for he was a grumpy old coot. But Pony was nothing like Mule.

I held Pony's gaze a few seconds, slightly dumbstruck by him, and then carefully pulled myself up into the saddle. I was still inexpert in this maneuver, but he held steady for me as I scrambled up.

"Are you really going to do this, Silas?" Mittenwool asked incredulously.

He was standing in back of me, so I turned to answer. The

sun was setting directly behind him. It almost looked like rays of light were coming through his body.

"I told you," I answered. "I feel it in my bones. Can't explain it more than that."

He rolled his shoulders, defeated.

"You know half your face is covered in blood, right?" he pointed out.

I looked down at my bloodied hands. I could only imagine what my face looked like, but I made no attempt to wipe it. "Are you coming with me or not?"

He took a deep breath. "I told you I would."

I smiled gratefully, to which he responded with another unhappy shrug. Then I nudged Pony with my heels to get him going. Not that I needed to. He knew to go. And where to go. Cautiously, slowly, he stepped through the thicket, and then nosed his way into the crack in the wall of ironwoods. It was only a sliver, big enough for a small boy atop a small horse. I pictured Pa, being as tall as he was, on that giant charger of a horse, having to bend down at the waist to get beyond it.

Then we were inside the Woods, and it was dark.

The trail, if it could even be called a trail, was a shallow rut winding through the trees. The branches intertwined just above me like long bony fingers clasped in prayer. They reminded me of the vaulted ceiling in the only church I'd ever been inside, in Boneville, which Pa had taken me to once after I'd professed a mild curiosity about the "man of sorrows." One visit was all I needed, which suited Pa fine, as he was not a believer. I was not a disbeliever.

The farther I went inside, the more my heart started racing. My cheeks felt flushed. The air was thick and smelled of musk and damp earth. I was feeling unsteady.

"How are you doing there, Silas?" Mittenwool called out from behind me. I knew he could tell I was getting anxious, just like I could tell he was no longer miffed at me.

"I'm fine," I said, trying to control my breathing.

"You're doing real good."

"It just got so cold all of a sudden."

"Is your coat buttoned?"

"I said I'm fine!" I found it irritating, the way he fussed over me sometimes.

"All right. *Steady on,*" he replied calmly. This was a phrase of Pa's.

I buttoned my coat. "I'm sorry about before. The *empty arms* remark."

"Don't worry about it. Just focus on the task at hand."

I nodded, too shaky to say anything else. Even though I felt cold to the bone, I was sweating now. My teeth were chattering. My heart was racing.

Steady on, I dared myself, cupping my hands over my mouth to keep them warm.

"Fare thee well," Mittenwool started singing softly. *"I must be gone and leave you for a while . . ."*

This was a tune he used to sing to me when I was little and couldn't fall asleep.

"Stop it," I whispered, embarrassed. But then, "No, keep going."

"But wherever I go, I will return, if I go ten thousand miles."

He hummed the next verse, so softly it melded with the sound of Pony's hoofbeats and the din of the Woods. It was like a sound from far away, and it soothed me, I must admit. It was a great comfort, truth be told, having Mittenwool there with me. I resolved to be less impatient with him.

About a stone's throw from where we'd entered, the trail opened up around a smooth slab of rock, which rose at an angle off the ground. I prodded Pony to climb it, and when he was at the highest point he could get to, I stood tippy-toed in the stirrups to look all around me.

"Do you see anything?" Mittenwool asked.

I shook my head. By now, my skin was gooseflesh. My hands were trembling.

Mittenwool climbed up next to me. "Why don't you call for him one last time, and then we'll go home?"

"Paaaaaaaa!" I shouted in the damp air.

My call was met with the startled cry of a multitude of invisible forest creatures, cawing and shrieking in reply. I could feel, though not see, the rush of small movements in the branches all around, like a wind slapping through them. When it settled, I waited for a more familiar sound to come to me. *Silas, I'm over here, son. Come here.* But nothing came.

I shouted several more times, and each time heard the same mix of loudness and silence.

There was only the faintest light to see by now. The air was blue and the trees were black. Maybe in the summer, when the branches were full of leaves, one could say the forest was green. But right now there were no other colors in the world, as far as my eyes could tell, but blue and black.

"Come on now. You've done all you can do," said Mittenwool. "We should head back, before it's too dark to find the trail out."

"I know," I answered softly. He was right. I knew he was. But even so, I found myself unable to move right then, to turn Pony around and go home.

I had been feeling quivery this whole time, my heart pulsing inside my ears, but it was getting louder now, that thumping sound. It was like a drumbeat. *Boom. Boom.* Coming from inside me. A quickening. Mixing with the buzz of the Woods I'd been hearing all along. The murmur of invisible forest creatures, and the rattling of branches, and Pony's tail whisking, and the hum of insects, and the squishy sound of hooves on uncertain ground. It felt like these noises were rushing into me, coursing into my ears like a river. And suddenly, the memory of what I had heard last time all those years ago, when I was with Pa and got so scared, came flooding back to me. For I was hearing it again now.

A rumbling. Whispers and moans, everywhere around me. That is what I had heard back then. The hushed roar of voices.

But this time, I steeled my nerves against what I told myself were the delusions of my mind. My own *grand imagination* at work, as Pa phrased it once. *They are not voices,* I thought, *only the sounds of the forest.*

Yet, for all I tried to listen for those forest sounds now, it was only strange utterances that I heard, the wisps and mumbling of words rising and falling in the air. Closing in on me. Like they were carried on a fog. The air was so thick with words, I felt like I could choke on them. Like they would pour into my throat and into my nostrils. Deluge my ears. Liquefy my bones.

"Silas, we need to go *now*!" yelled Mittenwool.

"Yes!" I cried, and tried to turn Pony around. But I could feel his muscles tensing under my legs, resisting me. His ears started twitching madly. He tossed his head and took some cautious steps backward down the rock. I pulled hard on the reins, for I was truly frightened now, and wanted to turn and get us out of the Woods as fast as possible. But this impulse only startled him, or it could be that he was hearing what I was hearing. Whatever it was, something caused Pony to suddenly rear. And then he bolted off the rock, his tail up, neck forward, and took off at full gallop. Left and right he threaded through the trees, me holding on to his mane for dear life, folded over his neck to keep my head from getting sliced off by the tangle of branches above me. My face got whipped and scratched anyway.

I don't know how long Pony ran buck wild like this. Was it ten minutes or an hour? A few thousand feet or ten thousand miles? When he finally slowed, his coat drenched in sweat, I remained low against him. I did not lift my face from his neck. My fingers stayed entwined in his mane. He was panting fitfully, and so was I, and I could feel his heart beating under my left leg. Who knows how much more time passed before he came to a full stop, but even then it took me a while to open my eyes.

I had no idea where we were. At this point, I could barely tell the difference between up and down. From where I was looking, the whole world was bent sideways. We had reached a clearing of some sort, encircled by sleek bare trees that looked like maypoles. It had gone dark now. Not pitch-black yet, but everything was shadows. Still, at least it was quiet here. That much I noted at once. There were no muffled voices. No words hanging in the air to drown me.

"Mittenwool?" I called out softly, for I could not feel him near me. I sat up then to look around, but I saw no trace of him.

I have stated that Mittenwool has been my companion for as long as I can remember, but I don't mean to imply that he is by my side at all times. He has always come and gone, willy-nilly, as he pleases. Hours will go by when I don't see him. Sometimes, a whole day will have passed without me catching sight of him. But by nightfall, he always comes back. I'll see him walking nearby, or sitting on the chair in my room, whistling or cracking some joke or other, keeping me company until I fall asleep. So I was accustomed to his absences. But right now, in the middle of these diabolical Woods, the idea that he was not nearby filled me with a panic that I cannot describe. For the first time in my life, it occurred to me that maybe I could lose Mittenwool. Or maybe he could lose me. I did not know the rules of our existence together.

"Mittenwool!" I cried out. "Where are you? Can you hear me? Please come!"

I heard the snap of a branch and turned around. There, at the foot of the clearing, a barrel-shaped old man with a snow-white beard was pointing a shiny silver pistol right at me.

"What in blazes?" said the old man, surprised at the sight of me.

"Don't shoot, please!" I cried, my hands in the air. "I'm only a child."

"I can see that. What are you doing here?"

"I'm lost."

"Where'd you come from?"

"Boneville."

"Who is Mittenwool?"

"I'm looking for my pa."

"Mittenwool is your pa?"

"I'm lost! Please help me."

The old man looked confused. He sighed. I heard in that sound a kind of irritation, like he regretted finding me. He holstered his gun.

"You shouldn't be out here all by yourself, kid," he said gruffly. "A boy your size. There are panthers in these Woods that would rip your belly out and lick your bones dry faster than you could know. Best get off your horse and follow me. I have a camp set up about a hundred yards from here. Hurry up now. I was about to start a fire."

That is how I made the acquaintance of Enoch Farmer.

5

WHEN EVENTS ARE BEYOND REASON, one tends not to ask a lot of questions. I climbed off Pony, led him by the reins, and followed the old man out of the clearing through a tight cluster of trees.

"Grab any big sticks you can find as you're walking," he instructed me, not looking back. "Avoid poplar, though. Makes an awful black smoke. We need tinder, too, so try to pick up some softwoods. Careful not to prick yourself. They're sharp as needles."

He kept walking, me following about five paces behind him, until we reached a little stream, no wider than I could jump across. On the other side of it was a small glade with a cluster of maple trees dotted with red buds. These bordered a clearing on which were piled a mess of burnt logs and ashes from previous campfires. I dumped the sticks and branches I had picked up onto the slab, and then led Pony to a tumbled maple about a dozen feet away. This is where the old man's horse, a gloomy brown mare with close-set eyes, was tied to a branch. The moment we approached, the mare bared her teeth at us, like a mean dog would, but Pony paid her no mind at all. He simply flicked his tail, not deigning any further reply, as I tied him a few feet away.

When I returned to the little clearing, the old man was standing by the wood mound, poking at the pile of timber.

"Did you bring any matches?" he asked, not looking up.

"Yes, sir." I pulled the box of matches from my satchel.

"You ever start a fire before?"

"In a firebox. But not out in the open like this, no."

"If you can't start a fire out here, kid, you're as good as dead." He sat down wearily, rubbing his knuckles into his back. "I'll show you how to do it. What's your name?"

"Silas Bird."

"I'm Enoch Farmer," he said. "Did you bring anything to eat, Silas Bird?"

"Just some salted meat and bread."

"I was chasing down a rabbit when you got in my way," he said sharply, kicking off his boots. "But I'm too tired to go back out hunting again."

"You can have some of my food."

He smiled kindly at that. "Well, thank you, Silas Bird. That's a funny name." His beard was like a short white broom hanging off his face. "So, Silas Bird, why don't you get a little fire going while I rest my aching back here, and we'll make a stew of that salted meat? Then you can tell me what the dickens you're doing out here in the middle of nowhere. Sound good to you?"

"Yes, sir."

"Wipe your face, by the way. It's covered in something."

"Yes, sir," I answered, spitting into my palm to clear my face of the blood that had dried there earlier.

"Is that blood? You get hurt or something?"

"No, sir."

He rubbed his hands together, watching me warily, and then showed me how to make a fire, how to stack the wood, where to light the tinder. He didn't talk as much as grunt all his words. I soon learned he was the kind of man who belched and farted and cursed freely. Very different from Pa.

I got the fire going, and then he had me strip some bark off an ironwood and curl it into a kind of bowl, which I used to boil water. We put the salted meat inside it and made a nice stew of it, which I sopped up with the bread. I hadn't realized how hungry I was.

He lit his pipe and regarded me curiously as I ate. The bowl was still half full when I offered it to him, but he waved it away.

"I'm not that hungry after all," he said gruffly. "You go on and finish it up."

"Thank you."

"So," he said once I was sated, "I think it's time you tell me your story, Silas Bird. How the hellabaloo did you end up here in the middle of these Woods?"

The fire warmed me. The food softened me. I had not had a chance to think too much about my situation until now, so absorbed was I by the tasks at hand, so when he engaged me with something like camaraderie, I felt my emotions untether. I pretended I was wiping my eyes because of the sparks and smoke coming from the fire, but it was the day's events catching up to me. I told him what had happened up until that point. How three riders had taken Pa in the night. How Pony had come back for me, which I took as a sign to look for Pa. How I ended up in the Woods. And how I was lost. The end.

Mr. Farmer nodded and took it all in, as if he were inhaling my story along with the pipe. Billowy gusts of smoke came out of his nostrils, like tendrils. His fingers, curled around the pipe, were thick and gnarled.

"So these riders," he finally said, "they came out of the blue, just like that? Your pa never saw them before? Had no run-ins with them before?"

"No, sir."

"What's your pa do for a living?"

"He's a boot-maker by trade, but now he's a collodiotypist."

"A collodio-*what?*"

"A type of photographer."

"Like a Daguerrean?"

"Yes."

"What's his name?"

"Martin Bird."

Mr. Farmer twisted his beard, like he was digesting the name. "So, who is this Mittenwool you were calling out for?"

I had not mentioned Mittenwool in any of my explanations. I guess I was hoping he would have forgotten my calling out the name before. I looked down and didn't answer.

"Look, son," said Mr. Farmer. "You're in a heap of trouble, out here by yourself. It's sheer luck your ending up in this neck of the Woods instead of the Bog. That swampland will eat you alive. If I hadn't found you, I don't know what would've happened to you, frankly. So I don't mind bringing you out of the Woods tomorrow morning, even though it's out of my way. But you got to level with me here, Silas Bird. Did you come here alone, or is there someone else out there who I should know about?"

"No, you don't need to know about anyone else."

He narrowed his eyes and scrunched up his face as he scrutinized me.

"I have a grandson your age, you know," he said. "What are you, nine, ten?"

"I'm twelve."

"You are?" he answered, amused. "You're a tiny thing for your age, aren't you? Lookee here, Silas Bird." He reached into his coat pocket and pulled out a tin badge. He held it up for me to see across the fire. "You know what this is?"

"It's a badge."

"That's right. I'm a United States federal marshal," he replied. "I'm tracking down some outlaws who are heading east. We got a tip they're holed up in a cave on the other side of the big ravine. They're about three days ahead of me, give or take. It just may be that you and I are looking for the same group of men."

"Are you looking for Rufe Jones?" I asked excitedly.

"I don't know that name, no."

"Seb and Eben Morton? They're brothers."

"No. Were those the men who took your pa?"

I nodded. "They were sent by someone named . . . Oscar something? I can't really remember." But as I was speaking, the other name popped into my head. "What about Mac Boat? Do you know him?" I babbled this without thinking.

Here, finally, Mr. Farmer reacted.

"Mac Boat?" he exclaimed, eyebrows raised. "Was Mac Boat one of the men who took your pa?"

His reply made me instantly regret saying the name aloud. I don't know why I did. I should have kept my big mouth shut.

"No," I said, "they just mentioned his name. I don't know why, exactly."

"Well, Mac Boat is one of the most wanted fugitives around!" he croaked, almost admiringly. "I haven't heard that name in years. But if he's somehow connected to what happened to your pa, then our paths have indeed converged, kid. Because the men I'm tracking, they're part of the biggest counterfeiting ring in the Middle West. And Mac Boat, well, he was one of the best counterfeiters there ever was."

THREE

I am a poor wayfaring stranger,
traveling through this world of woe.

—Anonymous
"Wayfaring Stranger"

1

MEMORY IS A STRANGE THING. Some things come to you crisp and bright, like fireworks on a long black night. Others are as dim and fuzzy as dying embers. I have always endeavored to provide order to my memory, but it can be like trying to put lightning in a box.

Still, I have defeated lightning, so there's that.

I don't remember exactly when Mittenwool appeared that night, which was the first of several I'd spend in the Woods. All I remember is waking up as the fire crackled and seeing the canopy of trees above me, through which only slivers of the night sky were apparent, shaped like broken glass. The stars dotted the black sky like tiny candles flickering somewhere far away.

What gives those stars their light? I wondered. And then, *What lies beyond those stars?*

I was half asleep.

"Silas," said Mittenwool.

"Mittenwool!" I whispered happily, sitting up. "You're back!"

Mr. Farmer was sleeping across the fire from me. I could hear him snoring loudly. But I did not want to wake him, so I kept my voice as hushed as I could.

"I thought I lost you," I added.

"Just took me a while to catch up," he answered, smiling

reassuringly. He patted my head as he sat down next to me. It was only when I reached up to squeeze his hand that he understood the extent of my relief. "Gosh, did you really think I wouldn't find you?"

I shook my head, a bit overtaken by my emotions.

"Silly billy," he said gently. "Look there. The fire's going out. You should stoke it. Add more wood."

I hadn't realized how cold I was until that moment, even though I was using Pony's saddle blanket to cover myself. Chilled as I was, I got up and threw some more big sticks on the fire. The flames shot up and made a crashing noise. I sat down next to Mittenwool and warmed my hands under my armpits.

"Where were you?" I asked.

"Oh, you know, here and there."

I usually did not ask Mittenwool questions like that. I had learned long ago that he was vague about certain aspects of his Being. Not because he didn't want to answer these questions, I think, but because he simply didn't know himself. His own origin was something of a mystery to him.

"Who is that person asleep over there?" he asked.

"An old man named Enoch Farmer. He found me. Turns out he's a U.S. marshal tracking some outlaws. I think they may be the same men who took Pa."

Mittenwool seemed dubious. "Well, that would be quite a coincidence."

"It's not a coincidence. It was Pony's doing. He brought me here to him. I told you it was a sign, his coming back for me. He's bringing me to Pa."

He smiled wanly. "I hope so."

"I know so."

"Hey, Silas, I have to confess, I am still a little peeved at you."

"About the *empty arms* thing?"

"No. That you didn't keep your word about going into the Woods. You promised me."

"I know. I'm sorry."

"These Woods are no jest, Silas. You have no business being here all by yourself."

"I know! That's why it's good the marshal found me. He showed me how to start a fire, and how to make a bowl out of tree bark. He's teaching me how to track."

He stroked his chin thoughtfully. "And you trust him?"

"He seems all right. Told me he has a grandson my age."

He made a face, not completely convinced.

"Anyway, you should get some sleep now," he said.

I lay back again and pulled the saddle blanket up to my ears. He got down next to me, resting on his elbows, face up to the sky. I turned on my side and studied his profile for a while, a landscape more familiar to me than any other place on earth. Every once in a while, the sheer wonder of Mittenwool took hold of me. The strangeness of us.

I almost did not want to ask, because I did not want to disturb the peacefulness of the moment, but I asked anyway.

"You heard them, too, right? Just before Pony ran off. I wasn't imagining it."

He clenched his jaw. "No, I heard them, too."

"It wasn't a bear, was it? That time with Pa?"

"No. It wasn't a bear."

"Who are they? What are they?"

"I don't rightly know."

"Are they like you?"

He thought about this for a second. "I honestly don't know." He was looking up while he talked, at the same starry night as I was. "There are so many things I don't know, Silas."

I nodded, for it occurred to me that if life is full of mysteries, death must be, too.

"It's kind of like these Woods right now, I think," he continued thoughtfully. "We can hear all the hoots and cries coming from everywhere around us. Branches falling. Creatures dying and being born in the darkness. But we can't see them. We just know they're there, right? We're *aware* of them. That's how it is with you, I think. You're special, Silas. You're aware of things that other people aren't aware of. That's a gift."

"I don't want it. It's not a gift. It's a curse."

"It may help you find Pa."

I reflected on that. "I guess that's true. And it makes it possible for me to see you. That's something, I suppose."

He smiled and nudged me with his elbow. "Don't go getting sentimental on me, lunkhead."

I chuckled. "You're the lunkhead!"

"Shh!"

I had gotten loud without realizing. We both looked over at Mr. Farmer to see if I'd woken him, but the old man just stirred a bit before rolling over on his side.

"We should stop talking or you're going to wake him up,"

Mittenwool said. “Get some sleep. I have a feeling you’re going to have to be wide awake these next few days. You need your rest.”

“But you’ll stay here, right?”

“Of course I will. Now close your eyes.”

I closed my eyes. “Mittenwool?”

“Hmm?”

“What do you think about the name Gringolet?” I whispered without opening my eyes.

“Was that Sir Gawain’s horse? Seems a bit highfalutin for Pony,” he answered.

“What about Perceval?”

“Perceval. Hmm. That doesn’t seem right for him, either.”

“No, I guess not.”

“Now go to sleep.”

I nodded. And then I fell asleep.

2

DAWN BROKE, BUT I SLEPT through it. By the time I wakened, it was a blinding bright day. The light didn’t come down from above as much as it shimmered on the mist that blew through the trees. It glimmered on the branches wet with dew. It fell like rain.

“Well, about time, sleepyhead!” Mr. Farmer groused. He had

his boots on and was tending to his droopy mare. He looked about ready to go.

"Morning, Mr. Farmer," I mumbled.

"*Marshal* Farmer," he corrected. "I tried to wake you but you were dead to the world. Come on, rise and shine."

I got up and rubbed the sleep out of my eyes. It felt like my face was encrusted with tree dust, and my tailbone and legs hurt from all the horseback riding. My bones were *weary to the marrow,* as they say.

"Is there any breakfast?" I asked, to which the old man made an angry face.

The fire had gone out, with nothing but white cinders left, and I was cold. When I breathed, a little cloud of smoke blew from my mouth. As I put on my hat, I caught sight of Mittenwool, leaning against a tree at the edge of the clearing. I only slightly acknowledged him. I didn't want the marshal to catch me being strange.

"You talk in your sleep," said Marshal Farmer, regarding me with some suspicion.

"I know. Pa's told me I do."

"You said that name in your sleep. Mittenwool."

I raised my shoulders and pouted my lips as if to say, *Hmm.*

"So who is he?" Marshal Farmer persisted. "This Mittenwool. That's who you were calling for when I found you. Is he a friend?"

I went to make water in the trees, where he couldn't see me. I didn't answer.

"Is he a friend of yours?" he asked again when I came back. He was intent on knowing.

"Just tell him I'm a friend from back home," Mittenwool called out.

"He's a friend from back home, yes, sir," I replied, picking up the saddle blanket and bringing it over to Pony.

"And he came with you to the Woods?" Marshal Farmer said, eyeing me curiously.

It was the first time I was actually able to see the old man's face clearly, in the dappled light of morning. He was much older than I had thought. He'd been wearing a hat last night, but now I could see he was practically bald, with long tufts of scraggly white hair sprouting here and there like weeds. He had a broad face, weathered as rawhide. Crinkled around the eyes, which made him seem friendly. Red-nosed. That shock of white beard under his chin.

"Mittenwool came with me to the edge of the Woods, yes, sir," I answered quietly, laying the blanket over Pony's back. "When I went inside the Woods, he stayed behind."

"So is he waiting for you where he left you?"

"No. I don't think he's waiting for me, no."

"When I take you to the edge of the Woods," he answered impatiently, "are you going to know how to get back to your house all by yourself? Because I don't have the time to take you all the way back to wherever it is you live."

"No, you don't need to do that," I said quickly. "I mean, I don't want to go home, Marshal Farmer. I'd like to go with you, if that's all right with you."

He snickered and jerked his head as he tightened his horse's stirrups. "That's certainly *not* all right with me."

"Please," I implored. "I have to find my pa. I'm sure those men who took him are connected with the people you're after. If you find them, you'll find my pa."

He was feeding an apple to his horse.

"Maybe they are connected and maybe they're not," he answered, "but either way, you're not coming with me."

It peeved me to see him feeding an apple to his horse and not sharing it with me, given that I had offered to share my meal with him yesterday, but then I thought of how I had cost him a rabbit. Still, my stomach yearned for that apple.

"Please, sir," I said. "Let me come with you. I don't have anyone at home waiting for me."

"Your pa told you to wait for him," he answered brusquely, not looking up. "You should do what your father says."

"But what if he's in trouble?"

He leaned over his horse's back and rested his elbows on the saddle to look at me.

"Kid, your pa is *obviously* in a peck of trouble," he replied, "but that doesn't mean you can help him out of it. You're just a little twig of a thing. You don't even have a gun."

"But you do."

He chuckled. There was a bit of a warmth to him, and I think he regarded me like he would his own grandchild. "Look, son," he said thoughtfully. "Go back to your house. Wait for your pa there, where you'll be safe and sound. I'll be on the lookout for him, all right? Martin Bird was his name, right? What's he look like?"

"He's very tall. And lean. And he has black hair with some

gray at the temples. He has piercing blue eyes, and very fine teeth. He's a handsome man. That's not just me saying that. I've seen how ladies lower their eyes when he talks to them. He has a dimple in his chin like I do, but you can't see it when his beard grows in."

"All right, I've made note of his appearance," said Marshal Farmer, tapping his forehead, "and I'll be sure the deputies are apprised of it, too, so he doesn't get hurt in any crossfire."

"What do you mean, crossfire?"

Marshal Farmer frowned. "You don't think I'm taking on a big counterfeiting ring all by myself, do you?" he said. "As soon as I've tracked them down and found their headquarters, I'll round up a posse in Rosasharon. That's a town on the other side of the ravine. The banks have a reward out for whoever catches these counterfeiters, so I'll have plenty of volunteers. Now, come on, mount up already, or I'll fall so far behind I won't be able to track them."

He mounted his horse, clicked, and turned the horse around.

I finished cinching Pony's saddle and pulled tight on the strap. Pony eyed me, and I thought for a second he was wishing I had an apple to give him. But then something in his expression made me think he was simply responding to my mood. His eyes had a human quality to them, the way they regarded me now. Like he understood everything that was happening.

"The marshal's right," Mittenwool said.

I glared at him, since I couldn't voice my reply.

"Don't dally now!" Marshal Farmer yelled.

"I'm not!" I answered sullenly.

"Going back to the house is the wise thing to do, Silas," Mittenwool continued.

I put my foot in the stirrup and swung my leg over Pony without looking at him. It was bad enough having the marshal tell me I couldn't go with him. I didn't need Mittenwool hectoring me about it, too. I was starting to feel hot anger rising in me at both him and the marshal equally.

"The edge of the Woods is about an hour from here," Marshal Farmer announced, pointing vaguely to his right. "I'll take you as far as the birch copse. From there it's just a short ride out."

"Fine," I mumbled.

"Now, come on, kid, enough with the long face. I told you why you can't come with me," said the marshal, trying to get me to look at him. But I wouldn't give him the satisfaction.

"This is the right thing to do," Mittenwool insisted.

"Let's just go," I said, and nudged my heels into Pony to follow Marshal Farmer.

3

WE TROTTED IN THE DIRECTION Marshal Farmer had pointed to, until we came upon a trail too narrow for us to ride side by side. He signaled for me to go ahead of him, and he followed behind. Mittenwool kept his distance as he walked parallel to us, bobbing in and out of the trees.

"Say, what's that thingum hanging from the back of your saddle?" Marshal Farmer asked at one point. His voice was light.

I pretended not to hear him, for I was in no mood to talk.

"Did you hear me, kid? What's that thing you got there? Looks like a tiny coffin."

"It's a violin case."

"A violin case? Why'd you bring that with you?"

I didn't answer him. I could feel my fury rising in my bones, up through my legs, my spine, and culminating in my head, which was hurting. All of me was hurting.

"Why'd you bring a violin case with you?" he repeated.

"To protect the violin inside of it."

"Why'd you bring the violin inside it?"

"I don't know."

"You play the violin?"

"No!"

He made a sound like a penny flute, a long, slow whistle.

"Look, I know you're mad, kid," he continued softly. "I'm sorry I can't take you with me. And, I promise you, I'll come and check in on you, after all this is said and done. I'll come visit with you and your pa in your house in Boneville. You owe me a rabbit dinner, you know."

He was trying to be conciliatory in tone, but this only aggravated me more. I was planning on not speaking to him at all, but my silence failed me.

"What if he doesn't come back?" I said, my voice scratchy, like I'd swallowed fire. I didn't look up when I said this. I was saying it to myself as much as I was saying it to him. I was saying it to Mittenwool, too. I was even saying it to Pa, in a way. His leaving me felt like a fresh wound, even though I knew why he left. It hit me now that being left alone is just about the worst thing in the world that can happen to a person. And here I was, about to be left alone again by this big old red-nosed man I'd just met. It was almost more than I could bear.

"What am I supposed to do if Pa doesn't come back?" I said again, wearily.

Marshal Farmer cleared his throat. He didn't answer right away.

"Well," he replied solemnly. "Do you have any relations you could stay with?"

"No."

"Your ma?"

"She's dead."

"I'm sorry about that."

"She died having me."

"Does she have any family?"

"They disowned her when she married Pa, on account of his coming from nothing. So even if I knew where they lived, or what their names are, I wouldn't in a million years go to them. And before you ask me, no, my pa never had any family of his own. It's only me and him."

"I see," he answered, weighing his words. "So, all right, then maybe you could go live with friends."

"I don't have any friends."

"What about your friend Mittenwool? I'm sure his family would let you stay with them."

I could not help but snort. "No, I couldn't stay with Mittenwool."

"Why? Don't you like his family?"

"He doesn't have any family, either!"

"He doesn't? How old is he?"

I shrugged. I just wanted Marshal Farmer to be quiet, at this point. So many doggone questions.

"Silas, how old is this friend of yours?" Marshal Farmer persisted. "I was assuming he was a kid like you."

"No, he's not a kid like me," I answered loudly. "He's not really a kid at all. I frankly don't know how old he is."

"Silas, be careful now," Mittenwool cautioned me.

But I was done with this. I was tired of Marshal Farmer's questions. I was as done as I could be.

"For all I know," I continued, "Mittenwool could be a hundred years old. He could be a thousand years old. He doesn't tell me stuff like that."

"Why are you doing this, Silas?" cried Mittenwool.

"So he's not a child, is that what you're saying?" asked Marshal Farmer.

"Silas, think carefully before—"

"No, he's not a child. He's a ghost, all right?" I answered hastily. "He's a ghost! You couldn't see him even if you tried! He's a ghost!"

I practically spat out the last three words. Mittenwool was looking over at me, and when I was finished, he shook his head mournfully and continued walking through the trees.

4

I SHOULD EXPLAIN THAT a long time ago, when I was about six or so, we had all agreed—me and Mittenwool, and me and Pa—that I was never to discuss Mittenwool with other people. We reached this accord after an unhappy incident involving some children, who overheard me talking to Mittenwool one afternoon as I waited for Pa outside the general store in Boneville. The children had asked me who I was talking to, and I, being innocent of how people viewed these things, told them without any trepidation: "I am talking to my friend Mittenwool!" You might well imagine how they taunted me afterward! Mocked and ridiculed me mercilessly. One boy even started twisting my arm, yelling loudly with his eyes closed, "Begone, ye devil!"

When Pa came out and saw them, the quiet fury in his eyes was something to behold. The children scattered before him like ravens in a field. Then he picked me up and put me in the cart, and gave me the reins—a thing that had never happened before, since Mule was feisty and my hands were still so small—and we rode out of Boneville. Pa was sitting on my right, and Mittenwool was on my left. *Listen, Silas,* Pa finally said, *your friendship with Mittenwool is wondrous, and something to be treasured. But there are people who won't understand it because they can't see that kind of wonder. So maybe, and this is completely up to you, but maybe you should keep your friendship with Mittenwool to yourself, at least until you get to know someone very, very well. What do you think?*

Mittenwool nodded. "Your pa is right, Silas. No one else needs to know about me."

I regretted saying what I said to Marshal Farmer the moment I said it, but there was no going back. There was no going back on any of this, anything that had happened since those three riders showed up on our doorstep. I could no more unsay what I'd said than I could travel back in time. That was another thing Pa once told me: *The world only spins in one direction, which is forward, and it goes so fast we cannot feel it.* But I could feel it right now. The world was spinning forward, at dazzling speed, and it was only forward that I could go.

I was surprised that Marshal Farmer did not respond to my statement immediately. Instead, he let my words hang in the air a bit, let the birds swoop around them, the gnats float inside them, and all the wild Woods take them in.

We rode silently until we reached the birch copse, where we would take leave of each other. Marshal Farmer called for me to slow my pace, but I felt indifferent to his words just then. I was caught in the forward motion of Pony's steps, and I could not will myself to rein him in. So the marshal trotted his horse in front of me and then turned in his saddle to face me. I figured he was going to say good-bye, and I was half right.

He removed his hat and scratched his head with the hand that held the hat. A fly had attached itself to his cheek, and he tried to chase it away with the hat. But it kept alighting on the same spot as he spoke.

"Son, I need you to be serious with me now, you hear?" he said solemnly. "Why are you toying with me like this? What is your reason for telling me all that before?"

I looked him right in the eyes. "Telling you all what before?"

He put his hat on and pursed his lips. "That business about your friend. Mittenwool."

"You mean about his being a ghost?"

"God dangit," he hollered, uncomfortable at the mere saying of the word. "You don't really believe that, do you? You're just messing with me, right?"

I shook my head and took a deep breath. Meanwhile, Mittenwool walked over and stood right between our horses.

"Tell him you were just joking, Silas," he said quietly. "Let's end this right now and go home."

"I don't want to go home," I answered. "I just want to find Pa."

"I know you do, kid," Marshal Farmer answered.

"I'm not talking to you, I'm talking to Mittenwool," I said defiantly.

Marshal Farmer again tried to brush the stubborn fly from his cheek, but I think he was just biding time to think how to respond.

"So," he prodded cautiously, "you're telling me that you're talking to him right now. This Mittenwool is here right now?"

"Yes, he's standing between our horses." I looked at Mittenwool, who shrugged his disapproval at my course of action.

"Now you've gone and done it," he muttered.

Marshal Farmer studied me carefully. He was sorely chagrined, I could tell. He once again swatted at the stubborn fly hovering near his face as he contemplated what to answer.

I looked upward. Mostly because I didn't want to look at him, but also because I wanted to take in the sky, and the birds flying overhead. This part of the Woods was so much brighter than where we'd been, and like night and day compared to the dark blue Woods I'd entered yesterday. I was now acquainting myself with the fact that forests, like all living things, are not just one thing or another, but a mix of many things together.

"Listen here," the marshal finally said, breaking the silence of my thoughts. "I've had just about enough of this. I told you I'd bring you to the edge of the Woods, and here we are. If you follow this line of trees straight through, you'll avoid hitting the Bog and get to the open in about an hour." He pointed to the black birch trees that stood like pillars marking the way. "We're a little north of where I found you, but if you stick to this trail, you should be home in time to sleep in your bed tonight."

I knew he was looking at me, waiting for me to reply, but I just turned my face back up to the sky and closed my eyes. I'm sure he thought I was touched in the head. And it could be that I was. Am. Sometimes I don't know.

I think maybe only a few seconds passed, but it felt like much longer.

"Or . . . or," he stammered, "I suppose you can come with me."

He said this so casually, I thought for sure I'd misheard him. I looked his way immediately. He was staring directly at me, his expression stone-cold and serious.

"But if you do come with me," he continued, "I cannot guarantee your safety. And I won't coddle you. If you get in my way, I'll leave you behind. If you can't keep up, I'll leave you behind. And if you lie to me . . ."

"I won't!" I cried happily, shaking my head. "I swear, Marshal Farmer, I'll keep up with you! I won't get in the way!"

He held up his parsnip finger to me, as if to warn me. "And if I hear you talk about a ghost again, or any such nonsense, so help me, I'm sending you away. Do you hear me?"

"Yes, sir," I replied with humility.

"I don't cotton to folderol like that," he said hotly. "I'm a plain man and I speak plain English and I don't have time for your flights of fancy. Maybe your pa put up with that kind of jibber-jabber, but I won't. You hear me?"

He practically huffed the last few sentences, like he was saying the words through his nose in one long exhalation.

"Yes, sir." I bobbed my head quickly.

"You sure?"

"Yes, sir!"

He nodded approvingly at my change in demeanor, for I was sitting straighter in the saddle now, to impress him. Yes, I'm small for my age, but I wanted to show him that I could be fierce, too. It seemed to me Pony perked up as well. Pawed the ground as if to say, *I'm ready. Let's charge!*

All this time, I had done my best to avoid looking at Mittenwool, who I knew would be unhappy with this change of events. I spied him briefly some distance away, looking not at me but at the Woods before us. There was nothing to say to him, even if I could have.

"All right, then, now that we are agreed, let's go," Marshal Farmer said, wheeling his mare around and trotting past me. He veered away from the birch trees into a thicket, and I knew he was heading back into the heavy Woods. Taking a deep breath, like I was about to swim underwater, I turned Pony around quickly and trotted after him.

It is forward motion was all I could think of now. I was moving forward, not backward, on this quickly spinning earth.

5

I NEVER ATTENDED SCHOOL. When I was seven or so, I had gone for a brief time to the schoolhouse in Boneville run by a woman known as Widow Barnes. By then, however, word had spread that Martin Bird's son was "addled" (that is what they called it), and when Widow Barnes heard those rumors, she confronted me one day in front of the class. Even though I was good at lying about Mittenwool at this point, and told her what she wanted to hear, she made me write *There are no such things as ghosts* on the blackboard while the children laughed behind me. And then she rapped my hand with a yardstick for good measure, telling me she wouldn't abide any newfangled spiritualists in her schoolhouse, whatever that meant.

When I came home and Pa saw the welts on my hands, and heard my tearful explanation, he looked angrier than I had ever seen him look before. *People like that old Widow Barnes have no business teaching,* he said quietly, seething as he rubbed almond oil liniment on my knuckles. *She has no idea of the grandeur that lies inside your mind, Silas. I've known people like that my whole life. They have no imagination. No fire in their minds. So they try to limit the world to the paltry things they can understand, but the world cannot be limited. The world is infinite! And you, young as you are, already know that.*

He held up my pinkie.

You see this little finger? There is more greatness in this little finger of yours than in all the Widow Barneses of the world put together. She is not worthy of your tears, Silas.

Then he kissed my pinkie and told me I was never to set foot inside that schoolhouse again. He would be my teacher from now on.

Of course, this was the best thing that could have happened to me, because Pa was a far better teacher than old Widow Barnes. I say this not to brag in any way, but to point out that because of Pa's schooling, I know things a child my age has no business knowing. Conversely, there are things a child my age should know that I don't. But Pa says it'll all balance itself out by the time I grow up. This is what I was learning as I ventured farther into the Woods. All those bits of things he'd taught me were coming back to me. Things I didn't even know I knew, I was remembering.

Marshal Farmer and I made good time. We rode straight for most of the morning until we picked up the trail of the men we were pursuing. Four men on horseback leave their marks on the ground, especially when they don't know they're being pursued. The marshal pointed these signposts out to me as we went. Horse dung, which was the easiest to track because of the flies, like small fogs, that hovered over the mounds. Broken sticks on the forest floor. Bends in branches. Puddles too round to be natural. I got better at spotting these markers myself as the day progressed. And whenever I'd see a pressed twig on the ground, I'd think, *Maybe it was Pa who made this dent.* That alone was enough to keep me going, even though I was so tired at times I felt like I could sleep a hundred years.

We did not stop to eat at all, but sipped water from the streams that crisscrossed our path. It wasn't until sometime in the midafternoon that we entered the part of the Woods that Marshal Farmer kept referring to as the Bog. We had been riding parallel to it this whole time. I would catch glimpses of it every once in a while, the murky tangle of trees on my right, darker-hued, impenetrable-seeming, and my spine would tingle just thinking about the voices I'd heard inside there the day before. I remembered Pa telling me that giant reptiles had walked the earth once, *in the days of the primordial world,* and this is what the Bog seemed to me. Something from another time, belonging to creatures of another age.

Still, we had no recourse but to go in. The men we were pursuing had entered, so we would enter, too. I did my best not to show my fear to the marshal. *Steady on, steady on.* I sat ramrod straight in the saddle as we went inside. Put on a brave face. Did not let my eyes linger on the vines that coiled like snakes around the trees. Or the branches so knotted together above us, it was like giant black daggers hung from the sky. As we twisted our way through, trunk by trunk, everything dripping around us, wet to the touch, I tried hard to ignore the cold I started feeling in my bones. The smoke coming out of my nostrils. The very air seemed thicker here. Then a fog moved in. And I started to hear the voices again.

They were distant at first. I thought maybe they were the mosquitoes that buzzed everywhere around us. But the farther we journeyed on, the louder the buzzing became, and soon I heard them not as buzzing, but as voices. Cries and murmurs, same as yesterday. Same as all those years ago, when I first entered the Woods with Pa. How to describe that sound? It is like entering a vast room where hundreds of people are conversing at once, some loudly and some softly and some urgently. This time around, I did not even bother to tell myself they were part of some delusion of my imagination. I knew what they were. These were the voices of ghosts.

I was afraid Pony would bolt again, like he did yesterday, so I kept close behind Marshal Farmer, my head down, chin pressed against my neck. If I could have closed my eyes, I would have, but I needed to stay watchful to keep up. I kept telling myself, *Be brave, Silas! You have defeated lightning.*

Soon enough, out of the corner of my eyes, I started seeing forms among the trees. Not clearly, at first. They were only the motions of beings. They were not crisply drawn in my vision, but blurs of people walking through the morass. I dared not look at them directly, for fear that I would scream and have to explain myself to Marshal Farmer. I could feel the now-familiar flush of my cheeks, the quiver of my spine, the feverish shivers running through me. It was not only fear that my body was feeling, for that is a mental preoccupation, but the physical reaction of my body to theirs. I was a living boy, after all. And they were not living. They were the dead, all around me.

The farther inside the Bog we rode, the more the blurred figures took form in my eyes. Shapes in the shadows. Walking. Talking to themselves. Some whimpered. Some laughed. They were ghosts, each to their own purposes. Their own mysteries. Speaking their own stories. Young and old. Children, too. Drifting past us like water around a rock. If you were to ask me what they looked like, I couldn't tell you. I couldn't bring myself to look at them directly. I didn't want to see them at all.

One such form passed close enough to me that I thought she would touch me, so I moved my leg to avoid her. That was enough to cause her to look up at me, for at that moment she must have realized that I could see her. And though I had done my best to avoid looking at her directly, I had no recourse now. I took her in fully. Her one eye opened wide in terror. The other not there at all, for half her head was gone, a mass of pulp and blood.

I could not help but gasp, at which point all the ghosts looked up at once, alerted to my presence. Every one of them covered in the wounds that killed them. Gashed and slashed and shot and ripped and rotted and burned. Skin shorn off bones. Limbs oozing. Bloodied. They began to come toward me. To what purpose, I did not know. And I could not help myself now. I cried out.

"What's the matter?" Marshal Farmer yelled, turning around in his saddle to look at me.

But I was off before he could finish turning. Whether Pony was acting of his own volition or reacting to my sudden distress, I don't know, but he darted in front of the marshal's mean brown mare and we raced ahead, at full speed like we did yesterday, to wherever before us was free of ghosts.

FOUR

Any body, after having been exposed to light, retains in darkness some impression of this light.

—Nicéphore Niépce
Annual of Scientific Discovery, 1859

1

ALMOST EVERY NIGHT IN THE SPRING and summer, and sometimes even into the fall, Pa and I would sit on the front porch after supper and spend an hour or so there, taking in the sky as the cool breezes blew in across the prairie. Pa would read to me, usually from one of his journals. However difficult the subject matter, he always made it sensible to me. Or he would read me stories that he knew I would like. Tales about the Arthurian knights and musketeers and buccaneers and mariners. Magic carpets. Centaurs.

Some nights, he would put the books away altogether and outline figures among the millions of stars that filled the sky. How those stories of the constellations captured my imagination! Pa's soft, musical voice would transport me across deserts and oceans. He'd use words that sounded like make-believe. *Barmy,* for instance. As in, *Cassiopeia was a barmy queen if ever there was one.* Meaning foolish.

Soogh was the sound of a long, soft breeze blowing over the sea.

Amerand was what he called the color of grass in early spring.

It was only much later that I found out these aren't words from American English, but ones Pa carried with him from across the ocean.

As I waited for Marshal Farmer to catch up to me, once I had ridden out of the Bog, all I could think of was Pa saying to me, *You're in for a gowling, Silas.*

And he was right.

2

TO SAY MARSHAL FARMER WAS furious when he finally caught up to me would be an understatement. The old man was livid, his face tomato red. He could barely speak.

"I saw a bear" was the only lie I could think of in my defense. "I'm sorry."

He was out of breath, like he himself, and not his horse, had chased after me.

"A bear," he finally said through gritted teeth. "You saw a bear, and you didn't say peep? By gum, next time you see something, you holler it from the treetops! You hear me?"

I nodded. "I'm sorry, Marshal Farmer."

"What kind of bear was it? A black bear? A grizzly?"

I was still shivering from my encounter, and I just wanted to continue riding as far away from there as possible. "I don't know. It was a shadow. . . ."

"A shadow?" He puffed out his cheeks and exhaled a long breath, like someone blowing out a candle. "Why the sam hill I ever agreed to take you, I don't know," he muttered, more to himself than me.

I thought it best not to answer him.

"You're lucky you didn't get too far ahead of me, kid, that's all I have to say," he continued, waving his large bent finger at me, "because if you had, let me tell you, I would not have bothered to find you! Let the wolves eat you, for all I care! Just listen good now: if you ever do that again . . ."

"I won't! It won't happen again. I promise."

He pulled angrily at his beard for a while, teeth still bared in fury, until he started calming down. When he was finally done being angry, he wiped his palms over his face.

"Well," he then said, looking around, "I guess this is as good a place as any to make camp for the night."

"No, please. Could we ride out a little farther?" I was still trembling.

His eyes bulged like he could not believe I had the gumption to disagree with him.

"Please. Just a little farther away from the Bog?" I pleaded.

"What makes you think we're not still in the danged Bog!"

There are no ghosts here, I thought.

"The ground is less wet here," I said.

"Exactly! The ground is dry!" he yelled, shaking his fist at me. "Which is why we should make camp here!" He pushed up his sleeves. "Now get off your horse and get a fire going! It's almost dark. We've been riding twelve hours straight and the horses need rest."

He got off his horse and took a long stretch, holding his hand on his hip. I couldn't help but notice that his back stayed bent at an angle, even when he tried to straighten himself out. When he spied me watching him, he roared, "I said to get off that dod-rotted horse! Go find us some firewood! Hurry up, while there's still some light to see by!"

I dismounted, tied Pony to a nearby tree, and hastily started looking for kindling.

3

I WAS SOME DISTANCE AWAY, my arms full of wood, when Mittenwool came up to me.

"How are you doing there, Silas?" he asked sympathetically.

"I can't let him hear me talking to you," I whispered, glancing back at Marshal Farmer to make sure he wasn't watching me. "I don't want to get him riled up again."

"I don't like the way he talks to you."

"I shouldn't have let Pony run off like that."

"He got startled."

"So you saw what happened back there? In the Bog?"

He clenched his jaw. "I did."

"There were so many of them, Mittenwool. Covered in blood. It was the most scared I've ever been in my life."

"I know. But you're all right now."

"What if they come here tonight, though, while I'm asleep?"

"They won't. They don't leave the Bog."

"Why?"

"It's just how it is."

"But why? Why do they not leave the Bog? And how do you know that? Just yesterday you said you didn't know what they were."

"And I didn't, not for sure. But today I *saw* them, just like you did. It's obvious what they are."

"They're ghosts."

He grimaced and nodded.

"You *saw* them," I said. "But they didn't see you."

He shrugged, like he wasn't sure how to respond.

Then it hit me. "Maybe some ghosts don't know they're dead."

He stood silently for a few seconds, his hair falling over his eyes as he looked down at his feet.

"I can't tell you what some ghosts know or don't know," he replied softly. "Death is different for everyone. Just like life is. People see the world they believe in. And you see the world they believe in. I know it's not easy for you."

He brushed the hair away from his face and looked at me intently. "Those ghosts in the Bog don't mean you any harm, Silas. They're just passing through, same as you. Maybe they linger because that ground holds some meaning to them. But they'll move on when they're ready. Either way, it's nothing to do with you. So you don't need to worry about them coming here tonight. All right? You'll be fine."

"Darnation and hellfire!" Marshal Farmer bellowed from the other side of camp. "What is taking you so long, kid?" He was looking for me through the trees.

"I'm coming!" I called back. Then, to Mittenwool, "We should get back before he has another conniption."

"Go on. I'll see you tomorrow."

"Wait. You're not coming with me?"

"I'd rather stay put, if that's all right. I can still hear you from here."

"Is this because you don't like him?"

He glanced over at the marshal, who was by now furiously kicking out his bedroll, stomping and cussing and throwing a fit that I hadn't started the fire yet. "Like I said before," he said, "it bothers me the way he talks to you. He's a mean old fogy."

"I know he is, but he's going to help me find Pa. That's all I care about."

"Well, he better start being nicer to you, or else."

"Or else what? You going to give him a drubbing?" I chuckled.

"Oh, you don't know what I can do!" he replied comically, balling his hand into a fist. "Anyway, I'll be right here if you need me. Go get some sleep. Good night."

"Night."

I started to walk back to camp, then remembered something.

"What about Aethon, by the way?"

He weighed the name. "What is that from?"

"One of Hector's horses."

He repeated it a few times. "I still like Pony better."

I frowned. "Hmm. All right."

"Keep thinking, though."

"I will."

4

MARSHAL FARMER DIDN'T UTTER two words to me once I returned to camp, not even when I offered him some morels I had foraged after I made the fire. He just waved me away brusquely, lit his pipe, and stared into the flames. I was fine not talking to him, either. Happy not to have to talk, quite frankly. At least, at first I was. As the night went on, though, and the memory of the ghosts in the Bog kept swirling in my mind, the silence started wearing on me. It seemed like wherever my eyes turned, I'd see that woman's face in the darkness. The bright red blood. The horror of her demise so plain to see. I could not shake the questions taking turns in my mind, until finally, I had no choice but to break the silence.

"Marshal Farmer?" My voice sounded like a little squeak in the night, even to my own ears. "Can I ask you a question?"

He looked at me warily. "What."

I chose my words very carefully. "Did something happen back there once? In that Bog we passed through?"

"You mean the place where you *saw a bear*?" he sneered, then spat into the fire.

I ignored his tone. "I remember my pa telling me there were a lot of skirmishes in these parts. Between the settlers and the natives."

"This was all disputed territory, if that's what you're talking about," he answered, throwing a little stick into the fire. "But we drove them out."

"Who is *we*?"

"The government."

"Drove them out where?"

"Indian Territory! God blast it, with all your questions!"

I thought of the ghosts.

"I don't think they were *driven out*," I noted quietly. "I think they were killed. Some of them, at least."

"There was killing on both sides."

"My pa says it's repugnant what's been done to the natives," I answered.

Marshal Farmer harrumphed and tossed another stick into the fire.

"I think it's repugnant, too," I added.

"Well, you're just a small fry. You don't know much."

"Let us fight; and, if we must, let us die; but let us not conquer."

"That something else your pa says?"

"Fénelon wrote it. Do you know who that is?"

"Another one of your ghost friends, I wager."

"He was a writer," I answered. "François Fénelon. He wrote *The Adventures of Telemachus*. Do you know it?"

He looked surprised by the question.

"I'm not exactly a bookish man, kid. In case that wasn't obvious."

"Well, it's one of my favorite books in the world," I answered. "Fénelon wrote it for the king of France when he was still a boy. Anyway, he wrote that war is only ever justified if it's fought to bring about peace. But our government isn't fighting for peace. It's fighting for territory. So I don't think it's justified at all."

Marshal Farmer dug his canteen out of his coat and took a long drink from it.

"I mean, you can't just take someone else's land and expect them to be at peace with it, can you?" I continued.

He rubbed his eyes. "Well, when you got the big guns on your side, you can do anything you want."

"That's a terrible attitude to have!" I yelled.

He raised his chin at me, his eyes luminous, and I thought for sure he would rebuke me.

"You're a pistol, kid," he answered, and burped.

That's when I realized it wasn't water in the canteen, but something that made him that much more agreeable.

"I bet you don't even know who Telemachus is," I said.

"And you would win that bet," he answered.

"Do you want to know?"

He raised his eyebrows and gave a short whistle. "Sure, kid. I'm dying to know."

Again, I pretended not to note his sarcasm.

"Telemachus was the son of Ulysses," I said, "Ulysses being the cleverest of all the Greek warriors who fought in the Trojan War. But Ulysses did something that made the gods mad at him, so they punished him by making him get lost on his way home to Ithaca, after the war was over. Twenty years went by, and Ulysses still hadn't come home, so Telemachus, the son he'd left behind when he was just a baby, goes looking for him, to bring him back home."

Marshal Farmer crossed his arms and tilted his head at me.

"Why the goose are you telling me all this?" he said wearily.

"I don't know," I answered. "I guess I'm thinking it's kind of like me looking for my pa." This was actually a connection I had not made until this moment, and it pleased me to share it. "And Telemachus, he's accompanied on his adventures by a man named Mentor, and that's kind of like you, don't you think? I mean, the way you're teaching me about the Woods, and how to make a fire, and things of that nature."

I thought maybe this would flatter him, but he only huffed. He held the canteen up to me, like he was going to toast me or something.

"You're a very chatty kid, you know that?" was all he said.

I flushed, feeling suddenly foolish.

"I thought you'd find it interesting, that's all," I answered regretfully. "Pa told me the ancient Greeks put a lot of store in long travels, and homecomings, and all that."

"I told you, I'm not one for books," he grumbled. "Anyway, it's getting late." He drained the last of his canteen. "And frankly, you chirping like a dad-blasted bird is putting me to sleep. Good night."

"Good night." My voice quavered slightly.

"You could tell me more about the book tomorrow, if you want," he added in a way that I think was meant to be conciliatory. By now he had taken off his hat and placed it on top of his face. "Ha," he added from under the hat. "Chirping like a bird. And your name is Bird. I didn't even mean to be funny when I said that." He pushed up the brim of his hat and peeked at me. "That was funny, don't you think? Aw, I'll be hanged. You're not crying, are you?"

"No."

"That dog won't hunt with me!" he growled.

"I'm not crying!"

"Good!"

"I know you think I'm strange." I wiped my eye with my knuckle. "Not the first time someone's thought that."

He groaned. Or maybe it was a long sigh.

"I wouldn't say strange, exactly," he answered, not unkindly. "But you're not like any other kid I've ever met before, I'll tell you that much."

I sniffed in my tears and looked away. "That's probably not even water in your canteen."

"Sure, it is! It's my special nectar water."

I shook my head disapprovingly.

"I'll tell you what, kid," he slurred softly. "There's nothing in the world that doesn't look better in the daytime than at night, so just close your eyes and get some sleep. You'll feel better in the morning."

"The moon does," I replied, trying to keep my voice from breaking.

He looked at me blankly for a bit, until what I'd said made sense to him.

"Ha," he said, nodding his head. "You got me there, kid. Good night."

Then he covered his face with his hat again, and was snoring before I could count to ten.

5

***THE MOON DOES,* I HAD SAID.** It was a good retort. I wondered if Mittenwool had heard it. He would think it a clever reply to this unclever old man. Pa would've liked it, too.

Just thinking of Pa made my heart skip a beat.

I could see the moon above me, showing through the tops of the trees. A full white moon against a bone-black sky. *Pa could be looking at it right now,* I thought. *What's he doing at this very moment? Is he thinking about me?*

It was only a month ago that Pa and I had been on our front porch, taking a picture of a full moon just like this one. Well, not really like this one. Was it really only a month ago? Felt like ages.

(My mind was doing that thing again where my thoughts went in all directions at once.)

The plan had been to enter the photograph in a contest advertised in one of Pa's science journals. The best "lunar picture" would win a cash prize of fifty dollars and be exhibited by the Royal Astronomical Society at the Great London Exhibition of 1862.

"Fifty dollars for a photograph of the moon?" I had remarked skeptically when Pa showed me the announcement over breakfast. This was back in November some time. "Seems like easy money to me."

Pa had chuckled. "Oh, it's harder than you'd think, son," he said gently. "First of all, a person would need a big telescope, at least six or seven feet long. Maybe longer. The kind Foucault presented to the Academy of Sciences a few years back. With silvered glass for the reflector. Not speculum, mind you, which is what most of these so-called gentleman amateurs still use. They'd have to grind the glass, coat it with silver nitrate, and ammonia, maybe some potash. Milk sugar. Build a clockwork of some kind. Something to mount the whole thing on. No, no, it's a heap of work, son. That's why no one's been able to do it well since De la Rue. It's a big, big undertaking."

"Pa, you know what?" I said. "You should do it. You should enter this contest!"

"Ha," he said lightly, thinking I was joking.

"Why not? You would win!"

He raised his eyebrows at me. "Do you know how much time and money it would take to build a telescope of that kind?"

"But you already built a telescope."

"Not like that one, son."

"And we've been making good money from your irontypes."

"Which is for your schooling someday."

"But we could go to London if you won, Pa! You could wear one of those tall fancy hats to the exhibition!" I held my arm above my head to indicate how high his hat would go.

"Well, that would be a sight," he replied, amused. He leaned back in his chair.

"Come on! It'll be fun. I'll help you."

He smiled and sighed at the same time and then, after a few seconds, said, "You'll help me, aye? Do you remember what I taught you about the moon's orbit? What does *perigee* mean?"

"It's when the moon . . ." I hesitated.

He smiled. "It's the point in the moon's orbit when it's closest to the earth."

"Closest to the earth," I agreed quickly.

He nodded and reached for his reading spectacles. Then he picked up the *Farmers' Almanac* on the table and started leafing through it. He stopped at a page and ran his finger down a chart. *"March the seventh, 1860: The full moon will occur near perigee,"* he read aloud, and peered up over his glasses at me. "That would be the time to take it. When the full moon is closest to the earth. Won't get any brighter or bigger than that for the rest of the year."

"Does that mean we're going to do this?"

He closed the almanac. "Well, since you promised to help me . . ."

I clapped. "Hurrah! We're going to London!"

"Now, now, don't get your hopes up too high. March seventh is only four months away, and we have a lot of work to do before then. There are no shortcuts for hard work."

He was not exaggerating about that! The amount of work Pa ended up doing, every night, over those next four months, was nothing short of astounding. Building a telescope. A clock drive. A wooden mount. Experimenting with colloidal mixes. Adapting his camera box. All this while still fulfilling boot orders and taking portraits at the studio by day. Every night, I'd go to sleep leaving him bent over the table full of books, and every morning, I'd find him in the same spot. Not that he ever complained. If anything, he seemed to relish the work, even when his palms started bleeding from hours of grinding lenses on sandstone, then polishing the glass.

As the big day drew closer, it became the focus of all our conversations. What if it snowed that evening? What if it was cloudy? What if it was too cold and the lens fogged? What if it was too windy and the camera moved? By the time March 7 rolled around, I was giddy with anticipation. And Pa, who was generally cautious with his enthusiasm, could barely contain his own excitement.

When the day dawned and it turned out to be crystal clear, with not a cloud in the sky, we could not believe our good luck. It was like heaven had conspired with us to create this work of beauty, and we were ready for it. We had rehearsed the events of the evening countless times by then, to make sure everything went off without a hitch. Pa had painted X's on the wooden planks where the mount should stand, and enclosed the porch with a screen to keep the wind at bay. We brought out the telescope as soon as the sun started sinking in the sky. It was not a particularly elegant contraption on the outside, just a long rectangular box made of rough, unpolished walnut. But that box housed a meticulous array of mirrored glass lenses that would, Pa said, *bring the cosmos within our reach.* At the base of the telescope was the camera attachment, which Pa affixed carefully. Then, when he was done adjusting the angle and securing the base, he sat down next to me on the porch steps, and we waited for nightfall in silent wonder. When the moon started to rise above the hill line, it was sheer magnificence.

"Wow," I whispered reverentially. "It looks as bright as the sun."

"It's the sun that's making it shine," he whispered back.

"But the sun's not even out."

"It sure is." He tousled my hair. "Even if we can't see it, the sun never stops shining. Always remember that."

"All right."

"I think the sky's dark enough now." He stood up and brushed off his pants. "Are we ready to do this?"

"Ready!" I said, hopping up happily.

He poured the collodion over the glass plate, which would become the negative, tilting it slightly to let the solution cover the entire surface. Then, under cover of a large black cloth, he sensitized the plate with silver nitrate and slid the plate-holder into the camera box. He made a few slight adjustments to the focus reflector before slowly removing the cloth.

Finally, once everything was ready, he took a deep breath and gingerly lifted the cover off the lens to begin the exposure. We counted backward from twenty . . .

Six. Five. Four. Three. Two. One.

He replaced the cover. It was only then, after he exhaled, that I realized he had been holding his breath the whole time.

Once the lens was covered, he quickly removed the wooden plate-holder from the camera and proceeded to the darkroom in the cellar, which was lit by a single ruby-colored lantern. He poured his irontype solution over the glass plate to bring out the latent image of the moon.

It has always been a wonder to me, and always will be, to see something invisible be made visible. Slowly, magically, the negative of the moon took form on the glass plate inside the bath.

Pa lifted the glass plate by the very edges and gently rinsed it in a separate tray of rainwater. Then he held it up close to his face to examine it thoroughly in the dim red light. The water dripped from the bottom of the glass onto the floor.

"I must admit, Silas," he said slowly, smiling as he scanned every corner of the plate, "this exceeds my greatest expectations. The edges are crisp. The shadow areas are well defined. You can see the finest details—even in the craters. This really might do it for us!"

"Can I see? Can I see?" I asked excitedly.

"Of course, but be very careful."

He handed me the glass plate, and no sooner were my fingers curled around its edges than it slipped from my grasp. In an instant, the glass was in a million tiny shards around my feet.

I gasped, like my lungs had been punctured.

"Oh no," I said breathlessly. My hand covered my mouth. "Oh no. Oh no."

I started to moan. I could not believe what I had just done.

"It's all right, son."

I could not look at his face. "Oh, Pa . . ."

Words would not form on my lips. They were like pieces of glass in my mouth.

"It's all right, son," he repeated softly, rubbing my shoulder. "I promise. It's all right."

I was overtaken by a frenzied sobbing then, a quaking of tears that tore through my entire body. My stupidity! My clumsiness! Widow Barnes was right. *Addled!* That is what I am!

I might have collapsed into the pile of glass shards then and there, but Pa picked me up and carried me to the kitchen. I was wailing so hard, my head started hurting. My eyes were stinging. I hadn't realized my ankles were full of tiny bits of glass until I saw the blood.

Pa sat me on the edge of the table and meticulously removed the glass fragments from my legs while I tried to calm myself down. He whispered soothingly as he wiped away the little pinpricks of blood with tincture of iodine. "It was never really about the exhibition, or the prize money, right? What really matters is, we did it. Silas. We took a picture of the moon. That's all that matters, son. That we did it."

He tried to get me to look at him, and when I did, he smiled and placed his palms on my cheeks, wiping my tears with his thumbs.

"There'll be other moons," he assured me, looking deeply into my eyes. "Don't you worry."

Then he hugged me, and I knew everything would be all right.

He carried me to my room, and sat on the edge of my bed until I fell asleep.

I woke up a few hours later, my eyes puffy from the tears I had shed. Pa was no longer sitting in my room, but Mittenwool was there.

"Did you see what happened before?" I asked. "I broke the moon."

"I saw. I'm sorry."

"Is Pa asleep?"

"He's on the porch."

I crept down the ladder and peeked out the kitchen window. Pa was indeed on the porch, leaning against the column next to the telescope. There was only a hazy yellow mist where the moon had been earlier, but Pa was looking up at the sky like he could still see it. His eyes were shining in the dark.

He looked so peaceful, I did not interrupt him. I went back to my bed.

"There'll be other moons," said Mittenwool, repeating what Pa had said.

"Not like that one," I answered, and pulled the covers over my head.

Now, as I lay inside these unknown Woods, on unknown ground, looking up at a full moon infinitely paler than the one we had briefly captured, all I could think of was Pa's eyes peering up at the sky, shining a thousand times brighter than any moon ever could.

Looking back, I knew it wasn't the sun that lit the moon that night. It was Pa.

FIVE

We do not know why they can come,
nor why they can not.

—Catherine Crowe
The Night-Side of Nature, 1848

1

I WAS AWAKE BEFORE MARSHAL FARMER the next morning, ready to go. Ready to move. As soon as he was up, too, we got on the horses and took off. No chitchat. No taking time to eat.

Luckily, we did not have to go into the Bog again. The men we were pursuing must have hated that swampland as much as we did, for they had taken a path around it rather than venture through it. I was relieved, of course, not only because it spared me further acquaintance with the ghosts in the Bog, but because I'd been bitten up mercilessly by the mosquitoes there.

"How come they don't go after you?" I whined, noting as we paused at a brook to let the horses drink that Marshal Farmer had not a single bite on him. Meanwhile, I was making myself bleed from all my scratching.

"My skin is too tough for them, I guess," he crowed. "That's what happens when you get to be as old as I am."

"How old are you?"

"Hmph. You know, I'm not sure," he muttered. He squinted into the trees on the far side of the brook. "Truth is, I've spent so much time in these Woods, chasing fugitives this way and that way, I lose track of time. What year is this, anyway?"

"Eighteen sixty."

"Huh. That seems about right. I'll tell you, kid: time gets swallowed up in these Woods. Let's go."

He spurred his mare and I followed dutifully.

I had noticed this, too, about time inside the Woods. I had no concept if it was morning or afternoon when we were riding. Minutes seemed like hours. Hours flew like seconds. Sometimes we'd be riding, and it felt like we were seeing the same trees, the same groves, the same small knolls full of bloodroot and chickweed, over and over again. But then all of a sudden, we'd happen on a bright little glade, and it was like heaven had come down to earth on sunbeams. Every tree, every branch, sparkled in gold light, and when I looked straight up, I could see the sky glowing blue above the canopy of trees. It was wondrously beautiful.

I came to see that time is like the dappled light inside the Woods. It comes and goes. Hides and shines. And all the while, we're just running through it. I felt a bit like Jonah in that mighty whale of his, cut off from the world, with the trees rising around me like enormous ribs, and Pony, my little boat, tossing on the sea. Not that I've ever been to sea before, but this is how I imagined it.

We made only one longish stop that day. I think it was mid-afternoon, but I don't know, could've been earlier. I jumped down from Pony and started plucking fiddleheads while Marshal Farmer got on his haunches to examine the trail, which had become a bit vague in the brush here. Again, I could not help but note how corkscrewed his back was.

"What are you gaping at?" he gnarred at me when he caught me watching him.

"Nothing!"

Really, he was such a cantankerous old man, I could hardly stand it at times.

"I got some fiddleheads we can eat later," I said, pointing to the ferns next to me.

"Those are the poison kind," he remarked indifferently.

"What?" I hastily dropped the fiddleheads and wiped my palms on my coat.

"Help me up here."

I put out my hand, and he used it to hoist himself to his feet.

"Only eat the ones with brown sheaths," he said when he was standing. "Now let's get a wiggle on. I know which way they went."

I mounted Pony and watched as he struggled to get on his mare because of his back pain.

"My pa can help you with your back, by the way," I said cautiously once we got the horses at a pace. I was riding alongside him in a wide but dark clearing. "When we find him, I mean. He can realign the vertebrae of your back, like he did to mine."

"What're you jawing about now?"

"After my brush with lightning a couple of years ago," I continued, "my back got out of sorts because of the fall I took, so my pa got ahold of every anatomy book he could find and, lo and behold, he cured my spine! He could cure yours, too!"

He gave me an angry side glance, so I looked away quickly.

"Really, he could've been a doctor, my pa," I continued, careful not to look at him, like a wild animal you don't want to look in the eye. "He knows so much biology and things of that nature. Or a scientist."

"Thought you said he's a boot-maker."

"That's what he does for a living," I answered. "But he knows about a lot of other things. You never met a smarter man, Marshal Farmer! Something of a genius, you might say."

"That so."

"That's why they took him, I think."

"What do you mean?"

"They probably thought he could help them with all that canter-fitting stuff."

"Counterfeiting."

"Counterfeiting."

"You don't even know what that is, do you?"

"No, sir."

"You know who Fénelon is, but you don't know the word *counterfeiting.*"

If his intention was to make me feel foolish, he succeeded. "I didn't say *I* was a genius," I mumbled.

"A counterfeiter is someone who makes fake money," he explained.

"Fake money? How do they do that?"

"There are different ways," he answered. "Basically, they wash old banknotes clean of ink, and then print them with higher denominations that look real enough to pass for genuine money."

"How do they wash them clean?"

"They use chemicals and the like."

I could not keep from exulting. "Then my theory makes sense! Pa uses chemicals to print pictures on paper, Marshal Farmer, whereby the image doesn't just rest on the surface, like it does with albumen prints, but is dyed into the paper fiber itself. He took out a patent on it and everything."

He leaned back in the saddle and gnawed on his cheek, like he was actually giving my words some thought.

"Well, chemicals are a bit above my bend, I'll allow," he said after a few moments, "but you could be right about that, kid. These counterfeiters are always looking for new ways to do things. No matter what the banks do to try and outsmart them, the counterfeiters are two steps ahead of them."

"It doesn't even seem so bad to me, printing fake money," I then jabbered on, without thinking through what I was saying. I don't know why around Marshal Farmer words just seemed to pour out of my mouth like spittle.

"You don't think it's so bad?" he yelled angrily, flipping around in his saddle to literally gnash his teeth at me. They were the color of dirt, the few he had. "If you had a hundred-dollar note and it turned out to be worthless, how would you feel about that?"

My mouth dropped open. "Marshal Farmer," I answered truthfully, "I can't know how I'd feel, as I've never had a hundred-dollar note in my whole life!"

I think my unexpectedly honest reply caught him by surprise. He snorted as he shook his head.

"Tell you what, kid," he replied. "If your pa can fix my back, I'll pay him double that in real money."

"That's a deal!" I answered, feeling good that I had gotten him to be amiable.

"All right, now. Enough of this gabbing. Gig your horse and let's get moving."

"Wait, Marshal Farmer. Look!" I cried, pulling Pony to a quick stop. I jumped down excitedly and ran over to the base of a tree where two little songbird eggs lay unbroken on some bracken. I held them up for him to see. "One for you and one for me!"

"Fine, fine, let's go." He snapped his fingers at me impatiently.

I carefully put the little eggs in my coat pocket and hopped back on Pony.

"What did you mean before, by the way?" he said after a few minutes, looking at me sideways as we rode. "Your *brush with lightning*. What does that mean?"

"Oh. I got struck by a lightning bolt a couple of years ago," I answered without any flourish.

He snorted again, shaking his head. Then he spurred his mare to go faster.

"It's true!" I called out after him, kneeing Pony to catch up. "It left a mark on my back. I can show you when we make camp later."

"No, kid, it's fine." He didn't even look my way when he said this.

"Pa says it means I'm lucky," I added.

"Lucky?" he hissed, and suddenly all the mirth in his voice was gone. "You're out here in the middle of nowhere, chasing a band of outlaws. How's that lucky?"

"Well. Finding you was lucky, wasn't it?"

He was his old muffled self again. Face-forward in the saddle. Mouth twisting down at the sides.

"How about you give your mouth a rest, all right?" he murmured. "Never knew anyone who could talk as much as you do!"

And that was the end of our conversation for the rest of the day.

2

WE MADE CAMP SHORTLY BEFORE DUSK. Marshal Farmer sat down with a groan, his back against a large tree, while I went about making the fire to boil the eggs, which I had carefully candled. My hunger had caught up to me finally. I was feeling genuine pangs in my sides now, under my ribs. My head was sappy. I watched the eggs cook and my mouth watered.

This was now the end of our third day together in the Woods.

The marshal and I sat in silence, as usual, on opposite sides of the fire. I resolved that tonight I would not start up any conversation with him at all. I'd had enough of his barbs about my talkativeness. If he wanted to talk, let him do it. I gazed at the fire while he pulled out his canteen and took several long drinks. I daresay he must have had a dozen bottles of his "nectar" stored in his poke bag, the way that canteen never seemed to run dry.

I think maybe he knew I was planning on not talking tonight, because he kept eyeing me as I cooked the eggs, like he was itching for me to speak up. Which I wasn't about to do.

Finally, as he was lighting his pipe, he broke the silence.

"You know, your talking about your pa before," he said, "it got me thinking some."

I stoked the fire, kept my face still.

"You sure he didn't know any of those men who came for him?" he continued.

I could feel my throat tighten. "I'm sure."

He nodded, raking his fingers through his beard. His whole body, in the demi-light of the fire, seemed to disappear into the tree trunk he was leaning on. "I'm just asking because that Mac Boat was a clever fellow. He'd have been interested in that chemical stuff you were talking about earlier."

I hated myself for having prattled on about any of that.

"Did I even tell you what Mac Boat did?" he queried.

"Just that he was a counterfeiter."

"That's what he *was,*" he blurted. "It's not what he *did.* Want me to tell you?"

I lifted my shoulders to my ears, like I didn't care one way or another.

"The man took your pa. You're not even curious?"

"I never said *he* took my pa," I answered quickly. "Just that Rufe Jones mentioned his name, that's all."

"I'm just surprised at your lack of curiosity."

"Fine, then. Tell me."

He rearranged himself on the tree, like he was getting ready to tell a long story.

"You ever hear of the Orange Street Gang?" he asked, pointing his pipe at me. "No. Of course you haven't. The Orange Street Gang was the biggest counterfeiting ring in New York. This is going way back, of course, before you were born. They had operations running from the Five Points all the way up to Canada, that's how big they were. Anyway, Mac Boat came up in the Orange Street Gang."

"All right." Again I shrugged, trying to feign indifference.

"Now, the authorities had been after this gang for years," he continued, enjoying the telling of this story enormously. "And one day, out of the blue, they got a tip about a big exchange going down. That's when counterfeit notes get swapped out for real money. So, they got a huge posse together. Sheriffs, policemen, marshals. About twenty lawmen in all. Surrounded the headquarters on Orange Street. There was a big gunfight. Six lawmen were killed. But by the end of the day, they got them all. The whole gang either killed or arrested—except for one. Want to know who?"

He looked at me, eyes bulging eagerly.

"Mac Boat," I answered reluctantly.

"That's right," he said, taking another long whiff of his pipe. "And to this day, no one knows how he did it. Not only did he get away from the lawmen that day, but he made off with a trunk full of gold coins. Twenty thousand dollars' worth of newly minted Liberty Heads."

I could not help but gasp. "Twenty thousand dollars? Where'd he go with all that money?"

Marshal Farmer leaned back. "Nobody knows," he answered.

"The gold coins never made it back into circulation. They might be buried somewhere. Or melted into gold brick. He could've taken them with him to Scotland, which is where he was from. Truth is, no one knows what happened to Mac Boat. It's like he disappeared into thin air. That's why when you mentioned his name to me, out of nowhere, my ears perked up. It's all very mysterious, don't you think?"

I looked down at the fire. I cannot say what I was thinking, for I myself did not know.

"It made me realize," the marshal continued, "if Mac Boat is in cahoots with the men I'm pursuing, there's a good chance I might solve the mystery of that twenty thousand dollars when I catch them. That would be a real feather in my cap, wouldn't it?"

The boiled eggs were ready. The truth is, I had lost my appetite. I took the bowl off the fire and spooned one egg out of the water with a forked stick, not from any desire to eat, but to keep myself from looking at the marshal.

As I peeled the egg, I could feel the marshal's eyes glowering at me.

"It's not the reward money I'm after, mind you," he continued. "I'm after these fellas to settle a score, that's all. A few years back, my partner was killed by the head of this particular ring, a man by the name of Roscoe Ollerenshaw, and I—"

"That's the name," I said, looking up quickly.

"What's that?"

"That's the name I couldn't remember the other day. *That's* the man who sent Rufe Jones to get my pa. Not Mac Boat."

"Roscoe Ollerenshaw? You sure?"

"Certain of it."

"Well, don't that beat all," he hissed, scratching his cheek. "That's the man I've been after for years now! Swore on my partner's grave I'd find him someday. I'll be darned!"

As he was saying this, I bit into the top of the peeled egg. Then I immediately spat it out, stifling the urge to throw up.

Marshal Farmer grinned.

"It's a wild egg, son," he tittered softly.

"But I candled it!"

"Sometimes you can't tell it's pipping until you take the first bite. I figured you knew that."

"No, I didn't know that!" I replied bitterly, taking a big sip of water from my canteen while hurling the egg into the fire.

"Try the other one," he said. "It might be fine."

I threw the other egg into the fire, too, and wrapped my arms around my knees.

"If you're really hungry," he offered, "you can always dig for cutworms. They don't taste half bad if you fry them on a stick."

"I'm not hungry!"

"Up to you." He took his canteen out and started drinking from it. "Anyway, what I was saying before—"

"Look, if you don't mind!" I interrupted, for I felt like I really might retch. "I don't want to talk about these things anymore. I don't want to hear about gunfights and posses and counterfeiters. I just want to go to sleep now. That all right with you?"

The fire sputtered.

"Fair enough," he replied, amused. "But throw some wood on the fire before you turn in, will you?"

I rolled my eyes, threw a few large sticks at the cracklings, and then laid out the saddle blanket.

"Good night," I said, curling onto my side, away from the fire.

He burped. "Hey, let me ask you one more thing." His voice was a bit skewed, his tone mischievous.

I groaned. For some reason, I knew exactly what he was going to ask. "What."

He took a second to swallow his drink. "Why'd you call him Mittenwool, anyway? What kind of name is that? Why not Tom? Or Frank?"

"I didn't *call* him anything. That's his name."

"That's the kind of name a little kid would make up. Like Penny Doll. Or Lumber Jack."

I finally turned around to look at him. "What kind of man lets a boy bite into a pipped egg? That's what you should be asking yourself!"

"Hee-hee-hee! The kind of man who figures a boy with a ghost knows what's what in the world! I assumed your invisible friend was looking out for you, making sure you didn't eat half-cooked chickabiddies."

I narrowed my eyes at him. "Well, my *invisible friend* isn't here right now. And you want to know why? Because he doesn't like you, Marshal Farmer! Not one bit! And I can't say I blame him."

I hadn't realized just how much fury was in my voice until he looked at me, his eyebrows raised high, his lips closed tight. Then he let out the biggest laugh I'd heard out of him yet. He cackled so hard that it ended up making him cough.

I just plopped back down on the blanket.

"I'm glad you're enjoying yourself," I said, rolling over on my side.

"No, kid," he answered, laughter still in his voice. "Please, I'm just having a little fun with you, that's all. Don't be like that."

"I sure as heck don't think you're funny," I shot back from under the blanket.

"Don't be mad, kid. It's just old Marshal Farmer having himself a little laugh. Truth is, I've been on my own for so long, I think I plumb forgot how to be around people."

"The only reason I'm here with you is because you're helping me find my pa. That's the *only* reason."

"I know, kid."

"And I don't care one iota whether you believe me or not," I continued. "Not about lightning bolts or ghosts or anything at all. Pa always says, *The truth is the truth. Doesn't matter what other people believe.* So you go ahead and believe anything you'd like, Marshal Farmer. Have yourself a little laugh. I don't care in the least. I'm going to sleep now. Good night!"

The fire crackled and its warmth spread across my back. A few seconds passed.

"He sounds like a good man, your pa," Marshal Farmer said gently.

I swallowed hard. "Best man there is."

"I'm going to find him for you, kid. I promise you that."

He sounded like he really meant it. I didn't answer him.

"Good night, kid."

I didn't answer him.

3

MY MIND WANDERED IN CIRCLES after that. Marshal Farmer, in his inimitable way, had sparked little fires inside my head a hundred times hotter than the campfire at my back. Thoughts swirled like smoke. My head ached.

Mittenwool.

Pa told me it was one of the first words out of my mouth when I was a baby. Not *Pa.* Not *goo-goo.* But *Mittenwool.* How peculiar I must've seemed to Pa back then. I can't imagine what he thought. But he always made it seem so ordinary. Never once gave me grief about it. Never once made me feel foolish, or doubtful.

It's not that I haven't pondered the mystery of Mittenwool before, of course. I may be young, but I am curious, too. And while I've come to accept the unknowables of our world with all due respect, I was always reasonable enough to form the questions for which I had no answers. I even directed these queries to Mittenwool on occasion, as I've mentioned, but he was ever vague. He doesn't know beans about himself, truth be told. And there's no rhyme or reason to the little he does know. The rules of chess. A dislike of pears. His disdain for shoes. The only thing he knows for sure is that he doesn't know anything for sure.

This is what I have come to believe: some souls are ready to depart the world, and some are not. That's all there is to it. The ones who are, like my mother, they just go. But the ones who aren't, they linger. Maybe their deaths came too suddenly, so they attach themselves to the place where they last remember being alive. Something familiar. Where their bones rest. Or maybe they're waiting for someone. They have unfinished business. Something they want to see through. And when they do see it through, they move on, just like Mittenwool said.

As to why I can see them and others can't, that I don't know. I remember my surprise as a youngster when I first realized that other people couldn't see Mittenwool. *How can that be? He is so vivid to me! I can hold his hand! I can see his teeth when he laughs! His clothes have wrinkles! His fingernails get dirty! He is real as real can be. Flesh and blood. How can people not see him? How can Pa not see him?* It seemed impossible to me.

Nor was he the only ghost I'd ever seen. There were always others, at the edges of my vision. Fleeting shadows in Boneville. Figures lurking behind trees. I would shut my eyes to them, though. I didn't want to see what I couldn't unsee.

It was never like that with Mittenwool. There wasn't a moment in my life when he wasn't there. Like a big brother. My unceasing companion.

As to *why* he came to me in the first place, how we are connected—that is what I may never know. I suppose that's the way it is with everyone in life. Every day, people pass each other on the street, and they have no idea if they're connected in any way. If maybe their grandmothers knew each other once. It doesn't occur to the lady buying sugar in the mercantile that the stranger in front of her is a distant cousin. Folks just don't think that way. They don't wonder when they meet each other, *Did our ancestors know each other? Did they fight each other, perhaps? Did they love each other? Back in ancient times, when tribes of people roamed the desert, were we kin?* Heaven knows the connections that bind us! And if that is the way it is with the living, then that is the way it must be for the dead, too. The mysteries that govern us, govern them as well. If life is a journey to the great unknown, then death must be a journey, too. And while some people, like my mama, might know exactly where they're going, other people might not. Maybe they meander a little, not sure where they're headed, or feel a bit lost. Maybe they need a map, like foreigners in a new country. They're looking for landmarks. A compass. Instructions on where to go. Maybe Mittenwool is just traveling through, and his time with me is a stop on the road for him.

I simply don't know.

But I have made my peace with everything I don't know. I have made my peace with all the laws of physics that are broken, and the unnatural biologies at play, and the inconsistent proofs of Mittenwool's existence. I have made my peace with the delicate logic of his Being and all its fragile manifestations. The only thing I do know, with absolute certainty, is that he has always been there for me. And that's all I need to know.

So if old Marshal Farmer wants to have himself a good laugh over it, what is it to me? Let him laugh. Doesn't matter to me what he believes. The truth is the truth, like Pa says. That's all there is to it.

This is what I told myself as the campfire warmed my back and the night-side of the world echoed in the dark. *The truth is the truth.* And that soothed me like a balm.

It was the other part of my conversation with Marshal Farmer that kept me up, though. The one having to do with Mac Boat and a trunk full of gold coins. That was what my mind could not quiet, what my heart could not put to rest. Those were the thoughts that kept floating around in my head now, bumping into one another like moths inside a lamp. It was a whole other kind of unknowable.

I suppose that somewhere in my heart of hearts, I might have known the truth. Or believed I would find it on the other side of these Woods. But the heart is a mysterious country. You can travel thousands of miles, over strange lands, and still never find anything as unknowable as love.

4

WE GOT AN EARLY START the next morning. It was brisk and windy. I was tired and testy, for lack of sleep.

"A storm is coming," Marshal Farmer said.

I glanced up. The day looked cloudless to me, but I wasn't going to waste my time disagreeing.

"Will we reach the ravine today?" I asked.

He grunted something. Could have been yes or could have been no. I did not bother responding.

It was now my fourth day in the Woods. Did a part of me think, *Well, if I'd just stayed home and waited, Pa would've been home in a few days, anyway*? Did a part of me think, *Maybe if I'd listened to Mittenwool, I would've avoided the mosquitoes and the hunger, and the sore bones from riding all day, and the memories of bleeding dead people*? Yes, I did think these things. But I also thought, *Forward motion is forward motion. There is no turning back the clock.*

We rode the horses at a fast pace and reached the ravine within an hour.

After so many hours of traveling, with "the ravine" as the place we were looking to reach, coming upon it so quickly this morning seemed both remarkable and unremarkable at the same time. I was somehow breathless, like I'd been running blind this whole way and now, suddenly, the sun was bright in my eyes. Things were moving faster now. I could feel myself tingling, my senses heightened. We were here.

I had not realized, until I looked across the span of the ravine, that we had been climbing so high inside the Woods these last several days. What had seemed like a gentle slope was, in actuality, much steeper than I had imagined, for when we stood at the top of the ravine, it was like we were on the edge of the world. I had never been anywhere so high up in my twelve years of life, and for a few moments, as I looked down the side of the cliff, I felt my soul swoon as if it were leaving my body. I had to get down on my hands and knees and crawl back to where we had left Pony and the brown mare, a few dozen feet from the rock face. Merely watching the marshal pacing to and fro on the precipice made my very spine twitch and my knees go wobbly.

There was a name for what I was experiencing, which I remembered Pa teaching me once, but the word wouldn't come to me. It, like a million other words, swirled around in the space between me and the earth below.

I could not watch Marshal Farmer any longer and buried my face in Pony's mane. The way this horse whickered at me in return made me think fleetingly of Argos, who would make these sweet little yapping sounds when I petted his stomach, and suddenly a wave of despair came over me. *How is Argos doing? What am I doing here? How in the world did I come to be on the edge of a ravine so far from home?*

I looked around for Mittenwool. I had not seen him since the night before. It aggravated me when he wasn't somewhere nearby. He'd promised me he would stay close.

Marshal Farmer waddled over, mumbling something to himself. He was not in a jolly mood, to say the least.

He had lost the trail. That much I could tell. Here on the rocky ledge of the impossibly high cliff, there were no hoofprints in wet earth to follow, or bent twigs. We had searched high and low for horse manure or signs of a camp. It was as if the men we pursued, Pa in tow, had vanished off the face of the earth.

"So, what do we do now?" I asked.

"Hanged if I know," he rumbled, his voice like gravel.

"I'm thirsty," I said, not so much to him but simply to speak my feeling aloud. But this caused him to anger.

"Will you stop your yammering while I'm trying to think!"

I wanted to respond that I had not talked at all that morning, but I held my tongue. He went back to the rock face and got down on his knees. The mere sight of him bending, his back corkscrewed, made me wince. He scooted himself to the very edge, then lay prone, so that his head was completely dangling over the side of the cliff. I was full of admiration for his courage, until I heard him call me.

"Kid, come over here," he said.

"No, thanks, I'm fine here," I answered, my face buried in Pony's neck.

"Come over here!"

I rolled my eyes, and crawled up to the vicinity of where he was, lingering by his boots.

"No, up by me," he commanded. "My eyes aren't so good. You have to look and tell me what you see."

"My eyes aren't so good, either," I replied.

"Come over here now," he said. His mouth was clenched when he said this, his face red again.

I hesitated, but I knew that on the other side of this ravine was Pa, somewhere, and in my bones and in my marrow and in my heart and in my every fiber, I believed he needed me. So I let go of my fear as best I could and, lying down, my stomach pressed against the smooth rock, pushed myself upward until I had reached Marshal Farmer. With my hands clutching the edge of the cliff, I lay shoulder to shoulder with him, our heads hanging over the chasm below.

"Look down there," he ordered me. "What do you see?"

I felt like I would faint looking to where he pointed, but I didn't. Below was an unquiet creek, not quite as big as a river, winding its way through a narrow trench between the rock walls.

"I see a creek," I answered.

"No, over there!" he prodded impatiently, pointing across the chasm to the wall on the other side, which was about a stone's throw away.

"Nothing but the cliff," I said.

"Then over there and there!" he commanded, sweeping his arm left and right over the side, which I took to mean I should be looking everywhere for something.

"What am I looking for?" I asked.

"I don't know! Just use your eyes, confound it."

So I looked for heaven knows what. I made a careful sweep of the entire cliff wall across from me, looking to the right and the left. There was nothing but more of the same yellow rock face, and I was about to say so when something at the top of the cliff caught my eye. It was Mittenwool! Standing on the edge, waving at me. That was where he'd gone to! It was all I could do to contain my joy, seeing him there, and of course I didn't say anything to Marshal Farmer.

Mittenwool was motioning for me to look beneath him. He stood directly above where the cliff curved inward on itself, billowing like a curtain. I dropped my gaze straight as a plumb line to the bottom, and there, about twenty feet above the creek, I spotted a crude, oblong pocket in the rock face. It seemed unremarkable, except for the fact that there was another one, more or less the same size, about three feet below it, and then a few more below that one. There were six in all, somewhat parallel to one another, leading down to the creek.

"I see small indents over there," I said to Marshal Farmer, pointing to the left. "Kind of like ladder rungs carved into the wall."

He followed my hand, but couldn't see a thing for all his squinting. He pushed himself back from the edge and nudged me with his swollen knuckles to do the same.

We went back to the horses and rode them about a quarter of a mile through the Woods, parallel to the ravine, and then repeated what we had done before. Here the rock was much steeper, so to be able to lean our heads over the side of the cliff required more upward pulling than my arms could muster. I thought Marshal Farmer would help yank me up, but he only bullied me into it.

"Come on, kid! Get your puny little self up here," he said harshly.

I pulled and pulled, and finally managed to peer over the edge to get a closer view of the other side of the ravine. There, to my relief, was Mittenwool, still standing where he had been before. And far below him were the six indents above the creek. But from this vantage point, at the juncture directly opposite the cliff wall, I could see what I had not been able to see before. Above the "ladder," where the wall folded inward, was a large ledge leading to a hole in the rock face. It was maybe a dozen feet high and across, but was far back enough on the ledge to be hidden from view unless you were right across from it. Otherwise, just a few feet left or right, you'd completely miss seeing what was most certainly the mouth of a cave.

5

"HOLY MACKEREL," MARSHAL FARMER whispered gleefully, "we've found it, kid. We've found it."

"Are you sure?" I asked.

"Look for yourself! Even my old eyes can see it's a cave. It should be pitch-black in there, right? But it's not. Why do you think that is?"

"Because it's lit inside?"

He nodded. "Exactly!"

"So Pa is in there?" I asked, my heart jumping.

"I'd bet money on it," he answered. "They use those holes in the wall like a ladder to climb up from the creek bed."

"But how do they get down to the creek bed from up here?"

"That I don't know. There's got to be a way, either down or across. What's over that way?" He motioned for me to look to our left, where, much farther upstream, the creek seemed to fork around a narrow waterfall. "Is that a cascade up there? I feel like I can hear something like that. Dang these old eyes and ears."

"There's a waterfall, yes, sir."

"Let's go."

He slid back down the rock and I followed him.

We rode for another half hour, Pony keeping to the tree line like he knew I didn't want to be able to see over the edge, and the marshal riding alongside the ravine, though not close enough to it that he could be spotted from across the chasm.

When we finally stopped, the marshal motioned for me to come over, and it was all I could do to stay steady when I rode up next to him. We stood on an overlook that faced out over the ravine and, across from us, another overlook a few feet below ours. It was about a six-foot leap to the other side. Between the two overlooks was nothing but a straight drop to the frothy creek below. This was the narrowest point of the ravine, for immediately to our left the gully widened, dividing into two separate landforms that rose steeply like the sides of the mountains they were.

I couldn't even look over the edge without getting dizzy, my knees rattling. I walked Pony back to the trees a good dozen feet or so from where Marshal Farmer stood looking for whatever it was he was looking for, which I imagined was a magical way across the narrow chasm.

"Silas!" said Mittenwool, walking out of the Woods toward me.

"You found the cave," I whispered gratefully, careful the marshal wouldn't hear me.

"He's in there, Silas! Pa's in the cave. I saw him."

I covered my mouth to keep from gasping.

"His feet are shackled, but he seems all right," he continued. "There are men in the cave with him. I don't know how many because they were coming and going. Their horses are at the foot of the Falls. There's a path down to the creek on the other side, which you can't really see from here because it's right behind the waterfall."

"How do we get to the other side?"

"We're going to have to jump," said Marshal Farmer, who had approached from behind and thought I was talking to him.

I turned around quickly.

"What do you mean, jump?" I asked.

"The path down to the creek must be on the other side of the Falls."

"I know, but—"

"What do you mean, you *know*? How can you know?"

"I just mean I'm *assuming*. But it doesn't matter anyway if we can't get to the other side of the chasm."

His nostrils flared. "There is a way to the other side, and that is to jump!"

I found this so ludicrous, I practically laughed. "We can't do that!"

"He's right, unfortunately," Mittenwool murmured, still standing next to me. "It's the only way across."

"We are not jumping over the ravine," I stated loudly, not believing what I was hearing. From the marshal, maybe, but from Mittenwool, who was always so protective of me?

"I spent all night searching for a safer path," Mittenwool

said, staring past me at the chasm. "There's no way across. Maybe if we went all the way back down the way we came, we'd find a bridge or something, but that could take a whole day."

Marshal Farmer was talking at the same time as Mittenwool, so I only heard the last bit of what he was saying. ". . . horse of yours will get you over."

I looked at the other side of the ravine. "But I . . . I never even rode a horse before a couple of days ago," I stammered.

Marshal Farmer clucked his tongue, like I wasn't telling him anything he hadn't guessed. Then he came up next to me to check the girth on Pony's saddle. He pulled on the cinch strap to tighten it, then patted Pony's shoulders and nodded admiringly.

"This is a fine horse you have here, kid," he said, sounding gentler than he'd ever sounded before. "Just keep your heels down, and hold on tight. You'll be all right. Arabians are good jumpers."

"Arabians?"

He chuckled softly, like he'd just let me in on some secret, and mounted his horse. Then he snapped his fingers at me impatiently to do the same. I glanced at Pony, who puffed through his nose, like he was assuring me that he could do this.

Mittenwool had walked to the edge of the cliff and was peering over the side, looking more worried than I'd ever seen him look before. I was sure he was going to tell me to turn back now. It was what he'd been saying all along, after all. And here we were, about to see all his fears borne out on this reckless jump across an abyss.

Instead, when he caught my eye, he said, "You can do this, Silas."

My mouth dropped open, that's how surprised I was.

"Pony'll get you over," he said assuredly, his eyes bright.

I held his gaze for a long second, my eyebrows still high up on my forehead, and then I shook my head in disbelief. "Well, all right, then," I whispered.

"That a boy!" whooped the marshal. "Now come over by me."

I took a deep breath and exhaled slowly, like I was blowing out a candle. Then I climbed into the saddle. Only a few days ago, I could barely scramble up there, and now it was the most natural motion in the world to me.

I kneed Pony to follow Marshal Farmer's mare onto the overlook. There, at the very edge of the ravine, Marshal Farmer and I let our horses take it all in: the six-foot jump across, the chasm between the cliffs, the raging creek far below.

The marshal nudged me.

"I got my bearings now," he said, gazing down into the chasm. "This here is called the Hollow. And those woodlands across from us, that's Hollow Forest on a map. Straight up the mountain is Rosasharon, not more than a two-hour ride that way." He swept his arm to the left. "I know the sheriff there. He's a good man. After we find the path down to the creek, we'll head right back on up to Rosasharon, raise a posse, and be back here with a dozen men by late afternoon. If all goes well, I'll have Ollerenshaw clapped in irons by tonight and you'll be with your pa again! Doesn't that sound good to you?"

"Yes, sir," I answered.

"Told you I'd find him, didn't I?"

"Yes, you did!"

His face widened in a satisfied smile. Then he turned his mare around and trotted back to the trees to get a good run on the jump. I followed close behind.

"I'll go first," he said when I sidled up next to him. "You come right after me. Heels down. No hesitating. If you hedge even a little, your mount will know it and pitch you over the cliff. Trust me on that."

"I won't hedge."

"It's fine to be afraid. Just don't hedge, or your horse will know it."

"I won't hedge."

He clapped his big callused hand on my shoulder, which was such an unexpected gesture, I flinched without realizing. This made him grin so wide, I saw his bottom teeth clearly for the first time, like three brown peas stuck randomly in his gums.

"All right, kid!" he thundered happily. "I'll see you on the other side!"

Then he clicked his tongue, slapped the reins, and spurred his horse hard. The mare bolted forward quite majestically, running at a full gallop onto the overlook. About twelve giant strides in, she quickened her pace and leapt over the ravine with a kind of wild abandon. It stirred me to see that dour horse take off so, like she was flying. But no sooner had she landed on the other side than I heard a horrible crack, like a gunshot fired across the chasm. The sound of bone crunching reached me before my eyes even understood what was happening; that the horse had tumbled forward onto the bare rock. The marshal flew headfirst over her neck onto the stone, flipping a few times before landing dead-still, his body crumpled up like a string puppet. But the mare, still not finished in her wild fall, then skidded into him, long legs askew, and rolled over him. The cascade of noises echoed through the ravine. The clang of horseshoes on stone. The braying, like a long, shrill cry. Followed by a stillness that I was afraid would crush me.

I did not hesitate, at this point, but drove my heels into Pony and put my faith in his limbs and muscles, and we galloped at full speed over the rock ledge and jumped over the abyss.

SIX

Take courage, my heart; you've been through worse than this.

—Homer
Odyssey

1

PA HAD A SERIES OF BOOKS THAT I loved to peruse at night called *A History of the Earth, and Animated Nature.* It was made up of four volumes, but the one I liked the most was the second volume, which told the history of all the animals of the world. It was filled with luminous depictions of every creature imaginable. The moment Marshal Farmer uttered the word *Arabian,* I could picture the page in the book that read, *Of all the countries in the world where the horses run wild, Arabia produces the most beautiful breed.* How had it not occurred to me before? All along, Pony had seemed familiar to me. His profile. The arch of his neck. The high carriage of his tail. It was there in the book, in those drawings of his desert forebears.

And could he jump? Pegasus himself could not have done a better job leaping over that chasm, with me astride, gliding through the air with graceful majesty.

Pony landed easily on the other side, without so much as a skid or a bump. I jumped out of the saddle and got down on my knees by Marshal Farmer's head. He was breathing, but there was a trickle of blood coming from his mouth, and his body was bent at an unnatural angle. I felt light-headed just seeing him like that.

"Marshal Farmer," I called out, gently slapping his face.

"Ho there," he said feebly, opening his eyes. "You get across all right, kid?"

"Yes, sir, I'm fine."

"How's my horse?" He lifted his head to look for his animal, who had gotten back on her feet but was hobbling. *A broken foreleg,* I thought. When Marshal Farmer made note of this, he cursed. And then let his head fall back onto the rock again.

"Get me some water, will you?" he said.

I quickly went over to the mare and got his canteen and put it to his mouth. The "water" dripped over the sides of his mouth without going into him. He waved at me to stop, so I did, and waited for him to tell me what to do next.

"Well, ain't this a pickle," he muttered.

"Are you in pain?"

He shook his head and frowned. "Not really. Can't feel much of anything."

"What should we do?"

He took a deep breath to assess the situation. "Well, we don't have lots of options here, kid. You're going to have to go to Rosasharon to get some help."

"I can do that, sure."

"Good. I guess it was good I let you come here with me, after all."

"What do I do when I get there?"

"The sheriff's name is Archibald Burns. I haven't seen him for years, but he'll remember me. Tell him about this bind I'm in, and that Roscoe Ollerenshaw is holed up in a cave down in the Hollow, just south of the Falls. He'll know where that is. Tell him to raise a posse of a dozen men and come back here today, without fail. You got all that?"

"Yes, sir," I said.

"What's the lawman's name?" he tested me.

"Archibald Burns."

"And what's the outlaw's name? See if you have it now."

"Ros-coe Ol-le-ren-shaw," I said.

He managed a weak smile as he patted my arm. "Good boy."

"But are you going to be all right?" I asked.

"Oh, me? I'll be right as rain, kid," he assured me. "This isn't the first scrape I've been in like this, I assure you. Now leave my canteen right over here where I can reach it, and get going."

"Let me cover you with a blanket first," I said.

"I'm fine, kid! Don't coddle me. Just shuffle off and begone!"

I nodded, too stunned to truly think for myself just then, and got on Pony and set off through the forest.

2

I DON'T REMEMBER MUCH OF THAT ride. Just me keeping my head low over Pony's neck while he charged through the forest like he'd gone through there a hundred times before. It was a steep path upward, and I had to duck to keep the branches from swiping me, but the ground was far less dense on this side of the ravine. That I recall surely.

It is not the circumstances of the ride that I recollect the most, though, but the feeling I had while riding. A feeling like I had done this before, like I had dreamed this once upon a time. Something familiar in the color of the light, maybe. In the sound of the hooves trampling the earth. Like a storm plowing through a field of tall grass.

When I got to Rosasharon, it did not feel like strange country at all. Maybe because it was a town not unlike Boneville. Brick buildings. A dry goods store. A post office. A clapboard church at the end of the square. It felt odd seeing people again, dressed in ordinary clothes. I must have looked like a vagabond to them, riding down the main street in my mud-caked clothes. Luckily the county jail was easy to find, tucked between the saloon and the two-story courthouse.

I tied Pony to a post and charged through the large white door of the sheriff's office. I was met with surprise and curiosity by the only lawman in the room.

"Are you Archibald Burns?" I said with a certain new gravity, for although only four days had passed since Pa had left, it was like I had grown a year and a day in that time.

The man behind the desk, whose feet were crossed over a mess of papers, didn't know what to make of me or my intrusion.

"What in heaven," he replied. "Who are you?"

"I'm Silas Bird," I answered quickly. "Marshal Enoch Farmer sent me to find Archibald Burns. I have to speak to him now, if you please."

The man, who was young and thin and clean-shaven, with a mop of curly brown hair, leaned forward on his chair. "Who is Enoch Farmer?"

"He's a United States marshal," I answered. "Listen, I don't have time to dillydally. Marshal Farmer fell off his horse and is badly hurt. He was on his way here to raise a posse, for he's found Oscar Rollerensh's headquarters by the Falls." That name, for whatever reason, was one I just could not master in a pinch.

I thought all this information would spur the young lawman behind the desk into some kind of action, or at least trigger some kind of excitable response. But he looked at me like my words were much less meaningful than I was perceiving them to be.

"Oscar Rollerensh . . . ?" he finally responded. "Do you mean Roscoe Ollerenshaw?"

"Yes!" I answered madly.

"Down by the Falls?" he repeated.

"Yes!" I said, exasperated. "Look, can you find Archibald Burns for me, please? Marshal Farmer told me he's the one to talk to. We need to raise a posse of twenty men and charge the headquarters today."

"Charge the headquarters," repeated the man, looking at me like I was crazy. "Look, little fella, I've heard of Roscoe Ollerenshaw, for sure. I don't know what lawman hasn't. But I've never heard of a Marshal Enoch Farmer. And Archibald Burns? He was the sheriff before I got here, but he's been dead about five years now."

3

I WAS NOT AS TAKEN ABACK as one might think by this news about Archibald Burns. Marshal Farmer had warned that it had been years since he'd seen him. But I was aggrieved, for I did not think that the young lawman before me, with his curly hair and dimpled cheeks, was up to the task before him.

"Well," I said, "it doesn't matter about Archibald Burns, then. What matters is, you need to raise a posse, quick."

He shook his head slowly and finally stood up, his hands holding a felt campaign hat like he was undecided about whether to put it on or not. He was taller than I thought he'd be, and wore a dented tin badge on his shirt.

"Look, Silas," he said. "That's your name, right? Silas, you look like you've been through a lot, and I want to hear all about this Marshal Farmer and how you came to find Roscoe Ollerenshaw, who is indeed a fugitive from the law with a big bounty on his head. But why don't you sit down and have something to eat first, and then we can have ourselves a nice long chat."

"I don't have time for a long chat!" I yelled, feeling my throat tighten. "Marshal Farmer is hurt. His body's all mangled. We have to go back to get him. There's no time to waste."

Just then, another lawman entered the building and saw me squaring off against the tall man.

"Desimonde, what do we have here?" the large man said,

patting my head as he passed by me to sit down by the curly-haired man's desk. He eyed me with humor. His breath smelled of ale. "Who is this tiny child?"

"He says a U.S. marshal sent him," the curly-haired man answered. "Enoch Farmer. That name sound familiar to you?"

"No."

"Wants us to raise a posse."

"What the devil for?"

"Says he knows where Roscoe Ollerenshaw is."

"Roscoe Ollerenshaw?"

"We don't have time for this!" I exclaimed, throwing my hands in the air.

"Look, Silas," the curly-haired man then said to me. "I'm Sheriff Chalfont, and this here is Deputy Beautyman. We will help you in any way we can, but you got to slow down and tell us your story, from beginning to end. Who you are. Where you're from. And what it is you need from us. All right? Calmly and clearly. Sit down in this chair right next to you, and start from the beginning."

I felt like I would cry if I let my guard down just then. I was so tired, and in such a rush, and all this while, time had been speeding up on me. It had circled around me like floodwaters, and I was afraid I would be carried away by the torrent and swept out to sea. Here, Sheriff Chalfont was throwing me a rope to help me stay afloat in the deluge. And I desperately wanted to cling to it.

So I sat down and told him everything I could, save about Mittenwool, and the Bog ghosts, and the fact that pacing in the room behind him was an elegant young woman, about twenty years of age, holding both her hands over a wound on her chest that flowed with blood.

After I was done, Sheriff Chalfont didn't say anything, but let my words gestate in his mind. Deputy Beautyman, on the other hand, snickered as he bit off a wad of tobacco.

"Well, ain't that a load of bunkum right there," he scoffed, chewing noisily. "Come on, sonny boy. You must have more fables than that to tell us."

"Nothing I told you is a fable," I said directly to Sheriff Chalfont. I didn't even look at the deputy, who I took an instant dislike to.

"Oh, come now!" the deputy challenged. "You want us to believe you went chasing down Roscoe Ollerenshaw's men all by yourself? What are you, six years old?"

"I'm twelve! And no, I didn't go by myself, exactly," I answered. "I knew the pony would know the way because he had come through the Woods with those riders, the ones who showed up at our house and took my pa. So I knew he would lead me to them."

"Ah, yes, manhunt by means of magical pony!" Deputy Beautyman said sarcastically, nodding with a big fat grin on his face that I would have loved to wipe away. Then he nudged the sheriff, who had his arms crossed as he took me in. "Tell me, Desimonde, why don't we ever take magical ponies with us on our manhunts, huh?"

I was in a lather, at this point. Not only at the deputy, of course, but at myself for having so stupidly told them about Pony's part in recent events. How many times do I have to be rapped on my knuckles to learn that most adults don't give a whit what children have to say? They're not like Pa, who always heeds me. I should have known better!

"I never said my horse was magical!" I answered, my fury catching in my throat. "Just that I knew he would follow the trail back to where he'd come from. Which was a logical assumption. And it turned out to be right! For I'm here, aren't I? And I can lead you, right now, to a hidden cave, just above the banks of a creek, in which a band of counterfeiters are running their operations. Less than a two-hour ride from here, practically under your nose. Don't you want to catch them? What kind of lawmen are you? Or are you too afraid of being led by a magical pony, Deputy Beautyman?"

Well, Deputy Beautyman did not like this at all, but Sheriff Chalfont looked down and smiled. He put on his hat and patted the deputy on the arm.

"Looks like you've been bested by a six-year-old, Jack," he ribbed gently.

"I'm not six!" I shouted.

Sheriff Chalfont pointed at me, the smile still on his lips. "Listen, Silas. I'm with you, I really am, but you're going to have to stop yelling at us, all right? We're going with you! So calm yourself. And go easy on old Jack here. He's nicer than he acts and smarter than he looks, I promise you."

He pulled my hat down over my eyes, grabbed a couple of canteens full of water, and tossed a strip of jerky to me. "Eat something while we ready our horses, then meet us out front. Come on, Jack."

He left quickly, and Deputy Beautyman, sighing theatrically, narrowed his eyes into tiny slits, like he was being sinister. And then, as strange as it may sound, he stuck his tongue out at me before following his boss out the door.

4

IN HINDSIGHT, I HAVE REALIZED, I am able to see the many connections that were unknowable once. That is one of the tricks of memory: that we can see some of the invisible threads that bind us, but only after the fact. Later, I would find out more about Sheriff Desimonde Chalfont, and what he was all about in life, and what kind of man he was. But all I knew as we rode through the forest back toward the Falls was that I liked him. I trusted him. And that, for the time being, was enough.

I cannot say the same about Deputy Beautyman. How could this oafish dunderhead be a lawman? I wondered. Every time he regarded me, it was only to jape at my expense. Still, beggars can't be choosers, as they say, and he and Sheriff Chalfont were all I had. Despite my protestations, Sheriff Chalfont had refused to raise a posse until he had talked to Marshal Farmer himself, and taken stock of the Roscoe Ollerenshaw situation in the cave.

So we rode like demons through the forest to the Falls, going downhill the whole way. It had started to pour, which made the going much more slippery, but Pony charged through the trees without fear or hesitation. Sheriff Chalfont was on a big white mare, majestic as a painting, and Deputy Beautyman rode a muscular dun he called Petunia. Behind him he trailed a fourth horse for Marshal Farmer to ride, a shaggy but sturdy draft. But none of those big horses could keep up with my Pony as he galloped through the forest. Several times, the sheriff had to call for me to slow down, and finally one time he yelled, "Stop! Stop! Stop, Silas!"

I wheeled Pony around and saw that Deputy Beautyman had been parted from Petunia's saddle and fallen in the mud. He was not hurt, but mad as a cat—at me!

"Desimonde, you got to tell that kid to stop riding like a maniac!" he yelled at the sheriff, flicking muck off his shoulders as he got up. He was not a fit man, to say the least, and covered in mud as he was, he looked like a wet bear.

"Guess you could use yourself a magical pony," I observed coolly.

"It's not my fault the blamed draft can't keep up!" he shot back.

"Stop that," scolded Sheriff Chalfont, snapping his fingers at me. "Come on, Jack, hurry up." Then he pulled his horse next to me and said quietly, but sternly, "Silas, you need to go slower. It won't do anyone any good if we hurt ourselves before we even get to where we're going."

I made a solemn face, and watched Deputy Beautyman get up on his horse. Maybe at this point I even felt a twang of remorse.

"What kind of name is Beautyman, anyway?" I said.

"It's a name for a beautiful man," he grumbled. He answered so quickly that I realized he must have been asked that a hundred times before.

Once he was back in the saddle, I made sure Pony went at a more reasonable pace through the forest. We reached the rocky ledge above the Falls about an hour later. It had stopped raining, but the ground was soggy from the downpour as we made our way up to the overlook. Which was empty.

5

I HAVE GOTTEN USED TO A VARIETY of mysteries in my life, to be sure. That I have grown up with a companion no one else can see is one. That I have visions and hear the voices of people no longer alive in this world is another. That I have been marked by lightning, and lived to tell of it, is a third. So I guess I have come to expect a degree of uncertainty in my life, young as I am.

But I was not prepared for Marshal Farmer not to be where I had left him. I had steeled myself for the prospect of his dying there on that rocky ledge before I could reach him, yes. But that he was completely gone, with no sign pointing to where he'd gone to? That was a mystery for which I was not prepared.

"You sure this is where you left him?" Sheriff Chalfont asked me calmly from atop his horse.

I had gotten off Pony and was circling the overlook where, not four hours earlier, I had left the wounded man.

"Yes!" I said. "I left him right here!"

Deputy Beautyman, to his credit, had gotten off his mare and was poking around the shrubs near the rock face. "What about his horse?"

"She was standing right where you are now," I answered.

Deputy Beautyman bent down to inspect the ground, and then looked around a few feet in all directions. He shook his head. "Nothing to track here. The rain swept everything away."

"I swear, Sheriff Chalfont," I said, stomping my foot. "I left Marshal Farmer right here."

Sheriff Chalfont nodded. "I believe you, Silas," he replied intently.

"Are you thinking Ollerenshaw's men got him?" Deputy Beautyman asked.

Sheriff Chalfont's brow furrowed. "Either that, or he rode away on his lame horse. Could that have happened, Silas?"

"I suppose so," I replied, stupefied. "I mean, he's a tough old codger."

"Come on, get on your pony," said the sheriff. "Show us where you saw that cave you were talking about."

I glanced at the overlook on the other side of the chasm.

"We'd have to jump to that side," I answered.

"Hold on. *You* jumped across that?" Deputy Beautyman asked, peering over the edge of the cliff incredulously. "No, you didn't. No, he didn't, Desi."

"Why would I lie?" I countered.

"Why would the boy who cried wolf lie? Because he was a runty little liar. That's why."

"I'm not lying!"

"Tell him there's a path behind the Falls," said Mittenwool, appearing out of nowhere. He actually startled me, for I had not seen him approach. "Sorry, I didn't mean to surprise you!"

"There's a path behind the Falls," I said to the sheriff, catching my breath.

"I went down to the cave to see how many men were there now," Mittenwool explained.

"I can take you there, Sheriff," I continued fervently.

"Desimonde," cautioned Deputy Beautyman, eyeing me suspiciously, for he had seen me gasp when Mittenwool surprised me. "Something is offish here, I'm telling you. If *anything* this kid is saying is true—and I'm not sure even *he* knows what's true or not—but if what he's telling us about this cave is true, there could be a dozen men holed up inside. There are just two of us, if you haven't noticed." He spat a wad of tobacco juice on the ground, as if to make his point.

"There are seven men in the cave," Mittenwool said.

"There are only seven men in the cave!" I said.

"Now, how the devil would you know that?" Deputy Beautyman snapped.

"Marshal Farmer told me," I lied.

"This kid's off, Desi. I'm telling you!" the deputy insisted.

"I swear I can take you to the cave!" I proclaimed.

We were both looking at Sheriff Chalfont, waiting for him to speak, but he wasn't going to do that until he was good and ready. That much was clear. He was the kind of man who listened carefully and moved quietly. Not unlike Pa.

"Listen, Desi—" the deputy started saying.

"Hold on, Jack," the sheriff interrupted, palm in the air. "I think Silas is telling the truth. But whether he is or isn't, we're in this now, one way or the other. We're here. That's the long and short of it." He pulled one of his rifles out from its scabbard and laid it across the pommel of his saddle. "So let's just go take a look for ourselves, all right? I'd like to see what we're up against *before* we're actually up against it." He mounted his horse.

"But what if what we're up against is twelve sharpshooters in a cave?" the deputy asked skeptically.

"We'll just have to do what we've always done, Jack!" the sheriff answered cheerfully. "Either shoot real straight, or run real fast. Worked for us in the Rio Grande, didn't it?"

"Landed us in jail, if I recall," the deputy muttered, heaving himself onto his dun.

"But it kept us alive, partner!" laughed the sheriff. "That's all that matters in the end, right?" Then he turned to me, still laughing, and said jubilantly, "Now let's get going, Silas! Lead us to this hidden cave on your magical pony!"

SEVEN

**From there we came outside
and saw the stars.**

—Dante Alighieri
Inferno

1

THE STORY GOES THAT PA MET MAMA at an engraver's office somewhere in Philadelphia. She was there to see to the design of her wedding invitation. He worked there as a typesetter and was tasked with printing the invitation. Mama recited to Pa the words that were to appear on the invitation, including her name, which was Elsa. But Pa noted the sad expression of her eyes as she said the name of her intended, and it touched him. Since she was there with her mother, however, he could not engage her in polite conversation or make artful inquiries. After she left the shop, as Pa relates the story, he could not stop thinking about the beautiful young woman named Elsa or the melancholy in her eyes.

It took him three days to design the plates and set the type, but since she had chosen silver ink for the printing, which was a luxury even for the wealthy, he took a carriage to her estate to get her approval of the mechanicals. This was just a pretense to see her again, to be sure, but it was a good one, and as he knocked on the large wooden door of her home, he smoothed his hair with his hands and straightened his tie. Pa was in his early thirties by then, and had lived a life of work and privation and little love, so his feelings surprised him, for he had believed himself impervious to the call of his heart. He was let in by the butler and told to wait in a room decorated with full-length portraits in ornate gold frames. He sat down on a red velvet sofa. On a small table with lions' heads carved into the wooden legs was a tiny book, which he picked up, that instantly flipped open to a page set crudely in Garamond type.

As I've mentioned, Pa has a prodigious memory, and can but glance at a page and recall its contents in detail. So when my mother walked into the room, Pa rose to his feet, the book closed in his hands, and recited the following:

O Joy! O wonder, and delight! O sacred mystery!
My Soul a Spirit infinite! An image of the Deity!

My mother was, of course, delighted.

"Are you familiar with the work of Anonymous of Ledbury?" she asked.

Pa smiled and shook his head. "Not at all," he responded, opening the book in his hands. "Though his typesetter leaves much to be desired."

(When he tells this story, this is the point at which Pa raises his hand and makes it tremble to describe how his bones were quivering. He says he had never, in his whole life, seen such kindness shine in a person as it did in Mama, like she was a glass vessel filled with glowing light.)

Mama sat down on the dark green chaise with embroidered yellow orchids opposite the red sofa on which Pa sat. She was smiling. One dimple in the left cheek, Pa would always note, which she gave to me.

"Last year my family spent the summer with friends in Herefordshire," she answered, "and while we were there, the workers making renovations to the cellar found a trove of forgotten manuscripts, including the works of an unknown poet. I felt a deep connection to this particular poem. It's called 'My Spirit.' My host, quite graciously, had a copy set and bound, just for me."

"It's lovely," Pa acknowledged.

"The poem speaks to me," she said. "I've been reading a lot about the spirit since the passing of my younger brother last spring. From scarlet fever."

"I am sorry for your loss."

"Thank you. Do you like poetry, Mr. Bird?"

Pa said he'd felt keenly aware of his worker's clothes just then, so gray and drab against the colorful furniture. He'd also felt, in her question, a measure of detection. Not judgment, just curiosity.

"I'm not inclined to religious poetry, no," he replied truthfully.

"You think spiritualism is a religion?" she countered playfully.

"I only mean, I don't put much stock in any philosophy that gives credence to notions of an afterlife, or spirits, or things of that nature. I am the kind of man who only believes in what I can see and touch and smell. Maybe that is a folly. I mean no disrespect."

She seemed wistful. "Not at all. Who's to say what is folly? All I know is that I've been reading a great deal about it, and I do believe there's something to it all. *All things are but altered, nothing dies; And here and there the unbody'd spirit flies,* as Dryden has said."

"I believe that was Ovid," Pa answered gently.

"No, sir!"

"It's a translation. I will wager on it."

She laughed. "Oh my goodness, you are probably right!"

"Do you know this one? *Overcoming me with the light of her smile, she said to me, 'Turn now, and listen, for not only in my eyes is Paradise.'* "

"I don't."

"Dante."

"I am outmatched."

"By no means, no."

"Where are you from, if I may ask? I hear a trace of an accent."

"From Leith, originally. Near Edinburgh."

"Scotland! We were there last summer, too!" Mama answered, delighted. "I loved it very much. Such a magical place. You must miss it."

"I know very little of it, to be truthful." He did not say *because I grew up inside a poorhouse.* This, and much more, he would tell her later. "When I was twelve, I stole away on a ship, and here I am."

She looked at him intently. "Here you are."

Pa, who was a quiet man by nature, but not shy, found himself at a loss for words because of the light in her eyes.

"I've brought the mechanicals for your wedding invitation," he said clumsily.

"Oh yes, of course. My mother is coming downstairs to look at them with me," Mama answered, and suddenly her voice took on the detachment of the other day. "It was his family we went to visit in Herefordshire," she added, sighing. "The man I am going to marry."

"Oh," answered Pa, "but you won't be marrying him. I am certain of that."

Pa says the words just came out of him, without hesitation. And it was done.

They were married three months later. It was quite a scandal for Mama's family. Her father set his deerhounds on Pa the first time they attempted to come back to visit her parents after their quiet nuptials. Pa says he only had to whistle for the deerhounds to stand down and lick him, which set Mama's father into even more of a fit. Mama was so deeply hurt by their treatment of Pa that she resolved never again to enter the house. She took with her only one thing from her home: her Bavarian violin.

Mama's father, determined to end their marriage, then used his connections in Philadelphia to deprive Pa of his employment at the engraver's shop. What's more, he began making inquiries about Pa with the local police, pushing them to concoct all kinds of fabrications. So Pa and Mama decided to head west and start their lives fresh in California. Pa was going to open a daguerreotype studio. Mama was going to plant an orchid garden near the sea.

They got as far as Columbus before they realized that a baby would soon be joining them on their adventures, and so they bought a little parcel of land outside of Boneville, in a location as removed as it could be from the intrusion of people. It was here that Pa built the house for Mama.

To me, that is the best story in the history of stories, and I have made Pa tell it to me a hundred times, at least, for I like to picture it all in my mind. The red velvet sofa. Pa fidgeting nervously. Mama's tender eyes.

There are stories we hold near in times of darkness, and this is mine.

2

MITTENWOOL WALKED IN FRONT of me as I led Pony to the far side of the rock, where it sloped downward toward the Falls. Sheriff Chalfont was behind me, and Deputy Beautyman behind him. As we got nearer to the chute of water, the roar became so deafening that we could hear neither the clip-clop of the horses nor our own voices. Even my very thoughts felt muffled.

By the time we reached the Falls, the air had gone from damp and misty to a constant spray of water, a kind of sideways rain. The cascade sounded like thunder now. *This must be what the ocean sounds like,* I thought, and then found myself wondering where all the water came from. Probably some itty-bitty spring somewhere miles away, winding its way down the mountain. You would not think that so small a trickle could become so large, though I'm sure Pa would say that this is how everything in the world begins: with a trickle. A trickle of an idea. A trickle of rain on an acorn. *Only love and lightning come all at once.* (I remember him saying this, though I don't remember the details of when or why he said it.)

Mittenwool stopped and turned around. "It's all downhill from here," he said, pointing to a path between the shrubs. "You should leave the horses, Silas. It gets pretty steep."

"We should leave the horses here," I advised, and then repeated it louder when Sheriff Chalfont cupped his ear. I got off

Pony and tethered him to a young maple tree, and watched as both lawmen did the same. The deputy gave his horse a quick kiss on the muzzle before turning to me, a scowl on his face.

"Lead the way, Runt," he ordered.

I spun around and followed Mittenwool downward on the path. They, in turn, followed me.

It touched and pleased me that these two men were putting so much trust in me right now, and I wondered how they would feel if they knew that it was really a ghost who was leading the way. Actually, I did not have to imagine it. I knew how they would feel.

3

THE PATH TO THE CREEK was hidden on one side by a tangle of trees teetering on the edge of the cliff, and on the other side by a wall of rock covered in shrubs and roots. Thick brown vines crisscrossed between the trees and the wall like a spider's web, and we had to weave our way in and out until we reached the edge.

I followed Mittenwool as he, barefoot as always, biting his lip as he concentrated, led us down the side of the mountain. I stepped cautiously into his footsteps, reminding myself not to look over the edge, to focus only on the path ahead of me. It was just a few feet wide, enough for a sure-footed horse, and it had me wishing I was riding Pony instead of sloshing in the mud. About twenty feet down, the path corkscrewed sharply around, and then again another twenty feet below that, until we came to a large opening in the mountainside. It looked like some ancient monster had taken a bite out of the rock. This was the innards of the Falls, a place from which we could see the cascade falling in front of us like a river tumbling down from the sky. We were soaked and unable to hear a thing.

Mittenwool motioned for me to follow him down the last stretch of the path on the other side of the cavern, but when I looked back, I could tell that Deputy Beautyman was winded. He was pale, and I thought it best to let him catch his breath. Sheriff Chalfont made note of my gesture, subtly signaling his approval, like we shared a confidence. He then came closer and asked me something, which I couldn't hear at all, so he pantomimed his question by walking two fingers on the palm of his hand and raising his shoulders.

"It's just another twenty minutes and we'll be there," answered Mittenwool.

I held up both my hands to the sheriff, splayed my fingers out wide, twice.

The sheriff signaled that he understood and then motioned that we should move on. The deputy, still panting, sucked in his stomach and nodded briskly, like he was ready. We headed down the last part of the path.

I realized at just this moment that it wasn't heights I was afraid of so much as ledges. The feeling of being at the edge of a precipice, that was what was terrifying. Because even though we were only forty or fifty feet above the ravine at this point, the rest of the path was barely a lip on the rock, bordered by a sheer drop to the bottom. The mere thought of that edge made me feel like I would sway and fall, and I could not help but hug the wall as I stepped sideways down the path. The sheriff was right behind me, I noticed, agile and fearless.

Deputy Beautyman, on the other hand, was as afraid of heights, or ledges, as I was. I didn't see this until I reached the bottom and looked back, of course. The poor man had his cheek pressed to the wall, his arms stretched out like he was trying to embrace the entire side of the mountain, his fingers clawing at the rock face. It was both painful and comical to watch him, feet shuffling, inch by inch down the path, and at that moment I took pity on him, for I knew how scared I myself felt on that same rocky ledge.

Once we were, all three of us, down at the base of the Falls, we wound our way upstream along the bank to where a promontory jutted out into the creek, like the prow of a ship. This is where, maybe a hundred feet above, I had made the jump across the chasm. I couldn't see from up there, but now I understood why this was called Hollow Falls. There was a large open space at the bottom of the promontory, forking the creek, enclosed by an overhang that sparkled with tiny flecks of iron ore. The underpass was an almost ethereal little meadow, covered in short blue grasses and yellow reeds, in the middle of which six horses were peacefully cropping. I recognized Rufe Jones's spotted horse immediately. And next to it was the large black charger that had taken Pa away.

4

I REALIZED, AS SOON AS I SAW how Sheriff Chalfont took command of the situation, that I had been too hasty in my assessment of him before. I had mistaken his baby-faced good nature as a sign that he was too docile for the task at hand. I had wanted Marshal Farmer to lead the charge against Roscoe Ollerenshaw, truth be told. A spark of pure fire. The sheriff had not seemed as capable, to my eyes. How wrong I was!

The moment we saw the horses, Sheriff Chalfont brought his rifle up to eye level. He motioned for me to stay back, then crooked his finger at the deputy, who had likewise pulled out his rifle, and they cautiously stepped out from the bushes toward the horses. They circled the area until they were sure there was no one else there. Just the six horses, bridled but untethered, their saddles in a heap on the ground. A makeshift gate of sticks and twine had been placed along the bank, so there was nowhere for the horses to go unless they swam across the creeks on either side.

"How far is it to the cave?" Sheriff Chalfont asked me, putting his rifle down.

"About a half mile up the creek," I answered.

"More like a whole mile," Mittenwool corrected.

"Or maybe a whole mile," I quickly added. "We were on the other side of the ravine, so it's hard to gauge from down here. The creek bends around so steeply you don't actually see the cave until you're directly in front of it."

Sheriff Chalfont nodded.

"Is Marshal Farmer's horse one of these?" he asked.

I shook my head. I had already checked for his broody brown mare, but she was not there.

"That paint is the one Rufe Jones rode," I said. "And this big black one here is the one my pa rode off on." I patted this horse's neck, thinking of that night, which now seemed like moons ago.

"Why'd they take your pa, again?" Deputy Beautyman asked grumpily, putting a fresh wad of tobacco in his mouth. He had heard the whole long story when I related it earlier, so this question annoyed me.

"I don't know," I answered. "Like I told you before, they thought he was somebody else."

"Who'd they think he was?" he asked.

"It doesn't matter, does it?"

"Sure, it does."

"Someone named Mac Boat."

At this, Sheriff Chalfont turned to look at me.

"Mac Boat?" he exclaimed. "You didn't tell us that before."

"I didn't think it mattered," I lied. "Why? You heard of him?"

"Everyone's heard of Mac Boat."

"I never heard of him."

"What's your pa's name again?" he asked.

"Martin Bird. He's a boot-maker," I answered.

Both men looked at me, nodding without saying anything.

"He's also a collodiotypist," I added. "He does a kind of photography that uses paper coated in iron salts to make a picture. Marshal Farmer thought that maybe the counterfeiters wanted to use this method to help them print their fake money." This was not exactly the truth in that it was my thought, not Marshal Farmer's, but it sounded more powerful if it was presented as his idea.

Both of them still just stood there contemplating me, without making any comment or asking any questions. I knew what they were thinking.

"My father is not Mac Boat," I assured them.

5

SHERIFF CHALFONT PATTED my shoulder.

"No one is saying he is, Silas," he said.

Deputy Beautyman spat.

"*He* is thinking it, I can tell," I mumbled accusingly, looking at the deputy.

"What *I* am thinking is none of your danged business!" he retorted testily, and I went back to detesting him again. The man definitely stirred my emotions, I can say that for sure.

"Look, the real question," said Sheriff Chalfont in his calm way, "is what do we do now? Do we go back to Rosasharon and raise a posse? Or should we try and get the jump on the men in the cave? Jack, what do you think?"

Deputy Beautyman scratched the side of his face and frowned.

"We can't get the jump on them if they know we're coming,"

he answered hastily, "and they'll know we're coming if they got ahold of the marshal. The fact that the marshal's horse isn't here with these others doesn't mean a string bean. If the horse was lame, they would've shot it and dumped it into the creek. Could've done the same to the marshal, too, for all we know."

"If that's the case," answered the sheriff, "then we won't find anyone in the cave anyway. Ollerenshaw will have packed up and left, figuring the law's already on its way."

Deputy Beautyman agreed and spat.

"But if they didn't find Farmer, it's a whole different story," the sheriff continued. "Seven against two, *and* we have the element of surprise on them."

"That's assuming the kid is right about that number," said the deputy.

"I'm right about the number," I piped up.

"Why do I still get the feeling you're trying to bamboozle us?" the deputy snarled at me.

"I don't know!" I blustered, stopping myself from glancing at Mittenwool, who was literally standing next to him.

"If you're walking us into some kind of ambush . . . ," the deputy threatened, poking my shoulder.

"Why would he be walking us into an ambush?" the sheriff countered.

"I don't know! But I *do* know when someone's trying to hide something from me. And I'm telling you—"

"Come on, Jack," scolded the sheriff. "We have a decision to make. Do we raise a posse, or go after Ollerenshaw ourselves? What's your preference?"

"My preference," the deputy answered, his eyes flaring wildly, "is to be back in town right now eating a big fat roast chicken and guzzling down a pint of ale! That is my preference, Desi! But if you ask me what I think we should do, I'll tell you this much: if I climb back up that blasted cliff, I'm not coming back down again. Not if I had three hundred Spartans behind me. I'll take the long way down, wherever that is."

"That would be the way we came," said Mittenwool.

"It would take a whole day to ride down the mountain!" I cried.

"Why does this pesky gadfly keep dinging in my ear?" the deputy muttered to the sheriff.

"What did I ever do to you?" I yelled.

"Enough, enough," Sheriff Chalfont said quickly, wiping the air with his hands as if to separate us. "So, Jack, confirm: your preference is to go after Ollerenshaw now. Is that right?"

"Yes!" replied the deputy, nodding with great exaggeration.

"Mine is, too!" I said eagerly.

Sheriff Chalfont looked at me. I realized then that I shouldn't have uttered a word. I should have tried to disappear, hoping they would forget my presence, because I knew what was coming.

"Whoa, Silas," the sheriff said gently. "I know you're not going to want to hear this, but we're not taking you with us, make no bones about it." He continued to talk over me as I began my protestations. "You're going up that path to stay with the horses until we return. And if we don't come back, you're getting on that speedy little pony of yours and riding to Rosasharon for help."

"No," I said, "everyone keeps leaving me. Please . . ."

"I know you've had a tough time of it, Silas, but—"

Whatever else he uttered was lost on me, because Mittenwool was suddenly right next to me. "Someone's coming."

"Shh!" I commanded.

"Now hold on!" the sheriff replied sternly, thinking I was shushing him.

"Someone's coming!" I whispered, putting my fingers to my lips.

"What are you—" barked Deputy Beautyman, but Sheriff Chalfont pushed him to be quiet, and for a few seconds we were all frozen, listening.

All that could be heard was the sound of the Falls, which was now like a noise inside our minds, and the nickering of the horses, and the slapping water of the cataracts left and right of us. Deputy Beautyman, who was looking at me like he was ready to throttle me, was about to break the silence when a different sound reached us. The sound of splashing, a little heavier than the slap-slap-slap of the cataracts. Then the sound of men's voices.

The three of us crouched low to the ground and hugged the shadowed wall. We watched as Seb and Eben Morton waded waist-deep through the creek on the right of us. They held their rifles over their heads, as well as sacks containing what I presumed were their clothes, since they were shirtless in the water. They had obviously not seen us, nor had any inkling of the danger that awaited them on this side of the creek.

That could only mean one thing, of course. Marshal Farmer, bless his soul, had not been caught.

EIGHT

People only see what they are prepared to see.

—Ralph Waldo Emerson
Journal entry, 1863

1

IT IS A MISCONCEPTION AMONG people who believe in these things that ghosts are somehow all-seeing, or all-knowing. They are not. They are bound by the same laws of the universe as the living. They'll know what's happening in the house they occupy, for instance, but won't know what's happening in a house down the street. Not if they're not there. Maybe they can see a little more clearly and hear a little better than we can, but it's not because the world is different for them than it is for us. It's only because their perception is slightly different. Just like one person might see a color and perceive it to be blue, while another person can look at that same color and perceive it as green. Sure, you could argue that blue is blue and green is green, but have you not seen the way colors bleed in and out of each other, and change with the light, and reflect the things around them? Look at how a sunset bleeds into the sky. Or how a river is full of a multitude of colors. Anyway, ghosts go places and come places, but they are not everyplace at once. They are not gods. They are not angels. They are just people who have died.

I say this because, although Mittenwool knew that the Morton brothers were crossing the creek before I did, he did not know anything more about them than that. He didn't know why they were coming, or if they knew we were here. As he crouched next to me in the shadows, I could tell he was as nervous for me as I was for myself. His heart was pounding.

"You stay down, Silas," he whispered to me, as if the others could possibly hear him. "Stop playing the hero."

". . . not my fault there's no food," one of the Morton brothers was saying as they approached. "It's the Plugs that eat so much, not me. They should be the ones out hunting, not us. I'm sick and tired of apples."

I could not tell their two moon-round faces apart, so in my head the one who'd just spoken was Seb. The other one, who was slightly taller and broader than his brother, was Eben.

They had almost finished crossing the creek and were now in knee-deep water, trudging through the current in their drawers.

"I personally don't mind getting out of that cave," Eben replied. He was in front. "Just so much of that stench a man can take."

I immediately thought of the smell of sulfur, and how Pa's collodion chemicals stank like rotten eggs.

"All I'm saying is, I don't see why it's only us doing the dirty work," Seb griped.

"Who else is going to do it? It's not like we're smart enough to do the other stuff," replied Eben. "So quit your whining. I'm sick of it."

"I'm just cold, that's all," his brother whined.

"*I'm just cold, that's all.* You're sounding like Rufe now."

They had cleared the water and thrown their dry clothes and rifles on the ground to wring out their wet drawers. It was precisely then that Sheriff Chalfont and Deputy Beautyman charged out of the bushes and tackled them with a fierceness I had not foreseen. It happened so quickly, and with such precision, there was barely a scuffle. The sheriff had his man facedown in the mud, rifle pointed at his cheek. The deputy's man was pinned faceup, rifle pointed between his eyes.

"Say a word and I blow your head off," Deputy Beautyman warned him.

"Silas," Sheriff Chalfont called out, "get some rope. I saw some by the saddles."

I did as he asked, and in no time the two brothers were tied fast, the ropes wound all the way around their mouths.

"Were these the men who took your pa?" Sheriff Chalfont asked me.

"Yes, sir. Two of them," I reported. "Their names are Seb and Eben Morton. I don't know which one is which." I could tell from their reactions, the way their eyes took me in, that they remembered me well.

Sheriff Chalfont nudged the one I'd named Eben in my head with the tip of his rifle. "You answer my questions truthfully," he said, "and I'll tell the judge to go easy on you boys. He might even let you go free. Otherwise, you're looking at quite a lot of time in the penitentiary. Just know this: if either one of you yells out, or does *anything* to annoy me, I'll let my partner here kill your brother. He is very good at killing. We served together in Mexico, so I know what I'm talking about."

Deputy Beautyman raised his eyebrows and nodded, almost comically. I could tell he and the sheriff had a long history together, the way they seemed to know each other's minds. I also wondered if what the sheriff said was true about his deputy. I somehow believed it.

"So, here's what's going to happen. I'm going to take the rope off your mouth," Sheriff Chalfont continued, speaking to Eben, "and you're going to answer my questions. If you do anything I don't like, your brother's a dead man. You understand?"

Both brothers blinked yes in exactly the same way, and Sheriff Chalfont lowered the rope from Eben's mouth. Eben coughed and spat.

"Is it just the two of you out here?" Sheriff Chalfont asked him.

"Yes, sir," answered Eben, his eyes dull and wide and scared.

"Is Roscoe Ollerenshaw in the cave?" asked the sheriff.

"Yes, sir."

"Who is with him?"

"We don't know all their names. But there's Rufe Jones. There's a little fella from up north. Don't know his name, but his fingers are completely blue. And then there are two of Mr. Ollerenshaw's men. His personal bodyguards. Don't know their names, either, but Rufe says they're Plug Uglies from Baltimore, so we call them the Plugs behind their backs. Plug One and Plug Two."

"What about my pa?" I said. "Is he there?"

"Of course he's there. Wasn't counting him."

"And what are they doing there?" asked Sheriff Chalfont.

"They're printing money. That's not really a crime, is it?"

"Why did they take this boy's father?" asked Deputy Beautyman.

"He's Mac Boat," answered Eben.

"He is not!" I yelled, lunging at him.

Deputy Beautyman caught me by my collar and lifted me up, one-handed, like I was a puppy being picked up by the scruff of his neck.

"I'm just telling you what they told me!" Eben replied defensively. "They said he was a chemist or something like that, and Mr. Ollerenshaw needed his help figuring out this newfangled method for printing money because the little blue-fingered man, who was supposed to know how to do it, made a mess of things. Honestly, I don't understand half of what they say."

"Is the boy's father cooperating?" asked Deputy Beautyman.

"Yes, sir," Eben answered. "Mr. Ollerenshaw told him he'd let him go if he figured out how to print the banknotes. Which he did! Those banknotes look perfect now. You'd never know they weren't real."

"So they're going to let him go!" I cried, still collared by the deputy.

Eben blinked a few times. "Well, that's not what I heard, exactly."

Deputy Beautyman released my collar now. I stumbled on the ground. He steadied me.

"What did you hear, *exactly*?" asked the sheriff.

Eben breathed in sharply. He avoided my gaze. "Just that, well, Mr. Ollerenshaw wanted him for something else, too—though we didn't know about that at first! Apparently, there's this trunk full of gold buried somewhere, and Mr. Ollerenshaw thinks Mac Boat—or whoever he is—knows where it is. That's why we were supposed to bring the kid back with us, you see. Because Mr. Ollerenshaw was going to use the boy to get the father to tell him where the gold was hidden."

Eben glanced over at his brother, who nodded at him to keep talking.

"Mr. Ollerenshaw was fit to be tied when we showed up without the kid," Eben continued. "And on top of that, we lost his horse on the way back. A little white-faced thing, got away from us in the Woods. I've never seen Mr. Ollerenshaw look so mad! Anyway, Rufe Jones offered to go back and get the boy, but Mr. Ollerenshaw sent the blue-fingered man instead. The boy was gone by the time he got there, of course. Though the dog was there still. Bit his leg up awful bad."

"Argos," I whispered.

"How do you know all this?" Sheriff Chalfont asked him.

"Because the blue-fingered man got back to the cave yesterday," Eben replied, "leg covered in chiggers. Most disgusting thing we ever saw. Almost threw up, we did."

"What did Ollerenshaw do when Blue Fingers showed up without the boy?" Sheriff Chalfont asked.

Eben raised one of his shoulders, like he was trying to scratch his ear. "Well, sir," he drawled reluctantly, "he had the Plugs give Mac Boat a real working-over, that's what he did."

I felt my heart clench at those words. Breathless, they left me.

"He gave him until tomorrow morning to tell him where the gold is, or else," added Eben.

"But my pa doesn't know where the gold is!" I cried.

Eben looked at me, openmouthed, blinking that slow blink of his. "Well, Mr. Ollerenshaw thinks he does."

I clasped my hands over my head, looking at the sheriff with desperation. "We have to go get my pa now!"

The sheriff would not allow for distractions. "What about the marshal?" he continued calmly. "Did you find an old man in the Woods?"

"An old man? No, sir!"

"Please, Sheriff, we have to go get my pa!" I pleaded.

But Eben had more to say.

"Look, Mr. Sheriff, sir," he entreated, staring up at the sheriff with puppy dog eyes now. "You see how much I'm cooperating, right? I've told you everything I know. Will you please let us go? Truth is, we didn't even know Mr. Ollerenshaw before a couple of months ago. My brother and me, we were just heading to California to pan for gold. We were going to find ourselves a gold mine, strike it rich, and open up a candy shop somewhere. That was the plan. But we ran out of money by the time we got to Akron, and that's when we met Rufe Jones. He told us we'd make a lot more working for him than we would mining for gold. So that's what we did. It was such easy work, too! He'd give us money to spend, and our job was to spend it!"

"But it was counterfeit money you were spending," replied

Sheriff Chalfont. "You knew that, didn't you? You were boodle carriers. What you were doing was illegal."

"Well, we knew it was illegal, but we didn't know it was a crime!" blubbered Eben, his cheeks shiny with tears. "We thought it was a nice idea, frankly, printing enough money so everyone could have some. Didn't seem like it could hurt anybody."

Deputy Beautyman snickered.

"But we see the error of our ways now!" Eben avowed quickly, his eyes darting back and forth between the two lawmen. "We are very, very repentant, sirs. And right now, really, all we were doing was hunting rabbits for those bad men. That's all. We don't want to be mixed up with any of this anymore. Please, let us go. We won't tell Mr. Ollerenshaw you're here. We'll just get on our way to California."

"You ever kill anyone?" asked the sheriff.

"No! We have never. I swear on the Almighty!"

I only now realized how young the brothers were. Not yet eighteen, from what I could tell, for all the tufts of hair growing on their chins. They were big, and had soft faces and delicate lips. They were not monsters, but fools.

Sheriff Chalfont scratched his forehead. "What do you think, Jack?"

The deputy pursed his lips, then spat a fresh wad of tobacco juice in front of Eben.

"Is there only one way in and out of the cave?" he asked him fiercely.

"Yes, sir. Just one entrance," said Eben, plainly frightened of the deputy. "You can only get to it by either climbing up the ladder from the creek or lowering yourself on a rope from the top of the cliff. That's how we got all the supplies in the cave when we first got here last month. The blue-fingered man brought a wagon to the top of the cliff, and he lowered the barrels using ropes and pulleys. He's the only one that goes up that way, though. Me and my brother would never climb up that cliff on account of being afraid of falling."

"And there are no other men coming to the cave? Just the ones you named?"

"Yes, sir. As far as I know."

The deputy gave a slight nod, satisfied with the reply.

"So," said the sheriff, and he started counting off on his fingers. "That's Ollerenshaw, the two Plugs, Rufe Jones, and Blue Fingers. Five in all. Not the worst odds we've ever had, Jack."

Deputy Beautyman shrugged. "Not the best, either."

"I just don't see how we can ride back to Rosasharon, raise a posse, and get back here before tomorrow morning. Do you?"

The deputy didn't respond, but I know he glanced at me.

By now I had dropped to the ground, my face in my hands, racked by everything I had just heard. I couldn't look at either of them, so scared was I that they'd say no to rescuing Pa.

"Ah, dang blast it," the deputy finally huffed. "Fine, let's just get this over with."

"Thank you," I breathed.

"Don't thank us yet!" he answered sharply. "We need a plan before we do anything."

"I'm working on that," said the sheriff, dumping the contents of the brothers' sacks onto the ground. He skewered a shirt with the end of his rifle and held it up to the deputy. "How about this, Jack? You think you can squeeze into this man's little green shirt?"

"It's not green, it's blue," Eben pointed out innocently.

Deputy Beautyman reached forward and tucked the rope back over the young man's mouth.

"It's green, you toad," he corrected before clubbing Eben's head with the butt of his rifle and knocking him out cold. Then he did the same to the other brother.

2

SHERIFF CHALFONT AND Deputy Beautyman trussed the brothers together, feet to hands, as they lay unconscious, and lashed them to a tree with leather reins. Then they started putting the brothers' clothes on.

Sheriff Chalfont pulled this off fairly well. His body was leaner than the twins' but near enough in height that, from twenty feet away, you might think he was a Morton brother. Deputy Beautyman, on the other hand, was too "bountiful," as he put it, to fit neatly into Eben's clothes. He barely managed to close two buttons of the shirt around the chest, much less the belly. The duster fit well enough over him, though. And with the hat on, he was close enough in appearance to pull it off. The hats made all the difference in the deception, as the twins wore identical white melon hats with wide yellow bands. I remembered them well from the night they came to the house. They were distinctive, and even Deputy Beautyman's bountiful head fit nicely inside.

The plan was for the two lawmen to approach the cave near nightfall, heads down, hats on, dead rabbits slung over their shoulders. The hope was that none of the men inside the cave would take note of the deception, at least until the lawmen had gotten close enough to get the jump on them. It seemed like an impossibly simple plan, but Sheriff Chalfont was in remarkably good spirits about its prospects. He had also concocted another ruse, just as simple, that involved stuffing their own clothes with leaves and dirt and topping them with their hats. These decoys would be placed at some distance from the cave so that the men inside, in the dim light of dusk, would think there were more men surrounding the cave than just the two.

The plan for me remained the same as before. I was to proceed up the path to stay with the horses until they returned. If they did not come back after a few hours, I was to go at full speed to Rosasharon and report everything to the judge in the courthouse. If things did go well, I would be reunited with Pa tonight. That was the plan.

There was not a big chance that any of this would work, of course, but enough to pin my hopes on. Some hope is better than none, after all. And now more than ever, I was realizing how my being here really did have a touch of providence to it. I had come through the Woods because I knew in my bones that Pa needed me, and here I was now, by a creek at the bottom of the world, watching events unfurl like wings. There was nothing I could do now but hold on for dear life and pray. *Steady on!*

It took about an hour for the sheriff to hunt the rabbits, while the deputy worked on the decoys. When the lawmen were finally ready to go, I pleaded with them one more time to let me come with them. Not only would they not comply, they warned they would not go forward with the plan unless they saw me climb back up the path behind the Falls. That's how little they trusted me not to follow them.

I was bitterly unhappy about this. Before I left them, I described what Pa looked like in detail, and made them promise they would try their best not to accidentally shoot him.

"We'll do everything we can," asserted Sheriff Chalfont with great earnestness. He was reloading his rifles as he said this. Both he and the deputy had six-shot repeating rifles. Two each. I'd never seen these kinds of long arms before.

"Did you really fight in Mexico?" I asked.

Sheriff Chalfont bowed his head yes.

"Not on the winning side, though," added the deputy, with a smirk.

I looked at him quizzically, for I had no idea what he meant by that.

"Off you go, Silas," said the sheriff, who had finished reloading.

"I know who the Spartans are, by the way," I blurted to the deputy.

He, too, had finished reloading, and now cocked his head at me. "What?"

"You said before, even if there were *three hundred Spartans* behind you," I reminded him, "you wouldn't climb down . . ."

I didn't even finish my sentence, for he was looking at me like I was the dumbest person he'd ever known.

"You do know what happened to the Spartans, right?" he said.

"Off you go, Silas!" the sheriff repeated louder. His face had become tight now. His mind was already on the next thing. I knew that expression.

With great reluctance, I walked up the bank to the path behind the Falls. I didn't look back or say good-bye to them. I'd been left behind, yet again, by living men, and I was left, once again, with only ghosts for company. There was nothing more to say.

3

I SIGNALED ONCE I NEARED the top of the cliff, to let them know I'd arrived. Then I watched them make their way past the Falls and down the left bank of the creek, keeping close to the wall. Rabbits slung over their shoulders. Decoys dragging behind them. After about ten minutes, they reached the first bend in the creek, then they disappeared from view.

"If we climb up that little bluff over there, we'll be able to see them," Mittenwool said, pointing somewhere.

"You go ahead. I want to check on Pony."

He looked over at Pony, who was grazing peacefully by the sheriff's white mare.

"Pony's fine, Silas. Are you all right?"

"I'm just tired. You go. Let me know if there's anything to see."

He hesitated. "I will. But I won't be long. Don't worry."

He went off.

Pony nickered when I came over. He lowered his head and softly bumped it against mine as I rubbed my cheek against his muzzle. I closed my eyes. This is what I needed just then, though I could not have told that to Mittenwool. I needed something warm to hold, something I could wrap my arms around and hug with all my might. Pony was so strong and bold, and I felt myself so lost and small. I just wanted to breathe him in. Breathe in his might. And I don't know how, but Pony seemed to know that. It was like he knew my heart, the way he nuzzled me. It had only been four days that we'd been traveling together, but it felt like a lifetime, in a way. Like we'd known each other forever. I suppose we were bonded now, like men in war, soldiers at arms. . . .

Even as I had this thought, though, fleeting as it was, I rejected it. Wished I'd never had it. Actually got mad at myself for even thinking it. *Bonded? Like men in war?* Why did my mind go to these ludicrous places? What did I know about men in war?

Nothing but some old stories in tattered books! No wonder the deputy had looked at me like I was an idiot. This paltry country boy, with his magical pony, talking about Spartans. I knew nothing of the real world!

That much was clear to me from these last four days in the Woods. Four days in which I'd seen more of the real world than I'd seen in my previous twelve years on this earth. What happened to those ghosts in the Bog. Children younger than me. *That* was the real world. The riders coming for Pa. The marshal talking about gunfights. The Morton brothers, bound in ropes on the bare ground. That was all the *real world.*

I'd been spared that until now. Me in my cocoon in Boneville with Pa and Mittenwool. I'd been protected my whole life. Yet here I was, peeking over to that other side, thinking I knew the first thing about any of it. *Bonded like men in war. Spartans.* I felt foolish. And childish. That was why they didn't want me to go. *Stay home, Silas. Go back, Silas.* Both Pa and Mittenwool knew there'd be no going back for me. You can't unknow what you know. You can't unsee what you've seen.

I was finally understanding that. Realizing only now what had been done for me. Pa, with his books and stories, working like a dog for twenty-five cents a boot. And Mittenwool, keeping me company all my solitary days. I never even realized how lucky I'd been.

And maybe, in the end, that was the whole point of it. Keeping that other world at bay. Preserving that time, the before time, for as long as possible.

I suppose, in a way, that's the real world, too. The fathers and the mothers and the ghosts, the living and the dead, spinning butterflies out of thin air. Holding them gently in their hands, for as long as they can. Not forever, but infinitely. Beckoning the wondrous. But never for themselves. Just for us. If only for a little while. It's not the fantasy of it, but the trying of it that matters. That's the real world, too.

This is what I was thinking when the young woman I had seen in the jailhouse walked out from behind some trees toward me.

"Where did Desimonde go?" she asked me, her hands daintily pressed over her heart as the blood from her wound flowed freely through her pale fingers and over the bell sleeves of her yellow dress.

"He went down the creek bed after some bad men," I answered, trying hard not to look at her wound. Her eyes were cinnamon-colored.

"Ah," she said, nodding with a slight smile. "Desimonde is good at fighting bad men. Are they slavers?"

"I don't know."

"We came west to be free-staters, my family did."

I nodded, though I didn't know what that meant.

"Can you point the way, please?" she asked. "Where he went to?"

"Down this path." I gestured to where she should walk.

She looked at the path.

"Can you take me to him?" she asked politely.

I tilted my head at her.

"I'm afraid I can't," I answered. "Desimonde told me to stay here with the horses. What's your name—do you mind my asking?"

"Matilda Chalfont."

"Are you Desimonde's wife?"

She laughed. "No, silly. I'm his sister. Well, I should go find him now. Thank you."

"Good luck."

She went around me and started on the path down the cliff. But then she turned to me.

"If I don't find him," she said, "will you give him a message for me?"

"Sure, if I can."

"Tell him I left Mother's plum pudding in the bread box for him, but I ate most of it and I'm sorry about that. Will you tell him?"

"Yes."

"Thank you," she replied, smiling. Her cheeks were dimpled exactly like Sheriff Chalfont's, and she had similar curly hair.

Mittenwool had come over to me by now and we both watched her disappear down the path. I wanted to say to him, *What strange creatures you are.*

"What do you suppose that was about?" I asked him.

"I guess she felt bad about the pudding," he answered casually, not giving it much thought. "I saw the sheriff set up the decoys. They look good!"

"Is that all it takes, then?"

"Hmm? Is that all what takes?" He looked at me, eyes wide, and I knew he truly did not understand my question.

"Is that all it takes to cause a person to . . . stay behind?" I asked, mystified. "Feeling bad about some *pudding*? Seems like such a small thing to hold on to. I thought for sure it would have to be something bigger than that. *Pudding!* It just doesn't make sense to me. Why do some stay and some go?"

He knit his brows, and looked down at the palms of his hands as if there were some clue to an answer in them. "Darned if I know, Silas."

"Mittenwool, are you my uncle?"

He looked up at me, surprised. "Your uncle?"

"My mother had a brother."

"No, Silas. I don't think I am."

"Then who are you to me?" I asked impatiently. "How are we connected? How come you came to me? How can you not know?"

He rubbed his forehead and seemed to be struggling to think it all through.

"I really don't—" he started to say.

"Please stop telling me you don't know!" I yelled, for I was suddenly filled with so much emotion I couldn't bear it. "I'm so tired of hearing that, Mittenwool! *I don't know, Silas! I don't know!* How can you not know?"

He didn't answer right away. When he did, his voice was serious.

"But I really don't know, Silas," he whispered, and I knew he was telling me the truth. "Do you think I wouldn't tell you if I did? You think I would keep it from you? Dash it! You say you're tired of not knowing. Well, I get tired, too! Or maybe what you're really saying is that you're tired of *me*! Is that it, Silas? Are you saying you want me to leave you or something?"

This took me completely unawares. "No! Of course not. That's not what I'm saying at all."

"Then stop asking me these kinds of questions!" he cried, and I'd never seen him look at me the way he was looking at me now. Like I had hurt him deeply. "Stop asking me about things I don't know! When you *know* that I don't know! When I've told you a million times that I don't know!"

"All right!" I said, my cheeks burning. "I'm sorry! It's just . . ."

"It's just what?"

"If all it takes is some *pudding,*" I said, "then why doesn't everyone come back? Why hasn't she . . ." My voice caught. "Why hasn't *she* ever come to me?"

I could barely finish the sentence. I was suddenly choking on tears. I'd been holding that thought inside me for so long.

Mittenwool sighed. Finally, I think he understood. He let a second pass before he answered.

"Maybe she has, Silas," he answered softly. "In ways you can't see. Ways I can't know. I mean, look at Pony there, how he brought you all the way here."

"That's not what I'm talking about," I whispered, wiping my face with my palms.

"I know." He looked down at his hands again, as if they might hold better words. "I know it's not. Look, I'm sorry—"

"No, I'm the one who's sorry. Obviously, I don't want you to leave me. I'd never want that. Not in a million years. I would be lost without you."

He smiled wearily, and leaned back against the tree behind him like he was tired.

"Well, that's good," he replied, relieved, "because I don't want to leave you, either."

"Even though I can be a lunkhead sometimes?"

He gave my shoulder a little push. "I'm the lunkhead."

I resolved, then and there, to never ask him these kinds of questions again. It was all too painful. For him. For me. Whatever mysterious connections we had between us, whatever reason he had come to me, didn't matter in the end of things. All that mattered was that he was here with me, always, until the end of things.

Then a thought occurred to me.

"I should go with her," I said to him. "She asked me to take her to the sheriff, and I should do that."

"You should always do what your heart tells you to do, Silas."

"I should do what my heart tells me to do."

4

MATILDA CHALFONT HAD NOT gotten far when we caught up to her. I had taken Pony with me, for I knew I would need him soon enough. He was sure-footed down the narrow path, as I knew he would be.

Matilda seemed happy to see me.

"Would you like to ride?" I asked gallantly, extending my hand.

"Why, yes, thank you!" she answered, and with her bloodied hands wrapped around mine, she put her foot in the stirrup and climbed onto the saddle behind me. Pony did not stir an inch.

We continued down the side of the cliff behind Mittenwool. Strangely, I couldn't tell whether Matilda could see him or not, so wide-eyed was she in her aspect. She literally giggled when we got sprayed by the mist behind the waterfall. It was almost like she'd just been born.

When we reached the Morton brothers, who had by now woken up, bound and gagged, where we'd left them, they glared at me with tearful eyes. Perhaps I felt a touch of pity for them, lying in their drawers on the cold earth, but then I quickly recalled how mean they had looked on the night they took Pa. We were all in peril now because of their heartless actions, and I steeled my own heart against them. I got down from Pony and went looking for their rifles, which the deputy had tucked away next to the wall.

"Are these the bad men Desimonde was after?" Matilda asked me, gazing at them with pity from the saddle.

"They are on their way to being bad men," I answered, taking one of the rifles off the grass. "Perhaps this will set them on a better path."

I didn't care one bit if the brothers heard me talking to "no one."

"They look cold there on the ground," she said.

I wanted to ignore her, but could not bring myself to do it, so I went over to the pile of saddles and pulled two blankets out. Then I laid a blanket over each of the brothers, avoiding their grateful eyes.

Matilda smiled at me as I climbed back on Pony.

"Snug as two bugs in a rug," she said sweetly.

It took us no time at all to reach the same bend around which Sheriff Chalfont and Deputy Beautyman had disappeared earlier. There was about twenty feet of embankment between the cliff wall and the creek. Large round rocks, slick with wet moss, covered every inch. Down here, the creek looked so much bigger than it had from above. Wilder, like a raging river. It was not deep, but swift, and the waves slapped loudly, almost like the sound of a million hands clapping together.

"Mittenwool," I called out.

He stopped, not more than ten feet in front of us, and turned.

"Can you cross over to the other side of the creek and signal me when I'm nearing the cave?" I asked.

Mittenwool looked across the creek, which the brothers had shown us was only waist-high at its deepest, and shook his head. "I'd rather stay with you, if that's all right."

His eyes got shiny. And suddenly it occurred to me that he was afraid of the water. It seemed impossible that I had never known that about him before.

"Of course," I said, trying not to show how puzzling I found this.

Was it reasonable for a ghost to be afraid of water? It wasn't as if he could drown, after all. But then I thought, *Maybe he can.*

We don't know the rules. Either way, it is enough to have died once. That much was evident from the look on Mittenwool's face, the quiver of his chin.

"I'm sorry, Silas," he said meekly, afraid of disappointing me.

"Silly billy," I replied gently, and for the first time in our lives together, I felt like I was the older of us.

"I can go across!" said Matilda cheerfully. "I like the water." And just like that, she jumped off Pony, ran into the creek, and dove into the current. I lost sight of her immediately.

We walked on for about another quarter of a mile. I had some sense of where we were from having seen it earlier from above. It was hard to believe that it was only this morning that I had been up there with Marshal Farmer, peering down over the edge of the chasm, my knees wobbly. From down here, there was no sign of the trees and shrubs up there. All I could see was the sharp steep walls rising into the sky. They had looked yellow, like clay. But now they were bright purple, the color of dusk. And everywhere above me, the whole sky, was lavender.

Somewhere far away, the sun was setting. Its light was reflected in the glistening overhangs at the top of the cliffs, sparkling like orange jewels. But the sunset itself seemed to belong to another world right now, one far beyond my reach. Here, there was no west or east or north or south. There wasn't even up or down. There was only the winding of the creek. Forward and backward. And the looming walls that kept out that other world, the one with cardinal points and towns and oceans. I thought of Scylla and Charybdis, and how Ulysses—

"You should leave Pony here," Mittenwool whispered. "It wouldn't be good if he whinnied or made any noise. . . ."

I blinked hard, snapped out of my musings.

"And you've got to concentrate, Silas!" he admonished. "There's no time for daydreaming right now. You have to be wide awake and alert."

I nodded. He was right, of course. It was like he had splashed cold water on me.

Silas, awake now!

I dismounted and hitched Pony to a large rock on the creek bed. I was afraid that he might try to follow me, but he seemed to understand that he was to stay put. Really, if I could find the words to explain how sure I was that this creature could read my thoughts, I would! But I can't.

Nor can I explain why I had brought him down to the creek with me. I really hadn't needed to. All I can think is that somewhere inside me, from that place as ancient as these rock walls, I knew Pony would have a part to play in the events that were about to unfold.

5

IT WAS NOW FULL-ON DUSK. The air felt thick, the shadows had taken on the dark blue cast of night, and the edges of everything blurred into one another. There is something that happens at this time of day, those minutes between light and night, that has always seemed dreamlike to me. *It is the hour of redcaps and powries,* Pa used to say, *demon elves and goblin kings.* And this is how it seemed to me now, like I was watching myself walking from somewhere far above, a knight-errant on a quest. I was not me, but he.

Here I was, doing it again! Letting my mind travel. I don't know why my thoughts kept wandering! Mittenwool was right. I needed to concentrate. Banish the whirling thoughts.

Mittenwool elbowed me.

"I'm awake!" I replied.

"Shh!"

He pointed to where, on the near side of the sharp bend of the creek just ahead of us, lay the first of the decoys that Sheriff Chalfont and Deputy Beautyman had placed. It was leaning on its elbows over the top of a large rock, a long stick in its arms that looked like a rifle pointed at the cave. Just ahead of it was the second decoy, similarly deployed. They were quite effective, I must admit. I had thought it a silly plan before, but they looked like sharpshooters from where I stood, which was a good sixty feet closer to them than the cave was.

I could tell from the direction the decoys were pointing their "rifles" that the mouth of the cave was not too far ahead. I remembered how the walls here looked like billowing curtains, and the cave was tucked deep inside where two large folds converged.

I slowed down and hugged the wall as I rounded the first bend. Once on the other side of it, I could see the two lawmen clearly, walking about a hundred feet ahead. They were ambling side by side, their feet splashing in the water, making no attempt to be quiet or secretive in their approach to the cave. Their heads were down and they were feigning easy discourse with each other, laughing amiably, trying to look like the Morton brothers. Draped over their shoulders were the dead rabbits. In their hands, casually held, were their rifles. In the indigo air of twilight, they looked just like the twins coming back from the hunt. The ruse was working!

Ahead of them, about thirty feet, was the entrance to the cave. It was a little bigger than I remembered it looking from across the chasm. Two burly men were sitting by the entrance, smoking, their legs hanging off the sides. These were the Plugs, I imagined. They took little notice of the lawmen as they approached, even when Deputy Beautyman (who was a brazen man, for sure!) had the audacity to wave to them. Neither of the Plugs became suspicious.

The lawmen were just a dozen feet away from the cave now, and I could hear one of the Plugs say to them from the ledge, "It's about time you came back!"

And then Sheriff Chalfont, without looking up, said, "We'll toss you the rabbits so we can climb up easier." He even pitched his voice higher, to sound like the brothers.

The Plugs lowered their rifles to prepare to catch the rabbits, but at that moment, a man with a blanket over his shoulders came out of the cave. He hollered down at them, "Just climb up the ladder, you white-livered sapheads!"

I recognized the voice immediately. It was Rufe Jones. And I think the moment I recognized him was the exact same moment he recognized that the lawmen were not the brothers. Quicker than my mind could absorb, the lawmen snapped their rifles upward and shot at the Plugs from below. The crack of gunfire echoed in the chasm, and one of the Plugs tumbled headfirst down the side of the cliff onto the creek bed. The other stumbled back, hit but not dead. Rufe Jones dropped to the floor and crawled back into the cave.

From inside the cave could be heard a great commotion, and I saw the two lawmen scramble for cover against the wall. Deputy Beautyman sprinted across the narrow beach to the bend on the other side of the cave.

The wind had picked up, and there was a sudden chill in the air.

"Listen up!" Sheriff Chalfont shouted to the men in the cave. "Roscoe Ollerenshaw! We have you surrounded! Come out with your hands in the air!"

He had not even finished his sentence when several rifle shots ricocheted near him and he snapped back against the wall. Deputy Beautyman returned fire from the bend he was hiding behind.

"It's no use, you're surrounded!" yelled Sheriff Chalfont.

As he shouted this, he shot a couple of rounds at the cliff wall across the creek, in the direction of the decoys. The sound ricocheted through the ravine, and the men in the cave instantly started shooting at the decoys. This gave the lawmen cover to fire into the cave, which was good, of course, but I could see clearly from my vantage point that they were too close and too low to get off a good shot inside. They could only hit the roof of the cave near the entrance. The Plug must have realized this, too, because he got down on his stomach and started crawling toward the front ledge of the cave. Neither of the lawmen could see him, but I could, since I was far enough away.

"Rufe Jones! We know who you are!" Sheriff Chalfont called out, reloading his rifle. "We're after Ollerenshaw, not you! So drop your gun and come out, and you'll be given—"

The Plug had reached the edge and shot his gun from under the lip of the cave floor. Sheriff Chalfont once again snapped back against the wall, but not fast enough this time. I could tell from the grunt he made that he had taken a hit. Deputy Beautyman leapt in front of the cave now and took out the Plug with one well-placed shot.

"Desi?" he shouted, jumping back against the wall.

"I'm fine, just grazed my arm!" Sheriff Chalfont called back.

By now, there was barely any light left in the sky, and the sound of distant thunder could be heard. The wind was at our backs, swooping in and howling. A storm was coming in fast.

"Ollerenshaw!" Sheriff Chalfont yelled, stepping away from the wall, rifle shouldered, arm bleeding from the forearm. "Another man down! Just one to go. The jig is up, you see! Come out and let's end this!"

"The jig is not up!" replied a deep voice from inside the cave, which must have been Ollerenshaw. "Not by a long shot."

Just then, I noticed Matilda across the creek, waving her

arms at me wildly, and I followed her line of vision to the top of the wall above the cave entrance, where I spotted a man with bright blue fingers pointing his rifle at the sheriff below.

"Sheriff, above you!" I screamed. He looked up just as a flash of lightning lit the sky and everything beneath it went to pieces.

NINE

That was the river,
this is the sea!

—The Waterboys
This Is the Sea

1

I DON'T REMEMBER FIRING my rifle, but the shot came from the rifle I was holding. The man who was about to kill Sheriff Chalfont jerked forward and went flat on the ground just as the thunderclap that followed the lightning broke, and the recoil from the rifle hurled me backward into the creek. I rolled farther than I thought I would into the water, for the wind had whipped the current into rapids, and I could not for the life of me grab hold of anything to keep myself from being carried away. What I remember most of my sloshing and sliding under the water is feeling like I was being pulled down by a giant sea monster, and wondering if I had just killed the blue-fingered man. I prayed to Mama, *Let me not have killed him!* for I didn't want that to be my last action on this earth. I also prayed to her that she come meet me on the other side, if it was to be my time, for I sorely missed her. I was thinking all these things at once when a fierce hand gripped the top of my head and pulled me out by my hair like a fish on a line. Gunshots were ringing in the air as I gulped my first breath, though it felt like my lungs had been crushed. It was Deputy Beautyman who had pulled me out, his left hand latched on my head while his right hand kept shooting his rifle. He hurled me to safety against the cliff wall just as the top part of his left ear was blown off by a bullet.

Deputy Beautyman stumbled backward, covering his bleeding ear with his left hand, but continued shooting with his right. The rain only added to the chaos, for it was coming down in buckets now, and it had become night almost in the blink of an eye. It was too dark to see anything except when lightning flashed and lit the air with explosions of luminous yellow.

There was a brief reprieve of gunfire as Deputy Beautyman sprang back against the wall to reload. With another explosion of light, I saw that Sheriff Chalfont was looking at us from the other side of the cave. The deputy gave him the all-clear sign as he finished reloading. Then another flash of illumination revealed the sheriff slowly inching his way to a spot under the entrance of the cave. This part of the embankment was almost all gone now, as the creek had swollen so quickly from the rain that the water lapped directly against sections of the cliff wall.

It was clear that we were at a standstill. We were too close to the cave itself, the angle of our shots too steep, to be able to shoot inside the cave. Nor could they get a clear shot at us. It was simple geometry.

Deputy Beautyman slid down onto his haunches to reload both his rifles.

"Thank you for saving me," I said, having coughed up all the water that I had swallowed.

"Not now, Runt."

I nodded, and leaned against the wall next to him. His ear was bleeding all over his neck and shoulders.

"Want me to try to bandage your—"

"Shut up."

I imagine he felt bad then, because without looking at me, he said, "That was a good shot. You saved Desi's life."

"I hope I didn't kill the man."

"Well, I hope you did!" he spat. "But I don't think you did, if it's any consolation. That's him firing at us right now."

"I think it's Rufe Jones."

"It's both of them," he corrected, handing me one of his rifles. "Which is why, if anyone comes down here, you have to shoot them, you hear me? None of this *Gosh, I hope I didn't kill anyone* nonsense. This isn't a game, Runt. No magical ponies are going to come rescue us, you got that?"

"Yes."

"Roscoe Ollerenshaw!" Sheriff Chalfont shouted, his voice booming over the rainstorm like a thunderclap. "Come on out. Give yourself up. There's nowhere for you to go, as you must know. All we have to do is wait you out. You're going to run out of food and water eventually. Might as well just give up now, save us all the trouble."

"Save us *all*?" came the reply. "There are only three of you, by my count. Those are decoys across the creek. You think I'm an idiot?"

"Yes, we do!" Deputy Beautyman taunted gleefully.

"More of my men are coming any minute now!" bellowed Ollerenshaw. "They'll make mincemeat out of you!"

"Do you mean the two baby boys we got roped up on the creek?" the sheriff replied. "Or are you talking about the blue-fingered man up there on the cliff, who's probably bleeding to death as I speak?"

"I have a proposition for you!" shouted Ollerenshaw.

"If it's about trying to bribe us, don't bother!" answered the sheriff.

"Hear me out! There's enough money at stake to make you and your friends out there rich beyond your wildest dreams," said Ollerenshaw.

"If I cared that much about money," answered the sheriff, "I'd be digging for gold out in California."

The deputy nudged me. "We actually did go digging for gold once."

"What I'm talking about *is* gold!" answered Ollerenshaw. "Not counterfeit bills, either. But real gold! Twenty thousand dollars' worth! Hidden away somewhere. The man I have with me here is none other than Mac Boat, and he said he's going to tell me where it is!"

My heart froze.

2

A LONG SILENCE FOLLOWED. The sheriff glanced over at me, maybe because he was thinking about what to say next. The rainstorm that had flooded our senses had suddenly quieted, if only for a while, and the silence gave us all the opportunity to think our thoughts through. The sky had cleared. Things sparkled in the moonlight.

"I'm not sure how to tell you this," the sheriff answered matter-of-factly, "but that's not Mac Boat you got there! I'll tell you what, though. You let that man go, and I'll make sure the judge hears about it. You might even get a couple of years lopped off for cooperating with us. Rufe Jones, you listening? That goes for you, too!" As he talked, he signaled something to Deputy Beautyman, walked his fingers in the air.

"You stay here, Runt," Deputy Beautyman whispered to me, pushing his finger into my forehead to keep me back against the wall. "Don't move from this spot."

Then, pressing himself as flat as he could against the rock face, cheek squished against the stone, he started scaling the rock face. I thought about how afraid he'd been on the cliff earlier, and how brave he was being now to clamber up like that.

"So you're telling me you're not interested in twenty thousand dollars in gold!" Ollerenshaw screamed from inside the cave.

"Of course I'm interested!" answered the sheriff, in an almost friendly manner. I knew he was buying time for the deputy to climb. "Who wouldn't want twenty thousand dollars? I just don't think you know where it is, that's all!"

"But Mac Boat *does* know where it is, and I got him right here!" Ollerenshaw yelled back. "I'll wager that he'd be happy to make a nice deal with you, here and now, to avoid jail time! Which is something I'm willing to do, too! Twenty thousand dollars goes a long way! So let's end this strife! You put your weapons down. I'll put my weapon down. We'll all come to an equitable business arrangement!"

Sheriff Chalfont let out a scornful laugh. "If that fella didn't tell you where the gold was when your men were beating the daylights out of him," he replied, "why do you think he's going to give it up now? Just face it, Ollerenshaw, you got the wrong man. He's not Mac Boat!"

"It *is* Mac Boat! And he's about to tell me where the gold is."

It was at that moment that I saw, of all the things in the world to see, Marshal Farmer making his way across the creek! It was such a shock to see him there, barreling through the frothy water, his eyes gleaming. I'd given him up for dead not more than two hours before, but there he was, shining in the moonlight, charging through the rapids like some kind of mad bull.

"Come on, Ollerenshaw, this is getting tiring!" the sheriff shouted. He had not yet spied the marshal, even though the old man had reached the embankment and was now snaking his way through the mud toward the ladder. "Let's end this now!"

"You end it first! Drop your weapons!"

"But why would we drop our weapons?" the sheriff shouted, laughing. "We have the upper hand, you idiot! You got no cards left to play! You got no men! You got no gold! You got nothing!"

"Does this look like nothing to you?"

That is when Ollerenshaw pushed Pa, mouth gagged, feet and hands in manacles, to the front of the cave, where we could all see him. Ollerenshaw himself was close behind him, pressing a revolver into Pa's back.

I gasped, seeing Pa like that, his body bent, his face battered.

"THIS IS MAC BOAT!" Ollerenshaw screamed wildly, his pale face glistening in the moonlight. Like white marble, his head looked to me. A stone marker in a graveyard. "He admitted it to me! Told me he'd TAKE ME TO WHERE THE GOLD IS BURIED!"

"You're bluffing!" shouted the sheriff.

"If I'm bluffing, then I have no reason to keep him alive! Drop your gun—or I'LL KILL HIM RIGHT NOW!"

Marshal Farmer, covered in mud from head to foot, had gotten to the bottom of the ladder and was now pulling himself up rung by rung.

"Let him go, Ollerenshaw!" the sheriff yelled calmly. Then he stepped away from the cliff wall so Ollerenshaw could see him holding his rifle above his head. "I'll let you walk if you let him—!"

"I SAID DROP YOUR GUN!" Ollerenshaw screamed crazily, shoving the pistol harder into Pa's temple. "DROP IT OR I'LL SHOOT HIS BRAINS OUT!"

"I'M DROPPING IT. LOOK!" the sheriff shouted, throwing his rifle to the ground, his palms up in the air.

"THE FAT ONE, TOO! You think I don't know he's climbing up?"

"Jack!" yelled the sheriff, and the deputy dutifully jumped down from the cliff wall and put his hands in the air, palms out, to show he had dropped his rifle. "There! You see? We've dropped out weapons. Now let the man go!"

"There were three of you!"

"No, it was just two of us!" shouted the sheriff as the deputy glared at me to stay hidden. "We have repeating rifles!"

"There were three guns. I know it!" screeched Ollerenshaw.

Marshal Farmer had, by now, reached the top of the ladder and was hiding just under the lip of the cave. Slathered in mud as he was, he seemed to disappear into the cliff wall. It was miraculous that no one had spotted him yet.

"Look, Ollerenshaw," the sheriff continued, his palms up in the air, fingers splayed out. "Here's what we're going to do! We're going to cross the creek to give you time to come down! Then you can make your way to the Falls, get your horses, and be on your way. Just let the man stay behind, and you go."

It was at that moment that we heard the unlikeliest of sounds, for Ollerenshaw started laughing.

"Did you think I was ever going to walk away from twenty thousand dollars in gold coins? RUFE, SHOOT NOW!"

That is when a couple of things happened all at once.

3

THE FIRST THING WAS RUFE JONES, in his long yellow duster, stepping onto the ledge to shoot the lawmen, who were out in the open now, defenseless. The second thing, what I will remember until the day I die, was a piercing shriek echoing through the ravine, like a cry from another world. It was Pony, squealing as he charged down the embankment toward the cave! In the darkness, all anyone could see was that white face of his, nostrils flared, teeth bared, like a disembodied skull flying through the air. No one but me saw Mittenwool, of course, sitting astride him, goading him into a full gallop. It was a sight to behold!

Rufe Jones instantly raised his rifle to shoot at the charging skull, thinking it must have been the third lawman gunning for him. This gave the sheriff and deputy just enough time to retrieve their guns and take cover against the cliff wall.

"SHOOT AT THE SHERIFFS, NOT AT THE HORSE, YOU FOOL!" Ollerenshaw yelled. But the moment the lawmen started firing at him, Rufe Jones abandoned the cause and scurried back into the cave.

"YOU IDIOT!" shouted Ollerenshaw, who started shooting at the lawmen himself.

This was all the distraction Pa needed. Swerving his body around, he rammed his elbow deep into Ollerenshaw's ribs, then, as Ollerenshaw doubled over, swung at him again, bringing his manacled fists down like a cudgel onto the top of his head. Ollerenshaw collapsed to the ground, but before Pa could come at him a third time, he rolled to the edge of the cave, flipped onto his back, and pointed his gun at Pa. Just as he pulled the trigger, Marshal Farmer lunged up from under the lip of the cave and grabbed the front of the pistol. There was a loud popping sound then, like something wet hitting rock, as the gun exploded point-blank into Marshal Farmer's massive hands. For a brief second, the old man stood teetering on the very edge of the cave, looking at the bloody stumps at the end of his arms, then he fell backward, straight as a tree, off the side of the cliff. I didn't even hear a splash when he hit the water.

I had no time to think on that, though, for inside the cave, Ollerenshaw was banging his pistol against the wall, like one does after a misfire, as Pa was charging at him with a giant barrel hoisted on his shoulders. Ollerenshaw managed to get off one wild shot before Pa heaved the barrel at him, which would have killed him had it connected. But Ollerenshaw twisted out of the way just enough that the barrel only clipped him before smashing to bits against the floor. In an instant, white powder spewed out of the broken barrel, covering the entire cave with silver smoke. I couldn't see anything inside after that.

Deputy Beautyman and Sheriff Chalfont rushed up the ladder and threw themselves into the cave. I heard the sound of scuffling and Ollerenshaw's unmistakable voice shouting, then a sudden silence. Nothing could be heard after that. I was about to climb the ladder when, out of the corner of my eye, I spotted the yellow duster climbing down a rope off the far ledge of the cave.

"No, you don't, Rufe Jones!" I yelled, pointing the rifle at him.

"Oh, hang it all!" he growled, and then turned his head upward like he was going to climb back into the cave. But he jumped on me instead! Flattened me out completely. Little stars exploded inside my head and I lost sense of where I was for a split second, but then I realized I was on my back and he was trying to get up off me. The rifle had been knocked out of my hand, but I was not helpless, for all I could think of was him showing up in the night and taking Pa, and this fury filled me with strength I did not know I had.

I grabbed on to his leg as he got up, wrapping my arms around him with all my might. No matter how hard he tried to shake me off, even when he pulled my hair and it felt like every strand was being ripped out of my skull, I would not let go. Finally, he started peeling my fingers back, one by one, at which point I bit him in the thigh as hard as I could. He shrieked bloody murder, and then kneed me in the face with his other leg, which is when I at last let go, as I could feel the bone in my nose shatter and my mouth fill with blood.

As I fell on my back, he spun around to make his getaway, but out of nowhere, suddenly, Pony was rearing up in front of him, ten feet tall on his haunches, squealing like mad. People don't think of horses as being roaring creatures, like lions or elephants, but that really was the sound Pony made as he pummeled Rufe Jones with his hooves. He was roaring. Mouth frothing. Eyes open wide. Rufe Jones raised his arms to shield his face as he stumbled backward against the cliff wall, but it was of little help. Pony's hooves were like hundred-pound mallets bludgeoning him. I've no doubt he would have been smashed to death then and there had he not been socked on the head by Deputy Beautyman, who had descended the ladder, covered in dust. Rufe Jones went down like a puddle, which is what saved his life in the end, for it was only then that Pony stopped attacking him.

I was about to say something to the deputy, I don't know what, when he pulled me to my feet and practically hurled me up the ladder.

"Hurry," he said to me, with an urgency I had not expected.

I climbed the ladder and jumped headfirst into the cave. Everything was covered in that white powder, but the first thing

I made out was Roscoe Ollerenshaw lying motionless next to the broken barrel. And then, by the wall, was Sheriff Chalfont tending to Pa. He was bleeding from his stomach, the sheriff moving quickly to bind his wound.

"Pa!" I cried, falling to my knees next to him.

Pa looked at me with utter disbelief. His face was covered in the fine white dust. Except his eyes. His eyes glowed blue.

"Silas?" he said, barely able to comprehend the seeing of me.

"Silas, move back, give him room," said Sheriff Chalfont, using his jacket to stanch the bleeding.

"He was shot?" I asked, not comprehending what I was seeing.

"How did you get here, Silas?" Pa whispered.

"I came for you, Pa," I said, holding his hand. "I brought the sheriff. I knew you needed us."

"I did," he answered. "I thought if I helped them, they'd let me go, but . . ."

"Save your strength," said Sheriff Chalfont, whose hands were drenched in Pa's blood.

I squeezed Pa's hand.

"I should never have left you, Silas," he said. "I didn't know what else to do. I just wanted to keep you safe."

"I know, Pa."

"I promised her I'd keep you safe."

"I know."

The blood continued to spurt out of him. It seemed unnaturally red against the white powder that coated everything.

"Is Mittenwool with you?" he whispered.

Mittenwool nodded.

"Yes, he's right here. He's next to you, Pa."

Pa smiled and closed his eyes. "Your mama tried to save a boy from drowning once. Did I ever tell you that?"

Mittenwool blinked and looked at me.

"No, Pa," I answered.

Deputy Beautyman came up behind me now, and placed his hand gently on my shoulder. This is when I knew that Pa was going to die.

"I brought her violin with me," I said. "I don't know why. . . ."

"You brought it?" His eyes opened wide, as if I'd answered a question that had always been a mystery to him. He reached out his other hand and put it on top of mine. He held my hand tightly between his own.

"You're a good boy, Silas," he said. "You're going to have a fine life. You'll do good in the world. Being your pa has been the best thing that's ever happened to me."

"Pa, please stay. I don't want to be alone."

But he was gone.

4

IT IS SOMETHING, TO SEE a soul rise from its moorings. I am not sure why I'm gifted with the ability to see these things, or why the line between the living and the dead has always been so blurred for me. I don't know why some souls linger and some don't. Mama's did not linger. Pa's did not, either. It rose from his body and hovered briefly, unencumbered by weight. Have you seen the way heat rises above a shiny field and melds the edges of the world contained beyond it? This is what a soul leaving the earth looks like. To me, at least. It may look different to others, but I can only catalog my own perceptions.

Mittenwool closed Pa's eyes softly. I could not even cry, for the wonder of it all was with me. To this day, and it has been years, I cannot be too saddened by the passing of souls between worlds, for I know how it is, how they come and go for us through the ages, in our lifetimes. It is not unlike Pa's irontypes, I've come to realize. We don't see the images until the action of sunlight, or some other mysterious agency, gives form to the invisible. But they are there.

Sheriff Chalfont looked up at me, over Pa's body, and I could see how pained he was. "I'm so sorry, Silas," he said.

I couldn't form any words. He lowered his head, and sighed deeply. Deputy Beautyman, who was still behind me, his hand on my shoulder, wrapped his arm around me and held me tight with that one arm. He pressed his chin on my other shoulder and hugged me.

It was strange to feel that tenderness from him, but I grabbed hold of his arm with my hands and held him tighter than I had ever held anything in my life, for he was living and breathing. And I needed that.

5

WE STAYED IN THE CAVE for the rest of the night. The details of that evening are a bit of a fog to me. I know that after the dust had literally settled, we saw how the cave opened into an enormous cavern, maybe forty feet high by a hundred at its widest. It was well ordered, like a storehouse. In every corner and nook and cranny were barrels full of chemicals, and stacks of counterfeit money piled up as tall as a man. All covered in a fine dust of what no one had to tell me was silver nitrate. I recognized the smell immediately.

Deputy Beautyman had brought Rufe Jones up into the cave and tied him back to back with Ollerenshaw, who was still unconscious. For whatever reason, whether it was because Rufe Jones knew a judge might show him leniency if he cooperated, or because he wanted to expunge his conscience, the sly man got very talkative in the cave that night. Despite the fact that he'd lost a mouthful of teeth, and one of his eyes was swollen shut, he started rattling off details about the counterfeiting operation as if the sheriff and the deputy were asking him questions. They weren't. They knew a man lay dead. Silence was all that was called for. But that didn't stop Rufe Jones.

"That contraption over there," he said, in that same singsong voice that I remembered from the night he took Pa, "that's the geometric lathe. We didn't really use that too much this time around. We were trying something new. That room to your left there?" He pointed his chin to the left side of the cave. "That's where we used solvents to wipe the banknotes clean of any ink. I bet you want to know where we got the banknotes from, right?"

"Just shut up," said the deputy.

Rufe Jones, spitting out another loose tooth, shrugged. "I thought you'd want to know all the details of the operation, is all."

"I should kill you right now for shooting my ear off," answered the deputy.

"That wasn't me! I'm a terrible shot."

"Just shut your mouth."

"I'll testify against Ollerenshaw, by the way. I know all the details of his operation. I'll cooperate fully in exchange for some leniency. You make sure to tell the judge that."

"Stop talking," said the sheriff.

All this was happening behind me somewhere as I was still sitting next to Pa's body, which had been covered with a blanket. Mittenwool was next to me, his arm draped over my shoulder. I hadn't moved from that spot the whole time.

"I just want you to know, I didn't think it would get this ugly!" Rufe Jones blathered on. "I'm not a violent man by nature. I'm a counterfeiter, not a killer. You could ask anybody."

"You really need to shut your clamshell," Deputy Beautyman warned him.

"This was all Doc Parker's fault, as far as I'm concerned," continued Rufe Jones. "He was supposed to be the brains of the operation, but he couldn't figure out the chemical stuff to save his life! Didn't even know enough to keep his fingers from turning blue. *He* is the one who told Ollerenshaw about the photographer in Boneville, by the way! That was all *his* doing! Told Ollerenshaw there was a photographer who had taken his wife's portrait, who knew how to print photographs on paper. So, Ollerenshaw rode to Boneville to see what he could dig up on this man, and when he heard that he was a Scotsman? Well, that was all it took to convince him that it was Mac Boat, the legendary counterfeiter, living under an alias. Had us all convinced of it, too!"

I think he was looking at me the whole time he talked, but I didn't look up at him once.

"Anyway, when Ollerenshaw came back here," Rufe Jones prattled on, "he ordered me to take the twins and a couple of extra horses and bring that photographer back here to the cave. Which is what I did. It was nothing personal. And remember, if I *had* brought the kid back with me like I was supposed to, he'd be dead as a doornail right now, same as his old man. So, in a way, I'm kind of the one who saved his life, which is what I'm hoping you fellas tell the judge, if he—"

He didn't finish his sentence because Deputy Beautyman, who had come up behind him, socked him on the head for the second time that evening, knocking him unconscious once again.

"Finally," Sheriff Chalfont said, sounding exhausted.

"People need to know when to shut up," replied the deputy, going back to bandaging his ear, which was still bleeding profusely.

The cave got eerily quiet without Rufe Jones jabbering on. I was feeling a bit strange just then. Like I was floating in the cave, disembodied, peering down at myself from somewhere above. I could see how pitiable I looked. How small. And how alone. Half my face smeared with dried blood again, like it had been before I entered the Woods. Not just my own blood this time, but also Pa's, for I had lain my face upon his chest before they covered him with the blanket. *This must be the mark of my destiny,* I remember thinking. *My face, half red, for I live half in this world and half in the next.*

"Hey, Silas," the sheriff called to me, his voice gentle. "Why don't you come over by me awhile?" He was sitting next to a basket of apples. It was the only food the counterfeiters had in the cave.

"I'm fine," I answered. My nose had stopped bleeding by then, though it was swollen and painful. But I was just about numb everywhere else.

"Are you hungry?" he asked, holding an apple out to me. His arm, where the bullet had grazed him, had stopped bleeding, but his sleeve was covered in blood. That might have been Pa's blood, too. I don't know.

I shook my head.

"Say, Jack," said the sheriff. "When you're done tending to your ear there, why don't you try to locate those rabbits we shot earlier? Let's make Silas a nice hot stew. There's nothing else to eat here but apples."

"I'll go now," said the deputy. He replaced the blood-soaked banknotes he'd been using to bandage his ear with a fresh wad, kept in place by the melon hat, and started down the ladder.

"And, Jack," the sheriff called out after him. "Check on the pony while you're down there, will you? Make sure he's tied to something so he doesn't roam off."

"Pony won't run off," I said quietly.

"Toss me a couple of those, Desi," the deputy said. "That magical pony deserves a reward for taking down that windbag over there. You should have seen how he pelted him with his hooves. Never saw anything like it."

The sheriff tossed him a few apples, and the deputy climbed down the ladder to the creek.

A few hours later, the cave smelled of rabbit stew. The sheriff offered me some, actually bringing the spoon to my lips like I was an infant, to entice me to eat, but I couldn't swallow a thing. Both he and Deputy Beautyman took turns checking on me for the rest of the night. They were kind men.

TEN

I now fear neither seas nor winds.

—François Fénelon
The Adventures of Telemachus, 1699

1

EARLY THE NEXT MORNING, Sheriff Chalfont scaled the side of the cliff to see if there was any sign of Doc Parker, but the blue-fingered man, injured as he had been by my bullet and Argos's teeth, had taken off long before. I was relieved, though I didn't say it aloud, for it meant I hadn't killed him. Even though he was the reason Pa had been dragged into this whole mess, I didn't want him dead. I'd seen enough of death.

"They'll arrest him soon enough," the sheriff said when he returned to the cave. "Not too many men with blue fingers in the world." And he proved to be right about that, for Doc Parker was apprehended only a few days later while trying to stow away on a steamboat to New Orleans.

"Want to know how his fingers turned blue?" asked Rufe Jones, like a child trying to impress his teachers. Even with his hands and feet bound, and his face swollen with hoofprint-shaped bruises, he was as talkative now as he'd been the night before. "Because of the sil-ver ni-trate."

"Because of the ferric tartrate, you idiot," I muttered.

Rufe Jones grinned. Most of his front teeth had been knocked out, I noted, and his mouth was still bleeding. "Look at that, Roscoe!" he exclaimed, elbowing Ollerenshaw, who had finally woken up after being unconscious all night. "The kid knows his stuff! Maybe we should've taken *him* instead of his pop."

"Just say the word, young man," Ollerenshaw said to me, his deep voice reminding me of a cow's moo. "You can come and work for me as soon as I get my business up and running again."

"If either of you says one more word . . . ," Deputy Beautyman warned them, holding up his fist.

Rufe Jones instantly quieted, but Ollerenshaw laughed like he had not a care in the world. He had the swagger of a man who's used to being boss, and it was clear from his silk tailcoat and slim cravat that he fancied himself more refined than the other men in the cave.

"You'll what, Deputy?" he said, smiling smugly. "Do you have any idea what's going to happen to you when I get out of jail?"

"You're not getting out of jail," snickered the deputy. "We got you dead to rights. Besides, your partner there can't wait to peach on you."

"That's not true!" cried Rufe Jones, terrified.

"It matters not in the least," answered Ollerenshaw, smooth as ice. "Rufus Jones knows that any man who crosses me doesn't last long in the world. As for me, there's not a judge from here to New York City that I can't bribe."

Deputy Beautyman took another menacing step toward him, but Ollerenshaw seemed unperturbed. The deputy got down on his haunches right in front of him.

"It's not too late, Deputy," Ollerenshaw continued. "There's plenty of money here, as you can see. More than enough to go around! No one will be the wiser if you—"

He didn't finish the rest of his sentence because the deputy spat a mouthful of tobacco juice into his smirking face. This shut Ollerenshaw up well enough, at least for a while.

When it was time to go, the sheriff went first and waited by the creek while the deputy forced Ollerenshaw and Rufe Jones down the ladder at gunpoint. Then they lashed their wrists together with chains that had been pulled off the lathe, and threaded them around their ankles. There was no way the criminals could get away, even if they had somewhere to hide. But in the clear light of morning, the cliff walls on either side of the ravine were just as tall as they'd been the night before. *Like the walls of Troy,* I thought, looking up at them.

"Reminds me of the walls of Troy," said Mittenwool, like he could read my mind.

He was standing right next to me, and now reached for my hand as the lawmen started lowering Pa's body down from the cave with ropes. They had wrapped him in a fresh blanket, which covered him from head to foot like a shroud, so I was spared seeing his limbs falling limply against the cliff wall. I think it would have made it harder, seeing him flail like that.

Once Pa was down on the creek bed, the three of us, the two lawmen and me, lifted his body and laid it gently over Pony. We secured the blanket with ropes, which we wrapped under the cantle and then over the pommel, so Pa wouldn't slide off the saddle. The blanket was green, with tiny yellow flowers embroidered all over it. It was very pretty in the morning light.

We walked back along the bank of the creek toward the overhang behind the Falls. Rufe Jones and Ollerenshaw shuffled along, side by side, between the two lawmen, while I followed with Mittenwool, next to Pony and Pa. It seemed to me, and I don't believe I was imagining it, that Pony stepped with great delicacy upon the rocks. His gait was always very smooth and steady, as I've noted, but there was a gingerliness to it now. His hoofbeats echoed quietly in the quiet morning air of the ravine.

I suppose to anyone who didn't know better, it would have looked like Pony was carrying a rolled-up carpet on his saddle. They wouldn't have known that in the green blanket was the quiet boot-maker of Boneville and the smartest of men, who could memorize books in one sitting and had invented a formula for printing photographs on iron-salted paper. They wouldn't have known that inside the green blanket was the greatest pa a boy could ever have hoped for. Or that the boy was crying entire rivers inside.

When we got to the overhang, we found the Morton brothers where we had left them, shivering in their drawers under the saddle blankets that, because of Matilda Chalfont's kindness, I had thrown over them. When the two of them saw Rufe Jones and Roscoe Ollerenshaw bound and gagged, they started to bawl like babies.

Sheriff Chalfont made the decision, then and there, to let them go free. He said he put faith in their contrition, and believed they would be scared away from a life of crime after all they'd seen. Deputy Beautyman wasn't so sure, but I was fine with the decision. The sheriff gave the twins their two horses back, and their white hats, one of which was colored dark red from the deputy's blood.

"Now people can tell you apart," said Deputy Beautyman, pulling the bloodied hat down hard over Seb's ears. Or maybe it was Eben's ears, I don't know.

Their guns were not returned to them. Nor their clothes, which the lawmen were still wearing.

"I don't want to ever see you in these parts again," Sheriff Chalfont warned them sternly.

"No, sir!" they said in unison, reeling from disbelief at being let go. Then, still in their drawers, with the saddle blankets draped over their shoulders, they wheeled their horses around and took off as fast as they could through the forest. I hope they ended up in California and found themselves a gold mine. I harbored no ill will. I was tired.

We buried Pa under the overhang, where the short spring grasses grew between the two sides of the creek.

"Do you want to say any words?" Sheriff Chalfont asked me after we had lowered his body into the ground.

I shook my head. I had many words to say, but none out loud.

"Was your pa a religious man?" he asked gently. "Do you want me to say a prayer?"

"No," I said. "He was a man of science. He was a genius. But he was not religious, no."

Mittenwool looked at me from the edge of Pa's grave.

"O Joy! O wonder . . . ," he reminded me. It was that poem my mother had loved.

"O Joy! O wonder, and delight! O sacred mystery!" I said aloud. *"My Soul a Spirit infinite . . ."* I could not remember the rest. Even if I could have, my voice fell short.

Sheriff Chalfont patted my back, and he and Deputy Beautyman then pushed the dirt from the edges of the grave on top of Pa's body. They found a smooth rock to use as a marker. They carved the words:

HERE LIES MARTIN BIRD

2

IT WAS LATE AFTERNOON by the time we climbed up the path behind the Falls. The lawmen's horses were exactly where we'd left them. We'd brought the other horses up the cliff with us, but even though there were more than enough horses for everyone to ride, Deputy Beautyman made Rufe Jones and Ollerenshaw share a mount. He put them both on the sturdy draft horse that we'd brought for Marshal Farmer.

"This is outrageous," Ollerenshaw seethed. "I demand you let me ride my own horse!" He was looking at Pony when he said this.

"No, that there's a demon horse," Rufe Jones mumbled, shuddering.

"That horse is worth more money than you'll see in your whole lifetime," drawled Ollerenshaw. "Listen, you hayseeds!" he yelled at the lawmen. "If you think I'm letting you country bumpkins take my horse, you're even stupider than I thought. I had him imported from Cairo just two months ago! Direct from the court of Abbas Pasha!"

"I take it you like fancy horses," answered Deputy Beautyman, riding up alongside him.

Ollerenshaw quickly turned his face away, thinking he was about to get tobacco-juiced again. Instead, the deputy deftly lifted him off the saddle and flipped him around, so that he was now riding backward, facing the horse's rear.

"Look, Desi!" the deputy guffawed. "One horse-ass riding another!"

Ollerenshaw fumed. "You're going to be so sorry," he raged slowly through his teeth. "As soon as I get out of jail, Deputy, I'll get my horse back, and then I'm coming for you, and you're going to wish you'd never been—"

He didn't get to finish whatever he was going to say because the deputy took the bloody bills bandaging his ear and shoved them into his mouth. He pushed them in there pretty deep, then secured them with a rope. Ollerenshaw was rabid at this point, his eyes practically popping out of his head, the veins in his forehead like blue worms on his face. These hysterics only made the deputy chuckle gleefully, of course. He glanced back at me, to see if I approved of his handiwork.

And then he trotted Petunia back up to the front of the line.

Unfortunately, comical as it might have seemed to the deputy when he did it, he had not realized that this particular positioning left Ollerenshaw facing me the whole way back to

Rosasharon, since I was still bringing up the rear of our little procession.

As we rode through the forest, Ollerenshaw took sport in glaring at me with a most malicious expression. Even gagged as he was, he succeeded in unnerving me. Something about the smoothness of his face, like a wax effigy, and the way his eyes sought mine to taunt me. I don't know whether it was because I was riding his horse, or because it was my father who had been his undoing, but I had honestly never come across that degree of cruelty before. This is how well Pa had protected me, my whole life, that I had never come close to this kind of malignity in a human being. Sure, Widow Barnes had not been kind, and those laughing children could have been nicer. But unkindness is not the same as cruelty. It is, perhaps, the precursor to it, the first step down a path toward that inevitable end. But it is still not quite the same. And as I witnessed this cruelty now, directed at me, I was stung not only by the action itself, but by the sheer malice of it, that a grown man would choose to spend his time trying to terrify a young boy whose father he had just killed. With all the ghosts I'd seen, none had ever seemed as devoid of humanity to me as Roscoe Ollerenshaw.

I had not shed tears until now, for Pa's death was still something I was reckoning with, and I felt the need to contain my emotions until I was safely on my own somewhere. But Ollerenshaw's unflinching glower rattled me. I could feel myself becoming shaky, my eyes starting to water. My heart pulsed in my ears.

"That's enough," Mittenwool said. He was walking on my right, next to Pony, his hands in his pockets. At first I thought he was talking to me, but then I realized it was Ollerenshaw he was addressing.

What surprised me to the core, though, was that Ollerenshaw snapped his head to the left, like he had heard Mittenwool's voice himself. This was something new.

Mittenwool then walked up to the draft horse, and got up close to Ollerenshaw's face.

"Murderer," he said quietly.

Ollerenshaw's face twitched. Again, he looked around him, to see who was saying the word. That he could hear Mittenwool, even if he could not see him, was a revelation to me. Never in my whole life had I seen Mittenwool resort to this kind of corporeal tactic, where he was literally haunting someone. Taunting someone.

"Murderer," Mittenwool repeated, and now Ollerenshaw's eyes widened. If he had not been gagged, he might have cried out. "Murderer!"

Ollerenshaw looked at me now to see if I could hear what he was hearing. I saw in his eyes a look of total horror. I registered no expression.

"Murderer!" Mittenwool yelled loudly again. The word carried on the wind. It echoed through the air. Over and over again he screamed it. "Murderer! Murderer! Murderer!"

At this point, Ollerenshaw was half crazed and undone, looking wildly all around him. If he could have covered his ears with his hands, he would have, but they were tied behind him. No way to shield himself from Mittenwool's voice. He started shaking his head left and right, jerking his shoulders up and down as if to rid himself of the sounds in his head. It was like he was being stung by invisible hornets, the way his whole body convulsed.

"What is the matter with you, Roscoe?" Rufe Jones muttered, trying to look behind him.

But Ollerenshaw didn't answer, probably because he couldn't hear him over the sound of his own caterwauling. Even after Rufe Jones elbowed him to get him to stop, Ollerenshaw continued to moan. His eyes were closed, his teeth chattering, like someone with a grave fever. His face was white as ash.

It was only then that Mittenwool stopped screaming at him. Instead, he got as close as he could to Ollerenshaw's ear. I think Ollerenshaw might even have been able to feel his breath, for his eyes opened wide.

"If you ever go near this child again," Mittenwool whispered slowly, "or so much as look at him, you will *never* have another moment's peace again for the rest of your life. I will make sure that every person you ever murdered rises from the dead to torment you, just like I will, every day and every night for as long as you live. Do you hear me, Roscoe Ollerenshaw?"

Tears came from Ollerenshaw's eyes then as he looked blindly in front of him. He nodded wildly and wept.

"And that pony of yours?" Mittenwool continued. "That's not *your* pony anymore. It's *his.* If you tell anyone otherwise, or if you try to take it away from him, I will come—"

"No, no, p-please," sobbed Ollerenshaw, who had somehow bitten through the wad in his mouth, his teeth covered with blood. He cowered and once again closed his eyes. "Please, please, please . . ."

Mittenwool stepped back, his face looking like I'd never seen it look before. Pale and hard and frightening. He was completely winded, as any movement in the material world always took a lot out of him, and this was more than anything he'd ever done before. He slowed down so I could catch up to him. Then he reached up and took my hand.

"He won't be bothering you again," he said.

"Thank you," I whispered.

He lifted my pinkie. "You see this little finger?" he said.

I caught my breath. He did not need to say the rest, but when he did . . .

"There is more greatness in this little finger," he whispered, his eyes shining, "than in all the Roscoe Ollerenshaws of the world. He is not worthy of your tears, Silas."

It took us about three hours to get back to Rosasharon. We could have gotten there faster, but we wound through the forest slowly.

3

AS WE GOT NEARER TO THE TOWN, the trees began to thin and the wild fields slowly gave way to farmland, bordered by tall hedges and fences. The horses, sensing they were getting closer to stables, quickened their pace. I could feel my heart beating faster, too. A part of me just wanted to ride back through the forest into the Woods to hide in the deep blue night, not seeing or talking to anybody ever again.

It was at this moment that Sheriff Chalfont slowed his horse down and shuffled over to me. Mittenwool, who was walking next to me, moved aside to give him room. I could tell, from just this simple gesture, that he liked the sheriff.

"How are you doing there, Silas?" the sheriff asked me softly.

"I'm fine," I answered.

"How's your nose? We'll have the doctor look at it when we get back to town."

I shook my head. "Oh, it's fine, thank you. How's your arm?"

He smiled. "It's fine. Thank you."

We rode in silence for a while, and then he turned to me. "I was wondering, Silas, do you have anyone back in Boneville you'd like us to contact? Any relatives?"

"No. I don't have anyone."

"Friends? Neighbors?"

"There's a hermit named Havelock lives about a mile away from us," I answered, "but he's not a friend, exactly."

He nodded. His white mare, who seemed taken by Pony, bumped her muzzle into Pony's neck. We watched in silence as the two horses exchanged a series of gentle nips and pushes.

"Well, you know," he said, "you can stay with me and my wife, Jenny, in Rosasharon, if you want. At least until you're ready to go home."

"Thank you, sir."

"You can call me Desi."

I cleared my throat. "Desi."

At this point, we had lagged quite a bit behind the rest of the group, but we made no effort to catch up.

"Thank you for everything you did, by the way," I then said. "For coming with me to the cave, and all that. If you hadn't, I wouldn't have had the chance to see him again."

His face fell. His voice was raspy. "I'm glad you got that chance, Silas. I'm just sorry we didn't get there sooner. . . ." His voice trailed off.

"There was nothing that could have been done differently. From the moment this pony came back for me, this was how it was going to be."

He looked at me like he was going to tell me something, but he either couldn't think of the right words or decided against saying anything at all, for he simply nodded sadly and turned his face away. I knew there was something on his mind, though. I knew he'd heard what Pa had said to me. It took him another few minutes to work up the nerve.

"Silas, do you mind if I ask you something?" he finally inquired, almost in a whisper.

"Not at all."

"Who is Mittenwool?"

I was ready with my answer.

"Oh, he's nobody," I said, shrugging. "He's just an imaginary friend. I guess that's what you'd call him. That's what my pa called him."

Sheriff Chalfont smiled, almost like he'd expected that answer.

"Ahh," he replied, looking straight ahead of him. "My sister used to have those. Imaginary friends. When she was little, she had two ladies who would come and have tea with her every day. She called them her *companions.* It was very sweet. I was a terrible big brother, I must admit. I used to tease her about it. It always made her cry that I couldn't see them, too. . . ." He drifted off toward the end of that sentence.

"What happened to them?" I asked. "Your sister's companions?"

"Her companions? Oh, well," he answered, sighing. "She outgrew them, you could say. Or at least she stopped talking about them, when she was about sixteen or so, a few years before we moved out west." He paused to see if I was interested in what he was saying, and when he realized I was, he continued. "My family was from up north originally. Our father was a minister, a man fiercely committed to abolition, and he moved our family to Kansas so we could be free-staters. About a year after we got there, though, poor Matilda, my sister, got caught in the crossfire between some border ruffians and a couple of jayhawkers. Just about broke my heart, as you can imagine."

I looked at him. "They stay with us, you know."

He scratched his nose. "They sure do."

"No. Really. They do." I didn't want to keep looking at him just then. His eyes seemed too eager. "That connection between people, it doesn't get broken. They hold on to us, just like we hold on to them. Did she like plum pudding, your sister? I bet she did."

I wasn't looking at him directly now, as I said, but I could see, out of the corner of my eye, that his mouth opened a little, and his eyebrows came together in the middle of his forehead.

"She did, as a matter of fact," he answered slowly.

"I bet there were times when she was sorry she ate more than her fair share."

He swallowed hard and tried to laugh off the tremor in his chin. He seemed at a loss for words.

I reassured him. "Who doesn't love pudding?"

It was at that moment that I saw Matilda Chalfont, who had been walking nearby, smile at me before disappearing into the trees.

Sheriff Chalfont had taken his hat off and was scratching his head. Finally, he put his hat back on, pinched his nose, sniffed deeply, and coughed into his fist.

"My wife is going to like you, Silas," he said, his voice catching a little.

"Why do you say that?"

"I just know she will."

"Does she make pudding?"

This made him laugh a little. "She actually makes wonderful pudding."

"I've never had pudding myself," I answered.

And then suddenly, out of nowhere, I started to cry. Not just slow tears rolling down my cheeks, but that shaking, sobbing crying where my head started hurting and my eyes couldn't see.

He leaned over and put his arm around me.

"You're going to be all right," he said kindly. "Everything is going to be fine. I promise. My Jenny's going to take good care of you."

I ran my hands across my face, grateful for the soft words, and we rode together silently for the rest of the way back, our two horses side by side. It wasn't until we got into town and caught up with the others that the sheriff took note of Roscoe Ollerenshaw's petrified expression on the back of the draft horse in front of us. His face was cast down, blanched of color, his eyes closed tightly. He was trembling.

The sheriff nudged me.

"He looks like he's seen a ghost," he remarked lightly.

I could not help but smile.

4

THE CAPTURE OF ROSCOE OLLERENSHAW was big news, both in the Middle West and in the Northeast, from where he'd come originally. A newspaperman journeyed all the way from New York City to Sheriff Chalfont's house a few days after our return, just to interview me about my role in the capture of this notorious criminal. News had spread about the "Demon Horse" that had come charging up the creek, providing just the distraction the lawmen needed to gain the upper hand in the gunfight. It was Rufe Jones who spread that colorful story, talkative as ever even in the county jailhouse. Several years later, while still in the penitentiary, he would write a memoir called *Five Years an Outlaw, Being an Account of My Former Life Among Counterfeiters, Smugglers, and Boodle Carriers.*

The newspaperman, who had brought a wet-plate camera with him, took a picture of Pony to print in his gazette. He asked me what the name of my horse was, and I thought of all the various names I had discarded. I answered, simply, Pony, but I could tell from the newspaperman's face that this was an unsatisfactory reply. That is why, I'm assuming, he kept the more dramatic "Demon Horse" for the newspaper headline.

After he took the picture, we chatted about his camera for a while. He was impressed by my knowledge of pinion gears and albumen mixes. When I told him that my pa had used a combination of iron salts, silver nitrate, and tartaric acid for his solution, he remarked, *What a brilliant innovation on the Herschel method!* It made me proud to think of how ahead of his time Pa had been.

It was from the newspapers that I learned more details about Roscoe Ollerenshaw's dozen years of criminal activity. His counterfeiting ring had extended all the way from the cave in the Hollow to the Black Swamp and east to Baltimore. All in all, five hundred thousand dollars in counterfeit banknotes had been confiscated, their design lifted from currency printed by the American Bank Note Company, whose intricate shadings had been thought to be uncounterfeitable. This would have made them especially valuable, had they ever been distributed. According to the *Ohio Counterfeit Detector of 1861,* "Of the hundreds of counterfeit banknotes we have examined, we unhesitatingly report that these are the best we have ever seen. A work of pure genius."

Pure genius.

The name of Martin Bird was not mentioned, for which I was grateful. Nor was Mac Boat brought up anywhere. Actually, nobody ever said that name to me again.

One name that did come up, for it was an unresolved mystery to Sheriff Chalfont, was that of Marshal Farmer. The sheriff spent some time afterward trying to track down the old lawman, who I had described with such accuracy and who had disappeared so inexplicably. In the end, when he found no trace of him, Sheriff Chalfont concluded that the old man must have died from his injuries in the Woods somewhere. Naturally, I did not tell the sheriff what I had seen in the cave. There was no reason to. Neither he nor the deputy saw what I saw, of course. Nor had Rufe Jones, hiding under a blanket waiting to make his escape from the cave. And whatever Ollerenshaw saw or didn't see, he never breathed a word about it to anyone. After both Rufe Jones and Doc Parker testified against him at his trial, Ollerenshaw was sentenced to life in prison. It seems the judge he'd been so sure that he could bribe did not come through for him, after all. A few months after his conviction, it was reported that Ollerenshaw started hearing voices inside his cell. He was moved to an asylum for the criminally insane, which is the last I ever heard about him.

It was around the time of the trial that I came across an article listing, in the tiniest of fonts, the names of all of Roscoe Ollerenshaw's victims over the years. Toward the very bottom of the list was the name of Enoch Farmer, a U.S. marshal, killed while pursuing Ollerenshaw's gang into the Woods near the Hollow Forest in April 1854. Six years before I met him.

Whatever fates caused my path to cross with Marshal Farmer's, I am forever grateful. I would not have found Pa had it not been for him. I hope, now that Roscoe Ollerenshaw has been brought to justice, old Marshal Farmer has found some peace. I hope his back no longer hurts him. And that his canteen stays full with whatever makes him happy.

5

I WAS SITTING AT BREAKFAST one morning, about a week or so after arriving at the Chalfonts', when Jenny Chalfont looked out the red-framed window of her pretty white clapboard house and said, "Oh my. Now, what is that?"

I was still shy around her, so I smiled politely and looked back down at my plate of pudding. I was not used to the company of ladies, truth be told. I was not used to any company in general, or a house that smelled of freshly baked bread and the occasional wisp of sweet perfume. And I was unused to the tender ease with which people could talk to one another. As I've said, Pa was a quiet man by nature. He talked, but he did not chat. My longest exchanges had always been with Mittenwool.

Sheriff Chalfont's house was at the end of a lane with two other homes, up the hill from the center of Rosasharon. The stables were in the back, which is where we kept Pony. In front was a garden with a young oak tree, surrounded by rosinweed and yellow bunchflowers. The kitchen window faced the garden.

"What is it, darling?" Sheriff Chalfont asked, looking up from his plate at Jenny.

They had not been married long, and talked to one another with the gentle merriment that I hoped to have myself with someone someday.

"It's a dog," she answered, smiling. Her eyes, dark and deeply set, seemed always on the verge of laughing. "At least, I *think* it's a dog. He's just sitting there in the garden. Looks like he's been through some hard times, poor thing."

This piqued my curiosity, of course, and I went to the window.

Outside, sitting on the grass among the flowers, looking at the house, was Argos.

"That's impossible!" I cried. It was perhaps the most animated the Chalfonts had seen me so far. My hands flew up to my face, and I actually laughed. "It's Argos! It's my dog, Argos!"

"What?"

I bounded out the door, and Argos came bouncing over to me in his wobble-legged way, wagging his rat tail and barking joyfully. I threw myself to my knees and hugged him, letting him lick the tears on my face. I've never felt such bliss as I felt right then and there.

How did he come to be here? The Chalfonts could only surmise that, after taking a bite out of the blue-fingered man's leg, he followed the man through the Woods to the cave, where he then picked up my scent to Rosasharon. He was a hound dog, after all. It made sense.

I, of course, knew that it was Mittenwool who had guided him here. Mittenwool was standing right behind Argos, his arms crossed triumphantly, a self-satisfied smirk on his face. He had been absent for a few days, though I had assumed it was because he, too, was shy and unaccustomed to being around people. But now I knew what he'd been up to.

O my son, look thee out a kingdom equal to and worthy of thyself.

—PLUTARCH

1

THE CONNECTIONS THAT BIND us are astounding, as I've noted. The invisible threads weave in and around us, and tug at us in places and at times that we may not ever see, or that only make sense over time. This is what I have found.

The way we discovered that Jenny Chalfont had known my mother as a child was this. One late afternoon we were sitting in the parlor, and Jenny was reading aloud to us, as she did every evening before supper. It was a nice custom. Desimonde would smoke his pipe, a slight curl of smoke rising from the edge of his mouth as he listened, and I would sit rapt, spellbound, with Argos's head resting on my lap.

Anyway, we were sitting in the parlor, and Jenny finished a story from a book by Edgar Allan Poe.

"It is the beating of his hideous heart," she recited, then closed the book dramatically. "The end!"

Desimonde and I both gasped, followed by clapping.

"That was wonderful!" Desimonde said.

"I may never sleep again," Jenny quipped, fanning herself. And added comically, "Should I read another?"

"No more mysteries, please!" answered Desimonde, theatrically clutching at his chest. "My heart can't take it."

"Says the brave sheriff of Rosasharon!" Jenny replied quickly, putting the book back on the shelf.

As I've mentioned, this kind of patter was still a novelty to me. I found myself smiling a lot, and nodding agreeably, but not knowing how to be myself around them, kind as they were.

"How about instead of another story, you play us a song?" Desimonde suggested, taking a long puff of his pipe. "Jenny plays the harpsichord, Silas. She's a woman of many talents."

"Well, I don't know about *many* talents," she demurred in her self-deprecating way. "Let's just say I can play five songs fairly well, and ten songs very badly."

I laughed.

"In fact, I daresay Mr. Poe could write a terrifying story about my playing!" she continued, sitting down at the harpsichord. "The Tell-Tale Ear. The story of a young woman who confesses to murdering a song." She started to flip through the pages of her music book as she spoke, and then cast her gleeful eyes on me.

"Silas, I couldn't help but notice you brought a violin with you," she said. "Why don't you take it out and play along with me? I bet you're really good."

I felt my cheeks turning red.

"I don't play," I answered quickly. "The violin was my mother's."

"Ohh," she answered, smiling sadly.

Up until now, I had not talked much about myself to the Chalfonts. Whenever they had asked me simple questions about my life, I had answered vaguely, especially about Pa. And after I mentioned that my mother had died the day I was born, there wasn't too much left for them to inquire about.

"Well, if you ever want to learn how to play, I'm sure Jenny can teach you," Desimonde said.

"Me?" cried Jenny.

"Didn't you used to play the violin?"

"When I was a little girl!" she laughed, once again flipping through the pages of her music book. "And I was *absolutely* the worst player my teacher ever had! I'm convinced the only reason she continued teaching me was because she had no choice: I was her neighbor. Which is probably why she was thrilled when we moved out of Philadelphia."

"My mother was from Philadelphia," I offered casually.

"Really? What was her name?"

"Elsa."

Jenny stopped flipping through the book and looked at me.

"Not Elsa Morrow," she said.

"I don't know her last name."

"Do you know where in Philadelphia she lived?"

"No."

Jenny nodded, obviously taken by the notion of a possible connection. "Well, Elsa Morrow, *my* teacher, was about ten years older than me," she said. "She was a lovely girl, I recall. Very beautiful. With a hearty laugh. I would go to her house twice a week for my lessons. We lived next door to her family until I was about nine, which is when we moved to Columbus. I don't actually know what became of Elsa Morrow. I remember once hearing that she had left Philadelphia, though her parents remained."

"My mother left her family when she married my pa," I said. "Her parents didn't like him. Thought him too lowborn for her."

"It would be a rather unbelievable coincidence, wouldn't it?" Jenny pointed out. "Elsa is not that common a name."

"It's not that uncommon a name, either," Desimonde chimed in, the voice of reason.

"But an Elsa who played the violin in Philadelphia?" she insisted.

"What young ladies from those circles *don't* learn the violin?" Desimonde countered mischievously. "Violin or harpsichord, *c'est de rigueur* on Society Hill, *n'est-ce pas*?"

"You're terrible, *Monsieur* Chalfont," she teased, going back to flipping through the pages.

"Her father set his deerhounds on my pa once," I said, for it occurred to me.

This stopped Jenny cold.

"Oh my goodness," she whispered, bringing her fingers to her lips.

"Don't tell me Elsa Morrow's family had deerhounds!" Desimonde asked, somewhat dumbfounded himself.

Jenny's eyes were opened wide.

"They did," she answered slowly, looking at me as if mesmerized. "Oh, Desimonde, it can't be. . . ."

He had already taken his ledger out to jot down some notes.

"I'll telegraph a lawyer I know in Philadelphia tomorrow," he said. "He should be able to look up the county court records. Don't worry, darling, we shall get to the bottom of this."

"And here you had just said you didn't want another mystery," she answered, still looking at me with wonder.

Four days later, Desimonde came home from his office in the middle of the day, a big smile across his face as he jumped down from his buggy. He was waving a telegram, which he could barely restrain himself from reading aloud to me while we waited for Jenny to come running down the stairs.

"This just came from my lawyer friend," he said, almost breathlessly, when she arrived. And then he read the telegram aloud.

Dear Desimonde. Stop. I have found a marriage certificate for Elsa Jane Morrow and Martin Bird. Stop. It was signed by a justice of the peace in the county clerk's office on May 11, 1847. Stop.

Jenny covered her mouth with both her hands.

"Will wonders never cease!" she cried as tears started flowing from her eyes.

I could not quite comprehend it all myself, until she cupped her hands on my stunned face.

"Silas, you *are* Elsa's boy!" she said joyfully. "You sweet, darling child! You're Elsa Morrow's son! And here you are, with *us,* out of all the places in the world you might have ended up! Don't you see? Surely, it was Elsa who guided you here! So that I could take care of you! You *will* let me do that, won't you? You *will* stay and live with us, yes? Please say you will?"

I was too bewildered to understand everything she was saying, but her happiness filled me with something I had not felt for a long time. Not since the moment those riders had come out of the night and upended the world I had known. It was a sense that, somehow, I had come home. Maybe not to the place I'd left, but to the place I was meant to be.

I smiled at Jenny, somewhat bashfully, as I was feeling overwhelmed by emotion, and then she hugged me tightly. For a little while, as I closed my eyes, it was like Mama's arms were reaching down to me from heaven knows where.

For I was home.

2

THERE WAS ONE LAST MYSTERY, but it is not one I ever disclosed to any living person, though I share it here now.

I spent the next six years with Desimonde and Jenny Chalfont, who showed me every sort of familial kindness imaginable. I never wanted for anything while under their care. I ate like I had never eaten before. I had never thought of myself as poor, but I realized now that we had been poor, Pa and me. Not destitute, for we had something to eat every day, but we were poor by many people's standards. Unless you could eat books. By that measure, we were rich. When Old Havelock packed up the contents of our little house in Boneville, it was only books that filled the cart. And Pa's camera and telescope. Mule and Moo stayed with him. I don't know what happened to the chickens.

The Chalfonts sent me to the school in Rosasharon, where no one knew of my eccentricities, or thought I was "addled." I flourished there. I had a wonderful teacher, who did not belittle me for the things I did not know and praised me for the things I did know. I took to school with an eagerness and hunger I would not have thought possible after my time in Widow Barnes's classroom. Also, I had absorbed, by then, the wisdom of not revealing to people what they would not understand. I kept Mittenwool to myself. He approved of this, of course. We kept our world together a secret.

When Desimonde and Jenny had their two little girls, I became a big brother to them. This is how much a part of their family I had become. The older daughter was named Marianne. The younger was Elsa, who we called Elsie. For a while, when she was very little, it looked like Elsie could see Mittenwool herself. He would coo at her in her cradle, and she would beam and laugh as he made comical faces at her. I liked seeing him as he used to be with me, when I was little. But as she learned to walk and talk, he began fading from her vision, and then even from her memory.

To be truthful, as I became older myself, and my world became more and more occupied with the living among us, including new friends and teachers and acquaintances everywhere around me, I found myself spending less and less time with Mittenwool. At least, it was not the way it used to be between us. My earliest memories had always involved him being everywhere I was, playing hide-and-seek, or racing each other across the field behind the barn. Games of marbles and hop-skip, and spinning until we were dizzy in front of the house.

But nowadays, he would visit me less often. Once in a while, I would come back from a long day at school and find him reading in my room, and we would joke together and have a quiet laugh. Sometimes, I would see him walking near me on the street, and he would catch my eye and smile his loopy smile at me. But there were times when many days would come and go without my seeing him, or even thinking of him. There came a point when I got to be as tall as he was, which was strange. Even stranger was when I became older. For he would always remain sixteen, and I would become a man.

Mittenwool came with me when I went north for my college education. So, too, did Pony. I had not grown into a tall man, like Pa, but stayed of medium height and build. I sometimes wonder if my body had remained compact simply so I would never become too big to ride Pony. Marianne and Elsie had pleaded for me to leave Pony for them to ride, since they loved nothing more than bouncing on him as he glided around the pretty fields behind their house on the hill. But I could not leave Pony behind.

Instead, I left the girls my black charger, the same one that Pa had ridden off on all those years ago. The horse had technically become the property of the American Bank Note Company upon the arrest of Roscoe Ollerenshaw, but they bequeathed him to me as a reward for having helped in the capture of the notorious counterfeiter. I named the steed Telemachus, and he proved to be a gentle giant. The girls were delighted by him.

3

THE DAY I RODE OFF on the next big adventure of my life was harder than I thought it would be. Unlike the last time I had left my home, I had months to prepare and organize myself for the journey. I was older, and presumably wiser, with the proper clothes, a good education, and a real sense of finally belonging in the world. Still, with all that, when the day came to leave for my college studies, I was unexpectedly fragile. Like a child, I felt. Which was not a bad thing, for, despite all my privations and solitude, my childhood had had its enchantments. But it was the feeling of being at the whim of the world that brought me back to being twelve years old again, about to enter the Woods for the first time.

We said our good-byes at the train station. I stabled Pony in the horse car, then went back to the platform where the people who had become my family were tearfully waiting to say their farewells. The girls wept and squeezed me and begged me not to go away. I promised I would be home for Christmas.

Sheriff Chalfont, who now sported a big mustache and muttonchops that covered his boyish dimples, hugged me and patted my back. He told me that I should write often, with any needs I had, and that he would miss me and our many excellent conversations.

Jenny kissed both my cheeks tenderly, and blessed me. She

whispered in my ear, "Your mother would be so proud of you, Silas. So proud of the man you've become. I know I am."

"Thank you, Jenny. For all your many, many kindnesses."

She turned away before I could see her tears. She did not want to make me cry.

The person who did succeed in doing that, however, was Deputy Beautyman. Of all people. We had become close friends over the years. He still called me Runt and occasionally stuck his tongue out at me, but I had learned, as Sheriff Chalfont had told me years ago, that he was nicer than he acted and much smarter than he looked. He had grown his hair long to cover his mangled left ear, which he tried his best to keep tucked under a kepi hat.

This cap he now removed from his head, revealing the large scar on his forehead from a wound he'd sustained a few years before on the battlefield. Both he and Desimonde had joined the Forty-Third Ohio at the start of the War, and both were injured in the Battle of Corinth in '62. Desimonde's leg wounds healed quickly. Jack's head wounds did not. It took him almost a year in the hospital to recuperate, but he suffered from debilitating melancholia afterward, which the doctors put down to soldier's heart. I knew there was more to it than that, though.

I had met Peter, Jack's beloved, in the hospital when I'd gone for a visit one night, early on in his recovery. Peter was sitting vigil at Jack's bedside, holding his hand with great tenderness. He told me he was a cavalry officer, though he couldn't remember the details of his death, or where he was from, or even when he'd known Jack. But what he knew with absolute clarity was that

Jack had been the love of his life, and he wanted Jack to know that. It took me a few months to tell Jack all this, after he was better, as I wasn't sure how he would react. I was actually surprised by how unsurprised he was by my revelation.

"I always knew there was something strange about you, Runt" was all he said, but I knew he was glad I had told him. We never talked of it again.

Now, as he stood on the platform, he handed me the cap he had taken off his head.

"I want you to have this," he croaked in his gruff way.

"No, Jack, you keep it. I have a hat already," I answered, pointing to the dapper Continental derby I had just acquired for my travels.

"It was Peter's," he whispered in my ear. "His sister sent it to me, after he died. I want you to have it. As a keepsake."

I took the cap and turned it over in my hands. "Thank you, Jack."

He gave me a big bear hug, and then pushed me away rather brusquely. I felt my throat tighten, and tried to smile through the tears that flowed, but by then he had whisked Elsie up onto his shoulders and was spinning her around. He didn't look my way again.

I boarded the train. I leaned outside the window to wave at them as the train pulled away. I was headed to Philadelphia first. From there I would take the train to Boston, and then a carriage to Portland.

The nation had only just emerged from the bloody carnage of

its civil war, and the scars were still everywhere. As the train wound its way through the Pennsylvania countryside, I passed fields that had been ravaged by cannon fire, and houses pockmarked by bullets, standing crooked, skeletal, on the hills. One town had been completely burned to the ground, with nothing but the charred husks of buildings left here and there, and trees rising from the barren land like tall black spikes.

I had been too young to fight in the war myself, but everywhere I looked, I saw men who were as young as me on the platforms and in the streets. They seemed lost and weary, and murmured to themselves in that way I have come to know. The ghosts of soldiers traveling back home.

By now I've accepted that it is my lot in life to see these people, those who are caught between this world and the next, or are not quite prepared to move on. Although they often wear the wounds of their demises, and such things can be frightening to behold, I have become accustomed to the seeing of them. These souls look for nothing from me but recognition, perhaps a remembrance that they were here once, breathing the same air, not to be forgotten. It is a small price to pay that I can honor them this way, and occasionally talk to them, or pass on soothing messages to the loved ones they left behind. I wish I had known this back in the Bog. When I returned there years later, to find the woman and perhaps bring her some solace, she was gone. *They move on when they're ready,* Mittenwool had told me. He was right.

Several of the dead soldiers came to sit with me in the train car when I was alone, and told me of their wounds, or their regrets, their sorrows, their joys. Some asked me to send word to their mothers and fathers. Their friends. Their loves. Even when they didn't remember their own names, they always remembered who they loved. That, I've learned, is what we cling to forever. Love. It transcends. It leads. It follows. Love is a journey without end. One fellow, who had been bayoneted between the eyes, kept wiping the blood that ran down his cheeks like tears as he sang me the lullaby I was to sing to his baby girl, if ever I had the chance to meet her.

4

WHEN I ARRIVED IN PHILADELPHIA, I stayed at the house of Desimonde's lawyer friend, the same fellow who had searched out the marriage certificate confirming the nuptials of my mother and father. He lived just three blocks away from my mother's childhood home. I waited a few days before going.

I rode Pony to a house on Spruce Street, where a stableboy met me and took Pony to the stables. I climbed the stairs to a large paneled front door, flanked by tall marble columns. A butler showed me into the foyer after I told him I had business with the lady of the house.

"Tell her I am Silas Bird," I said quietly, taking off my hat.

I was told to wait in the parlor, a large room with full-length paintings in ornate gold frames. I sat on the red velvet sofa, and opposite me was a green silk chaise with yellow orchids. I had with me Mama's Bavarian violin.

An old woman came into the room with a nurse attending to her. She needed help to walk, and her eyes were gray and foggy, but she seemed well enough for her age. I judged her to be around seventy or so. I got up from the sofa and bowed my head politely.

She looked at me intently, and then pointed at me with her cane.

"Did you come for money?" she asked, her voice gravelly.

"No, ma'am," I answered. I felt absolutely nothing toward her, so I was not hurt, or surprised. I expected nothing from her. "I just thought you'd want to know I live. I am your daughter's son, Silas Bird."

She nodded, and for a second she held my gaze. "Where is she? Where is my Elsa?"

"She died on the day I was born."

The old woman then looked down, and seemed to shrink in size. The nurse's arm kept her from falling. "I knew it, I suppose," she said, her eyes welling with tears. "But I thought maybe . . . someday I would see her again."

You will see her again, I thought, but I did not say it.

"And you are fine?" she asked, recovering. "You look fine. You look taken care of."

I nodded. "Yes. I am off to college in Maine. My pa raised me until his death, when I was twelve. I have been living with a family in Rosasharon since then. The wife was a friend of my mother's when she was little."

"Oh? Who?"

"Jenny Chalfont. She was born Jenny Cornwall."

"Oh yes, the Cornwalls. They lived here a long time ago. I remember them."

"They have been quite kind to me."

"Good. Good. So what do you want?"

"Nothing."

"Is that Elsa's violin?" she asked tremulously.

"Yes, it is."

"Did you bring it for me?"

"No. It is all I have of her."

"So why did you bring it?"

"It is all I have of her," I answered.

Her mouth twitched, and perhaps something in my reply made her soften, for she said quietly, "Let me give you a daguerreotype of Elsa. Molly, will you get it for me? The one on the dresser upstairs?"

The nurse attending her, a young woman with bright red hair, helped her to sit down on the green chaise, and then left the room. I sat down again on the red velvet sofa.

We waited silently. I once thought there would be a million questions I would ask, if ever I was in this position, but none came to me.

"It's a Mittenwald violin, you know," she finally said, looking at the violin case on my lap.

I nodded politely. Then glanced up quickly. "I beg your pardon. What did you say?"

"Do you play?" she asked, not hearing my question.

"No, I don't. Did you say a *Mittenwald*?"

"Yes. We bought it for Elsa in Bavaria. They are the best violin-makers in the world. She had such a gift for music."

I smiled, and leaned back on the sofa.

"She could sing, too," she added. "There was one song she used to sing all the time. I wish I could remember the name. . . ."

I knew immediately what song it was. I could practically hear Mittenwool's voice singing it to me now. Suddenly, everything became very clear. But I didn't say anything. I let her words fade into the air like a lullaby.

Molly came back into the room. She opened the daguerreotype to show it to the old woman, who pursed her lips and waved her away. Molly handed it to me. There I saw, for the first time other than in my dreams, what my mother looked like. From the shiny mirrored image, her face looked out at me. Luminous eyes, daring and curious. She was probably about the age I was now. She was so beautiful, so full of life, it moved me to tears.

"Thank you," I said, hardly able to find my voice. I cleared my throat. "My father had no pictures of her. Sometimes I think that's why he became a photographer. To make up for the portrait he never took."

The old woman coughed. I think she did it because she did not want me to discuss Pa. So I got up quickly.

"Well, I should be going now," I said.

She wasn't expecting that.

"Oh, well, is there anything else you want from me?" she hastened to say. "I'm all alone now, you see. My boy died a long time ago. And then Elsa left us. And my husband's been gone for years now. You look like him."

"No, I don't think so. I look like my pa," I answered quickly, wiping my eyes with my knuckles. I put my dapper derby back on and tilted my head courteously. "You asked if I wanted anything. There is nothing I would like, but if you would grant me the pleasure of walking on your grounds a bit, I would be very appreciative. Jenny told me about a pond out back that my mother used to swim in. I would love to see that, and the gardens where my mother spent her youth."

My grandmother, for I suppose this is what she was to me, motioned to Molly to help her stand up, which she did.

"Of course," she said feebly, waving the back of her tiny hand at me. "Go where you'd like."

I thought I was being dismissed, so I began to leave, but as I passed the old woman, she put her hand out and touched my elbow. I stopped, and she, still looking down, gripped my arm. Then, without a word, she pulled me to her, and climbed her withered hands up my arms like she was ascending a ladder. She had more strength in her than I thought she would, as she wrapped her arms around my neck and pressed her cheek to mine. I felt like she was breathing me in, and I wrapped my arms around her frail body like I was holding a delicate seashell.

5

I RODE PONY AROUND THE grounds for several hours. It was a beautiful estate. The main house was a red-brick Georgian mansion with white-shuttered windows, and in the back there was a large greenhouse and a cherry orchard. The fishpond was at the end of the orchard, down a slope between a cluster of weeping willows.

I was far from the house by now. It was late in the afternoon. The sky was beginning to purple. The sun seemed to set the grass on fire. I could not help but think of that first night on my travels, when I was approaching the Woods. The landscape had looked ablaze then, too. Behind me, where the sun was setting, the world I had known was in flames. I had left my old life behind then, never to return. And yet here I was, in a way, continuing that same journey, like a pilgrim who has found the road again when they thought they had lost it. I had not lost it. I had not lost anything.

I dismounted and sat down on the bank of the pond and looked around. There was not a soul in sight. Only Mittenwool, who was sitting on a large rock looking at me. We had not said a word to each other for days. He was my companion, as always, and I loved him, as always. We did not need to talk.

I opened the violin case. It was the first time I had opened it in several years. The violin was as beautiful as I remembered it. The dark maple wood glowed in the golden-hour light, and the ivory pegs sparkled. I pictured my mother's hands playing, and it filled me with regret that I could not hear her voice singing the melody in my mind, even in my memory.

Then I lifted the violin out of the case, and looked through the fine filigree cutouts. There, on a label attached to the inside back panel, was the name of the violin-maker: *Sebastian Kloz, anno 1743, Mittenwald.* I had never noticed it before. Never thought to look for it. But there it was. This whole time. I inhaled, and let out a long breath. Then I set the violin down on the soft grass.

In the back of the violin case, under the burgundy velvet lining, was a small secret pocket I had only recently discovered. I imagine it was intended to hold extra strings, but that is not what it held. From inside this pocket, I removed a folded piece of paper. I opened it. It was a carefully drawn map, and on the back of it, in Pa's elegant scrawl, was written:

My dearest Elsa,

Now that I have told you everything, it is as if the greatest weight has been lifted from my soul. That you love me, still, is all I need as proof of the divine nature of the human heart. All I can offer you is a world of fresh starts and honest labor, but I will endeavor every day to be worthy of your love. And if, by chance, you decide on a different path, do not worry, my darling. For if I cannot be with you in this world, I will find you in the next. Of that you have convinced me. Love finds its way through the ages.

Yours,
Martin

I turned the page over and looked at the map, and saw the careful drawing made with all the scrupulous detail only my father could have noted. He, with his prodigious memory, would remember where every willow tree was planted, and the shape of the pond, and where the cherry orchard ended and the gently sloping hills began. It was all there, precisely drawn in black ink. My father was an artist in every way. He had been a skilled engraver once. A designer. A genius.

In red ink over the intricate map was a dotted line, which I followed now. It ended between the two willow trees at the far end of the pond. There, equidistant between these two trees, was a large X with a circle around it. I counted the steps between the trees, and then halved them and marked the spot with my boot. I pulled out the small pickax I had brought with me, but didn't need it. The ground was soft as I began to dig. I did not have to go too far before I hit it. A brass-framed trunk, which I pulled out of the earth. It was heavy but not impossible for me to manage on my own, as my father must have once. I had the key for it, too. My father had pressed it into my hand as he lay dying. He must have been keeping it in the secret chamber of his boot heel for all those years. I had not known what the key was for, but I kept it hidden away, and didn't tell anyone about it. Until now.

I put the key in the lock of the trunk, and turned it. The lock clicked, and the lid popped open. Inside, the gold coins sparkled. I leaned back and closed my eyes for a long time. A part of me had not wanted to find this, but if it was to be found,

I had wanted to know. And now I did. Were my parents planning on coming back for it someday? Or not? That part, I will never know.

I opened my eyes and called Pony over with a click-click of my tongue. He came. Into the four leather satchels hanging from all four corners of his saddle, which I had brought with me for just this purpose, I distributed the gold coins evenly. They were not too heavy for Pony. Then I put the trunk back in the earth, and covered it over so that no one would ever find it again.

"What are you going to do with it?" asked Mittenwool, who had come up beside me as I walked with Pony away from the pond.

"I don't know yet," I said. "But it will be something good. I promise you that much."

"Oh, I know, Silas. I know."

I had kept a single gold coin for myself, and fidgeted with it for a bit before putting it in my pocket.

"He was a good father to me," I said.

"Yes, he was," he answered sweetly.

"Whatever else he may have been, he was a good father."

"When you see him in Ithaca, do not expect to find him perfect."

"Yes. Yes. So true," I answered, clearing my throat. "You understand so well."

He patted my arm. He was smiling, but I could tell he was lost in his own thoughts.

Two dragonflies suddenly appeared out of nowhere and, after doing an aeronautic dance around us, disappeared over the pond.

The surface of the water glowed red in the sunset, as if it had been painted by light.

"You remember this pond, don't you?" I asked him gently.

He nodded, without looking at me.

"It's coming back to me," he said. He breathed in deeply and closed his eyes. "I remember her pulling me out of the water, right over there." He pointed vaguely in the direction we'd come from. "I was visiting her brother, I believe. I was a schoolmate of his, I think?" He shook his head and looked at me. "Those kinds of details, I don't recall much now. It was so long ago."

He bit his bottom lip, like he always did when concentrating on something.

"I forgot to take my shoes off," he continued quietly. "Went down like a stone the second I jumped in. She tried to save me. She tried so hard. And when she couldn't, how she wept over me. She'd only just met me that morning, but she wept so much. Oh, Silas, it moved me." He put his hand over his heart. "When my parents came to get me later that day, she was so gentle with them. So kind. She held my mother's hand while they wrapped my . . ." His voice faded.

He looked up at the pond again, and took in everything around it.

"She played the violin at my funeral," he added. "It was so beautiful. It stayed with me."

"And you stayed with it," I answered slowly.

His mouth opened a little.

"I guess I did," he whispered, nodding. "Someone asked her about her violin. *It's a Mittenwald,* she told them."

He looked at me, and for the first time in my life, I saw how young he was. Just a child, really.

"A Mittenwald," he murmured, his eyes opened wide in astonishment. Then he laughed a little, and covered his cheeks with his hands, almost like he was embarrassed.

"It's so strange, the things we cling to, Silas!" he continued, his voice trembling. "It was the first word I said to you, when you were born. It was the only word I could recall for a long time."

"Do you remember your name now?"

He took a deep breath. "Was it John, maybe? I think it was John." His eyes filled with tears. "Yes. John Hills."

We stopped walking.

"John Hills," I whispered.

"No." His voice broke. "It's Mittenwool to you."

"You have been such a good friend to me, Mittenwool," I said quietly.

He looked down.

"But if you need to go now, it's all right," I continued. "You can. I'll be fine."

He looked up at me and smiled slightly, almost shyly. "I think I will, then, Silas."

I smiled, too, and nodded. Then he hugged me.

"I love you," he said.

"I love you, too."

"I will see you again someday."

"I am counting on it."

He inhaled deeply, started walking toward the pond, and turned to wave one last time. Then he was gone.

A silence settled over the meadow. I stood there, looking all around me, as night fell. For the first time in my life, I was completely alone. But I was fine. The world was spinning. Dazzling. Beckoning me. And I would go to it.

I got on Pony, and nudged him gently down the slope.

"Off we go, Pony," I said.

And we went.

From the *Boneville Courier,* April 27, 1872:

A country gentleman of twenty-four, recently come into the inheritance of his late grandmother's estate in Philadelphia, has announced plans to convert the sprawling grounds into a school for orphans. The gentleman, only two years out of college, where he distinguished himself with the highest academic honors in physics and astronomy, cites as his inspiration the experiences of his immigrant father, which were hampered by misfortune, and his own reminiscences of becoming orphaned at the age of twelve. Longtime readers of this periodical may recall the story of a boy from Boneville who was struck by lightning many years ago. It is this same young man. The name he has chosen for the school is the John Hills School for Orphaned Children, named for a child who had died on the grounds years earlier. For the emblem, the young gentleman has chosen the image of a lightning bolt, emblazoned on the head of a bald-faced pony.

The End

OBSERVATORY, Cranford, Middlesex.
North Latitude......... 51° 28′ 57.8″
Min. Sec.
West Longitude......... 1 37.5
ENLARGED PHOTOGRAPHIC COPY
OF A PHOTOGRAPH OF
THE MOON
HOUR
SEPTEMBER 7, 1857, 14—15
The Original Collodion Positive was obtained in five seconds, by means of a Newtonian Equatoreal of thirteen inches aperture and ten feet focal length.
Sir John W. Herschel Bart.
with Warren De La Rue's
Compliments
Sept. 22/57

AUTHOR'S NOTE

I don't know what's to come, but I'll stay beside you,
I'll stay beside you through the ages.

—Cloud Cult
"Through the Ages"

I spent many years researching this book, and I hope none of it shows.

My family will tell you that my favorite place to be in the world, other than home, is in antiques shops. Artifacts of the past, with all their scratches and broken hinges, are deeply moving to me. I see them not as remnants of history as much as conduits to it, as I can almost hear the stories they have to share.

This book is a result of those artifacts, and a dream my older son once had, which he related with all the vividness a twelve-year-old can use to tell a story. That dream-story of a boy with a half-red face sparked, through a very circuitous route, the story that resulted in this book.

The artifacts themselves have also found their way onto these pages. I've been interested in photography since I got my first Pentax K1000, when I was in the seventh grade, and have been collecting daguerreotypes, ambrotypes, tintypes, and entire Victorian-era albums full of cabinet cards since I was a teenager. I used daguerreotypes and ambrotypes in the chapter openers of this book because they literally inspired some of the characters in this story, and helped form them physically and, in some ways, emotionally. A daguerreotype, because it has no negative, is a one-time-only keepsake, and if it's been separated from its keeper, it becomes an anonymous relic of another time. There's no way of knowing who these people were, which is perhaps why I find them so haunting, and can't help imagining stories for them. The daguerreotype at the beginning of this book, for instance, practically sums up this entire novel. A young father. A baby son. No mother in the picture. Some photos can speak a thousand words. Some, more than sixty thousand.

My love of photography is by no means limited to photographs. I am fascinated by the entire apparatus, both the physical machinery of cameras themselves, as objects, and the luminous science at work inside them. To research this book, I took a class in wet collodion photography at the Penumbra Foundation in New York City, which was invaluable in helping my understanding of early photographic processes and cameras.

The history of photography reads as one of the greatest thrillers ever told. It is not a linear history, but, like most sciences, a complicated and nuanced chronicle of groundbreaking discoveries happening simultaneously all around the world. Especially helpful to me were *The Evolution of Photography* by John Werge, 1890; *The Silver Sunbeam: A Practical and Theoretical Textbook on Sun Drawing and Photographic Printing* by John Towler, 1864; and *Cassell's Cyclopædia of Photography,* edited by Bernard Edward Jones, 1912. One has only to look at the scientific discoveries of a single year, let's say 1859, which are available in the *Annual of Scientific Discovery* for 1859, as well as other resources, to see how many great minds throughout history went to work on the same challenges, arriving at similar solutions, with varying degrees of success. Progress is measured by these successes and tends to overlook the failures, even though one cannot exist without the other. The scientists themselves are often reflective of these benchmarks, some achieving fame and fortune within their own lifetimes, and others not. Louis Daguerre and William Henry Fox Talbot, for instance, inventors of the daguerreotype and the talbotype, respectively, were household names in their own time, revered and well compensated for their considerable contributions. Frederick Scott Archer, on the other hand, who invented the wet collodion process in 1851, from which all modern photography is derived, died in poverty, having spent most of his meager funds on his own research. In *Pony,* Martin Bird's irontype is based on Archer's discoveries, as well as Sir John Herschel's argentotype, invented in 1842. Martin's proprietary sensitizer includes tartaric acid, a component that would, in real life, become part of a formula patented thirty years later as the Van Dyke process. There is no reason to believe that a man like Martin, a genius without the benefit of ample opportunity, who had to rely on his own ingenuity his whole life, could not have come upon this formula himself. Martin is the representation of so many people in the world whose successes have been lost to history. There are many unknown geniuses out there just like him, including my own father.

The advent and evolution of the science of photography coincided, curiously, with the rise and growth of the American spiritualism movement of the mid- to late-nineteenth century. This movement did not come out of any specific religious tradition, per se, but was a result of reports, often documented in books and newspapers, that went "viral" at a time when it took years, and not TikTok seconds, to become famous. The rise of spiritualism was abetted by the practice of borrowing scientific vocabulary and phenomena to explain what was generally accepted as unknowable. It used terminology similar to that found in photography, often referencing "mysterious agents," whether chemical or spiritual, through which something previously unseen becomes seen. In photography, that mysterious agent is sunlight, which in 1827 Nicéphore Niépce used, along with bitumen of Judea, to permanently "fix" a latent image on a pewter plate. In spiritualism, there was no equivalent fixing solution to capture the invisible world, though similar-sounding verbiage was often employed to ground it as a pseudoscience for its adherents. For a fascinating glimpse into that world, track down a copy of Catherine Crowe's 1848 bestseller, *The Night-Side of Nature,* Robert Dale Owen's *Footfalls on the Boundary of Another World,* 1860, or Charles Hammond's *Light from the Spirit World,* 1852. I thought the themes of photography and spiritualism tied together nicely, which is why they feature so prominently in this story. In the end, of course, it comes down to "faith in the great unknown," to quote a lyric from Cloud Cult's *The Seeker.* To each their own unknown.

In addition to old cameras and photographs and ephemeral prints, I love antique books. These have also found their way into this novel, including my 1768 edition of *The Adventures of Telemachus,* the 1859 *Annual of Scientific Discovery,* the aforementioned *The Night-Side of Nature,* an 1854 edition of *Roget's Thesaurus of English Words and Phrases,* and all four volumes of the 1867 edition of *A History of the Earth, and Animated Nature.*

Readers may wonder about the erudition of the young protagonist, Silas Bird, but the simple fact is, people used to read a lot in those days. Although there were popular pulp novels at the time, it's unlikely that Silas would have had access to anything other than classical literature in a home full of Martin Bird's books. Silas's verbosity and expressive language are a reflection of the flowery tone of many of these works, which would have formed him, both in character and spirit, as much as his friends and teachers might have, if he'd had any. As for his "brush with lightning," as unlikely as that might seem, this incident was inspired by a short chapter, "The Photographic Effects of Lightning," in the previously mentioned 1859 *Annual of Scientific Discovery,* detailing the "arborescent character" of imprints left on people's backs. As most writers will tell you, sometimes you really can't make this stuff up.

Lastly, in terms of antiquarian inspirations for this book, I should also mention my love of old musical instruments. I have a "coffin-shaped" violin case from the 1850s that set off what started out as a minor story line and ended up becoming key to the book. The epigraph of this book is a variation of an eighteenth-century folk ballad called "Fare Thee Well," also known as "The True Lover's Farewell," "Ten Thousand Miles," and "The Turtle Dove." It's come down through the years in various forms and with floating, interchangeable lyrics, but I've combined my three favorite verses for this book. It is quite possible that Elsa Morrow would have played this song on her "Bavarian violin," as it appeared in music collections of the time. As for violins, when researching what kind Elsa Morrow might have owned, I was drawn to the word *Mittenwald,* or *mitten im Wald,* which, in German, literally means "in the midst of the forest." The reasons, after reading the book, are probably obvious. The idea of the Woods as a kind of ancient impenetrable place, harking back to the dawn of known time, weaves its way in and out of these pages.

I did a great deal of research on counterfeiting for this book, and I hope the FBI doesn't come knocking on my door because of my Google search history. Particularly helpful were *A Nation of Counterfeiters* by Stephen Mihm, 2007; *Three Years with Counterfeiters, Smugglers, and Boodle Carriers* by George Pickering Burnham, 1875; and *Counterfeiting and Technology* by Bob McCabe, 2016. That the United States experienced a surge in counterfeiting throughout the nineteenth century, which coincided with the evolution of photography and the rise of spiritualism, seemed like too much of a thematic coincidence not to incorporate into this story.

In the novel, Elsa Morrow has a bound copy of the poem "My Spirit" by Anonymous of Ledbury. The poem is actually by Thomas Traherne, a seventeenth-century English writer and theologian. I was drawn to Traherne's fascination with what, for him, was the new science of "infinite space," as well as his reverence for the natural world, which he believed was the path to human "felicity." Although his work remained forgotten by the world for several centuries, lost inside the vaults of a Herefordshire family estate, it was discovered in the latter half of the 1800s, and subsequently published and attributed to him in the early twentieth century. That bits and pieces of Traherne's work, unattributed and unacknowledged, could have been found and published by private means is plausible if not factual. Antiquarian bookstalls are full of these "anonymous" works printed in crude type and adorned by engravers, so while I have no proof that such a book was ever printed, I have no proof that it wasn't. That's enough for a work of fiction.

As for what type of fiction, I know this may be labeled historical fiction because it takes place in the 1800s, but I offer a small disclaimer: my goal was not to portray real historical events here but to tell a small story that happens to be set within a certain time period. Historical novels can be seen as road maps through history, but this book is more like a river running through it. Silas embarks on a journey through nameless Woods outside a fictional town. Since just about every forest in the Midwest would have borne witness to uncountable atrocities enacted against Indigenous peoples by European and American invaders through the centuries, it is natural to assume that Silas, a boy who sees ghosts, would also encounter them as he traversed hallowed ground. I encourage readers to read the extraordinary *An Indigenous Peoples' History of the United States for Young People* by Debbie Reese and Jean Mendoza, adapted from the adult book by Roxanne Dunbar-Ortiz, for a comprehensive account of the many and diverse peoples who lived in these lands long before the Europeans arrived, and the many battles, broken treaties, "removals," and massacres they endured in the centuries that followed. All of Tim Tingle's novels—in particular, *How I Became a Ghost*—are beautifully written and take place in and around actual historical events. The Birchbark

House series by Louise Erdrich is also high on my list of recommendations.

This novel begins in 1860, just a year before the start of the American Civil War. One of the characters, Desimonde Chalfont, mentions that his family moved to Kansas as "free-staters" in order to be able to vote against the expansion of slavery in America. His younger sister, Matilda, was killed in the crossfire between "jayhawkers," who were abolitionists, and "border ruffians," who were militantly pro-slavery. While Desimonde's family history is not central to the narrative of the book, it speaks to the kind of man he is. For more about the abolitionist movement, there are no better books than those by Frederick Douglass, including *Narrative of the Life of Frederick Douglass, an American Slave; My Bondage and My Freedom;* and *The Life and Times of Frederick Douglass.* As for Deputy Jack Beautyman, he mentions having been on the losing side of the Mexican-American War because both he and Desimonde fought in the Saint Patrick's Battalion against the United States: Desi because he was against governmental expansion of slavery, and Jack because he'd heard that Santa Anna, the larger-than-life general of the Mexican forces, had once proclaimed himself the "Napoleon of the West." Jack hoped that Mexico, if victorious under Santa Anna, would adopt the Napoleonic Penal Code of 1810, inspired by France's 1789 Declaration of the Rights of Man and of the Citizen, which decriminalized homosexuality. Desi and Jack became fast friends while serving time in a Rio Grande prison for their allegiances, and after Desi's well-to-do father bought their "official" pardons, they moved to California to mine gold for a year before relocating to Rosasharon. This, of course, is just my backstory for them, having nothing to do with the events in the book, but I am so fond of the two of them, I thought I'd share their little histories here.

Even though most of the characters in this book are men of a certain time and place in American history, in my mind this is a book that is completely driven by a woman. A mother. She is the central character, off the page, connecting and propelling and protecting from afar within the limits of what she can do, which are unknowable. Ultimately, this is a book about love, which never dies, and the invisible connections that exist between people, both the living and the dead.

My world, my being, my life, my love for books, my everything, was guided, nurtured, inspired, and motivated by one person. My mother. This book is for her.

ACKNOWLEDGMENTS

Thank you, Erin Clarke, my incredible editor, for all your guidance and all your patience while I figured out this strange little book. I remember the calmness with which you received my news, about five years ago, that I had literally thrown out the four hundred manuscript pages I'd been working on and would be starting from scratch—*someday* in the unspecified future. That kind of unconditional support from an editor means a lot to a writer, and I'm relieved beyond measure that you think it was worth the wait.

Thank you to Barbara Perris, Amy Schroeder, Nancee Adams, Alison Kolani, and the ever-on-it Artie Bennett for your insightful and diligent copyediting, and for making my work better and stronger in every way. Thank you to Jake Eldred for putting this terrific team together and making sure all the pistons were firing and ready to go for the speedy turnaround. Thank you, April Ward, Tim Terhune, and the rest of the design and production group for making *Pony* exquisitely beautiful, inside and outside. To Judith Haut, John Adamo, Dominique Cimina: we have been on this adventure together since 2012, and I thank my lucky stars for having found my Team *Wonder* from the get-go. Barbara Marcus and Felicia Frazier, I've been blessed to have you two amazing women blazing paths and leading the enormously talented folks at Random House Children's Books. I look forward to riding *Pony* with you on whatever path he takes. It'll be a joyous journey. To Jillian Vandall Miao, one of my favorite people in the world, thank you for being the best traveling companion an author and friend could hope for, but especially for that phone call you made after you'd finished the manuscript. It meant more to me than you can possibly know.

Thank you to Professor John N. Low, JD, PhD, of the Ohio State University, director of the Newark Earthworks Center and a citizen of the Pokagon Band of Potawatomi, for lending your expertise in American Indian histories and Native identities to your very thoughtful read.

Thank you to Alyssa Eisner Henkin, my agent, for always having my back, and for being such a champion of all my books—especially this one. There's no one in this industry whose instincts I trust more, both from a literary and a business point of view, and I'm so grateful that I get to be one of the beneficiaries of all your talent and hard work. I feel like we've walked ten thousand miles together already, and I hope we walk another ten thousand.

Thank you to Molly Fletcher for your invaluable contributions to the book trailer. Your beautiful violin playing and composition for the solo in "Fare Thee Well," and your help with the production, elevated this project to heights I could not have imagined. Thank you to Lane at Moon Recording in Greenpoint for facilitating the socially distant recording, and to Aiden for his help on the video shoot.

Thank you to Rebecca Vitkus for being such a wonderful contributor to the trailer and for all your wisdom and patience with my grammar and copyediting queries. Most of all, though, thank you for bringing so much joy into our household in the strange year that was 2020.

Thank you to the doctors and nurses, the delivery people, the first responders, the teachers, and the postal and essential workers, who kept the world going during the COVID-19 months of isolation, which is when I wrote these pages.

Thank you to my Amalfi mamas for keeping me sane and laughing.

Thank you, Papi, for Ithaca.

Thank you, most especially, to my wondrous family, Russell, Caleb, and Joseph. Thank you for lending your prodigious talents to the book trailer—both in front of and behind the camera. Russell, what can I say? We did this together—all of it. *Thank you and you're welcome.* And, Caleb and Joseph, I am in awe of both of you, my wonders, and love you more than words can ever say. You make this world so beautiful.

Other books by the authors

For personally signed copies, go to **www.tiffanyhaugen.com**

COOKING SALMON & STEELHEAD
Exotic Recipes From Around the World
by Scott & Tiffany Haugen

Globe-trotting authors, Scott and Tiffany Haugen share some of the world's most exquisite flavors in this book. Whether selecting your fish at the market or catching it yourself, *Cooking Salmon & Steelhead* teaches you what to look for, how to care for your fish and offers unique and insightful ways to prepare this healthy meat.

Spiral SB: $24.95

ISBN: 1-57188-291-X

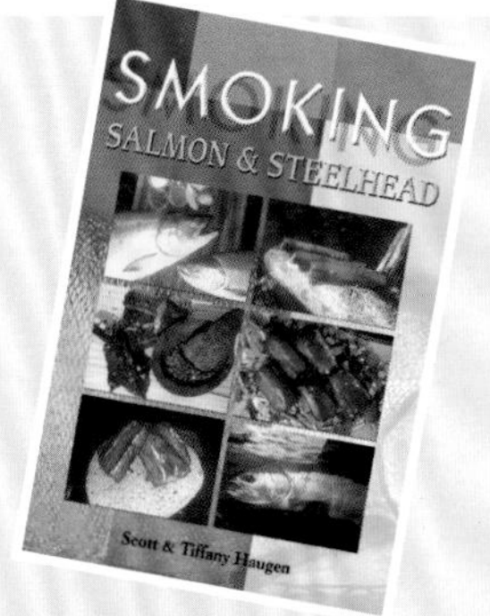

SMOKING SALMON & STEELHEAD
by Scott & Tiffany Haugen

With over 50 wet and dry brine recipes and tips on how to handle and prepare your fish, this book is packed with valuable information. With original recipes created by the authors to secret recipes gathered from fishing guides and seasoned anglers, there's something in this book for everyone. 6 x 9 inches; 96 pages, all-color.

Spiral SB: $19.95 **ISBN: 1-57188-290-1**

COOKING BIG GAME
by Scott & Tiffany Haugen

Game meat is one of the most nutritious forms of protein, and the Haugens, having lived a subsistence lifestyle, offer innovative twists in preparing big game. From family favorites to tastes the world over, more than 100 imaginative recipes will have you clearing your freezer in no time.

Spiral SB: $19.95
ISBN: 1-57188-407-7
UPC: 0-81127-00241-2

PLANK COOKING: THE ESSENCE OF NATURAL WOOD
by Scott & Tiffany Haugen

From the oven to the grill, plank cooking has made its mark in the culinary world. This book outlines how to master the art of plank cooking, from seasoning planks, choosing woods to detailed cooking tips in over 100 easy-to-follow recipes. Full color; 6 x 9; 152 pages.

Spiral SB: $19.95
ISBN: 1-57188-332-0

About the author

With a focus on healthy, creative meals that are easy to prepare, Tiffany Haugen is fast becoming a recognized and respected cookbook author and columnist. A major in health education, combined with a Masters Degree and several years of public school teaching, has helped shape Tiffany into the inspirational cookbook author she is today.

Her cooking skills stem from a lifetime of practical experience. Tiffany grew up with a passion for cooking. As an adult she has traveled to nearly 30 countries, and lived in such exotic places as Alaska's Arctic, Indonesia and Spain, where she cooked extensively with local foods. The background she's gained continues to stimulate her worldly approach on simple food preparation.

Having coauthored a variety of best-selling cookbooks on topics such as plank cooking, smoke-cooking, wild game, fish and more, this book echoes Tiffany's easy-to-follow style.

Tiffany Haugen lives with her husband, Scott, and two sons Braxton and Kazden, in western Oregon.

Recipe Notes

S

T

V

W

Z

Index

Pickled Pepper Relish

Ingredients

- 1 green bell pepper, diced
- 1 red bell pepper, diced
- 1 yellow bell pepper, diced
- 1 orange bell pepper, diced
- 2 cloves garlic, thinly sliced
- 1/4 cup extra virgin olive oil
- 1/4 cup rice vinegar
- 1 tablespoon sugar
- 1 teaspoon fresh oregano or 1/2 teaspoon dried
- 1 teaspoon fresh rosemary or 1/2 teaspoon dried, optional
- 1/2 teaspoon salt
- 1/2 teaspoon black pepper

Submerge chopped peppers in boiling water 1 minute. Drain well. In a large bowl, combine remaining ingredients and gently toss. Marinate, refrigerated at least 12 hours before serving for optimal flavor.

Fresh Salsa

Ingredients

- 6 roma-style tomatoes, chopped
- 1/2 cup bell pepper, chopped
- 1/2 cup onion, diced
- 2 jalapeños peppers, diced
- 2 tablespoons lemon or lime juice
- 1 teaspoon sugar
- 1/2 teaspoon salt
- 1/2 teaspoon cumin
- 1/2 teaspoon chili powder
- Black pepper to taste
- Hot pepper sauce to taste, optional

In a medium bowl, gently toss all ingredients until combined. If salsa is too hot, increase sugar until desired flavor is reached.

Orange Ginger Marinade

Ingredients

- 1 cup orange juice
- 1/4 cup teriyaki sauce
- 2 tablespoons honey
- 3"-5" fresh ginger root, sliced or grated

In a medium bowl or sealable plastic bag, mix all ingredients until thoroughly combined.

Red Wine Sauce

Ingredients

- 1 tablespoon olive oil
- 1 tablespoon butter
- 2 cloves garlic, pureed
- 2 tablespoons shallots or onions, minced
- 1/2 cup red wine
- 1/2 cup beef broth
- 1 tablespoon balsamic vinegar
- Salt and pepper to taste

In a medium sauce pan, melt butter with olive oil. Sauté garlic and onion on medium-low heat 5 minutes. Add all other ingredients and bring to a boil. Lower heat and simmer 20-30 minutes or until sauce reaches desired thickness. Uncooked Red Wine Sauce can be used as a meat or vegetable marinade or a mop.

Indian Rub

INGREDIENTS

- 1/2 teaspoon ground cumin
- 1/2 teaspoon ground coriander
- 1/2 teaspoon fennel seeds, crushed
- 1/4 teaspoon white pepper
- 1/2 teaspoon salt
- 1/4 teaspoon turmeric
- 1/4 teaspoon cinnamon
- 1/4 teaspoon cloves

In a small bowl, mix all rub ingredients until thoroughly combined

Parsley-Pecan Pesto

INGREDIENTS

- 1 cup fresh parsley
- 1/2 cup parmesan cheese, grated
- 1/4 cup extra virgin olive oil
- 1/4 cup pecans
- 2 cloves garlic
- Salt and pepper to taste

Place all ingredients in a food chopper or processor and puree until smooth.

Rhubarb Salsa

INGREDIENTS

- 2 cups rhubarb, finely chopped
- 1/2 cup bell pepper, finely chopped
- 1/3 cup red onion, finely chopped
- 1/4 cup cilantro, chopped
- 1 4-ounce can green chilies
- 2 tablespoons lime juice
- 1 tablespoon brown sugar
- 1/4-1/2 teaspoon cumin
- Salt and pepper to taste

Submerge chopped rhubarb in boiling water 2 minutes. Drain well. In a medium bowl, gently toss all remaining ingredients until combined. Chill well before serving.

Cilantro Mint Sauce

INGREDIENTS

- 1 cup cilantro, chopped
- 1/2 cup fresh mint leaves, chopped
- 2 tablespoons lime juice
- 2 tablespoons rice vinegar
- 2 tablespoons honey
- Salt and pepper to taste

Place all ingredients in a food chopper or processor and puree until smooth.

Soda Pop Marinade

INGREDIENTS

- 1 can cola, root beer or Dr. Pepper (not diet)
- 1/4 cup vegetable or olive oil
- 1/4 cup onion, minced
- 4 cloves garlic, minced
- 2 tablespoons Worcestershire sauce
- 1 teaspoon salt
- 1 teaspoon red pepper flakes, optional

In a medium bowl or sealable plastic bag, mix all ingredients until thoroughly combined. This recipe can also be used as a mop.

Super Soy Sauce

INGREDIENTS

- 1/3 cup soy sauce
- 2 tablespoons green onion or chives, finely chopped
- 2 tablespoons rice or white vinegar
- 1 teaspoon sugar
- 2-3 Thai hot peppers or 1-2 habanero, minced

In a medium bowl or sealable plastic bag, mix all ingredients until thoroughly combined. This sauce can be used for a marinade or sauce over meat, seafood or rice.

Cuban Garlic Sauce

INGREDIENTS

- 1/4 cup olive oil
- 6 cloves garlic, chopped
- 1/2 cup parsley and/or cilantro, chopped
- 1/4 cup lime juice
- 1/4 cup orange juice
- 1/2 teaspoon cumin
- 1/4 teaspoon oregano
- Salt and pepper to taste

In a small skillet, sauté garlic 5 minutes on medium heat. Do not let garlic brown. Remove from heat and cool. Place all ingredients in a food chopper or processor and puree until smooth.

Mango Salsa

INGREDIENTS

- 2 cups mango, cubed
- 1 red bell pepper, finely chopped
- 2 green onions, chopped
- 1/4 cup cilantro leaves, chopped
- Juice of 1 lime
- 1 tablespoon ginger, minced
- 1 tablespoon brown sugar
- 1 tablespoon fish sauce, optional
- 2-3 teaspoons chili sauce

In a medium bowl, gently toss all ingredients until combined. Let sit, refrigerated, at least 30 minutes before serving.

Sauerkraut Relish

INGREDIENTS

- 4 cups sauerkraut, drained
- 1 cup celery, diced
- 2/3 cup green pepper or jalapeño, diced
- 1/2 cup red onion, diced
- 1 4-ounce jar diced pimento
- 1/4 cup sugar
- 1/2 teaspoon celery seed
- Salt and pepper to taste

In a large bowl, mix all ingredients until sugar is dissolved. Marinate, refrigerated, at least 2 hours for optimal flavor.

Fresh Sage Marinade

Ingredients

- 1/3 cup fresh sage, chopped
- 1/4 cup olive oil
- 1/4 cup balsamic vinegar
- 1 tablespoon Worcestershire sauce
- Salt and pepper to taste

In a medium bowl or sealable plastic bag, mix all ingredients until thoroughly combined.

Lemony Spinach Pesto

Ingredients

- 2 cups fresh spinach
- 1/3 cup extra virgin olive oil
- 1/4 cup lemon juice
- 1/3 cup parmesan cheese, grated
- 1 clove garlic
- 1/4 teaspoon nutmeg
- Salt and pepper to taste

Finely chop spinach in a food chopper or processor. Add remaining ingredients and blend until combined.

Chili Rub

Ingredients

- 1 teaspoon salt
- 1 teaspoon ground coriander
- 1 teaspoon garlic powder
- 1 teaspoon chili powder
- 1/2 teaspoon white pepper
- 1/2 teaspoon ground cumin
- 1/2 teaspoon granulated garlic

In a small bowl, mix all rub ingredients until thoroughly combined.

Lemon-Herb Marinade

Ingredients

- 2 tablespoons olive oil
- 1 tablespoon garlic, minced
- Juice and zest of 1 lemon
- 1/2 cup fresh herbs (basil, sage, lemon balm, and/or parsley)
- Salt and lemon pepper to taste

In a medium bowl or sealable plastic bag, mix all ingredients until thoroughly combined.

Hot Citrus Marinade

Ingredients

- 1 lemon
- 1 lime
- 1 orange
- 1/4 cup honey
- 2 tablespoons lemon or lime juice
- 1 tablespoon hot pepper sauce or Asian chili sauce

Thinly slice lemon, lime and orange. Put 1/2 of the slices in a sealable plastic bag. Place meat, fish or vegetables on top of the slices and cover with the additional slices. Mix the lemon juice or lime juice, honey and hot sauce in a small bowl. Pour the marinade mixture in the bag and seal.

Hummus

Ingredients

- 1 15-ounce can garbanzo beans, drained
- 3 tablespoons tahini
- 2 cloves garlic
- 1-2 tablespoons water
- 2 tablespoons fresh lemon juice
- 1 tablespoon extra virgin olive oil
- 1/2 teaspoon cumin
- Dash of cayenne or hot pepper sauce

Place all ingredients in a food chopper or processor and puree until smooth. For flavored hummus, add 2 tablespoons roasted red peppers, fresh parsley or smoked garlic (page 102).

Strawberry Citrus Salsa

Ingredients

- 1 pint strawberries, sliced
- 1 orange, peeled and chopped
- 1-2 jalapeño peppers, diced
- 1 green onion, thinly sliced
- Juice and zest of 1/2 lime or lemon
- 1 tablespoon honey
- Salt and pepper taste

In a medium bowl mix lemon or lime juice with honey. Add all other ingredients, gently toss until combined.

Italian Salsa Verde

Ingredients

- 1/2 cup extra virgin olive oil
- 1/2 cup fresh parsley, finely chopped
- 1/3 cup fresh mint, finely chopped
- 1/3 cup green onion or chives, chopped
- Juice and zest of 1 lemon
- 2 tablespoons capers, rinsed and finely chopped

In a medium bowl, gently toss all ingredients until combined.

Mustard Sauce

Ingredients

- 2 tablespoons mayonnaise
- 1 tablespoon Dijon mustard
- 2 teaspoons parsley, minced
- 1 teaspoon lemon juice
- 1/4 teaspoon white sugar
- 4-6 dashes hot pepper sauce

In a small bowl, whisk all ingredients until thoroughly combined.

Rhubarb Ketchup

Ingredients

- 2 cups rhubarb, diced
- 2 tablespoons sherry
- 2 tablespoons orange juice
- 1 tablespoon red wine vinegar
- 1/4 cup sugar
- Zest of 1 orange, peel in large strips
- 1/4 teaspoon salt

In a medium saucepan, bring all ingredients to a boil. Turn heat to low and simmer 15 minutes. Remove zest from mixture and discard. Puree in a blender or with a hand-held blender. Serve hot or cold.

Grilled Vegetable Salsa

INGREDIENTS

- 3 cups smoke-grilled vegetables of choice, diced
  (Use vegetables from Rosemary Vegetable Skewers (page 14) or Grilled Vegetables in Raspberry Vinaigrette (page 22).
- 3 tablespoons extra virgin olive oil
- 2 tablespoons balsamic vinegar
- Salt and pepper to taste

In a medium bowl, gently toss all ingredients until combined.

Sweet & Hot Rub

INGREDIENTS

- 1 tablespoon brown sugar
- 1/2 tablespoon red pepper flakes
- 1 teaspoon garlic salt
- 1/4 teaspoon cayenne pepper

In a small bowl or sealable plastic bag, mix all ingredients until thoroughly combined.

White Wine Marinade

INGREDIENTS

- 1/2 cup white wine
- 3 tablespoons soy sauce
- 2 tablespoons extra virgin olive oil
- 1 tablespoon dill or dried parsley
- 2 teaspoons onion powder
- 4 cloves garlic, minced
- 1/2 teaspoon salt
- 1/2 teaspoon lemon pepper

In a medium bowl or sealable plastic bag, mix all ingredients until thoroughly combined.

Herb Rub

INGREDIENTS

- 1 tablespoon dried parsley, crushed
- 1 teaspoon garlic salt
- 1 teaspoon dried tarragon, crushed
- 1/2 teaspoon dried thyme, crushed
- 2 tablespoons lemon juice

In a small bowl or sealable plastic bag, mix all ingredients until thoroughly combined.

There are many reasons as to why we marinate foods. Flavoring and tenderizing is just the beginning. Marinading can improve nutritional value and help off- set any negative effects of high-temperature grilling. It is also a great way to have the flavors you desire already on the food, so you don't have to crowd the grilling space with spices. I typically only have salt and pepper by the grill for the final touch. It saves cleanup and prevents having spices spread all over the place.

One thing to keep in mind and try to avoid is the tendency to over-marinate food. Caution against keeping food in the marinade too long, which may have an overly salty end result, as well as over-spicing a marinade. You want to be able to taste your food and the wonderful flavors grilling and smoke bring to it. Keeping salt to a minimum is a good idea so people can salt as they wish once the food is cooked and served.

There are many ways to introduce marinades into food. Simply soaking in liquid is the most common way. Utilizing sealable plastic bags is a good approach—always place in a bowl or shallow dish in case of a leak—because most of the air can be removed from the bag and the meat is fully surrounded by marinade. These bags also work great for storage in the freezer. Pre-marinaded meats are not only a convenient time-saver, they can double as ice packs when camping or tailgating, whereby keeping other foods chilled. The marinaded food can be cooked up as soon as it is thawed. It's quick, easy and effective.

Occasionally, I use a vacuum sealer to quickly marinate foods. Usually the food absorbs enough flavor within 30 minutes so it does not need to be refrigerated if cooking immediately.

Injectors are another great way to put flavorful marinades into foods. These work especially well with large roasts and turkeys. When it comes to introducing marinades into foods, be creative, monitor your time, and you'll be amazed at how good the end-flavors will be.

Marinades, Rubs & More

Cherry-Smoked Sweet & Simple Fish

Ingredients

- 5 pounds salmon or steelhead
- 1 quart water
- 1 cup brown sugar
- 1/2 cup rock salt
- 2 tablespoons hot pepper sauce
- 1 tablespoon granulated garlic

Mix all brine ingredients. Submerge fish in brine, skin-side down on the bottom layer, meat side down on the next layer. Repeat layering skin to skin, meat to meat. Place a weighted plate on top of the fish to fully submerge all fillets. Soak fish in brine 8-12 hours or overnight in the refrigerator. Remove fish from brine and place in smoker. Smoke to desired texture. Cooking time varies from 3-10 hours, depending on the smoker, volume of fish being smoked and outdoor conditions. Check frequently so as not to overcook.

Wood Suggestion:

Smoke using cherry, apple, alder or Eastern Blend (page 98)

Eastern-Smoked Peppered Fish

Crack whole peppercorns using a mortar and pestle or give them a few pulses in a food grinder. Mix with sugars and rock salt. Lay fish skin-side down in a 9" x 11" glass casserole dish. Pour dry brine over fish. Let sit 2 hours, stirring occasionally. Cover and refrigerate, 8-12 hours. Rinse fish and place on racks. For a sharper pepper flavor, grind your choice of pepper over the moist fish. To balance the pepper, sprinkle a bit of white sugar over fish at the same time. Air-dry 1 hour. Smoke at 150°-180° 5-7 hours or to desired texture.

Ingredients

- 5 pounds fish
- 1/2 cup brown sugar
- 1/2 cup white sugar
- 1/3 cup rock salt
- 1 tablespoon cracked green peppercorns
- 1 tablespoon cracked white peppercorns
- 1 tablespoon cracked pink peppercorns

Wood Suggestion:

Smoke using Eastern Blend (page 98), alder, pecan or apple.

Apple-Smoked Soy Salmon

WOOD SUGGESTION:
Smoke using apple, alder, West Coast Blend (page 98) or hickory.

INGREDIENTS
- 5 pounds salmon or steelhead
- 1 cup soy sauce
- 1 cup water
- 2 cups brown sugar
- 2 tablespoons garlic
- 1 tablespoon basil
- 2 tablespoon dill
- 1 cup white wine

Mix ingredients in a large bowl. Cut fish pieces from fillets in 3/4"–thick strips, removing skin and fat. Soak fish in brine 15-18 hours in refrigerator. Drain on paper towels and blot dry. Place on smoker racks and air dry 15 minutes. Smoke at 150°-180° 5-7 hours or to desired texture. Let cool, cover in plastic wrap and refrigerate at least 6 hours.

Fruit-Smoked Salmon

INGREDIENTS
- 5 pounds salmon or steelhead
- 3 cups water
- 1 cup golden plum, peach or apricot jam
- 1/4 cup hot water
- 1/4 cup sugar
- 1/3 cup Morton's Tender Quick
- 2 Walla Walla onions, chopped

Mix jam with hot water and stir until liquified. Mix remaining ingredients and jam in a large bowl with a wire whisk until sugar is dissolved. Submerge fish in brine, skin-side down on the bottom layer, meat side down on the next layer. Repeat layering skin to skin, meat to meat. Place a weighted plate on top of the fish to fully submerge all fillets. Soak fish in brine 3-4 hours. Place on racks and air-dry 1 hour. Smoke at 150°-180° 5-7 hours or to desired texture.

WOOD SUGGESTION:
Smoke using any fruit woods, apple, cherry, pear, peach or apricot.

Alder-Smoked Herb Medley Salmon |

Rinse herbs and tear into small pieces. Mix all ingredients in a large bowl with a wire whisk until sugar is dissolved. Submerge fish in brine, skin-side down on the bottom layer, meat side down on the next layer. Repeat layering skin to skin, meat to meat. Place a weighted plate on top of the fish to fully submerge all fillets. Soak fish in brine 3-5 hours, the longer it soaks, the more intense the flavor. Place on racks and air dry 1 hour. Smoke at 150°-180° 5-7 hours or to desired texture.

INGREDIENTS

- 5 pounds salmon or steelhead, cut to desired size
- 3 cups water
- 1/4 cup Morton's Tender Quick
- 1/3 cup white sugar
- 1/4 cup fresh parsley
- 1/4 cup fresh basil
- 2 sprigs fresh rosemary
- 3 sprigs fresh dill
- 1 teaspoon white pepper
- 5 cloves garlic, crushed

WOOD SUGGESTION:

Smoke using alder, apple or Eastern Blend (page 98)

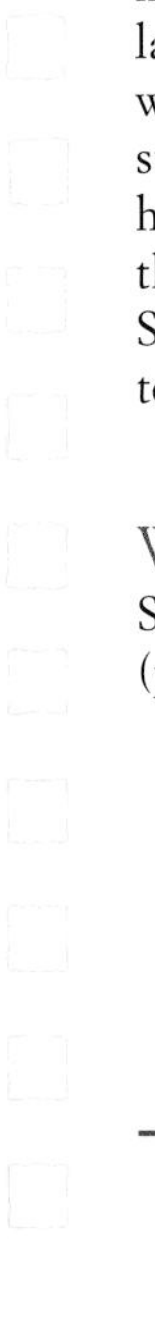

Rugged-Smoked Salmon Jerky |

WOOD SUGGESTION:
Smoke using Rugged Blend (page 98), alder, apple or cherry.

INGREDIENTS
- 2 pounds salmon
- 1/3 cup non-iodized salt
- 1/3 cup brown sugar
- 1/4 teaspoon white pepper

Remove skin from salmon fillet and cut into long, lengthwise, 1/2" strips. In a small bowl mix salt, brown sugar and pepper. Coat strips with salt, sugar mixture and lay in a large, shallow, glass pan. Refrigerate 1 hour. Rinse well under cold water and place on paper towels to dry. Place salmon on smoker racks. Do not let strips overlap or touch. Smoke at 150°, 3-4 hours or until salmon reaches desired texture. Store in refrigerator. For long-term storage, vacuum seal and freeze.

Mid-America Smoked Halibut |

INGREDIENTS
- 2-3 pounds halibut
- 1/2 cup Morton's Tender Quick
- Salt
- Black pepper to taste

Cut halibut to desired smoking portions. Place curing salt on a plate. Roll each piece of halibut in curing salt taking care to cover every side. Place covered fish in a shallow casserole dish. Let sit at room temperature 20 minutes. Rinse well under cold water and place on paper towels to dry. Place halibut on smoker racks. Sprinkle with black pepper. Do not let pieces touch or overlap. Smoke at 150°, 2-3 hours or until halibut reaches desired texture. Store in refrigerator. For long-term storage, vacuum seal and freeze.

WOOD SUGGESTION:
Smoke using Mid-America Blend (page 98), apple, alder or cherry.

West Coast Smoked Shrimp

Ingredients

- 1 pound medium shrimp, peeled and deveined
- Juice of 1 lemon
- 4 cloves garlic, pureed
- 2 tablespoons olive oil
- 1 tablespoon soy sauce
- Salt to taste
- Lemon for garnish, optional

Metal or wooden skewers (soak skewers at least 1 hour in water or white wine)

In a medium bowl, mix lemon, garlic, oil and soy sauce until thoroughly combined. Add shrimp and toss. Let sit 10-20 minutes. Thread shrimp onto skewers, 3-5 shrimp each.

Preheat smoker to 200°-220°. Place on smoker racks and cook 30 minutes or until cooked through. Serve with lemon slices if desired.

Wood Suggestion:

Smoke using West Coast Blend (page 98), alder, apple or cherry.

Cowboy-Smoked Whole Trout

Ingredients

- 6-10 whole trout, cleaned with heads removed
- 4 cups water
- 2 cups white wine
- 1/2 cup sugar
- 1/4 cup salt
- 1 lemon, sliced
- 1 lime, sliced

In a large casserole dish or crock, mix all brine ingredients until sugar is dissolved. Add trout and cover making sure all fish are submerged in the brine. Refrigerate at least 8 hours, rotating trout every few hours. Place on racks and air-dry 30 minutes. Preheat smoker to 180°-200°. Smoke 1-3 hours or until trout flakes easily.

Wood Suggestion:

Smoke using Cowboy Blend (page 98), alder, apple or maple.

Pacific Northwest Smoked Stuffed Clams

Ingredients

- 20 steamer clams, approximately 1 pound
- 1 tablespoon olive oil
- 1/2 cup pork sausage
- 1/2 cup celery, finely chopped
- 1/3 cup onion, finely chopped
- 1/2 red pepper, finely chopped
- 1/2 green pepper, finely chopped
- 1/4 cup fresh parsley
- 1 sprig fresh thyme or 1/2 teaspoon dry thyme
- 2 tablespoons clam water
- 1 tomato, diced
- 1/2 cup bread crumbs
- Lemon for garnish

Rinse clams well, discard any clams that are not clamped shut. Steam clams with lid tightly closed in approximately 1" water on medium heat for 15 minutes. Drain, reserving 2 tablespoons clam water. When clams are cool, carefully remove from shells and chop clam meat. In a large skillet, brown sausage on medium-high heat. Add olive oil, celery and onions and continue to sauté until onions are tender. Add peppers, clams and clam water, sautéing an additional 1-2 minutes. Remove mixture from heat and stir in parsley, thyme, tomatoes and stuffing. Stuff each clam shell with the stuffing mixture. Preheat smoker to 180°-200°. Place stuffed clams on a foil-lined smoker rack. Smoke 15 minutes or until clams have picked up desired smoke flavor. Serve with lemon wedges.

Wood Suggestion:

Smoke using Pacific Northwest Blend (page 98), alder or apple.

Maple-Smoked Honey Halibut

In a medium bowl, mix marinade ingredients. Add halibut and marinate 1-2 hours in the refrigerator. Let fish sit at room temperature 20 minutes prior to smoking. Preheat smoker to 200°-225°. Place fish on smoker rack. Cook 25-40 minutes or until internal temperature reaches 140°. Top with Herbed Honey Butter if desired.

Herbed Honey Butter Preparation

In a small bowl, mix all ingredients until thoroughly combined.

Wood Suggestion:

Smoke using maple, alder, apple or cherry.

Ingredients

- 2 pounds halibut steaks, 1" thick

Honey Maple Marinade

- 1/3 cup raspberry or white balsamic vinegar
- 2 tablespoons olive oil
- 2 tablespoons honey
- 2 cloves garlic, pureed
- 3/4 teaspoon salt
- 1/2 teaspoon maple flavoring
- 1/4 teaspoon black pepper

Herbed Honey Butter

- 2 tablespoons butter, softened
- 1 tablespoon fresh cilantro, parsley, basil and/or chives, chopped
- 1 teaspoon honey
- Salt to taste

Apple-Smoked Trout with Avocado Cream

In a small bowl, mix salt and spices.

Sprinkle liberally over flesh side of trout. Smoke skin side down in a preheated 300°-350° smoker 10-12 minutes or until fish flakes in large chunks. Serve with Avocado Cream if desired.

Ingredients

- 6-10 trout fillets

Smokey Fish Rub

- 1 teaspoon salt
- 1/2 teaspoon lemon pepper
- 1/4 teaspoon cumin
- 1/4 teaspoon chili powder
- Dash cayenne pepper, optional

Avocado Cream

- 1 large avocado
- 1/2 cup sour cream
- 2 tablespoons horseradish, optional
- 1 tablespoon lemon juice
- Salt and white pepper to taste

Avocado Cream Preparation

In a food processor or mini-chopper, blend all ingredients until thoroughly combined. Sauce can also be used as a sandwich spread or vegetable or chip dip.

Wood Suggestion:

Smoke using apple, alder or West Coast Blend (page 98)

Stovetop-Smoked Salmon

Ingredients

- 1 fillet salmon (3-6 servings)
- Salt and lemon pepper to taste

Place smoke, chips in smoker according to manufacturer's instructions. Season fish and place on rack. Seal smoker and place on medium heat. Once pan is hot and a whisp of smoke can be seen, cook fish 20 minutes. Remove from heat and let sit 5-10 more minutes before opening smoker.

Wood Suggestion:

Smoke using alder, apple or bourbon-soaked oak.

Simple Citrus Salmon

Place fillet skin side down in a shallow dish. Salt and pepper fish to taste. Squeeze orange over salmon, covering with juice. Let sit 15 minutes. Sprinkle fennel or dill over top of salmon and drizzle with olive oil. Place in a preheated 300°-350° smoker 20-30 minutes or until fish flakes in large chunks or reaches an internal temperature of 140°.

Ingredients

- 1 fillet salmon (3-6 servings)
- 1 orange
- 1 tablespoon fresh fennel or dill
- Salt and pepper to taste
- Olive oil for drizzling

Wood Suggestion:

Smoke using alder, apple, cherry or Tropical Blend (page 98)

Recipe Variation

Substitute any citrus for the orange and fresh herbs of choice for the fennel or dill. For a richer flavor substitute butter for olive oil.

Alder-Smoked Mustard Salmon

Wood Suggestion:

Smoke using alder, apple, cherry or Pacific Northwest Blend (page 98)

Ingredients

- 1 fillet salmon (3-6 servings)

Mustard Glaze

- 3 tablespoons butter, melted
- 1/4 cup white wine
- 1 tablespoon rice vinegar
- 1 tablespoon brown sugar
- 1 tablespoon Dijon mustard
- 1 teaspoon fresh thyme leaves
- 1/2 teaspoon salt
- Black pepper to taste

In a small bowl, mix glaze ingredients until thoroughly combined. Place salmon fillet on foil, turning up edges of foil to catch glaze. Brush glaze over fish and let sit 15 minutes before placing in smoker. Place in a preheated 300°-350° smoker 20-30 minutes or until fish flakes in large chunks or reaches an internal temperature of 140°.

Fish & Seafood
Smoke It!

West Coast Five-Spice Pork Jerky |

Follow JERKY PREPARATION steps outlined on page 127.

WOOD SUGGESTION:
Smoke using West Coast Blend (page 98), alder, apple or pecan.

INGREDIENTS
- 3-5 pounds pork, sliced to jerky size
- 1 quart water
- 1/4 cup honey
- 1/4 cup soy sauce
- 2 tablespoons Morton's Tender Quick
- 1 tablespoon Chinese 5-Spice
- 1 tablespoon granulated garlic
- 1/2 tablespoon white or black pepper

Alder-Smoked Chicken Jerky |

Follow JERKY PREPARATION steps outlined on page 127.

WOOD SUGGESTION:
Smoke using alder, apple or cherry.

INGREDIENTS
- 3-5 pounds chicken breast, sliced to jerky size
- 2 cups water
- 2 cups apple juice
- 1/4 cup honey
- 2 tablespoons Morton's Tender Quick or curing salt
- 2 teaspoons white pepper, optional
- 2 teaspoons granulated onion
- 2 teaspoons liquid smoke

Tropical Orange-Soy Pork Jerky

Follow JERKY PREPARATION steps outlined on page 127.

Wood Suggestion:

Smoke using Tropical Blend (page 98), apple, cherry or alder.

Ingredients

- 2-3 pounds pork, sliced to jerky size
- 3 cups water
- 3/4 cup orange juice
- 1/2 cup white sugar
- 1/4 cup Morton's Tender Quick
- 1/4 cup soy sauce
- 1/2 tablespoon granulated onion
- 1/2 tablespoon garlic powder
- 1 teaspoon white pepper

Cherry Teriyaki Turkey Jerky

Ingredients

- 2-4 pounds turkey, sliced to jerky size
- 3 cups apple juice
- 1 cup teriyaki sauce
- 1/3 cup brown sugar
- 2 tablespoons non-iodized salt
- 1 teaspoon garlic juice or 2 cloves garlic, crushed

Follow JERKY PREPARATION steps outlined on page 127.

Wood Suggestion:

Smoke using cherry, apple or Pacific Northwest Blend (page 98)

Pecan-Smoked Cajun Turkey Jerky

Ingredients

- 3-5 pounds turkey, sliced to jerky size
- 1 quart water
- 1/4 cup white sugar
- 1/4 cup Morton's Tender Quick
- 3-4 tablespoons cajun seasoning
- 2 teaspoons red pepper flakes
- 1 1/2 teaspoons cayenne pepper
- 1 teaspoon white pepper

Follow JERKY PREPARATION steps outlined on page 127.

Wood Suggestion:

Smoke using pecan, hickory or Cowboy Blend (page 98)

Flavor-Your-Own Jerky

Follow JERKY PREPARATION steps outlined on page 127.

WOOD SUGGESTION:
Smoke using any of your favorite flavors or a combination of woods.

INGREDIENTS
- 3 pounds beef or venison, cut into strips
- 1 quart water
- 1/4 cup Morton's Tender Quick or curing salt
- 1/4 cup white sugar
- 2-4 tablespoons seasoning blend of choice
- 2 teaspoons liquid smoke, optional

Apple Smoked Beef Jerky

INGREDIENTS
- 2 pounds flank or skirt steak, sliced to jerky size
- 1/2 cup apple juice
- 1/2 cup Worcestershire sauce
- 1/2 cup soy sauce
- 3 tablespoons honey
- 1-2 teaspoons liquid smoke
- 1 teaspoon red pepper flakes, optional

Follow JERKY PREPARATION steps outlined on page 127.

WOOD SUGGESTION:
Smoke using apple, Rugged Blend (page 98) or cherry.

Apple-Smoked Herbal Turkey Jerky

INGREDIENTS
- 3-5 pounds turkey, sliced to jerky size
- 1 quart water
- 1/4 cup non-iodized salt
- 1/2 cup white sugar
- 2 cups fresh parsley, chopped
- 1 cup fresh cilantro, chopped
- 5-6 sprigs rosemary, chopped
- 2 tablespoons coriander seeds, crushed
- 1 tablespoon dried oregano
- 1 teaspoon white pepper, ground

Follow JERKY PREPARATION steps outlined on page 127.

WOOD SUGGESTION:
Smoke using apple, cherry, alder or maple.

Southern-Smoked Pepper Jerky |

INGREDIENTS
- 3-4 pounds beef or venison, sliced to jerky size
- 1 quart water
- 1/4 cup Morton's Tender Quick or curing salt
- 1/4 cup white sugar
- 1 tablespoon black pepper
- 1/2 tablespoon white pepper
- 2 teaspoons granulated onion
- 2 teaspoons liquid smoke
- 1 teaspoons liquid garlic
- Additional black pepper to taste

Follow JERKY PREPARATION steps outlined on page 127.

WOOD SUGGESTION:
Smoke using Southern Blend (page 98) or apple.

Fiery Asian Jerky |

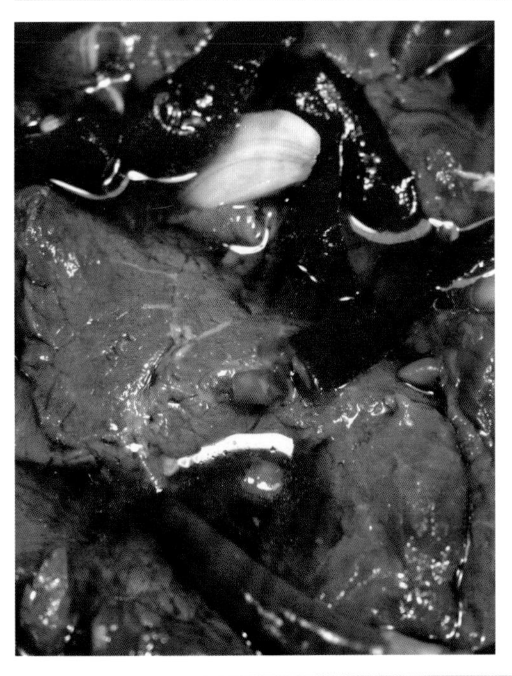

INGREDIENTS
- 3-4 pounds beef or venison, sliced to jerky size
- 1 quart water
- 1/4 cup Morton's Tender Quick or curing salt
- 1/2 cup brown sugar
- 2-4 hot red chilies
- 2-4 hot green chilies
- 8 cloves garlic, crushed
- 2" ginger, crushed

Follow JERKY PREPARATION steps outlined on page 127.

WOOD SUGGESTION:
Smoke using oak, maple or Cowboy Blend (page 98)

Jerky

is not an exact science. Jerky can be soft, hard, sweet, salty, full of exotic flavors or basic. There are endless ways to make jerky. In this section you will find tried and true recipes using a variety of flavorings and meats.

CUTTING JERKY—Cut To Desired Size.

When slicing meat for jerky, the traditional cut is in strips that go with the grain. For an easy-to-chew cut, meat can be sliced across the grain. Roasts can be sliced to make a circular piece of jerky or steaks can be cut into strips. Only the size of your smoker is a factor in how long your jerky pieces are cut. Keep in mind that thinly slicing meat will result in a dryer and possibly crisper end product. Thickly sliced meat will usually need to be finished in the oven or food dehydrator for proper preservation. The joy of making your own jerky is that you can cut the meat just how you prefer it.

BRINING JERKY—In a large bowl, mix until salts and sugars dissolve.

In preparing any brine, it's best done in a vessel that won't transmit foul tastes. Glass, crockery or plastic containers work well, as do stainless-steel bowls. Wood and aluminum bowls, when exposed to ingredients in some brines, undergo a chemical reaction and may taint meat. Always discard brine after one use.

SOAKING JERKY—Soak in the refrigerator 8-12 hours.

Unless you have a very cool place in the house to soak, meat should be refrigerated during the brining process if it is recommended to last more than a few hours. Unless specifically stated in a recipe, do not rinse brine off meat before putting on smoker racks.

LOADING JERKY—Place on smoker racks.

Keep smoker racks clean and free of debris. Give them a light coating of cooking spray before each use. When placing meat on smoker racks, take care to keep adequate space between each piece. Foods should never be touching during the smoking process. Once you know the hot spots in your smoker, place thicker cuts nearest to those spots. If additional flavors are desired, sprinkle or spray these on at this time while the meat is moist. Let meat air-dry 15 minutes to an hour to keep drips to a minimum in your smoker.

SMOKING JERKY—Smoke 3-6 hours, check often.

Follow smoking directions for your smoker. Cooking times vary greatly, depending on make and model of smoker and outside weather conditions. Try to keep the temperature of the smoker between 150° and 200°. Check for doneness after 3 hours.

FINISHING JERKY

Larger cuts of jerky can be finished on a baking sheet in the oven at 165°, check every 15 minutes. When jerky is done, place in a glass bowl and cover with plastic wrap until cool. This will allow the jerky to reabsorb moisture, making it softer. Refrigerate immediately once cooled.

STORING JERKY

Keep refrigerated or freeze if storing for an extended period of time. Vacuum sealing and freezing is a great way to preserve jerky for long periods of time. Smoke flavors hold up well and jerky can be enjoyed year-round.

Tropical Turkey Legs

INGREDIENTS

- 6 turkey legs, bone in

BALI MARINADE

- 1/2 cup onion, minced
- 1/2 cup orange juice
- 1/3 cup peanut butter
- 2 tablespoons olive oil
- 1 teaspoon salt
- 1 teaspoon curry powder
- 1 teaspoon orange zest, optional
- 1/2 teaspoon cinnamon
- 1/4 teaspoon cloves

In a medium bowl, mix all marinade ingredients until thoroughly combined.

Coat turkey legs and place in a shallow pan. Cover and refrigerate 8-12 hours. Preheat smoker to 220°. Smoke turkey 3-4 hours or until internal temperature reaches 180°.

WOOD SUGGESTION:

Smoke using Tropical Blend (page 98), cherry, apple or maple.

Pacific Northwest Smoked Turkey Breast

Basic Turkey Brine Preparation

Brine turkey breast 8-12 hours. Let sit at room temperature 30 minutes before smoking. Preheat smoker to 225°. Smoke 3-4 hours or until internal temperature reaches 180°. Serve with Cranberry Chutney if desired.

Cranberry Chutney Preparation

In a medium sauce pan, melt butter on medium heat. Cook onions until soft. Add remaining ingredients and bring to a low boil. Reduce heat and simmer 15-20 minutes. Remove from heat and cool.

Wood Suggestion:

Smoke using Pacific Northwest Blend (page 98), cherry, apple or pecan.

Ingredients

- 3-4-pound boneless turkey breast

Basic Turkey Brine

- 1 14.5-ounce can chicken broth
- 1 cup vinegar
- 1 tablespoon salt
- 2 tablespoons sugar
- 1 teaspoon white or black pepper

Cranberry Chutney

- 1 tablespoon butter
- 1/4 cup onion, diced
- 1 cup cranberries
- 1/2 apple, peeled and chopped
- 1/2 cup raisins
- 1/2 cup sugar
- 1/4 cup vinegar
- 1/2 teaspoon cinnamon
- 1/2 teaspoon ginger
- Salt to taste

Hickory-Smoked Ribs

Rib Mop

- 1 tablespoon butter
- 1/2 cup onion, finely chopped
- 1/2 cup red wine vinegar
- 1/2 cup water
- 1/4 cup molasses
- 1/4 cup firmly packed dark brown sugar
- 4 cloves garlic, pureed
- 1 12-ounce can tomato paste
- 3 tablespoons Worcestershire sauce
- 1 tablespoon chili powder
- 1 tablespoon dry mustard

Rib Mop Preparation

In a medium sauce pan, melt butter on medium heat. Cook onions until soft. Add remaining mop ingredients and bring to a low boil. Reduce heat and simmer 10 minutes. Remove from heat and cool.

Cut any loose fat and membrane off pork ribs. Cut ribs into serving portions. Add rub ingredients to a large sealable plastic bag. Place ribs in bag and work rub into every surface. Refrigerate 6-12 hours. Let ribs sit 30 minutes at room temperature. Wrap ribs in foil and bake in a 250° oven 1 hour. Preheat smoker to 250°. Remove top portion of foil and place ribs on smoker rack. Generously mop ribs every 30 minutes, 3 hours or until rib meat easily pulls away from bones. Serve with Strawberry Citrus Salsa (page 145), or Mango Salsa (page 147), if desired.

Ingredients

- 2 1/2- to 3 1/2-pound rack of pork spareribs

Rib Rub

- 1/4 cup firmly packed dark brown sugar
- 2 tablespoons sweet or smoked paprika
- 1 tablespoon garlic powder
- 1 teaspoon ground black pepper
- 1 teaspoon ground coriander
- 1/2 teaspoon salt

Rib Rub Preparation

In a small bowl, mix all rub ingredients until thoroughly combined.

Wood Suggestion:

Smoke using hickory, Cowboy Blend (page 98) or maple.

Southern-Smoked Pulled Pork

Ingredients

- 6-pound bone-in pork picnic or butt
- 6 cloves garlic, minced

Southern Rub

- 1/4 cup brown sugar
- 2 tablespoons paprika
- 2 tablespoons celery salt
- 1 tablespoon dry mustard
- 2 teaspoons white pepper
- 1 teaspoon dried thyme

Sweet & Tangy BBQ Sauce

- 1/2 cup Dr. Pepper or cola
- 1/4 cup balsamic vinegar
- 2 tablespoons spicy brown mustard
- 2 tablespoons honey
- 2 cloves garlic, minced
- 1 teaspoon salt

In a small bowl, mix all rub ingredients until thoroughly combined.

Massage rub into pork taking care to cover every surface. Refrigerate at least 6 hours. Let sit at room temperature 30 minutes prior to smoking. Preheat smoker to 220°. Place pork on smoker rack. Smoke 4 hours or until internal temperature reaches 140°-150°. Wrap pork in foil and place in a preheated 225° oven for an additional 3-4 hours. Rest pork up to 1 hour in foil before pulling or serving. To pull pork, use two forks to tear meat into bite-sized chunks. Remove any unwanted fat at this time. To keep pork warm for a longer time, wrap in several towels. Serve before temperature drops below 160°. Serve with Sweet & Tangy BBQ Sauce if desired.

Sweet & Tangy BBQ Sauce Preparation

In a small sauce pan, bring to a low boil. Reduce heat and simmer 10-15 minutes.

Wood Suggestion:

Smoke using Southern Blend (page 98), mesquite, maple or apple.

Fruit-Smoked Boneless "Wings"

Simple Rub Preparation

Cut breasts into bite-sized strips. In a small bowl, mix all rub ingredients until thoroughly combined. Massage rub into chicken. Preheat smoker to 250°. Cook chicken 35-45 minutes or until firm to the touch. Place smoked chicken in a large bowl and toss with Spicy Sauce. Serve with Ranch or Blue Cheese dressing.

Sticky Sweet Sauce Preparation

In a small bowl, mix all sauce ingredients until thoroughly combined.

Ingredients

- 4 chicken breasts, boneless and skinless
- Simple Rub or prepared BBQ seasoning

Simple Rub

- 1 teaspoon salt
- 1 teaspoon brown sugar
- 1/2 teaspoon pepper
- 1/2 teaspoons cayenne pepper

Sticky Sweet Sauce

- 3 tablespoons ketchup
- 3 tablespoons honey
- 2 tablespoons cider vinegar
- 1 teaspoon hot sauce or sambal
- 1 teaspoon granulated onion
- 1/2 teaspoon cumin
- 1/4 teaspoon chili powder
- Salt to taste

Wood Suggestion:

Smoke using any fruit woods, apple, cherry, pear, peach or apricot.

Oak-Smoked Jerked Chicken

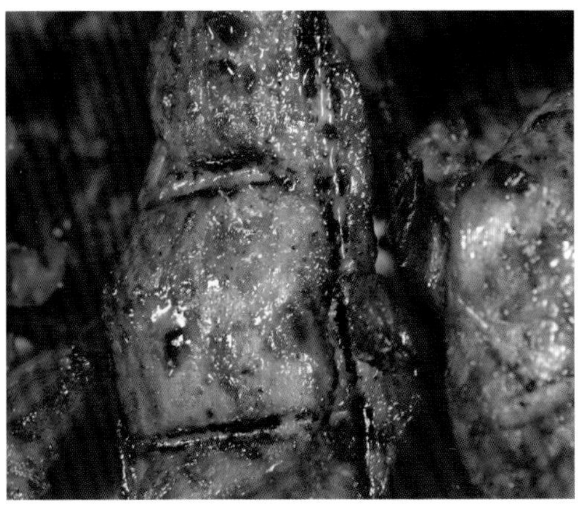

Cut breasts or thighs in half. In a small bowl, mix all rub ingredients until thoroughly combined. Massage rub into chicken. Preheat smoker to 250°. Cook chicken 35-45 minutes or until internal temperature reaches 180°. Serve with Super Soy Sauce (page 147), if desired.

Ingredients

- 2 pounds boneless chicken breasts or thighs

Jerk Rub

- 2 teaspoons onion powder
- 1 teaspoon brown sugar
- 1 teaspoon white pepper
- 1/2 teaspoon allspice
- 1/4 teaspoon cayenne pepper
- 1/4 teaspoon ground thyme
- 1/8 teaspoon nutmeg

Cherry-Smoked Stuffed Chicken Breasts

Ingredients

- 4 chicken breasts
- 1/2 cup blue or feta cheese
- 1/2 cup walnuts
- 1/4 cup dried cranberries
- 4 fresh sage leaves, chopped
- Salt and pepper to taste
- Olive oil for drizzling

Butterfly breasts and open. Season with salt and pepper. In a medium bowl, mix remaining ingredients. Evenly distribute cheese mixture among chicken breasts and fold closed. Place breasts on foil and drizzle with olive oil and salt and pepper to taste. Preheat smoker to 220°. Smoke 45-55 minutes or until stuffed breasts reach an internal temperature of 180°. Brush with additional olive oil if desired.

Wood Suggestion:

Smoke using cherry, apple, alder or Eastern Blend (page 98)

Mid-America Smoked Whole Chicken

Wood Suggestion:

Smoke using Mid-America Blend (page 98), cherry, hickory or apple.

Ingredients

- 1 whole fryer
- Salt and pepper to taste
- Olive oil for brushing

Wash bird well inside and out. Salt and pepper inside and out. Preheat smoker to 225°-250°. Place whole chicken on smoker rack. Smoke 3 hours or until internal temperature reaches 180°. Let sit 10 minutes before serving.

This is the most basic of smoking recipes. Several birds can be smoked at one time and meat can be removed from the bones and frozen for a quick meal. More flavor can be added by brining the bird in your favorite brine, using a rub or a mop, or injecting with marinade. See Marinades, Rubs and More (page 142) for a variety of sauces and salsas to accompany this recipe.

Double Fruit-Smoked Ham

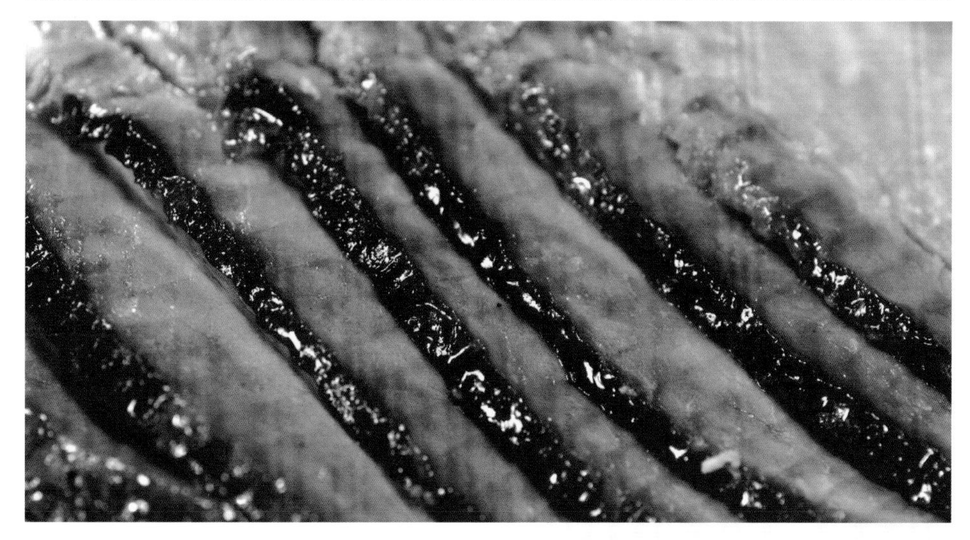

In a small bowl, mix all mop ingredients until thoroughly combined.

Place ham in a shallow ovenproof pan. Cover with half of the mop. Preheat smoker to 225°. Place ham in smoker. A fully cooked ham only needs to reheat to a temperature of 140°, approximately 2 hours. A partially cooked ham needs to reach 160°, approximately 3 hours. Glaze every 30 minutes, when glaze is gone, baste with liquid in the pan.

WOOD SUGGESTION:
Smoke using any fruit woods, apple, cherry, pear, peach or apricot.

INGREDIENTS

- 8-10-pound smoked, bone-in ham

WHISKY MOP

- 1/2 cup whiskey
- 1/2 cup sugar
- 1/4 cup ketchup
- 2 tablespoons Dijon mustard
- 1 teaspoon powdered onion
- 1 teaspoon powdered garlic

Eastern-Smoked Garlic-Rubbed Chops

In a food processor or mini-chopper, mix rub ingredients until thoroughly blended. Coat chops in rub mixture. Let sit 30 minutes at room temperature. Preheat smoker to 325-350°. Cook 40 minutes or until internal temperature reaches 160°.

Serve with Italian Salsa Verde (page 145) or Lemony Spinach Pesto (page 146), if desired.

WOOD SUGGESTION:
Smoke using Eastern Blend (page 98), hickory or maple.

INGREDIENTS

- 6-8 pork chops, 3/4"-1" thick

GARLIC RUB

- 10 cloves garlic, peeled
- 2 tablespoons oregano
- 2 tablespoons olive oil
- 2 tablespoons white vinegar
- 1 tablespoon salt
- 1 tablespoon colored peppercorns, cracked

Southern-Smoked Beef Brisket

In a medium bowl, mix all mop ingredients until thoroughly combined.

In a small bowl mix rub mixture until thoroughly combined.

Massage rub into brisket taking care to cover every surface. Refrigerate at least 6 hours. Let sit at room temperature 30 minutes prior to smoking. Preheat smoker to 225°. Smoke brisket 6 hours, mopping every 30-60 minutes. Remove brisket from smoker, generously mop one more time, and wrap tightly in aluminum foil. Cook in a preheated, 250° oven an additional 3-4 hours or until meat reaches desired tenderness. Let rest 30 minutes before opening foil and slicing. An alternative method to smoking brisket is to smoke until internal temperature reaches 180°-185°, remove from smoker, wrap tightly in foil and several towels. Serve before brisket temperature drops below 160°.

Wood Suggestion:

Smoke using Southern Blend (page 98), mesquite, maple or cherry.

Ingredients

- 1 center-cut, 4-5-pound beef brisket

Brisket Rub

- 1 tablespoon salt
- 1 tablespoon brown sugar
- 1 tablespoon smoked or sweet paprika
- 1 teaspoon chili powder
- 1 teaspoon onion powder
- 1 teaspoon garlic powder
- 1/2 teaspoon ground oregano

Beer Mop

- 1 can beer
- 1/3 cup cider vinegar
- 1/2 cup onion, minced
- 1/2 cup green pepper, minced
- 1/4 cup butter, melted
- 4 cloves garlic, minced
- 1 tablespoon hot pepper sauce
- 2 teaspoons salt
- 1 teaspoon chili powder
- 1/2 teaspoon black pepper

Cherry-Smoked Tomatoes

Remove tops from tomatoes and drain. In a medium bowl mix oil, garlic, pine nuts and seasonings. Stuff tomatoes with garlic mixture. Place tomatoes upside down snugly in an oven-proof pan, brush with olive oil and sprinkle additional spices if desired. Preheat smoker to 250°. Place pan on smoker rack. Smoke 45-90 minutes or until skins begin to separate. Serve as a side or puree for sauce.

Wood Suggestion:

Smoke using cherry, apple or Rugged Blend (page 98)

Ingredients

- 10 roma-style tomatoes
- 2 tablespoons olive oil
- 10 garlic cloves, chopped
- 1/2 cup pine nuts
- 1 tablespoon dried basil or 3 tablespoons fresh basil
- 1 teaspoon Italian seasoning
- 1 teaspoon salt
- Olive oil for brushing

Meat Smoke It!

Mesquite-Smoked Tri-Tip |

WOOD SUGGESTION:
Smoke using mesquite, oak or Rugged Blend (page 98)

INGREDIENTS
- 3-4-pound tri-tip roast
- 1/4 cup yellow mustard

THREE-INGREDIENT RUB
- 2 teaspoons salt
- 2 teaspoons garlic powder
- 1 teaspoon black pepper

In a small bowl, mix rub mixture until thoroughly combined. Massage rub into tri-tip taking care to cover every surface. Refrigerate at least 6 hours. Let sit at room temperature 30 minutes prior to smoking baste with a thin coating of mustard. Preheat smoker to 225°-250°. Place on smoker rack, fat side up. Smoke tri-tip 2-3 hours or until internal temperature reaches 140° rare, 150° medium-rare, 160° medium, 170° well-done. Let sit 10-15 minutes before slicing.

Cowboy-Smoked Pot Roast |

WOOD SUGGESTION:
Smoke using Cowboy Blend (page 98), hickory or alder.

INGREDIENTS
- 2-3 pound boneless beef roast
- 1 package Ranch dressing mix
- 1 package Au jus gravy mix
- 1 14.5-ounce can beef broth
- 4-6 small red potatoes, halved
- 3 carrots, peeled and chopped
- 1 onion, chopped

In a small bowl, mix dressing and gravy mix, divide in two. Massage 1/2 dressing/gravy mixture on roast, taking care to cover every surface. Let sit at room temperature 30 minutes. Preheat smoker to 225°-250°. Place roast on smoker rack. Smoke 3 hours. Place vegetables in a shallow roasting pan. Remove roast from smoker and place on top of vegetables. Mix remaining dressing/gravy mix with beef broth and pour over roast. Cover with foil and cook at 325° an additional 2 hours or until meat is tender. Let sit 10-15 minutes before slicing.

Hickory-Smoked Chuck Roast |

Ingredients
- 3-5-pound beef chuck roast

Sweet Coffee Brine
- 4 cups cold coffee
- 2 cups water
- 1/2 cup brown sugar
- 1/3 cup salt
- 1/3 cup molasses
- 4 tablespoons pickling spice
- 8 cloves garlic, mashed

Sweet Coffee Brine Preparation
Trim outer fat from roast. In a large bowl, mix all brine ingredients stirring until sugar is dissolved. Brine roast 8-12 hours in the refrigerator.

Black Bean Salsa
- 2 cups corn, fresh or frozen
- 1 15-ounce can black beans, drained
- 1 red bell pepper, diced
- 1 4-ounce can diced green chilies
- 1/2 cup red onion, diced
- 1/2 cup cilantro, chopped
- 2 tablespoons red wine vinegar
- 1 tablespoon olive oil
- 1-2 tablespoons taco or fajita seasoning
- 1 teaspoon sugar

Black Bean Salsa Preparation
In a medium bowl, gently mix all ingredients until thoroughly combined.

Dr. Pepper Mop
- 1/2 cup Dr. Pepper
- 1/4 cup cider vinegar
- 1/2 cup olive oil
- 5 cloves garlic, minced
- 1 teaspoon salt
- 1/2 teaspoon black pepper
- 10-20 dashes hot pepper sauce

Dr. Pepper Mop Preparation
In a medium bowl, mix all mop ingredients until thoroughly combined.

Preheat smoker to 225°-250°. Place on smoker rack. Smoke roast 6 hours, mopping every 30 minutes. Remove roast from smoker, generously mop one more time and wrap tightly in aluminum foil. Cook in a preheated, 250° oven an additional 2 hours. Let rest 30 minutes before opening foil and slicing. To serve mop liquid as a sauce, place in a small saucepan and boil 5 minutes on the stove. Serve with Black Bean Salsa if desired.

Wood Suggestion:
Smoke using hickory or Cowboy Blend (page 98)

Eastern-Smoked Corned Beef

WOOD SUGGESTION:
Smoke using Eastern Blend (page 98), mesquite, apple or pecan.

INGREDIENTS

- 1-2 pound flat-cut corned beef

LEMON LIME MOP

- 1 cup lemon lime soda or ginger ale
- 1/4 cup canola oil

LEMON LIME MOP PREPARATION

In a small bowl, mix all mop ingredients until thoroughly combined.

Let corned beef sit at room temperature 30 minutes. Preheat smoker to 225°. Remove from package and rinse under cool water. Pat dry and place on smoker rack. Smoke corned beef 6 hours, mopping every 30 minutes. Remove from smoker, generously mop one more time, and wrap tightly in aluminum foil. Cook in a preheated, 250° oven an additional 1-2 hours or until meat reaches desired tenderness. Let rest 20 minutes before opening foil and slicing.

Rugged-Smoked Flank Steak

WOOD SUGGESTION:
Smoke using Rugged Blend (page 98), mesquite, pecan or maple.

INGREDIENTS

- 2-3-pound flank steak
- 1 cup Italian dressing

Rinse steak and lightly score in a diagonal pattern. Place flank steak in Italian dressing, refrigerate at least 8 hours or overnight. Preheat smoker to 250°-300°. Let steak sit at room temperature 30 minutes. Place on smoker rack. Cook 50-70 minutes or until internal temperature reaches 140° rare; 150° medium-rare; 160° medium; 170° well-done. Let sit 10-15 minutes before slicing. Slice thinly, serve warm or cold as a salad topper.

Hickory-Smoked Wild Rice Stuffed Chops

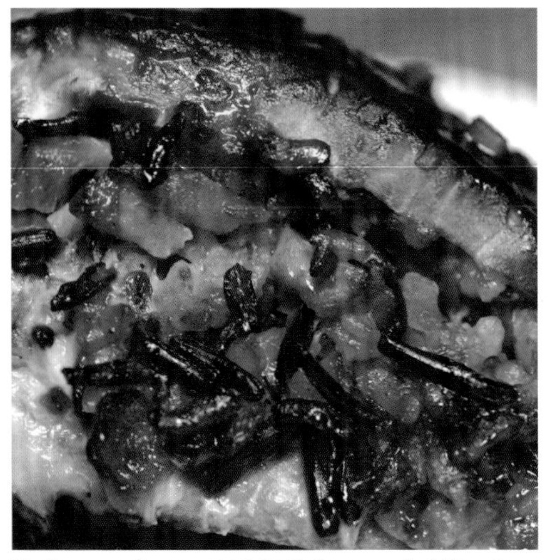

Preheat smoker to 220°-250°. In a small skillet, heat olive oil on medium-high heat. Sauté onions and celery until soft. Add remaining ingredients. Butterfly pork chops and open. Lightly season pork chops with salt and pepper. Divide stuffing ingredients evenly among pork chops. Place each chop on foil, turning up edges of foil to catch glaze. Brush glaze over each chop and place on smoker racks. Smoke 90 minutes or until chops reach an internal temperature of 160°. Brush with glaze often. Boil any remaining glaze at least 3 minutes to use as a finishing glaze.

Ingredients

- 6-8 pork chops, 1" thick
- 2 tablespoons olive oil
- 1/2 cup onion, finely chopped
- 1/2 cup celery or green pepper, finely chopped
- 1 5-ounce can water chestnuts, diced
- 1 cup wild rice, cooked
- 2 cups white rice, cooked
- 3 tablespoons Ginger-Hoisin Glaze
- Salt and pepper to taste

Ginger-Hoisin Glaze

- 1/3 cup hoisin sauce
- 1/4 cup soy sauce
- 2 tablespoons sherry
- 3" fresh ginger, minced

Ginger-Hoisin Glaze Preparation

In a small bowl, mix all glaze ingredients until thoroughly combined.

Wood Suggestion:

Smoke using hickory, mesquite, pecan or maple.

Maple-Smoked Pork Tenderloin

Ingredients

- 2-pound pork tenderloin
- Salt and pepper
- 4 slices maple-smoked bacon

Salt and pepper tenderloin. Let sit at room temperature 30 minutes. Preheat smoker to 220°. Wrap tenderloin in bacon. Place on smoker rack. Smoke 60-90 minutes or until internal temperature reaches 160°. Let sit 10 minutes before slicing. This recipe lends itself well to any spice combination.

Wood Suggestion:

Smoke using maple, mesquite, Southern Blend (page 8) or hickory.

Apple-Smoked Artichokes

WOOD SUGGESTION:
Smoke using apple, alder or cherry.

INGREDIENTS
- 10 baby artichokes or 4 regular
- 1 teaspoon salt

Trim stems and pull any discolored leaves from artichoke bottoms. Cut large artichokes in halves or quarters, cut baby artichokes in half or leave whole. In a large stock pot bring 5-6 inches of water to a boil. Add salt and artichokes. Lower heat and gently boil artichokes for 15-30 minutes or until leaves are slightly loose. Remove artichokes from water and drain on a towel. Preheat smoker to 200°. Smoke artichokes 30-45 minutes or until desired smoke flavor is achieved. Serve warm or cold with melted butter or mayonnaise.

Crunchy Smoked Salsa

INGREDIENTS
- 2 tomatoes
- 1 onion, halved
- 1 red pepper
- 1 green pepper
- 1 jalapeño pepper
- 2 tomatoes, seeded and chopped
- 1/2 red pepper, finely chopped
- 1/2 green pepper, finely chopped
- 2 jalapeño peppers, diced
- 2 cloves garlic, minced
- 1/2 cup fresh cilantro, chopped
- 1/4 cup fresh basil, chopped
- 2 tablespoons red wine vinegar
- 1 tablespoon lemon or lime juice
- 1 tablespoon sugar
- 1 teaspoon cumin
- 1 teaspoon coriander
- 1 teaspoon chili powder
- Salt and pepper to taste

Place first 5 vegetables listed on smoker racks. Smoke at 180°-200° 2 hours or until vegetables are soft. Remove from smoker, cool and chop. Add remaining ingredients and gently stir until combined. Refrigerate until ready to serve.

WOOD SUGGESTION:
Smoke using alder, apple or Cowboy Blend (page 98)

Eastern Twice-Baked Potatoes

WOOD SUGGESTION:
Smoke using Eastern Blend (page 98), alder or apple.

INGREDIENTS
- 3 medium baking potatoes
- 1/4 cup butter
- 1/4 cup milk
- 2 cloves garlic, pureed
- 1 cup cheddar cheese
- Salt and pepper to taste
- Garnish with fresh chives

Wash and dry baking potatoes. Pierce with fork in several places to allow steam to escape during cooking. Bake potatoes in an oven at 350° for 1 hour, or until soft. Remove from oven and cool slightly. Cut potatoes in half, lengthwise, and scoop out the inside leaving a thin shell. In a medium bowl, mash potatoes with milk and butter until fluffy. Add more milk if needed. Stir in cheese, garlic, salt and pepper to taste. Fill potato shells with mashed potato mixture. Preheat smoker to 250°-300°. Place potatoes on smoker racks. Smoke 30-45 minutes or until warm throughout. Top with chives and serve warm.

Pecan-Smoked Stuffed Mini-Peppers

WOOD SUGGESTION:
Smoke using pecan, Mid-America Blend (page 98) or apple.

INGREDIENTS
- 10-12 mini sweet peppers
- 1/3 cup sour cream
- 1/2 cup feta cheese, crumbled
- 2 tablespoons parsley, finely chopped
- Lemon pepper to taste

Chop tops off peppers and scoop out insides. In a medium bowl mix sour cream, feta cheese, parsley and lemon pepper. Fill peppers with cheese mixture. Place in a chili roasting pan or stack side-by-side, filled side up, in an ovenproof pan. Preheat smoker to 250°. Smoke peppers 20-35 minutes or until tops begin to brown.

Rugged-Smoked Stuffed Onions

Wood Suggestion:
Smoke using Rugged Blend (page 98), hickory, pecan, alder or apple.

Ingredients
- 2-4 medium sweet onions
- 2 tablespoons butter, melted
- 2-4 strips thick-cut bacon, finely chopped
- 4 cloves garlic, halved
- 1 sprig rosemary, optional
- Black pepper to taste

Peel onions and cut off tops and bottoms. Place root-side down. Use a small knife to cut a deep cavity out of the top of the onion. Evenly distribute chopped bacon and garlic into the onions. Place a small sprig of rosemary in each onion if desired. Brush onions with melted butter and pepper to taste. Preheat smoker to 250°-300° degrees. Place stuffed eggplant directly on smoker racks. Cook 90 minutes or until tender. Brush occasionally with melted butter if desired. Onions can be finished in a 325° oven if desired. Serve as is or chop and use in any recipe calling for onions. Smoked onions freeze well and retain a deep smoke flavor.

Alder-Smoked Potato Skins

Wood Suggestion:
Smoke using alder, apple or West Coast Blend (page 98)

Ingredients
- 4-6 medium baking potatoes, baked
- 4 slices bacon, finely chopped
- 1/2 cup onion, finely chopped
- 1/2 cup sour cream
- 1/2 cup cheddar or jack cheese
- 1 4-ounce can diced green chills, optional
- 1 green onion, sliced
- Salt and pepper to taste

In a small skillet, fry bacon until crisp. Add onions and sauté until tender and translucent. Set aside to cool. In a small bowl mix bacon, onion, sour cream, cheese and green chilies until combined. Cut baked potatoes in quarters, scooping out the middle of the potato. Place on foil or in ovenproof pan. Evenly distribute topping over potato skins. Preheat smoker to 250°-300°. Smoke potato skins 30-45 minutes or until topping is bubbly. Top with green onions and serve warm.

Oak-Smoked Stuffed Eggplant

Cut eggplant in half, lengthwise. In a large skillet, heat olive oil on medium-high heat. Fry eggplant cut-side down 5-7 minutes. Remove eggplant and set aside. In the same skillet, stir fry onion and peppers until soft. Adding extra oil if needed. Add tomatoes, salt and pepper. Simmer uncovered 10-15 minutes. Scoop a small amount of eggplant out of the middle to form a well. Mix basil with vegetable filing and distribute evenly among the eggplant. Sprinkle with parmesan cheese. Preheat smoker to 250°-300° degrees. Place stuffed eggplant directly on smoker racks. Cook 60 minutes or until tender. Eggplant can be finished in a 325° oven if desired.

WOOD SUGGESTION:

Smoke using oak, maple, alder, apple or Cowboy Blend (page 98)

INGREDIENTS

- 2-4 small eggplants or 1-2 large
- 1/4 cup olive oil
- 1 cup onion, thinly sliced
- 1 cup green bell pepper, thinly sliced
- 1 cup yellow pepper, thinly sliced
- 1/2 cup diced tomatoes, drained
- 1/2 teaspoon salt
- 1/4 teaspoon ground black pepper
- 1/2 cup fresh basil, sliced
- 1/2 cup parmesan cheese, grated or curled

Vegetables
Smoke It!

Tropical-Smoked Thai Tofu |

Combine all ingredients, except tofu, in shallow dish and mix well. Remove tofu from package, discard liquid. Gently press water out of tofu with several paper towels. Slice tofu into 1/2" slices. Place in marinade. Using a spatula, turn tofu over in marinade every 10-15 minutes for 1 hour. Tofu can be marinated up to 8 hours for more flavor. Preheat smoker to 200°. Place tofu directly on smoker racks. Cook 60 minutes or until tofu is dry to the touch or has picked up desired smoke flavor. Use smoked tofu as an appetizer, chopped up for a salad topping or sandwich filling, as a meat substitute or crumbled for a dip or pate. Tofu can also be grilled, brush with olive oil and grill 2-4 minutes per side.

INGREDIENTS

- 1 16-ounce block extra-firm tofu
- 1/4 cup peanut or canola oil
- 2 tablespoons red or green curry paste
- 2 tablespoons brown sugar
- 1-2 tablespoons fish sauce

WOOD SUGGESTION:

Smoke using Tropical Blend (page 98), West Coast Blend (page 98) or alder.

Smoked Tofu Pate |

In a medium bowl, mash tofu with a fork. Blend remaining ingredients. Serve with vegetables, chips or as a sandwich filling.

INGREDIENTS

- 1 cup smoked tofu
- 1/2 cup mayonnaise
- 1/4 cup celery, diced
- 1 tablespoon green onion or chives
- Salt and pepper to taste

Southern-Smoked Chicken Tofu

INGREDIENTS

- 1 16-ounce block extra-firm tofu
- 1 14.5-ounce can chicken broth
- 6 cloves garlic, minced
- 2" ginger, grated
- 1 tablespoon lemon juice
- 1/4 teaspoon salt

Combine all ingredients, except tofu, in shallow dish and mix well. Remove tofu from package, discard liquid. Gently press water out of tofu with several paper towels. Slice tofu into 1/2" slices. Place in marinade. Using a spatula, turn tofu over in marinade every 10-15 minutes for 1 hour. Tofu can be marinated up to 8 hours for more flavor. Preheat smoker to 200°. Place tofu directly on smoker racks. Cook 60 minutes or until tofu is dry to the touch or has picked up desired smoke flavor. Use smoked tofu as an appetizer, chopped up for a salad topping or sandwich filling, as a meat substitute or crumbled for a dip or paté. Tofu can also be grilled, brush with olive oil and grill 2-4 minutes per side. For extra garlic flavor, sliver garlic and imbed in tofu slices prior to smoking or grilling.

WOOD SUGGESTION:

Smoke using Southern Blend (page 98), alder, maple or oak.

Oak-Smoked Japanese Tofu

Combine all ingredients, except tofu, in shallow dish and mix well. Remove tofu from package, discard liquid. Gently press water out of tofu with several paper towels. Slice tofu into 1/2" slices. Place in marinade. Using a spatula, turn tofu over in marinade every 10-15 minutes for 1 hour. Tofu can be marinated up to 8 hours for more flavor. Preheat smoker to 200°. Place tofu directly on smoker racks. Cook 60 minutes or until tofu is dry to the touch or has picked up desired smoke flavor. Use smoked tofu as an appetizer, chopped up for a salad topping or sandwich filling, as a meat substitute or crumbled for a dip or pate. Tofu can also be grilled, brush with olive oil and grill 2-4 minutes per side.

WOOD SUGGESTION:

Smoke using oak, Pacific Northwest Blend or Eastern Blend (page 98)

INGREDIENTS

- 1 6-8-ounce block extra firm tofu
- 1 tablespoon soy sauce
- 1 tablespoon rice vinegar
- 1 tablespoon sesame oil
- 1 tablespoon green onion, finely chopped
- 1 teaspoon sugar
- 1 teaspoon wasabi powder

Sweet Pacific Northwest Almonds & Pecans

WOOD SUGGESTION:

Smoke using Pacific Northwest Blend (page 98), alder, apple or pecan.

INGREDIENTS

- 4 cups pecans and/or almonds
- 1 egg white
- 1/3 cup brown sugar
- 1 teaspoon vanilla
- 1/2 teaspoon cinnamon
- 1/4 teaspoon salt

In a medium bowl, whip egg white until frothy. Add sugar, vanilla, cinnamon and salt. Stir until thoroughly combined. Toss pecans and/or almonds into bowl and coat thoroughly. Spread nuts evenly on a pan with holes or a screen. Preheat smoker to 220°. Cook 60-90 minutes, stirring occasionally. Cool and continue stirring occasionally to break up larger chunks.

Mid-America Smoked Nuts

Ingredients

- 2 cups raw almonds, pistachios, pecans and/or hazelnuts, shelled
- 2 cups water
- 2 tablespoons salt
- 1 tablespoon honey
- 5-10 dashes hot sauce, optional

In a large bowl stir salt and honey in water until salt dissolves. Add nuts and hot sauce. Brine 1 hour at room temperature, stirring occasionally. Spread nuts evenly on a pan with holes or a screen. Preheat smoker to 180°. Cook 60-90 minutes, stirring occasionally. Remove from smoker and toss with more salt and any additional spices, if desired, while still warm. Grind any leftover nuts and add to cookies and cakes.

Wood Suggestion:

Smoke using Mid-America Blend (page 98), apple, maple or pecan.

Alder-Smoked Peanuts & Cashews

Ingredients

- 4 cups peanuts and/or cashews
- 1/4 cup butter, melted
- 1 tablespoon chili powder
- 1 teaspoon salt
- 1/2 teaspoon paprika
- 1/2 teaspoon onion powder
- 1/2 teaspoon garlic powder
- 1/4 teaspoon cayenne pepper, optional

In a medium bowl mix all spices with melted butter. Toss peanuts and/or cashews into bowl and coat thoroughly. Spread nuts evenly on a pan with holes or a screen. Preheat smoker to 180°. Cook 60-90 minutes, stirring occasionally.

Wood Suggestion:

Smoke using alder, Pacific Northwest Blend (page 98), pecan or cherry.

Alder-Smoked Stuffed Mushrooms

Clean mushrooms, discard stems and set aside. In a medium bowl mix remaining ingredients. Add finely chopped mushroom stems if desired. Generously fill mushroom caps with mix. Preheat smoker to 300°. Place mushrooms on smoker racks and cook 30-40 minutes or until mushrooms are tender and browned on top.

Ingredients

- 15-20 medium mushrooms
- 1/4 cup mayonnaise
- 1/2 cup cheddar cheese
- 1/2 cup jack cheese
- 1/2 cup bread crumbs
- 1 green onion, finely chopped
- 1/2 teaspoon paprika

Recipe Variation

For quick cheesy mushrooms simply add a square of pepper jack cheese to the mushroom and smoke. Top with pimento if desired.

Wood Suggestion:

Smoke using alder, apple, cherry, pecan, oak or maple (page 97).

Hickory-Smoked Bean & Eggplant Dip

Cut large eggplant in half or poke several holes in small eggplants. Preheat smoker to 250°. Place drained beans in a small oven-proof container. Smoke eggplant and beans 60-90 minutes or until eggplant is tender. Eggplant can be finished in the microwave if desired. Stir beans occasionally during smoke time to avoid drying.

Cool eggplant, peel and chop. Add all remaining ingredients to a food processor. Blend until dip reaches desired texture. Add more olive oil or water if needed. Serve with vegetables, pita or tortilla chips.

Ingredients

- 1 large eggplant or 2-3 small
- 1 15-ounce can white beans, drained
- 3 cloves garlic
- 1 tablespoon olive oil
- 2 tablespoons fresh parsley
- 2 tablespoons sesame tahini
- Juice from 1 lemon
- 1/2 teaspoon cumin
- Salt and pepper to taste

Wood Suggestion:

Smoke using hickory, apple or alder (page 97); Eastern Blend (page 98).

Hickory-Smoked Tostadas |

Wood Suggestion:
Smoke using hickory, apple, alder, cherry, pecan, maple or oak.

Ingredients
- 8-10 crispy corn tortillas
- 1 16-ounce can refried beans
- 2 tablespoons taco or fajita seasoning
- 2 cups cheese, shredded

Tostada Toppings:
- 1 cup lettuce, finely chopped
- 1 cup guacamole
- 1 cup sour cream
- 1 cup salsa
- 1 tomato, chopped
- 1/4 cup cheese, shredded

In a small bowl mix refried beans and seasoning until thoroughly combined. Evenly distribute beans and cheese over tortillas. Preheat smoker to 200-250°. Place tortillas on smoker racks and smoke-cook 15-30 minutes or until cheese is melted. Top with additional toppings and serve whole or cut into bite-sized servings.

Cowboy-Smoked Garlic Spread |

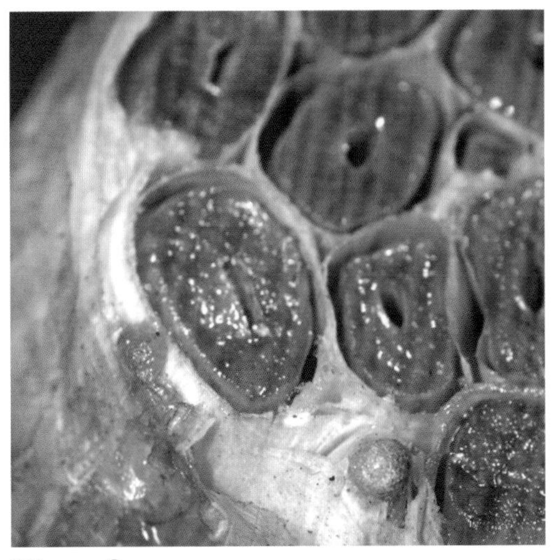

Wood Suggestion:
Smoke using Cowboy Blend (page 98), apple, maple or oak (page 97).

Ingredients
- 5-7 whole heads of garlic
- 2 tablespoons olive oil
- 4 tablespoons butter, softened
- 2 tablespoons fresh chives, chopped
- Salt to taste

Cut tops and bottoms off garlic. Place on foil or in a shallow pan. Drizzle with olive oil. Place in smoker and smoke at 180-220° 45-60 minutes or until garlic is soft. After cooling, pop garlic out of skins and mash with a fork. In a small bowl mix garlic, butter and chives until thoroughly combined. Any herbs may be added to this spread. Mayonnaise or margarine can be used in place of butter. Add Cowboy Smoked Garlic to any dish for an added smokey flavor.

Apple-Smoked Jalapeño Poppers

INGREDIENTS

- 12 jalapeño peppers, stemmed and seeded
- 4 ounces cream cheese, softened
- 1 tablespoon honey
- 1/2 teaspoon paprika
- 6 slices bacon

In a small bowl mix cream cheese, honey and paprika until thoroughly combined. Cut bacon strips in half. Stuff peppers with cream cheese mixture. Wrap bacon around jalapeño taking care to cover the open end. Secure bacon with a toothpick. Preheat smoker to 300°. Place on foil-lined smoker racks and cook 45-60 minutes or until bacon is crispy.

WOOD SUGGESTION:

Smoke using apple, alder, cherry, mesquite, pecan, maple or oak.

Appetizers
Smoke It!

When living in Alaska, for example, we often smoked fish in 50° below zero temperatures. Even with our smoker wrapped in a heat blanket, the meat had to be finished in the oven. When using the same smoker while living in Indonesia, the cooking time dramatically decreased. Now that we live in Oregon, our cooking times vary with the changing seasons. By knowing how your smoker reacts and performs in the environment in which you live, you will be able to turn out a quality product every time. These are points you may want to record and keep track of for future reference.

Be it walk-in or stovetop smokers, grill smokers, gas or electric units, there are many styles and brands on the market, and what you choose depends on personal preference. Many serious smoking fans have multiple units, finding they offer different cook-rates due to varying temperature controls. The key factor to which you prefer comes down to desired cooking time and convenience.

If using a smoker, a wood-chip pan will come with the unit. If smoking on a gas-grill style smoker, your unit may come with a smoker box. If so, fill this box with wood chunks (slowest burn rate), chips (moderate burn rate) or sawdust (fastest burn rate) and set it over a lighted burner until smoke arises, then lower heat to the target temperature. If your gas smoking unit does not come with a smoker box, these can be picked up from product-related websites or stores. You can also make your own chip pouch from foil. Simply wrap foil around a desired amount of chunks, chips or sawdust, poke a few holes in the top with a small knife and place beneath the grate, over a burner. Preheat on high until smoke is seen, then reduce heat to target temperature.

The recipes found in these pages can be applied to any style or brand of smoker. No matter what smoker you choose, be sure to always place it in a well-ventilated area, away from walls.

Do not use smokers on wood floors or decks and be certain all connections—be they gas or electrical—are solid and in place.

By preparing yourself with basic ingredients, quality food and an open mind, the world of smoke-cooking will open many culinary doors. Capturing unique flavors in your smoked food is simple, and once you discover how delectable and truly diverse they can be, you'll be wanting more.

CHIP-BLENDING RECIPES

Enough for one smoke packet and any foods cooked under 30 minutes.

Cowboy Blend: 2 tablespoons mesquite, 1 tablespoon pecan.

Southern Blend: 2 tablespoons hickory, 1 tablespoon pecan.

Eastern Blend: 1 tablespoon each of maple, oak and cherry.

Pacific Northwest Blend: 1 tablespoon each of alder, apple and maple.

West Coast Blend: 1 tablespoon each of apple, cherry and peach.

Tropical Blend: 2 tablespoons oak, 1 tablespoon lemon or orange.

Rugged Blend: 2 tablespoons each of hickory and mesquite.

Mid-America Blend: 2 tablespoons hickory, 1 tablespoon oak or maple.

Soaking Liquids

Another grilling/smoking debate surfaces, and that is to soak or not to soak your chips. After more than 20 years of experimentation with different wood types and flavors, I can attest that it comes down to personal preference. There are people who prefer the heavier smoke that may come initially when some woods are soaked, and others who find it makes more of a mess than it's worth. Some claim the liquid the chips are smoked in makes all the difference in the meal and some that say you can't detect any changes.

Just like the discussion over types of woods that can be used, I believe that if the cook has success with a certain method, it should not be debated. If the food is good, "the cook is always right!" Unless safe food-handling guidelines are not being met, differences in techniques and methods are a moot point, for it all comes down to personal likes and dislikes in the end product.

When experimenting I have found that woods soaked in wine or whiskey tend to hold a certain flavor, while adding fruit juices does add a touch of sweetness to the smoke. Beer tends to add a yeasty twang to the smoke. Even if it is simply adding to the aroma of the smoke, the effort may be worth it. Experiment, have fun, carry out taste tests and enjoy the experience for all it's worth.

Optimizing Flavor

Eating smoke-cooked food right from the smoker is preferred by many people. But if the smoke flavors are too sharp, refrigerate for a day, giving the food time to absorb the flavors. The end result is a more moist, rich and succulent flavored food that best represents the ingredients that went into creating it.

There are a few quick fixes when it comes to experiments or recipes that don't turn out quite as planned. If a food is over-smoked, too strong or too salty, adding it to something can tone down the flavor. Try making it into a dip or sandwich filling; chop the pieces small and use as a salad topper or add to the sauce of a rice or pasta dish.

Smoked foods may taste great but come out of the smoker too dry. A quick fix for this problem is to immediately put them in a sealable plastic bag or airtight container. Putting foods in a container while still warm causes moisture to be captured and reabsorbed into the food. Refrigerate immediately once moist.

Some foods acquire smoke flavor rather quickly. Smoke flavor can be optimized by burning more chips during the cooking process. In addition, by preheating the smoker and getting the chips burning prior to placing the food in the unit, a more intense smoke flavor will be delivered early in the smoking process.

If desiring a light smoke flavor, food can be smoked for a short period of time and finished off in a dehydrator or on low heat in the oven.

Know Your Smoker

Ultimately, the best smoked food will be achieved through practice. Unfortunately, at times these results are derivatives of trial and error. By experimenting with different recipes and learning the parameters of your smoker, what it's capable of doing, how it performs in varied climatic conditions and even seasons of the year, you'll optimize control of the overall smoking process.

With so many ways to add smoke flavor to grilled foods, the combinations and possibilities are endless.

sources, free of chemicals, pesticides and other unwanted residues. Never use soft woods, ones that have been pressure-treated or wood of unknown origin, in your smoker unit.

The Most Common Smoking Woods Are:

Alder: Common in the Pacific Northwest, gives off a delicate smokey flavor that is slightly sweet. Recommended for fish, poultry, pork and vegetables.

Apple: Preferred for its mild, fruity flavor with a hint of sweetness. Recommended for all smoked foods. Great also as a blend with stronger woods such as hickory and mesquite.

Cherry: Slightly sweet and fruity, this mellow wood is great for blending with stronger woods. Recommended most for poultry, this wood can be used with all foods.

Hickory: The most common wood used for smoking, bold and sometimes peppery with a hint of sweetness. Recommended most for pork, chicken and beef, also flavors well with mesquite.

Mesquite: Perfect for a short time on the grill, strong and tangy. Recommended most for beef, vegetables, pork and poultry, goes well with hickory.

Pecan: Common in the South, pecan is a versatile, mellow smoke flavor. Recommended for all smoked foods. Great also as a blend with stronger woods such as hickory and mesquite.

Oak: One of the most common fuels, oak has a subtle flavor that goes with a variety of foods and lends itself well to blending with stronger smoking woods. Recommended for all smoked foods.

Other Flavors Readily Available

Apricot: A mild, sweet fruit wood. Recommended for pork and poultry.

Birch: Similar to the fruit woods. Recommended for pork and poultry.

Lemon: Stronger smoke flavor, citrus woods pair well with milder woods.

Maple: One of the most versatile smoking woods, mild and slightly sweet, flavors can very in different regions. Recommended for vegetables and all other smoked foods.

Nectarine & Peach: Similar to pecan and the fruit woods. Recommended for pork, poultry and beef.

Pear: Similar to apple, a mild, sweet fruit wood. Recommended for all smoked foods. Great also as a blend with stronger woods such as hickory and mesquite.

In Addition to Wood, Try:

- **Corncobs**
- **Grapevines**
- **Hazelnut shells**
- **Coconut husks**
- **Dried seaweed**
- **Pineapple rinds**
- **Small amounts of dried or fresh herbs**
- **Pumpkin seeds in the shell**

appeals to my sense of smell. If the smoke coming from the smoker unit smells sharp, or has a bitter tinge to it, I won't use it; you should only use the kind of woods you like.

An important guideline when focusing on smoke flavors is to keep marinades and spices to a minimum in order to get the full effect and be able to taste the wood flavor in your foods. Find out the smoke flavors you prefer, then spice-up the recipes accordingly.

When working with chips, chunks or sawdust, it helps having a designated area in which to store different flavors of woods, using it much as you would a spice rack. The more you get into this form of cooking, the more diversified you'll want to become, and organization plays a big part.

In this day and age of Internet commerce, almost anything can be shipped to your doorstep. We tend to frequent sites that offer a wide variety of wood flavors as well as wood types like sawdust, chips or chunks. If placing on-line orders, be sure it's with a reputable business. Make certain the woods are from safe

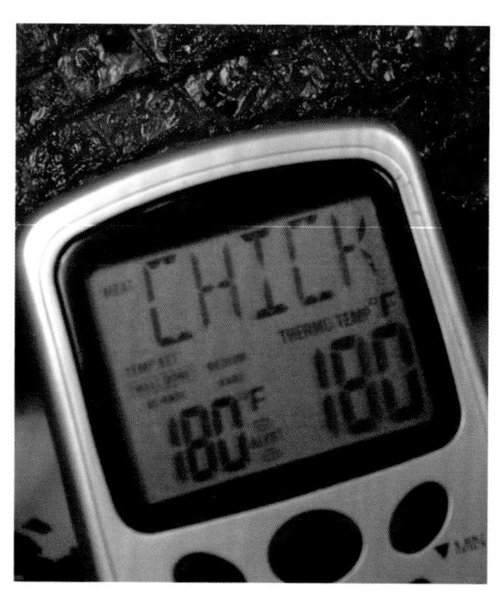

Keep in mind that food continues to cook even after it is removed from the heat source. It's often wise to pull foods 5° early, leaving the thermometer in to gauge when the food reaches its final temperature.

Hot-smoking occurs at a lower temperature, typically between 120°F and 200°F. These foods take longer to cook than when smoke-cooked, due to a lower cooking temperature. Jerky and some larger cuts of meat are common hot-smoked foods.

Cold-smoking, on the other hand, is preserving foods with smoke in temperatures of 100°F or lower, or below a temperature that liquifies or burns fats. Funneling smoke through ducts, into a cold-smoke house, is one way to achieve this. Traditionally, fires are built in one shelter, and smoke is piped under ground to the smoke house. This is a specialty approach to smoking, and delves into a whole different theme than what this book is intended for.

The process of smoke-cooking uses combinations of heat and smoke to break down the fibers within the meat (and other foods), while simultaneously releasing fats. The result is a tender piece of cooked meat, packed with flavor. The longer the meat is exposed to heat, the drier it becomes.

No matter what recipe you apply, the final outcome lies in attaining a well-textured food by creating a balance between salt, sugar, smoke and heat. Adding other spices and

The "lower and slower" a food cooks, the more pronounced the desired "smoke ring" becomes.

flavors you wish the meat to acquire is also part of the equation. Remember, smoke-cooking is not a form of preservation. Smoke-cooked food has a shelf-life very similar to that of regular cooked food, and if refrigerated, should not be kept more than a week. Vacuum sealing and canning are ways to keep some smoke-cooked foods for extended periods of time.

Alter To Your Taste

One of the rewards of smoking your own food is that you can create a flavor which appeals to your senses. Many of the recipes I've worked with over the years are quite different from their original form. When living in Alaska's Arctic, my husband and I smoked a great deal of fish and game, though were often limited to the ingredients on hand. As we moved to warmer climates with easy to access markets, not only did our smoking style change, but so did many of the ingredients. The result has been a collection of diverse flavors we never knew smoked foods could carry.

For this reason, I strongly encourage you to experiment with the recipes found in this book. If you like some of the ingredients but not others, switch them around to suit your liking. If you desire more of a sweet, salty, hot or tangy flavor, adjust the recipes accordingly. Some of these recipes may be simple starting points in your developing a more custom-fit flavor.

Smoke Flavors

Almost as numerous as the spices one can add to food, smoke flavors are many. When adding smoke to foods, I prefer using what personally

Introduction

Clearly defining what constitutes smoked foods is a tremendous task. For thousands of years cultures the world-over have smoked food. Some of the approaches are straight forward (as basic as tossing wood chips on an open fire), while others are hinging on science (addressing temperature control and smoke-flow levels).

Our ancestors primarily smoked foods to preserve them, because they had no refrigeration. Today, foods are mainly smoked to capture specific flavors, be they woods, brines or rubs. With today's ever-increasing accessibility to numerous wood-types, state-of-the-art smokers and creative recipes, smoking foods is reaching a new dimension.

Keep in mind that the process of curing and smoking foods is not an exact science. Many elements impact the final outcome of smoked foods, and the more you learn through personal experience, the more proficient you'll become at smoking foods. Patience is key, as is developing and adapting approaches to build on past experiences and enhance future outcomes.

The more you smoke foods, the more familiar you'll become with desired brining times; your smoking unit, where the hotspots are and how it performs on cold winter days or hot summer evenings; how wind impacts cooking time; the flavor of wood you like best, and more. Practice is the most practical way to become a proficient smoker cook.

Within this book you will find recipes that relate to smoke-cooking, that is, smoking foods while they cook. The foods which result from such high-heat smoking are intended for quick consumption-usually in the form of dinners or main meals-versus being stored for long-term. Generally speaking, smoke-cooking is anything that's cooked above 200°F in your smoker unit. When smoke-cooking, cooks need to rely more on the internal temperature of the food versus a specific time frame. Many smokers do not keep at a constant temperature due to either how they are built or how many times the doors open. Because of these possible inconsistencies it is best to use a thermometer that can be placed in meat and fish and be read outside the smoker. When the thermometer alerts that the target temperature has been reached, it is time to eat.

Follow Traditional Food Safety Guidelines When Smoke-Cooking Foods

Beef: Rare 140°; medium-rare 150°; medium 160°; well-done 170°

Poultry: White meat 170°; dark meat and whole birds 180°

Pork: Medium 160°; well-done 170°

Fish: 140°

Maple Chili Pork with Black Bean Salad

Place Chili Rub or taco seasoning in a sealable plastic bag. Drop meat into bag and massage, let sit 10 minutes. In a medium bowl gently combine all salad ingredients, vinegar and olive oil. Place papers on a flat surface and evenly distribute black bean mixture down the middle. Place marinated meat atop the black bean mixture. Fold papers with the grain and close, securing with a metal paper clip or heat-resistant band. Place filled papers on a baking sheet and bake in a preheated, 375° oven, or on a hot grill using indirect heat. Cook 20-25 minutes or until pork has reached desired doneness.

Ingredients

- 1 pound pork loin or chicken breast, cubed
- 1 15-ounce can black beans, drained
- 1 4-ounce can diced green chilies
- 1 cup bell pepper, chopped
- 1/2 cup corn
- 1/2 cup red onion, chopped
- 1 large tomato, chopped
- 2 cloves garlic, minced
- 1 tablespoon olive oil
- 2 teaspoons white wine vinegar
- 2 tablespoons Chili Rub (page 146) or prepared taco seasoning

4-6 prepared maple grilling papers, (See page 56, **Wrap Preparation**).

Coconut-Coated Stone-Fruit Wraps

In a large bowl, combine Grand Marnier, cinnamon and salt. Add stone fruit combination of choice and gently toss, coating all fruit. Let sit at least 20 minutes. Gently roll each piece of fruit in coconut. Place papers on a flat surface and evenly distribute fruit down the middle. Fold papers with the grain and close, securing with a metal paper clip or heat-resistant band. Place filled papers on a baking sheet and bake in a preheated, 375° oven, or on a hot grill using indirect heat. Bake 10-15 minutes or until fruit is heated through. Serve with Cheesecake Cream or ice cream.

Cheesecake Cream Preparation

In a medium bowl, blend all ingredients until smooth.

Ingredients

- 2-3 cups stone fruit, any combination of the following:
  peaches, peeled and chopped
  apricots, peeled and chopped
  plums, chopped cherries, pitted
- 1/4 cup Grand Marnier
- 1/4 teaspoon cinnamon
- 1/8 teaspoon salt
- 1 cup sweetened flaked coconut

4-6 prepared alder, maple or cherry grilling papers, (See page 56, **Wrap Preparation**).

Cheesecake Cream

- 4 ounces cream cheese, softened
- 1/3 cup sour cream
- 1 cup powdered sugar
- 1 tablespoon fresh lemon juice
- 1 teaspoon real vanilla

Flat-Wrap Halibut

INGREDIENTS

- 1 12-ounce halibut fillet
- 2 tablespoons butter, melted
- 2 tablespoons parsley, chopped
- 2 cloves garlic, pureed
- 9 slices zucchini
- Salt and pepper to taste

1 prepared cedar grilling paper,
(See page 56, **Wrap Preparation**).

In a small bowl combine butter, parsley and garlic. Place zucchini slices on prepared wrap. Salt and pepper to taste. Place fish atop zucchini layer and cover with parsley mixture. Place wrap, flat, on a preheated hot grill over indirect heat. Cook 25-35 minutes or until fish flakes in large chunks and is no longer opaque or reaches an internal temperature of 140°.

Cherry-Wrapped Trout with Herbs

INGREDIENTS

- 4-8 small trout
- 1 pint cherry tomatoes, chopped
- 1 bunch fresh parsley
- 1 bunch fresh cilantro
- 1 bunch fresh mint
- 4 rosemary branches
- Salt and pepper to taste

4 prepared cherry grilling papers,
(See page 56, **Wrap Preparation**).

Place papers on a flat surface and put fish in the middle, going with the grain. Salt and pepper fish both inside and out. Evenly distribute herbs and tomatoes among each wrap. Tuck herbs under and into fish. Fold papers with the grain and close, securing with a metal paper clip or heat-resistant band. Place filled papers on a baking sheet and bake in a preheated, 375° oven, or on a hot grill using indirect heat. Cook 15-25 minutes or until fish flakes in large chunks and is no longer opaque.

Alder-Wrapped Chicken Breast

INGREDIENTS

- 1 pound boneless, skinless chicken breasts
- 2 tablespoons olive oil
- 4 cloves garlic, minced
- Juice and zest from 1 lemon
- 1/4 cup fresh parsley leaves
- 1 tablespoon fresh rosemary and/or thyme
- Salt and pepper to taste

4-6 prepared alder grilling papers,
(See page 56, **Wrap Preparation**).

Cut chicken into long strips. In a medium bowl, mix remaining ingredients, add chicken and marinate up to 30 minutes, tossing occasionally. Place papers on a flat surface and evenly distribute chicken down the middle. Fold papers with the grain and close, securing with a metal paper clip or heat-resistant band. Place filled papers on a baking sheet and bake in a preheated, 375° oven, or on a hot grill using indirect heat. Cook 15-20 minutes or until chicken has reached an internal temperature of 165°.

Maple-Wrapped S'mores

INGREDIENTS

- 4 2"x2" brownies, quartered
- 40 mini-marshmallows
- 2/3 cup graham cracker crumbs
- 1/2 toasted almonds, finely chopped

4 prepared maple grilling papers,
(See page 56, **Wrap Preparation**).

Place papers on a flat surface. Sprinkle graham cracker crumbs down the middle of the wrap, going with the grain. Evenly top with brownies, marshmallows and almonds. Fold papers with the grain and close, securing with a metal paper clip or heat-resistant band. Place filled papers on a baking sheet and bake in a preheated, 375° oven, or on a hot grill using indirect heat. Cook 5-10 minutes or until brownies are warm and marshmallows begin to melt.

Alder-Wrapped Cilantro Lime Shrimp

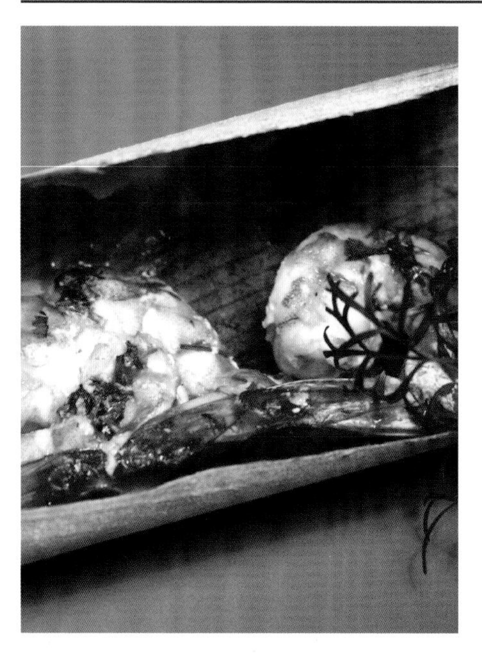

INGREDIENTS
- 1 pound raw shrimp
- Juice and zest from 1-2 limes
- 1 tablespoon soy sauce
- 1 tablespoon peanut oil
- 1/4 cup fresh cilantro, chopped

4-6 prepared grilling papers, (See page 56, **Wrap Preparation**).

Shell and devein shrimp. In a medium bowl, mix remaining ingredients, add shrimp and marinate 15 minutes, tossing occasionally. Place papers on a flat surface and evenly distribute shrimp down the middle. Fold papers with the grain and close, securing with a metal paper clip or heat-resistant band. Place filled papers on a baking sheet and bake in a preheated, 375° oven, or on a hot grill using indirect heat. Cook 6-10 minutes or until shrimp turns pink. Fish chunks can be substituted for the shrimp. Add at least 5 minutes to cooking time for fish.

Cedar-Wrapped Fish & Vegetables

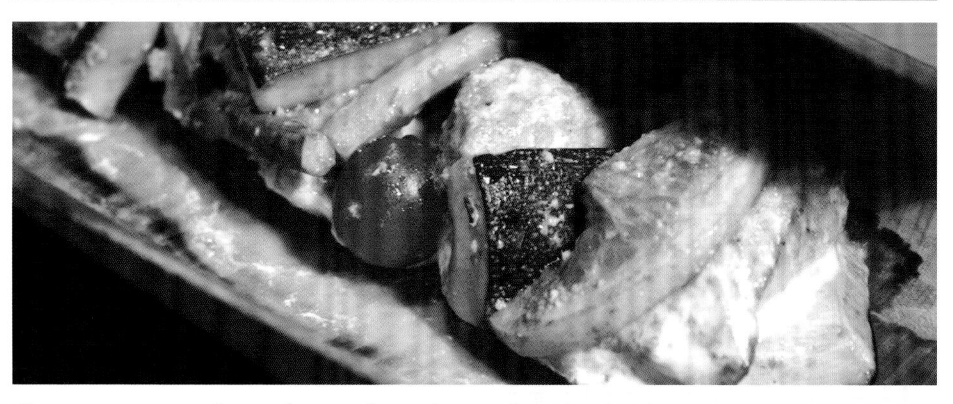

Place paper on a flat surface and evenly distribute all ingredients down the middle. Fold paper, with the grain, and close, securing with a metal paper clip or heat-resistant band. Place filled paper on a baking sheet and bake in a preheated, 350° oven, or on a hot grill using indirect heat. Cook 12-15 minutes or until fish reaches desired doneness.

INGREDIENTS
- 6 ounces skinless fish, cubed
- 2-4 cubes zucchini
- 1 stalk asparagus, chopped
- 1/2 tomato, chopped
- 1 clove garlic, minced
- 1 slice lemon
- 1 tablespoon melted butter
- Salt and pepper to taste

1 prepared cedar grilling paper, (See page 56, **Wrap Preparation**).

Cedar-Wrapped Teriyaki Salmon |

INGREDIENTS

- 4 6-8 ounce skinless salmon fillets
- Teriyaki Marinade (page 28)

4 prepared cedar grilling papers, (See page 56, **Wrap Preparation**).

Marinate fish in marinade at least 20 minutes. Place papers on a flat surface and put fish in the middle. Fold papers with the grain and close, securing with a metal paper clip or heat-resistant band. Place filled papers on a baking sheet and bake in a preheated, 375° oven, or on a hot grill using indirect heat. Cook 15 minutes or until fish flakes in large chunks and is no longer opaque.

Cherry-Wrapped Scallops |

INGREDIENTS

- 9-12 scallops
- 2 tablespoons fresh parsley, finely chopped
- 2 tablespoons fresh chives, finely chopped
- 2 tablespoons fresh basil, finely chopped
- Juice of 1 lime
- 1/4 teaspoon salt

4 prepared cherry grilling papers, (See page 56, **Wrap Preparation**).

In a medium bowl, gently mix all ingredients. Marinate 10-15 minutes. Place papers on a flat surface, put scallops down the middle. Fold papers with the grain and close, securing with a metal paper clip or heat-resistant band. Place filled papers on a baking sheet and bake in a preheated, 375° oven, or on a hot grill using indirect heat. Cook 8-10 minutes or until scallops are slightly firm.

Wrap It! *Plank It!*

Apple Crumble

Ingredients
- 3 tart apples, thinly sliced
- 1/4 cup sugar
- 2 tablespoons flour
- 1 teaspoon cinnamon

1 prepared plank, maple or fruit wood, soaked in apple juice or water (See page 57, **Plank Preparation**).

Crumble Topping
- 1/3 cup oatmeal
- 1/3 cup brown sugar
- 2 tablespoons flour
- 1/3 cup butter, softened

Place sliced apples in a large mixing bowl. Add sugar, flour and cinnamon, stirring just to evenly coat slices. Arrange apples in an even layer over prepared plank. Leave at least a 1/2 inch of plank space around the edges. Sprinkle crumble topping evenly over apples. Due to possible dripping, place plank on a cookie sheet or foil base to catch any sugary drips. Grill or bake at 375° 25-30 minutes or until apples are tender and crust is golden brown. Serve with ice cream.

Crumble Topping Preparation
In a medium bowl, mix dry ingredients. Cut butter into mixture and crumble with a fork.

Recipe Variation
Walnuts, pecans and/or raisins make a nice addition to this dessert. Rhubarb can be used in place of apples, increase sugar to 3/4 cup.

Toffee-Topped Pound Cake

Ingredients
- 1 pound cake, sliced 1/2"
- 1/2 cup chocolate toffee bar pieces
- 4 ounces cream cheese, softened
- 2 tablespoons butter, softened

1 prepared plank, alder or fruit wood, soaked in water (See page 57, **Plank Preparation**).

In a medium bowl, combine toffee pieces, cream cheese and butter. Spread toffee mixture evenly onto pound cake slices. Place on prepared plank. Grill or bake at 400° 8-12 minutes, until toffee mixture is lightly browned.

Triple Berry Tart

Ingredients

- 1 prepared pie crust
- 1 cup blueberries
- 1 cup raspberries
- 1 cup strawberries, stemmed and quartered
- 1/2 cup sugar
- 1/4 cup flour
- 1/2 teaspoon cinnamon
- 3 tablespoons butter

1 prepared plank, maple or fruit wood, soaked in water
(See page 57, **Plank Preparation**).

In a medium bowl, mix flour and sugar. Add berries, gently tossing to coat. Preheat prepared plank at 400° for 15-20 minutes. Place crust on hot plank and quickly place berries in the middle of the crust. Shape crust up over berries, leaving an opening on top. Divide butter into 3-4 pats and place atop berries. Due to possible dripping, place plank on a cookie sheet or foil base to catch any sugary drips. Grill or bake at 400° 35-40 minutes or until crust is golden brown. If a crispy crust is desired, finish tart on a hot pizza stone for the final 10 minutes of cooking time.

Recipe Variation

Any seasonal berries can be used for this dessert. If only using blueberries or blackberries, add 1 tablespoon lemon juice to fruit mixture. For Strawberry Rhubarb Tart, increase sugar to 3/4 cup.

Original Cedar-Planked Salmon |

Ingredients

- 1 fillet of salmon or steelhead (3-6 servings)
- 1 teaspoon Herb Medley Rub or fish rub of choice
- Juice of 1/2 lemon
- 1 lemon, sliced
- Olive oil for brushing

1 prepared cedar plank, soaked in water (See page 57, **Plank Preparation**)

Herb Medley Rub

- 1/2 teaspoon salt
- 1/2 teaspoon sugar
- 1/2 teaspoon dried thyme
- 1/2 teaspoon dried oregano
- 1/2 teaspoon onion powder
- 1/2 teaspoon lemon pepper
- 1/4 teaspoon dried rosemary

Place sliced lemons on prepared plank. Place fish, skin-side down on lemon layer. Squeeze 1/2 lemon over fish. Brush with olive oil and sprinkle with seasonings. Grill or bake at 375° 20-25 minutes or until fish is opaque and flakes in large chunks or reaches an internal temperature of 135°.

Herb Medley Rub Preparation

In a small bowl, mix all rub ingredients until crushed and combined. Or using a mortar and pestle, grind until combined.

Recipe Variation

There are hundreds of variations to the original cedar-planked salmon recipes. Salmon planks well with any wood flavor. Toppings can vary from Italian type seasonings to Asian flavors. Fish can be marinated prior to planking or basted during cooking time. Keeping simple ingredients to a minimum ensures the flavors of the wood smoke will come through in the final product. Don't forget that simply placing a cedar plank in the oven alongside a fillet of fish will minimize any unwanted lingering fish odors in your home.

Sour Cream & Chive Steelhead

Place fish, skin-side down, on prepared plank. Salt and pepper to taste. Spread sour cream in a thin layer over fish. Sprinkle with chives and lemon slices. Grill or bake at 375° 20-25 minutes or until fish is opaque and flakes in large chunks or reaches an internal temperature of 135°.

Ingredients

- 1 fillet of steelhead or salmon (3-6 servings)
- 1 lemon
- 1/2 cup sour cream
- 2 tablespoons chives, chopped
- 1 lemon, thinly sliced
- Salt and pepper to taste

1 prepared plank, alder or fruit wood, soaked in lemon juice or water
(See page 57, **Plank Preparation**).

Artichoke-Stuffed Halibut

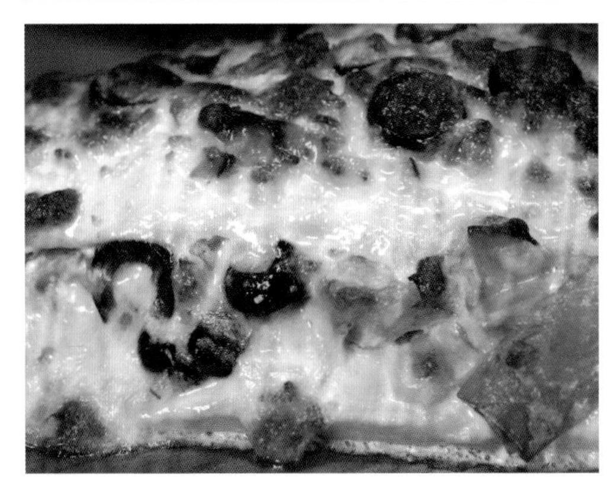

Prepare fish fillet by cutting lengthwise through the center of the fillet leaving equal thickness on top and bottom. Salt and pepper fish to taste. Fill fillet with stuffing mixture, reserving 3 tablespoons for the top. Place stuffed fillet on prepared plank. Top with additional stuffing mixture. Grill or bake at 350° 25 to 40 minutes or until fish flakes in large chunks and is no longer opaque or internal temperature reaches 140°.

Artichoke Stuffing Preparation

In a medium bowl, gently mix all stuffing ingredients until thoroughly combined. Keep refrigerated until ready to use. This stuffing also makes a great dip on its own. Place in an ovenproof pan and baked at 350° 10 minutes. Serve with tortilla chips.

Ingredients

- 1 2-3-pound halibut fillet
- Salt and pepper to taste

1 prepared plank, alder or fruit wood, soaked in white wine or water
(See page 57, **Plank Preparation**).

Artichoke Stuffing

- 1/3 cup mayonnaise
- 1/3 cup parmesan cheese
- 1/3 cup black olives, sliced
- 2 tablespoons diced green chilies
- 1/2 cup Monterey Jack cheese
- 1 6.5-ounce jar marinated artichokes, drained and chopped

Recipe Variation

A thick salmon fillet can be substituted for halibut. For a hotter filling, substitute sautéed or canned jalapeños for green chilies. Other cheeses can also be substituted.

Sesame Tuna

Add tuna steaks to marinade and let sit 20 minutes. In a large, dry skillet, toast sesame seeds at high heat, stirring constantly for 1-2 minutes. Remove sesame seeds from hot pan immediately. Remove fish from marinade and liberally coat both sides with toasted sesame seeds. Place on a prepared plank. Grill or bake at 3750° 15-25 minutes or until fish reaches desired doneness.

Ingredients

- 1-2 pounds tuna steaks, 3/4"
- 1 cup sesame seeds, toasted

1 prepared plank, alder or fruit wood, soaked in sake or water (See page 57, **Plank Preparation**).

Sesame Ginger Marinade

- 1/4 cup olive oil
- 3 tablespoons soy sauce
- 2 tablespoons toasted sesame oil
- 2 cloves garlic, minced
- 1 tablespoon ginger, minced
- 2 teaspoons honey
- 1 teaspoon chili powder

Sesame Ginger Marinade Preparation

In a medium bowl or sealable plastic bag, mix all marinade ingredients thoroughly.

Smokey Halibut with Salsa

Gently massage Smokey Rub in to all sides of the halibut. Let sit 10 minutes. Place fish on prepared plank. Grill or bake at 350° 20-25 minutes or until fish flakes in large chunks and is no longer opaque or internal temperature reaches 135°. Serve with Tomatillo Salsa.

Smokey Rub Preparation

In a small bowl, mix all ingredients until thoroughly combined.

Tomatillo Salsa Preparation

In a medium bowl, mix all ingredients until thoroughly combined.

Ingredients

- 4 8-ounce halibut fillets

1 prepared plank, cedar or hickory, soaked in apple juice or water (See page 57, **Plank Preparation**).

Smokey Rub

- 1 tablespoon brown sugar
- 1 teaspoon fresh ground black pepper
- 1/2 teaspoon granulated onion
- 1/2 teaspoon garlic powder
- 1/2 teaspoon salt
- 1/4 teaspoon cayenne pepper
- 1/4 teaspoon cumin
- 1/4 teaspoon liquid smoke, optional

Tomatillo Salsa

- 2 cups tomatillos, diced
- 1/2 cup onion, diced
- 1-2 jalapeños, seeded and diced
- Juice and zest of 1 lime
- 1/2 cup cilantro, chopped
- 1 tablespoon sugar
- Salt and pepper to taste

Curried Snapper with Peach Chutney

In a small bowl, mix yogurt and seasonings. Coat fish and place on prepared plank. Grill or bake at 375° 20-25 minutes or until fish flakes in large chunks and is no longer opaque. Serve with warm Peach Chutney.

Peach Chutney Preparation

Heat olive oil in medium skillet on medium high heat. Sauté onions and peppers 10-15 minutes. Add garlic, peaches, juice and sugar. Sauté an additional 10 minutes. Remove from heat and add mint.

Recipe Variation

Mango can be substituted for peaches in chutney and cilantro can be used in place of mint. Pollack, rockfish, or cod can be substituted for snapper.

Ingredients

- 4 8-ounce snapper fillets
- 2/3 cup plain yogurt
- 1 teaspoon curry powder
- 1/4 teaspoon turmeric
- 1/4 teaspoon salt

1 prepared plank, alder or fruit wood, soaked in water (See page 57, **Plank Preparation**).

Peach Chutney

- 1 tablespoon olive oil
- 1/2 cup onion, finely chopped
- 1 jalapeño pepper, seeded and finely chopped
- 2 cloves garlic, crushed
- 2 large peaches, peeled and chopped
- 1/4 cup orange juice
- 1 tablespoon brown sugar
- 1/4 cup fresh mint, finely chopped

Nut-Crusted Cod

In a shallow dish, mix flour, salt and cayenne pepper. In another shallow dish, beat egg until frothy. In a food processor or mini-chopper, finely grind nuts, coconut and bread crumbs. Coat fish with seasoned flour, dip in egg and then coat with nut mixture, pressing into fish. Place on a prepared plank. Grill or bake at 375° 20-25 minutes or until fish reaches an internal temperature of 135°. Serve with Tropical Salsa (page 31) or Green Sauce (page 42), if desired.

IIngredients

- 4-6 8-ounce cod fillets
- 1/2 cup macadamia and/or pistachio nuts, chopped
- 1/4 cup flaked coconut
- 1/4 cup bread crumbs
- 1 egg, beaten
- 1/4 cup flour
- 1 teaspoon salt
- 1/4 teaspoon cayenne pepper

1 prepared plank, cedar or oak, soaked water (See page 57, **Plank Preparation**).

Garlic Shrimp

In a medium bowl, mix all seasoning ingredients. Gently toss in shrimp, coating completely. Marinate 15-20 minutes. Thread 4-6 shrimp onto each skewer. Place on prepared plank. Grill or bake at 400° 5-7 minutes or until shrimp turn pink.

Recipe Variation

Prawns or scallops can be substituted for shrimp, place directly on prepared plank; skewers are not needed.

Ingredients

- 1 pound shrimp, cleaned and deveined
- 1/2 cup white wine
- 1/4 cup olive oil
- 1 teaspoon Herb Medley (page 79) or seasoning of choice
- 2-4 cloves garlic, minced

Metal or wooden skewers (soak wooden skewers at least 1 hour in water)

1 prepared plank, alder or fruit wood, soaked in white wine or water, add 1 cup lemon or lime juice to water if desired (See page 57, **Plank Preparation**).

Chili-Citrus Oysters

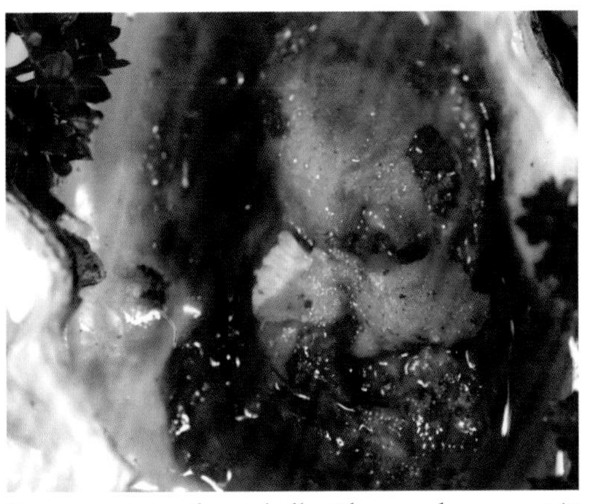

Remove oysters from shells. Clean and reserve 1/2 shell for each oyster. In a medium bowl, mix all marinade ingredients. Add shelled oysters to marinade and let sit 20 minutes, stirring occasionally. Place oysters into half-shells, spooning on 1 teaspoon of marinade. Place on prepared plank. Grill or bake at 400° 10-15 minutes or until heated through. Serve with fresh parsley and lemon slices.

Ingredients

- 20-25 oysters

2 prepared planks, oak or fruit wood, soaked in water, add 1 cup orange juice to water if desired (See page 57, **Plank Preparation**).

Chili-Citrus Marinade

- 1/4 cup orange juice
- 3 tablespoons olive oil
- 1 tablespoon parsley, minced
- 1/2 teaspoon chili powder
- 1/2 teaspoon salt
- Parsley and lemon for garnish, optional

Desserts
Plank It!

Fish & Seafood
Plank It!

Plank-Pressed Sandwiches

Prepare sandwiches according to taste. Brush bread with olive oil and place on a hot grill over indirect heat. Place dry plank atop sandwich and weigh down with a rock, brick or cast-iron skillet. Cook until cheese begins to melt and grill marks appear on sandwiches. Flip over and repeat on the other side.

Ingredients

- Artisan bread
- Pesto (pages 17, 74, 148)
- Mayonnaise
- Mustard
- Horseradish
- Deli meat
- Deli cheese
- Sautéed Vegetables

1 dry plank, any wood type.

Cajun Stuffed Pork Chops

Butterfly pork chops and open. Lightly season pork chops with salt and pepper. In a shallow dish mix flour and Cajun seasoning. Dredge all sides of chops in seasoned flour mixture. In a heavy skillet, heat canola oil on medium-high heat. Add chops and brown lightly on each side. Remove from skillet and place on prepared plank. In the same pan, add more oil and sauté onions and peppers 2-3 minutes. Sprinkle remaining seasoned flour over onion and pepper mixture. Place sautéed vegetables inside and on top of the chops. Cover with foil, tucking ends of foil 1/2" under plank to seal. Grill or bake at 375° 30-40 minutes or until internal temperature reaches 160°. Remove foil last 10 minutes of cooking time.

Ingredients

- 6-8 pork chops, 1"
- 1/4 cup flour
- 2 tablespoons Cajun seasoning
- 2 tablespoons canola oil
- 1 cup onion, sliced
- 1/2 green bell pepper, sliced
- 1/2 red bell pepper, sliced
- 1-2 jalapeño peppers, seeded and sliced
- Salt and pepper to taste

1 prepared plank, hickory or cedar, soaked in water (See page 57, **Plank Preparation**).

Crunchy Chicken Strips

Cut chicken breasts lengthwise into long strips. In a shallow dish, mix corn flakes, parmesan cheese and butter. In another shallow dish, beat eggs until frothy. In a third dish mix flour with salt and pepper. Dip chicken pieces in seasoned flour mixture, then egg, and finally into corn flake mixture. Place on a prepared plank. Grill or bake at 375° 20-25 minutes or until chicken is thoroughly cooked. Serve with Red Wine Sauce (page 149) or BBQ Sauce (page 62).

Ingredients

- 4 chicken breasts, boneless and skinless
- 1 cup finely crushed corn flakes or croutons
- 1/2 cup parmesan cheese, grated
- 2 tablespoons butter, melted
- 1/3 cup flour
- 1/2 teaspoon salt
- 1/4 teaspoon white pepper
- 1 egg, well beaten

1 prepared plank, alder or fruit wood, soaked in water (See page 57, **Plank Preparation**).

Recipe Variation

Any white meat fish can be substituted for the chicken. Decrease cooking time by 5 minutes.

Greek Chicken Bake

Cube chicken or fish into bite-sized chunks. In a large bowl mix remaining ingredients. Toss meat into vegetable mixture. Salt and pepper to taste and drizzle with olive oil. Place mixture on prepared plank. Grill or bake at 375°. Bake 20-25 minutes for fish and 30-35 minutes for chicken or until juices run clear. Serve with Hummus (pg, 146), if desired.

Ingredients

- 1-1 1/2 pounds chicken breast or fish, cubed
- 1 tomato, chopped and drained
- 1 cup green pepper, chopped
- 1 cup red onion, chopped
- 1 cup cucumber, chopped
- 10-15 kalamata olives
- 3 cloves garlic, pureed
- 1 teaspoon fresh oregano, chopped or 1/2 teaspoon dried
- 1 cup feta cheese, crumbled
- Juice and zest of 1/2 lemon
- Olive oil for drizzling
- Salt and pepper to taste

1 prepared plank, alder or fruit wood, soaked in water (See page 57, **Plank Preparation**).

Herb Roasted Chicken |

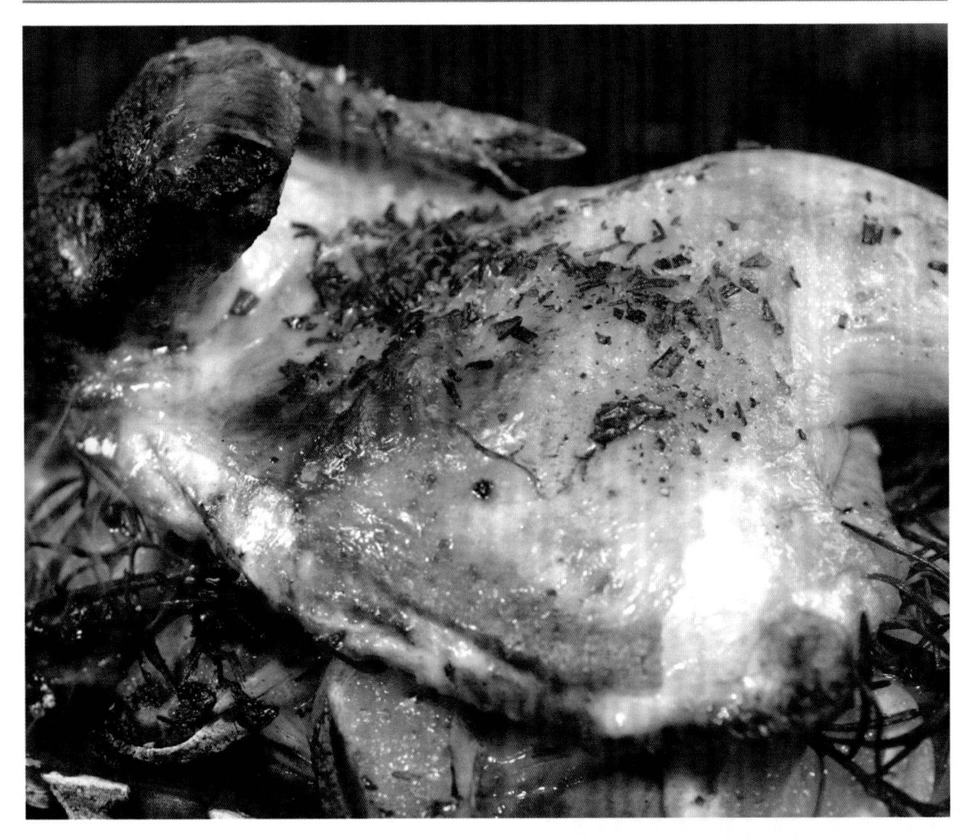

Place chicken in a medium bowl. Add olive oil, herbs, lemon juice, salt and pepper. Marinate chicken, turning occasionally, 1-6 hours. Place sliced oranges or lemons on a prepared plank. Place rosemary branches on top of oranges or lemons. Place chicken, skin side up, on top of rosemary. Grill or bake at 350° 50-60 minutes or until juices run clear and internal temperature reaches 170°. Serve with Fresh Salsa (page 149) if desired.

Ingredients

- 1/2 whole chicken
- 3 tablespoons olive oil
- 1/2 tablespoon fresh rosemary, chopped
- 1/2 teaspoon fresh thyme, chopped
- Juice of 1/2 lemon
- 1 orange or lemon, sliced
- Salt and pepper to taste
- 4 rosemary branches

Recipe Variation

Any combination of fresh or dried herbs can be used in this recipe. For a quick meal simply marinate chicken in prepared oil-based salad dressing of choice. Chicken pieces can be prepared using this technique.

1 prepared plank, maple or alder, soaked in white wine or water (See page 57, **Plank Preparation**).

Twice-Cooked Ribs

Clean any loose fat and membrane off pork ribs. Roll up and place in a crock pot on high heat. Cook 2 hours or until ribs are tender. Carefully remove ribs and place on a large prepared plank. Cover with a thin layer of rib sauce and grill or bake at 375 an additional 30 minutes or until tender. Continue to baste with rib sauce every 10 minutes. Serve with additional sauce and Mango Salsa (page 147) if desired.

Rib Sauce Preparation

In a medium saucepan, sauté pepper, onion and garlic in olive oil until tender. Add remaining ingredients. Bring to a light boil and reduce heat. Simmer 10-20 minutes on low heat.

Ingredients

- 1 rack pork spareribs

1 large prepared plank, hickory or pecan, soaked in vinegar or whiskey (See page 57, **Plank Preparation**)

Rib Sauce

- 1 tablespoon olive oil
- 1 cup green pepper, diced
- 1 cup onion, diced
- 3 cloves garlic, minced
- 1 cup orange or pineapple juice
- 1/3 cup ketchup
- 1/4 cup Worcestershire sauce
- 1/4 cup cider vinegar
- 1 tablespoon brown sugar
- 1/2 teaspoon salt
- 1/4 teaspoon ground black pepper
- Dash of hot pepper sauce, if desired

Sundried Tomato Pork Loin

In a food processor or chopper, thoroughly blend pesto ingredients. Cover pork loin with pesto and seal in a plastic zip-lock bag. Marinate 6 hours or overnight. Place seasoned pork loin on a prepared plank. Grill or bake at 375° 1 hour or until pork reaches an internal temperature of 160°. Let sit 10 minutes before slicing.

Ingredients

- 1 pork loin

Sundried Tomato Pesto

- 1 8.5-ounce jar sundried tomatoes in oil
- 5 cloves garlic
- 1/3 cup parmesan cheese
- 1/2 teaspoon ground black pepper

1 prepared plank, cedar or fruit wood, soaked in water or vinegar (See page 57, **Plank Preparation**).

Recipe Variation

Substitute Basil Pesto (page 17) for Sundried Tomato Pesto or marinate pork loin in Orange Ginger Marinade (page 149).

Three-Layered Pork Fillet

Ingredients

- 2-pound pork tenderloin
- 1/3 cup golden raisins
- 1/3 cup dried apricots, chopped
- 1/3 cup dates, chopped
- 2 tablespoons rum
- 2 tablespoons hot water
- 3 tablespoons butter
- 1/2 cup onion, thinly sliced
- 3 cloves garlic, minced
- 1 cup bread crumbs, plain or panko
- 1/4 teaspoon salt
- 1/4 teaspoon black pepper
- 1/8 teaspoon nutmeg
- 1 egg, beaten
- Salt and pepper to taste

1 prepared plank, alder or fruit wood, soaked in white wine or water (See page 57, **Plank Preparation**).

Prepare pork by dividing the roast into 3 equal sections, lengthwise. Lightly season with salt and pepper. Soak raisins, dates and apricots in rum and hot water. Soak until mixture cools. In a small skillet, sauté onions and garlic in butter until tender. Cool completely. In a medium mixing bowl, combine remaining ingredients. Evenly spread stuffing between two layers of pork, topping with final pork layer. Tie pork loaf together with string. Place on a prepared plank, cover with foil, tucking ends of foil 1/2" under plank to seal. Grill or bake at 375° 50-70 minutes or until internal temperature reaches 160°. Remove foil last 10 minutes of cooking time, baste with olive oil if needed. Let sit 10 minutes before slicing.

Lemon Pepper Chicken Breasts

Ingredients

- 4-6 chicken breasts, bone-in
- Juice of 1 lemon
- 1-2 lemons, thinly sliced
- Salt and lemon pepper to taste

1 prepared plank, alder or fruit wood, soaked in water (See page 57, **Plank Preparation**)

Drizzle lemon juice over chicken breasts. Rub salt into chicken, lifting up skin and massaging underneath. Rub a generous amount of lemon pepper into breast meat. If desired, place a slice of lemon under skin. Place lemon slices on prepared plank. Lay seasoned chicken atop lemons. Grill or bake at 375° 45-60 minutes or until internal temperature reaches 170°. Serve chicken hot or chill and serve on chicken salad.

Recipe Variation

Substitute Chicken Spice Rub (page 32) for lemon pepper or marinate in Southwestern Marinade (page 29), 2 hours before cooking.

Fajitas

Ingredients

- 1 pound beef sirloin, sliced into strips
- 1 onion, sliced
- 1 green bell pepper, sliced
- 1 red or yellow bell pepper, sliced
- 1 portabello mushroom, sliced
- 2 tablespoons fajita seasoning mix or Basic Beef Rub (page 27) with 1 teaspoon cumin and 1/2 teaspoon chili powder added
- 2 tablespoons olive oil
- Salt and pepper to taste

1 large prepared plank, oak or fruit wood, soaked in water (See page 57, **Plank Preparation**).

Place sliced beef in a large sealable plastic bag. Sprinkle in seasoning and massage into meat. Let sit at least 20 minutes. Place sliced vegetables in a large sealable plastic bag and coat with 2 tablespoons olive oil. Two separate bags can be used for onions and peppers if desired. Preheat a large plank on the grill or in the oven, at least 15-20 minutes. Place meat and veggies atop the plank. Grill or bake at 375° 25-30 minutes or until meat is done and vegetables are tender. Rotate food around with tongs to ensure even cooking. Serve with warm tortillas, salsa, sour cream and guacamole if desired.

Recipe Variation

Chicken or pork can be substituted for beef.

Vegetable-Topped Steaks

Ingredients

- 4-6 sirloin steaks or cube steaks, 1"
- Basic Beef Rub (page 27)
- 1/2 cup red pepper, chopped
- 1/2 cup green pepper, chopped
- 1/2 cup onion, chopped
- 1 tomato, chopped
- 1-2 jalapeño peppers, chopped
- Olive oil

1 prepared plank, cedar, hickory or alder, soaked in red wine or water (See page 57, **Plank Preparation**).

Sprinkle Basic Beef Rub over steaks and lightly pound with a meat mallet or tenderizing tool. Brush both sides of steaks with olive oil. In a bowl, mix peppers, onion and tomato. On a hot grill or skillet, sear steaks 30 seconds on each side. Place half of pepper mixture on a prepared plank. Place steaks atop pepper mixture and top with remaining pepper mixture. Grill or bake at 350° 20-25 minutes or until steaks reach desired doneness.

Horseradish-Stuffed Steak Rolls

Sprinkle both sides of thinly cut or pounded steaks with salt and pepper. In a medium bowl, combine all stuffing ingredients. Divide stuffing mixture equally among steaks. Roll steaks up, placing them seam-side down on prepared plank. Lightly brush with olive oil. Grill or bake at 375° 20-25 minutes or to desired doneness.

Ingredients

- 1 pound beef steaks, thinly sliced
- 1 cup spinach, finely chopped
- 2 tablespoons creamy horseradish
- 3 cloves garlic, pureed
- 1/2 teaspoon dried thyme
- Salt and pepper to taste
- Olive oil for brushing

1 prepared plank, cedar or oak, soaked in white wine or water (See page 57, **Plank Preparation**).

Recipe Variation

Substitute horseradish stuffing with cream cheese and Basil Pesto (page 17). Pounded, boneless, skinless chicken breasts can be substituted for beef.

Pot Roast

Place onion slices on prepared plank. Steam cut potatoes and carrots 4-5 minutes in the microwave. Place on plank on top of onions. Salt and pepper to taste and brush lightly with olive oil. Season roast with salt and pepper, place atop potato and carrot layer. Cover loosely with foil, tucking ends of foil 1/2" under plank. Grill or bake at 350° 45 minutes to 1 hour or until desired doneness, 145° (medium-rare) to 170° (well-done). Remove foil during last 10 minutes of cooking time. Let sit 10 minutes before slicing.

Ingredients

- 1 2-pound chuck roast
- 1 onion, sliced
- 1-2 baking potatoes, sliced
- 3-4 carrots, peeled and halved
- Salt and pepper to taste
- Olive oil

1 prepared plank, cedar or fruit wood, soaked in water (See page 57, **Plank Preparation**).

Stroganoff Tenderloin |

Ingredients

- 1 2-3-pound beef tenderloin
- Olive oil
- Salt and ground black pepper to taste

1 prepared plank, hickory or pecan, soaked in wine, vinegar or water
(See page 57, **Plank Preparation**).

Stroganoff Gravy

- 4 tablespoons butter,divided
- 1 cup mushrooms, thinly sliced
- 2 tablespoons flour
- 1 can beef stock
- 1/4 cup red wine
- 2 tablespoons ketchup
- 1 tablespoon Dijon mustard
- 1/2 cup sour cream

Trim fat and silver skin from tenderloin. Rub meat with olive oil and salt and pepper to taste. On a hot grill, sear grill marks into every side of the tenderloin, 1-2 minutes per side. Place on a prepared plank. Grill or bake at 375° 30-40 minutes or until internal temperature reaches 145°. Remove from heat and cover with foil, keep roast on the plank. Let rest 10-15 minutes. Cut into thin slices and serve with Stroganoff Gravy or sauce of choice.

Stroganoff Gravy Preparation

In a medium skillet, sauté mushrooms in 2 tablespoons butter. Remove from pan, set aside. In the same skillet, melt 2 tablespoons butter on medium heat. Add flour and whisk, cooking until lightly browned. Slowly add beef stock, wine, ketchup and mustard. Whisk until thick and smooth, 4-6 minutes. Add sautéed mushrooms and sour cream. Remove from heat and serve immediately.

Garlic Roast with Onion Relish

Puree garlic, sugar and spices in a food processor or mini-chopper. Pierce roast in many places with a fork. Coat roast completely with the garlic mixture. Marinate in the refrigerator 6-8 hours. Prior to cooking, let marinated roast sit at room temperature 30 minutes. Place on a prepared plank, cover loosely with foil, tucking ends of foil 1/2" under plank. Grill or bake at 350° 45 minutes to 1 hour or until desired doneness, 145° (medium-rare) to 170° (well-done). Let sit 10 minutes before slicing. Serve with Sweet Onion Relish.

Sweet Onion Relish Preparation

In a medium bowl, mix all ingredients until thoroughly combined. Marinate, refrigerated at least 12 hours before serving for optimal flavor.

Ingredients

- 1 1/2-pound beef roast or tri-tip
- 8-10 cloves garlic
- 1 tablespoon olive oil
- 1 tablespoon smoked paprika
- 1 tablespoon brown sugar
- 1 teaspoon black pepper
- 1 teaspoon salt

1 prepared plank, cedar or hickory, soaked in red wine or water (See page 57, **Plank Preparation**)

Sweet Onion Relish

- 2 cups sweet onion, finely chopped
- 3 stalks celery, diced
- 1/3 cup sugar
- 2 tablespoons cider vinegar
- 1 teaspoon salt
- 1/2 teaspoon celery seed
- 1/4 teaspoon white pepper
- 1 2-ounce jar diced pimento

Meat
Plank It!

Stuffed Sweet Potatoes

INGREDIENTS

- 3-4 orange-fleshed sweet potatoes
- 1 15-ounce can baked beans
- 1 15-ounce can kidney or pinto beans, drained and rinsed
- 1 8-ounce can crushed pineapple, drained
- 1/4 cup green pepper or green chilies, diced
- 2 tablespoons yellow mustard
- 5-10 dashes hot pepper sauce
- Salt and pepper to taste

Wash and dry potatoes. Bake at 350° for 30-45 minutes, or until slightly soft. Remove from oven and cool to the touch. Cut potatoes in half lengthwise, scooping out the middle of the potato. Make the center of the potato deeper to hold the topping. Set scooped out potato aside to use for pancakes or muffins. In a medium bowl combine crushed pineapple, green pepper, mustard and hot pepper sauce. Mix until thoroughly blended. Gently stir in baked and kidney or pinto beans. Salt and pepper to taste. Place sweet potatoes on prepared plank. Evenly distribute bean mixture down the middle of the potatoes. Plank cook potatoes 15-20 minutes or until warmed throughout.

1 prepared plank, cedar, pecan or fruit wood, soaked in vinegar or water
(See page 57, **Plank Preparation**).

Cornbread-Stuffed Portabella Mushrooms

INGREDIENTS

- 4-6 portabella mushrooms
- 1 tablespoon olive oil
- 1/4 cup celery, diced
- 1/4 cup bell pepper, diced
- 1/4 cup onion, diced
- 2 cloves garlic, minced
- 1/2 teaspoon tarragon, optional
- 2 cups cornbread, crumbled
- 1/2 cup parmesan cheese, grated
- Salt and pepper to taste
- 1/2 cup mozzarella cheese, optional

1 prepared plank, alder or fruit wood, soaked in white wine or water
(See page 57, **Plank Preparation**).

Clean mushrooms with a damp towel or mushroom brush. Remove stems and finely chop. Heat olive oil in medium skillet on medium-high heat. Sauté celery, peppers, onions and mushroom stems 7-10 minutes. Remove from heat, add garlic, tarragon, cornbread and parmesan cheese. Gently mix until combined. Brush both sides of mushrooms with olive oil. Salt and pepper both sides. Fill with stuffing mixture. Place stuffed mushrooms on a prepared plank. Grill or bake at 375° 25-30 minutes. Sprinkle with mozzarella cheese during last 10 minutes of cooking, if desired.

Tofu & Vegetable Kebabs

Ingredients

- 1 14.5-ounce package extra-firm tofu
- Spicy Sauce (page 36) or Teriyaki Marinade (page 28)

Use any combination of the following vegetables

- Red or yellow onion
- Yellow squash
- Zucchini squash
- Red bell pepper
- Green bell pepper
- Yellow bell pepper
- Cherry tomatoes
- Mushrooms

Metal or wooden skewers (soak wooden skewers at least 1 hour in water)
1 prepared plank, alder, oak or fruit wood (See page 57, **Plank Preparation**).

Remove tofu from package and press into paper towels to remove excess moisture. Cut to bite-sized pieces. Place tofu in marinade or sauce of choice and marinate at least 20 minutes. Cut vegetables into bite-sized pieces and marinate if desired or simply brush with olive oil. Thread vegetables and tofu on skewers. Place on a prepared plank. Grill or bake at 375° 20-25 minutes or until vegetables reach desired tenderness. Baste with marinade while grilling if desired.

Recipe Variation

Almost any vegetable can be prepared on a plank. For best results, steam or microwave vegetables that need longer cooking times prior to plank cooking.

Red Potatoes with Blue Cheese

Recipe Variation

Substitute baking potatoes for red potatoes and fill with desired fillings (cheese, chili, sautéed vegetables, bacon, chives and/or sour cream). Plank cook until toppings are warmed throughout.

Ingredients

- 8-10 small red potatoes
- 1/2 cup blue cheese, crumbled
- Salt and pepper to taste

1 prepared plank, cedar, hickory or fruit wood (See page 57, **Plank Preparation**).

Wash and dry potatoes. Place potatoes in a foil pouch and bake at 350° for 30 minutes, or until slightly soft. Remove from oven and cool to the touch. Make a small cut in the top of each potato and squeeze open. Top potatoes with salt, pepper and blue cheese. Place on prepared plank and grill or bake at 375° 10-15 minutes.

Shrimp-Stuffed Portabellas

Clean mushrooms with a damp towel or mushroom brush. Remove stems and finely chop. In a medium bowl mix cheeses with mayonnaise. Gently fold in olives, shrimp and mushroom stems. Brush both sides of mushrooms with olive oil. Salt and pepper both sides. Fill with stuffing mixture. Place stuffed mushrooms on a prepared plank. Grill or bake at 375° 20-25 minutes or until cheese mixture is bubbly and mushrooms are tender.

Ingredients

- 4-6 portobello mushrooms or 12-20 small mushrooms
- 1/2 cup cheddar cheese, grated
- 1/2 cup parmesan cheese, grated
- 1/2 cup mayonnaise
- 1/2 cup black olives, sliced
- 1/2 cup cooked bay or salad shrimp

1 prepared plank, cedar, oak or alder, soaked in white wine or water (See page 57, **Plank Preparation**).

Recipe Variation

This filling works well with small button or crimini mushrooms; reduce cooking time to 10-15 minutes. Chopped spinach or broccoli can be substituted for the shrimp.

Orzo-Stuffed Peppers

Ingredients

- 4 large red, yellow, orange or green bell peppers
- 2 tablespoons olive oil
- 1/4 cup onion, diced
- 2 cloves garlic, minced
- 1 1/4 cups orzo pasta, uncooked
- 1 cup fresh spinach, chopped
- 1 14.5-ounce can chicken broth
- 1/2 teaspoon Italian seasoning
- Olive oil for drizzling

1 prepared plank, cedar, pecan or fruit wood, soaked in white wine or water (See page 57, **Plank Preparation**).

Wash and dry peppers. Cut tops off peppers and discard all seeds. Set aside. In a large skillet, sauté onion and garlic in olive oil 3-6 minutes. Add orzo and stir until lightly browned. Add remaining ingredients and simmer until liquid is absorbed. Fill peppers with orzo mixture. Arrange peppers on prepared plank and drizzle olive oil over peppers. Grill or bake at 375° 35-40 minutes or until peppers are tender.

Recipe Variation

For a complete meal add 1 cup cooked and seasoned ground beef, turkey or sausage to the orzo stuffing.

Zucchini Parmesan

Ingredients

- 2-4 zucchini, cut into strips
- 1/3 cup Italian dressing or
- Rosemary Balsamic Marinade (page 50)
- 1/2 cup corn flakes, crushed
- 1/3 cup parmesan cheese, grated
- 2 tablespoons butter, melted

1 prepared plank, alder, oak or fruit wood (See page 57, **Plank Preparation**).

Place cut zucchini into a sealable plastic bag. Add dressing and let marinate at least 15 minutes. In a small bowl mix corn flakes, cheese and butter until thoroughly combined. Arrange zucchini strips on a prepared plank. Take care not to stack the strips more than two high. Sprinkle with corn flake mixture and grill or bake at 375° 15-25 minutes or until topping is toasted and zucchini is tender.

Vegetables *Plank It!*

Little Smokeys with BBQ Sauce

Ingredients

- 1 pound ground beef
- 1/2 cup soda cracker crumbs
- 1 egg
- 2 tablespoons onion, minced
- 2 teaspoons Worcestershire sauce
- 1/2 teaspoon salt
- 1/4 teaspoon black pepper

1 prepared plank, cedar or hickory, soaked in red wine or water
(See page 57, **Plank Preparation**)

BBQ Sauce

- 1/4 cup ketchup
- 1 tablespoon red wine vinegar
- 1 tablespoon Worcestershire sauce
- 1 tablespoon honey
- 1/2 tablespoon Dijon mustard
- 1/4 teaspoon salt
- 1/4 teaspoon liquid hickory smoke, optional
- 3-10 dashes hot pepper sauce

In a large bowl, mix all ingredients until well blended. Do not over mix. Shape into balls using one heaping tablespoon of meat mixture. Place meatballs on prepared plank and brush with BBQ Sauce several times while cooking. Grill or bake at 375° 20-25 minutes or until internal temperature reaches 160°.

In a small bowl, mix BBQ sauce ingredients until thoroughly combined.

Curried Drop-Meatballs with Raita

In a large bowl, mix all ingredients until well blended. Do not over mix. Using two spoons to shape, drop meat mixture by rounded spoonfuls onto prepared plank. Grill or bake at 375° 20-25 minutes or until internal temperature reaches 160°. Serve with Hummus (page 146) if desired.

1 prepared plank, alder or fruit wood
(See page 57, **Plank Preparation**).

Ingredients

- 1 pound ground pork, turkey or lamb
- 2 green onions
- 1/4 cup yogurt
- 1/4 cup ground almonds
- 1/4 cup oatmeal or oat bran
- 2 tablespoons fresh mint, finely chopped
- 1 tablespoon olive oil
- 3 cloves garlic, crushed
- Juice and zest of 1 lemon
- 1 teaspoon curry powder
- 1/2 teaspoon salt
- 1/2 teaspoon ground cardamom or coriander
- 1/4 teaspoon cayenne pepper

Cucumber Raita

- 3/4 cup plain yogurt
- 1 large cucumber, peeled and diced
- Juice of 1/2 lemon
- 1/4 cup finely chopped fresh chives
- 1/4 teaspoon salt

In a medium bowl, gently combine all ingredients.

Shrimp Puffs

In a small skillet, sauté shallots and mushrooms in butter until soft. Cool completely. In a medium bowl, gently combine remaining ingredients. Place one sheet of phyllo on a cutting board. Brush sheet with melted butter, top with a second sheet of phyllo. Cut the double layer of phyllo into 3 equal sections, lengthwise. Place a tablespoon of shrimp filling at the bottom of a section. Diagonally fold phyllo over the filling, taking corner to the opposite edge, like folding a flag. Continue folding, keeping the triangle shape all the way to end. Place puffs, seam side down, on prepared plank. Brush the tops of the puffs with melted butter. Grill or bake at 375° 15-20 minutes or until triangles are golden brown. Shrimp Puffs may be prepared in advance and refrigerated, add 5 minutes to cooking time.

Ingredients

- 3 tablespoons butter
- 1/3 cup shallots or onions, diced
- 1/2 cup mushrooms, finely chopped
- 1/3 cup green olives, finely chopped
- 1 cup bay or salad shrimp
- 1/2 cup sour cream
- 1/4 cup feta cheese, crumbled
- 10 sheets prepared phyllo dough (approximately 9" x 14")
- 1/4 cup melted butter, for brushing

1 prepared plank, alder or fruit wood
(See page 57, **Plank Preparation**)

Recipe Variation

Crab meat or ground sausage can be substituted for shrimp. Substitute capers or black olives for green olives.

Hazelnut Cheese Bites

RECIPE VARIATION

Substitute pepper jack cheese for cheddar cheese. Substitute a favorite pesto for the parsley and dry mustard. Any nuts can be used for the hazelnuts.

INGREDIENTS

- 1 1/4 cups bread crumbs
- 1 cup cheddar cheese, grated
- 1/2 cup hazelnuts, ground
- 1 tablespoon flour
- 2 green onions, finely chopped
- 2 tablespoons fresh parsley, finely chopped
- 1 teaspoon dry mustard
- 1/2 teaspoon salt
- 1/4 teaspoon white pepper
- 2 eggs, well beaten
- 2 tablespoons milk
- 2 tablespoons melted butter
- Melted butter for brushing

1 prepared plank, cedar, alder or fruit wood (See page 57, **Plank Preparation**).

In a medium bowl, mix all dry ingredients until thoroughly combined. In a small bowl, beat eggs until frothy and add remaining ingredients. Add egg mixture to dry ingredients and stir until blended. Divide mixture into 15-20 balls and form into desired shape. Place cheese bites on prepared plank and brush with melted butter. Grill or bake at 375° 15-20 minutes or until lightly browned.

Crab Cakes

RECIPE VARIATION

Substitute 1 cup cooked corn and jalapeños for crab. Any cooked and deboned fish can be used instead of crab.

INGREDIENTS

- 1 pound crab meat
- 1 cup seasoned bread crumbs
- 1 egg, beaten
- 1/4 cup mayonnaise
- 1 teaspoon Worcestershire sauce
- 1/2 teaspoon dry mustard
- 1/2 teaspoon salt
- 1/4 teaspoon pepper
- Melted butter for brushing

1 prepared plank, cedar, alder or fruit wood (See page 57, **Plank Preparation**).

In a medium bowl, combine all ingredients except for the crab. Gently mix in crab. If mixture is too dry to form cakes, add more mayonnaise. Shape mixture into small cakes. Place crab cakes on prepared plank and brush with melted butter. Grill or bake at 375° 10-15 minutes or until lightly browned. Flip cakes over once during cooking. Serve with Spicy Sauce or Green Sauce (pages 36, 42).

Caramelized Veggies & Brie

Heat olive oil in medium skillet on medium-high heat. Sauté onions and peppers 10-15 minutes. Add sugar and vinegar and cook an additional 10 minutes, stirring frequently. Remove from heat, add salt and pepper. Place cheese wedge on prepared plank, topping with sautéed vegetables. Grill or bake at 350° until cheese is warm and beginning to melt, serve immediately with bread, crackers or tortilla chips.

INGREDIENTS

- 1 7-ounce wedge brie cheese
- 2 tablespoons olive oil
- 1 cup onion, thinly sliced
- 1 bell pepper, thinly sliced
- 2 teaspoons sugar
- 2 teaspoons cider vinegar
- 1/2 teaspoon salt
- 1/4 teaspoon white pepper

1 prepared plank, maple, oak or alder, soaked in white wine or water (See page 57, **Plank Preparation**).

Confetti Sausage Balls

INGREDIENTS

- 1 pound seasoned sausage
- 1/2 cup biscuit baking mix
- 1 egg
- 1/2 cup fresh spinach, finely chopped
- 1/4 cup pineapple, finely chopped
- 1/4 cup red bell pepper, finely chopped

1 prepared plank, maple, oak or alder, soaked in white wine or water (See page 57, **Plank Preparation**).

In a large bowl, mix all ingredients until well blended. Do not over mix. Shape into balls using one heaping tablespoon of meat mixture. Place balls on prepared plank. Grill or bake at 375° 20-25 minutes or until internal temperature reaches 160°.

RECIPE VARIATION

Substitute diced green chilies for pineapple and sundried tomatoes for bell pepper. For cheesy sausage balls, add 1/2 cup of any grated or crumbled cheese.

Appetizers
Plank It!

Soak wrap in water.

Secure with a metal clip or kitchen twine.

Plank Preparation

STEPS

1. Soak plank in water or suggested liquid, minimum 1 hour, maximum 24 hours.

2. Preheat plank on grill at medium heat 5 minutes, or in a 350° oven 10 minutes.

3. Brush a light coating of olive oil onto cooking side of board.

Plank Cooking Options

Grill (Direct heat): Use the lowest setting on a gas grill or low charcoal heat. Place plank with food directly over the heat source. Cook with the lid closed so smoke surrounds food and infuses flavor. Plank should reach heavy smoke in 15-20 minutes. When plank begins to smoke, check often—use spray bottle filled with water to extinguish any flame on the plank. This method promotes a heavy smoke flavor.

Grill (Indirect Heat): Use a medium setting on a gas grill. If using charcoal, pile coals to one side. Place plank opposite the heat source. Cook with lid closed so smoke surrounds food and infuses flavor. Plank should begin to smoke after 15-20 minutes. The plank should not catch fire using this method. Cooking time increases due to the lower temperature. This method promotes a light smoke flavor.

Oven: Preheat oven and board to 350° or as stated in recipe. Place plank with food, directly on oven rack. Position a foil-lined baking sheet on the rack below the plank to catch any drippings. This method infuses a light smoke essence into food. Planks can be reused.

Warning: When cooking, never leave planks unattended. Avoid repeatedly opening grill cover as this can cause flare-ups and lost heat. When opening grill, take caution not to inhale or stand in direct smoke.

than others, which can greatly aid in the cooking of your food should you require more or less heat.

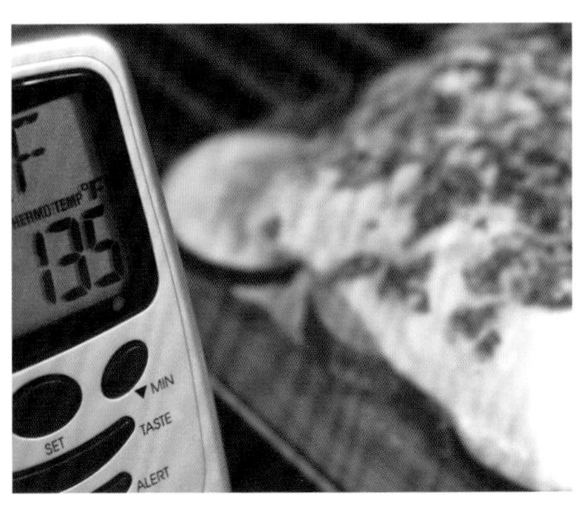

Grilling units featuring temperature-control devices are convenient, but not necessary. A standing temperature gauge works well, is inexpensive, and can be placed directly on the plank when cooking to give the truest reading of the unit temperature. A meat thermometer is a must, especially when cooking large cuts of meat such as a whole chicken, beef roast or pork loin.

When cooking over direct heat on the grill, that is, where the food is placed on the lowest rack, directly over the flame, use a low setting- if not the lowest setting possible. Cook with the lid closed so smoke completely engulfs the food to infuse flavor. The goal is to reach a level of heavy smoke in 15-20 minutes; doing so any sooner can result in uneven heating, likely burning the outer edges of the food. Once the plank begins to smoke, check often, spray bottle in hand, to extinguish any flames on the plank. This method promotes a strong smoke flavor.

When cooking over indirect heat on the grill, where food is placed away from the flame or in a hanging basket, use a medium heat setting. If using charcoal, pile the coals to one side and place plank opposite or elevated above the heat source. Cook with the lid closed, so the smoke surrounds the food to infuse flavor. Here, the plank should begin to smoke after 15-20 minutes. The plank should not catch fire when cooking over indirect heat. This method promotes a light smoke flavor, and takes longer to cook foods due to a lower overall internal temperature.

When grilling outside, weather conditions can be ever-changing, thus impacting cooking times. Outside temperature, humidity levels, even wind direction can impact the cooking rate of a grill. Cooking temperatures on the grill should range between 350-450 degrees. Knowing the anatomy of your grill and how it responds to varying climatic and seasonal conditions is important, and easy to learn with time.

Cooking With Planks and Wraps In The Oven

Cooking with planks and wraps in the oven is a great option. Though this approach is easy to maintain control over, it does not attain the concentrated smoke flavors achieved on the outside grill. Nonetheless, it is a very popular way of cooking, and it does impart a gentle woody essence into foods. One of the most appealing qualities to inside planking is the attractive aroma it introduces into the house.

For plank cooking, begin by preheating the oven and the presoaked plank, together, to 350°. Once oven has been preheated, oil the plank,

place food on plank and put directly on oven rack. It's a good idea to position a foil-lined baking sheet on the rack below the plank, to catch any drippings. Planks cooked in the oven can be used repeatedly. There are special, oven-only planks on the market, complete with internal adjustment rods to control warping. These specialized oven planks are considerably thicker when compared to grilling-style planks and can be pricey, but the extended cooking opportunities they promote make them a good value.

Many foods, such as fish, seafood and vegetables, benefit from a moist cooking environment. It is easy to apply this technique when plank cooking in the oven. Simply place plank in a shallow, ovenproof pan, partially submerging it in water or other liquids; do not let the liquids touch the food on the plank. Additional liquid may be added during the cooking to keep the plank moist and steaming.

When done cooking on a plank, be it in the oven or on the grill, quickly cool the plank. This will preserve the plank, ensuring it doesn't continue to cook or smolder on the underside, or internally. Cleaning the plank is the final step, if looking to reuse it. Thoroughly wash with warm water and mild dish soap. A solution of one part bleach to nine parts water can also be used to clean and sterilize a plank. Scrub to make sure all fat residues are removed and store the plank in a dry place, so molds do not form.

When reusing a plank that has become overly darkened, go over the cooking side with sand paper. Planks used in the oven can become laden with oils, masking the natural wood flavor. Sanding will recharge the plank, exposing fresh wood which allows for even cooking temperatures and better-tasting food. Be sure to soak the plank prior to each cooking session, and always preheat the plank which not only makes for more efficient cooking, but also sterilizes it.

Wood Types

Wraps (wood papers) are commonly found in cedar and alder but are now available in apple, maple and cherry. Use the same flavor guidelines as given for plank flavors.

Pecan

Cherry

Maple

Oak

PLEASE NOTE: WOOD TYPES ARE SUGGESTED IN EVERY RECIPE, BUT DO NOT LIMIT YOURSELF; EXPERIMENT AND FIND OUT WHAT FLAVORS SUIT YOUR TASTES BEST.

The Most Common Planking Woods

Alder: Common in the Pacific Northwest, gives off a delicate smokey flavor that is slightly sweet. Recommended for fish, poultry, pork and vegetables.

Cedar: One of the most diverse, Western red cedar produces a deep yet lenient wood flavor. Recommended for fish, pork, beef and any foods with bold spicy flavors.

Other Flavors Readily Available

Apple: Preferred for its mild, fruity flavor with a hint of sweetness. Recommended for all smoked foods. Great also as a blend with stronger woods such as hickory and mesquite.

Apricot: A mild, sweet fruit wood. Recommended for pork and poultry.

Birch: Similar to the fruit woods. Recommended for pork and poultry.

Cherry: Slightly sweet and fruity, this mellow wood is great for blending with stronger woods. Recommended most for poultry, this wood can be used with all foods.

Hickory: The most common wood used for smoking, bold and sometimes peppery with a hint of sweetness. Recommended most for pork, chicken and beef, also flavors well with mesquite.

Lemon: Stronger smoke flavor, citrus woods pair well with milder woods.

Maple: One of the most versatile smoking woods, mild and slightly sweet, flavors can vary in different regions. Recommended for vegetables and all other smoked foods.

Mesquite: Perfect for a short time on the grill, strong and tangy. Recommended most for beef, vegetables, pork and poultry, goes well with hickory.

Nectarine & Peach: Similar to pecan and the fruit woods. Recommended for pork, poultry and beef.

Pear: Similar to apple, a mild, sweet fruit wood. Recommended for all smoked foods. Great also as a blend with stronger woods such as hickory and mesquite.

Pecan: Common in the South, pecan is a versatile, mellow smoke flavor. Recommended for all smoked foods. Great also as a blend with stronger woods such as hickory and mesquite.

Oak: One of the most common fuels, oak has a subtle flavor that goes with a variety of foods and lends itself well to blending with stronger smoking woods. Recommended for all smoked foods.

Helpful Tips

For easy serving sizes, precut fish to the skin in the desired serving size. Place slices of lemons, limes or oranges, or perhaps herb leaves or sliced garlic, in the cut between each serving portion.

Placing meat or fish on a bed of vegetables, fruit or herbs, helps heat and smoke penetrate more evenly. The food placed underneath stays moist and acquires a great smoke flavor.

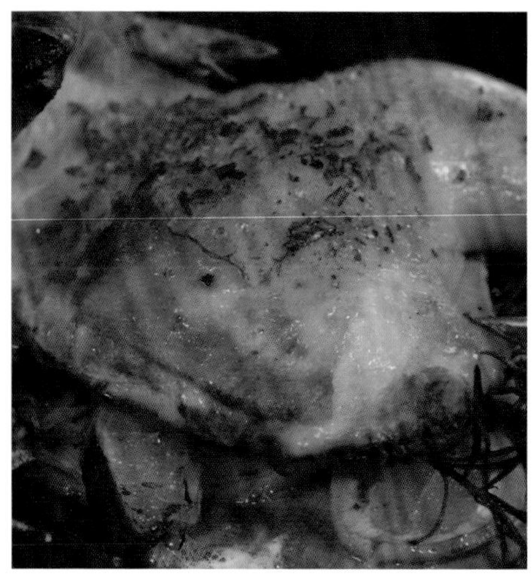

Always control flare-ups immediately. The goal with plank cooking is to bathe food in smoke, not burn up the plank.

For easier handling, if space allows, foil can be placed at the end of a plank to keep the area from excessive charring.

Bathing food in rich smoke flavors is the goal of outdoor plank cooking. Even foods that cook a short time will take-on tastes from plank cooking.

Several planks/wraps can be used at one time on the grill. Keep adequate space between each plank for airflow, and always watch food closely. Control all flare-ups immediately.

Wrap Preparation

STEPS

1. Soak wrap in water or suggested liquid 10-15 minutes.

2. Place food on moist wrap, roll closed and secure with a metal clip or kitchen twine.

3. Always cook on indirect heat on a grill and do not cook in an oven exceeding 350°.

WRAPS SHOULD NOT BE DRIED PRIOR TO COOKING. ALWAYS PLACE FOOD TO BE COOKED ON SOAKED WRAPS.

If looking for additional flavor, rub a clove of garlic over both sides of the dried plank or wet wrap. You can also lay a bed of fresh herbs, vegetables or fruits on the cooking side of the plank or wrap, placing the food to be cooked on top.

Wraps, narrow planks, and regular-sized planks that have been cut down in size, are great for dinner parties, with participants creating their own plank-cooked meals. Here, the food of choice, be it a fish fillet or veggies, can be dressed in herbs, spices, rubs or sauces by each individual. Each custom-created plank or wrap can be cooked simultaneously, and in the end, everyone can sit down and enjoy their special meal together.

Words of Caution

When cooking on a plank or wrap, never leave the area unattended. When cooking on a grill, avoid repeatedly opening the cover as this can cause flare-ups and lost heat. When opening the grill, do not stand directly over the unit, as smoke and heat will escape. Be careful not to inhale smoke or allow it to billow into the eyes. Always cook wraps over indirect heat.

When cooking fatty foods, note their tendency to cause flare-ups in the bottom of the grill, even on the plank itself. By close monitoring during the cooking process, excessive flare-ups can be kept in check.

When the plank begins to smoke, check to prevent undue flare-ups. Use a spray bottle filled with water to extinguish any flame on the plank. This approach not only prevents overcooking, it promotes a more robust flavor due to increased smoke production.

If serving food directly off a plank or wrap, or moving either with the food still on it, be certain to place it on a safe surface. The underside of the wood is extremely hot and can cause some surfaces to melt or catch fire. Having a large metal spatula with which to lift and transport the wood is a good idea and allows for easy placement onto a large plate. Take care not to bring a burning or even a smoldering plank or wrap inside the house.

If removing food from the plank while on the grill, be sure to also remove the plank from the grill surface. It's good practice to immediately douse the hot plank in water, by either running it under an outside faucet or submerging it in a bucket of water.

Know Your Grill

Plank cooking is one of those undertakings that is best mastered through repeated practice. One of the key steps is getting to know your grill and how it performs. Whether you cook on a side-by-side or front-to-back burner grill, or cook on a charcoal barbecue, it's critical to learn where the hotspots are. Some portions of the grill may burn hotter

Internet sites. Wraps are different from planks in that they are much thinner, and not meant to ever catch fire to produce smoke. Using a presoaked wrap helps to keep food moist while imparting a woodsy essence. Wraps can be used rolled or flat, in the oven or on the grill, over indirect heat.

Wraps can be found in several wood flavors. Cedar and alder are the most common but apple, maple and cherry are also available. Follow the same guidelines for choosing plank flavors when choosing wood wraps.

Unless you have special wood-working equipment that allows you to cut paper-thin sheets of wood, your best bet is purchasing the wraps.

Please note: All recipes in the plank section can be halved or quartered and cooked in a grilling paper. Wraps can be used flat, like a plank, and cooked over indirect heat on the grill or in the oven.

Soaking & Seasoning Planks and Wraps For Cooking

Prior to cooking with any plank or wrap, it should first be soaked. Soaking serves several purposes, the main goal being to foster the absorption of fluids which ultimately keeps food moist when cooking. This allows food to retain valued nutrients and results in a more distinct taste quality. In addition to keeping foods from drying out, soaking planks helps food cook evenly. This means food won't get overdone on the edges, while only partially cooked in the middle. The only exception to the soaking rule is if the plank is to be used in the oven to prepare a quick cooking food such as garlic bread or a very thin fillet of fish.

Soaking wood prior to cooking also reduces its burn rate when placed on the grill. The end result is a nice, woody smoke essence versus a harsh smoke flavor which can come from cooking on dry or charred wood.

If soaked and closely managed during the cooking process, some planks may be used repeatedly. Some of the harder woods, like oak or maple, can be used many times if properly cared for. Planks used in the oven can last through dozens of cookings, as they are not exposed to direct flames. Wraps can only be used one time; always dispose of them after initial use.

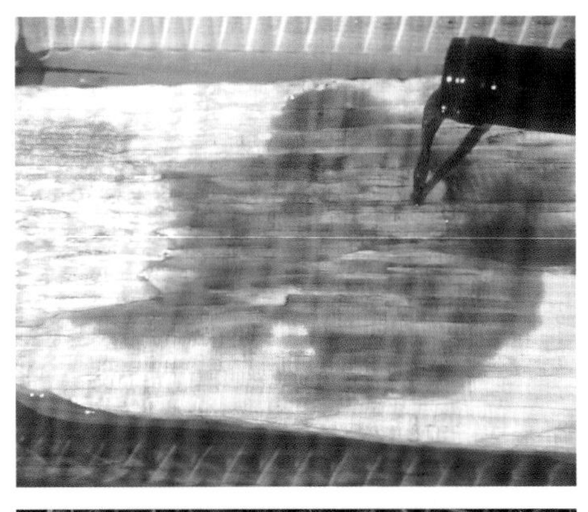

While water is the most common liquid in which to soak planks and wraps, fruit juices, vinegar, wine and other alcohols can also be used. Fully submerging a plank or wrap in these mediums imparts light flavors of the liquids into the foods being cooked. If wishing to tone down the flavor of the liquids which planks are soaked in, mix them with water.

Soaking times for planks can range from one to 24 hours, with one hour being the minimum. Wraps only need to soak 10-15 minutes. Depending on the size and type of wood, as well as personal preference, soaking times can vary. Tight-grained, larger planks can soak longer than thin, more open-grained woods.

Once soaked, remove the plank and place it on the grill, cooking side down, at medium heat and allow it to dry out and preheat for five minutes; be careful not to let the plank catch fire. If cooking in the house, place plank in a 350° oven for 10 minutes. Once heated in the grill or oven, brush a light coating of olive oil onto the cooking side of the board. The oil will season the wood for cooking, keep food from sticking to the wood and help the food retain moisture and nutrients.

Getting Started

What To Look For In A Plank

The more plank cooking you do, the more versed you'll become at targeting what tastes are most appealing. If you do a great deal of plank cooking, you may wish to explore outside the realm of the woods most commonly used; then again, you may be pleased with stockpiling general woods like cedar or alder.

When cooking on a plank, avoid using resinous woods such as pine, fir, juniper or poplar as these and other woods like them may contain volatile oils. If buying wood direct from a lumber yard or building supply store, be certain the woods have not been treated with any chemicals. You want either kiln or naturally dried hardwoods to cook on.

If you have access to raw wood—trees you can fall and split yourself—you'll find these natural wood *"sections"* make good planking material. Western red cedar, alder, maple and oak are some of the most commonly used woods in raw form, straight from the tree. The key to obtaining a good-quality, raw cooking plank is storing the split segments in a dry place where they can naturally cure without mold forming.

Due to convenience and safety purposes, many people elect to purchase prepackaged woods, ready to cook, from commercial producers of the product.

The more plank-proficient you become, the more you'll want to experiment with different wood types. Deriving individual wood flavors can be accomplished by soaking planks in different liquids, but for a true change of taste, cooking on different species of wood is the best way to find variety.

When obtaining planks, be sure the dimensions of the wood will fit inside your grill or oven, prior to cooking—if you have a way to cut larger planks to size, this is no concern. You'll also want to make sure that, prior to placing food on the plank, it will fit. The edges of planks tend to burn, so be certain the food can be situated on the plank with an inch or so to spare on all sides.

What To Look For In A Wrap

New to many cooks, wood papers or wraps are quickly finding their way to many specialty food stores and can be attained from many

The flavor of many foods, both savory and sweet, are dramatically accentuated when cooked on wood. In addition, an appealing, ready-to-serve presentation can be attained directly from the grill or oven. To many people, the novelty of preparing food on a plank or wrap is especially enjoyable for both indoor and outdoor entertainment, no matter what the time of year.

This book contains many recipes and handling techniques unique to plank cooking and cooking with wood papers. All recipes can be interchanged—plank recipes will work on wraps and vice versa. Wood wraps are not suitable for cooking times over 30 minutes and should not be used over direct heat. Plank recipes can be halved or quartered to fit on smaller wraps. Almost any recipe can be adapted to cook on a plank or wrap; the fun is in the experimentation.

Once the basics of plank cooking and cooking with wraps are mastered, a whole new world of preparing food presents itself. When you discover the scrumptious flavors and exquisite textures that cooking on wood has to offer, you'll be glad you learned the techniques sooner rather than later.

Plank It!

The process of cooking food on cut wood dates back to Native American cultures on both the East and West coasts of North America. This style of cooking results in tender, juicy, delectable foods, ranging from meats to desserts. Today, plank cooking and cooking with wood papers (wraps) has been refined to meet the needs of modern-day appliances, such as grills, barbecues and ovens.

Woods that have been cut, planed, sanded and sometimes kiln-dried, present abundant opportunities in which food can be prepared. Growing in popularity among restaurants and culinary institutes the world over, cooking on wood infuses food with a rich, smokey essence. Rather than waiting for smoke-cured meats to enjoy the flavor natural woods have to offer, now, by cooking on a plank or wrap, the alluring taste is only minutes away.

Vanilla Grilled Pineapple

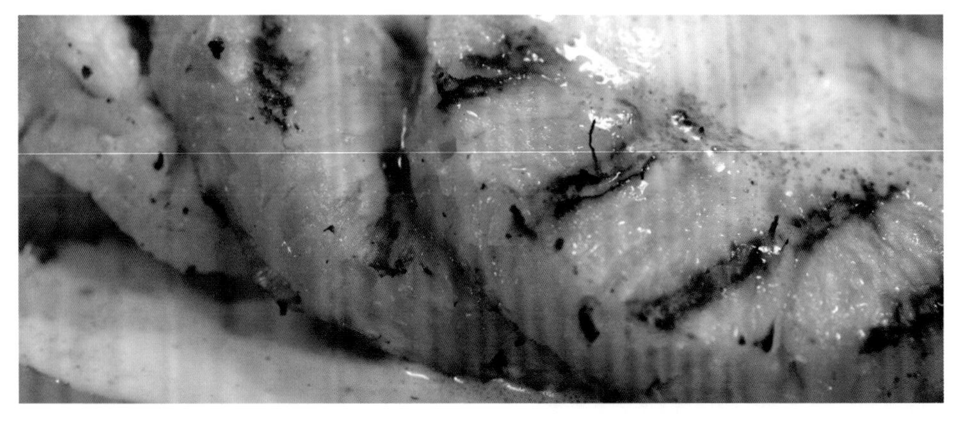

In a small bowl, combine oil and vanilla. Brush pineapple rings with oil mixture and place on a well- greased hot grill. Grill until grill marks appear, 3-4 minutes. Turn and repeat on the other side. Garnish with Cinnamon Clove Whipped Cream.

Cinnamon Clove Whipped Cream Preparation

In a large, cold bowl beat whipping cream with a whisk or electric mixer until fluffy. Add remaining ingredients and whip an additional 15 seconds.

Ingredients

- 1 pineapple, peeled, cored and sliced 1/2"
- 2 tablespoons canola oil
- 2 teaspoons vanilla

Cinnamon Clove Whipped Cream

- 1 pint cold whipping cream
- 1/3 cup sugar
- 1/2 teaspoon vanilla
- 1/2 teaspoon cinnamon
- 1/4 teaspoon cloves

Fruit Salad on a Stick

Use any combination of the following fruits

- 1 Pear
- 1 Mango
- 1 Banana
- 1 Kiwi
- 1/2 Pineapple
- 1 pint strawberries

Fruit Marinade

- 1 cup orange juice
- 1/4 cup balsamic vinegar
- 1/4 cup sugar
- 2 tablespoons light olive oil

Metal or wooden skewers

(soak skewers at least 1 hour in water)

In a bowl or large sealable plastic bag, combine all marinade ingredients. Cut fruit into bite-sized pieces and add to the marinade. Toss lightly, let sit 10-20 minutes. Thread fruit onto skewers. Grill at medium-high heat. If using wooden skewers, place a sheet of foil under the exposed wood to prevent them from burning. Cook 2-4 minutes per side. Baste with marinade while grilling. Serve with Marshmallow Cream Dip if desired.

Marshmallow Cream Dip

- 1 8-ounce package cream cheese, softened
- 1 7-ounce jar marshmallow cream
- 1/4 teaspoon nutmeg

In a food processor or with an electric mixer, whip ingredients until thoroughly combined.

Chocolate-Stuffed Bananas

INGREDIENTS

- 3-4 bananas
- 1 tablespoon canola oil
- 1 small bar milk or dark chocolate, broken into squares
- 1/2 cup toasted almond pieces
- Vanilla ice cream

Leaving peel on, cut bananas in half, lengthwise. Brush cut side with canola oil and place, skin side up on a well-lubricated medium-hot grill. Grill until grill marks appear, 3-4 minutes. Turn banana over and insert chocolate squares into cut side of the banana. Heat until chocolate begins to melt. Serve immediately with vanilla ice cream topped with toasted almonds.

Desserts
Grill It!

Seafood Pasta

Ingredients

- 2 cups cooked seafood
- 3 tablespoons extra virgin olive oil
- 3 cloves garlic, minced
- 1 cup fresh parsley, chopped
- 8-12 ounces pasta, cooked and drained

In a large skillet on medium heat, sauté garlic in olive oil 1-2 minutes. Add seafood, sautéing an additional 2-3 minutes. Toss in cooked pasta and fresh parsley, sauté until warm throughout and serve immediately.

Recipe Variation

Toss seafood and pasta with Lemony Spinach Pesto (page 146) or Cuban Garlic Sauce (page 147).

Tropical Fish Packets

Ingredients

- 4-6 servings white fish (tilapia, snapper, bass), cubed
- 1 green bell pepper, thinly sliced
- 1 tomato, chopped
- 1/2 onion, thinly sliced
- 1/2 cup fresh parsley, chopped
- Juice and zest of 1 lemon
- 1 can coconut milk
- 1/4 teaspoon curry
- 6-10 dashes hot pepper sauce
- Salt and pepper to taste

Cut fish into bite-sized pieces. In a large bowl, mix all ingredients except fish. Divide fish evenly, placing in the center of each piece of aluminum foil. Top fish with vegetable-coconut mixture, salt and pepper to taste. Loosely wrap foil around mixture, sealing packet at both ends. These packets can be prepared in advance and kept refrigerated. Add a few minutes to cooking time if putting on the grill directly from the refrigerator. Grill on medium heat 12-15 minutes or until fish is done and vegetables are tender. Serve with rice and Tropical Salsa (page 31) or Mango Salsa (page 147).

Garlic Mussels

INGREDIENTS

- 3-4 pounds mussels
- 1/2 cup butter
- 4 cloves garlic, pureed
- 1 teaspoon Italian seasoning or 1/4 cup fresh herbs of choice, chopped

In a small saucepan, melt butter on medium heat. Add garlic and cook 1-2 minutes. Remove from heat and add Italian seasoning or herbs. Set aside. Scrub mussels under cold water, discard any open or cracked shells. Place mussels on a hot grill over indirect heat. Grill 2-5 minutes until the shells open. Discard any mussels that do not open. Place open mussels on a platter and drizzle garlic butter into each shell. Serve immediately.

SMOKE SUGGESTIONS:
Pacific Northwest Blend (page 8), alder, cherry

Caribbean Salmon Steaks

INGREDIENTS

- 6-8 salmon steaks, 3/4" thick

CARIBBEAN MARINADE

- Juice of 2 limes
- 2 tablespoons canola oil
- 2 tablespoons honey
- 3 cloves garlic, minced
- 1/2 tablespoon red pepper flakes
- 2-6 dashes hot pepper sauce
- 2 tablespoons fresh basil or cilantro, chopped
- 1/2 teaspoon salt
- 1 lime, sliced
- Fresh basil or cilantro for garnish, optional

In a small bowl mix marinade ingredients until thoroughly combined. Place fish steaks in a shallow pan. Pour marinade over steaks, turning steaks over to coat both sides. Marinate 5-10 minutes. Place steaks on a well-greased, hot grill. Grill 4-5 minutes per side or until fish is opaque and flakes in large chunks. Serve topped with a slice of lime and fresh basil or cilantro.

SMOKE SUGGESTIONS:
Alder, pecan, Tropical Blend (page 8)

RECIPE VARIATION
Any fish can be substituted for the salmon steaks. Whole fillets or individual servings can be used.

Jumbo Shrimp with Green Sauce

Ingredients

- 16-20 jumbo shrimp, peeled and deveined
- Juice of 1 lemon
- 3 cloves garlic, pureed
- 2 tablespoons olive oil
- Salt to taste

Green Sauce

- 1 cup fresh cilantro leaves
- Juice from 2 lemons
- 2 tablespoons sugar
- 2 cloves garlic
- 2 large jalapeños, seeded and chopped
- 1/4 cup walnut pieces
- 1/2 teaspoon salt

Metal or Wooden Skewers

(soak skewers at least 1 hour in water)

In a small bowl, whisk together lemon juice, garlic and olive oil. Place shrimp in a shallow dish and drizzle with lemon mixture. Gently toss to coat and set aside for 10-20 minutes. Thread shrimp onto skewers, 2-4 shrimp each. Salt to taste. Grill at high heat on well-lubricated grill. Place a sheet of foil under the exposed skewers to prevent them from burning. Cook 2 minutes per side or until shrimp pinks and begins to curl. Drizzle with Green Sauce and serve immediately.

Green Sauce Preparation

In a food processor or mini-chopper, blend all ingredients until thoroughly combined. Serve immediately or keep refrigerated in a sealed container. This sauce is wonderful with any grilled food or used for a tortilla chip dip.

Smoke Suggestions:

Pacific Northwest Blend (page 8), alder

Mahi-Mahi in a Basket

Ingredients

- 1 pound mahi-mahi

Quick Fish Marinade

- 1 cloves garlic, pureed
- 1 tablespoon lemon juice
- 1 tablespoon fresh parsley, minced
- 1/2 teaspoon salt
- 1/4 teaspoon red chili flakes
- 1/4 teaspoon black pepper

Cut mahi-mahi to serving sizes. In a small bowl mix marinade ingredients until thoroughly combined. Place fish in a shallow pan or sealable plastic bag. Pour marinade over fish, turning over to coat both sides. Marinate at least 30 minutes. Refrigerate if marinating longer. Place fish in a well-greased fish basket and place on a medium-hot grill. Grill 3-5 minutes per side or until fish reaches desired doneness.

Smoke Suggestions: Alder, apple, cherry

Skinless Grill |

Ingredients

- 1 fillet of salmon or steelhead (3-6 servings)
- 1/2 cup butter, melted
- Juice and zest from 1 lemon
- 1 tablespoon seasoning salt (use your favorite pre-made or recipe below)

Fish Seasoning Salt

- 1 teaspoon salt
- 1 teaspoon black pepper
- 1 teaspoon garlic powder
- 1/2 teaspoon onion powder
- 1/2 teaspoon paprika
- 1/2 teaspoon dried dill, optional

In a small bowl mix butter, lemon juice and seasoning salt. Baste meat side of fish. Place fish skin side down on a well-greased hot grill. Grill 5 minutes or until grill marks appear. Using an extra-wide spatula, roll fillet over onto meat side. (Skin should peel away as you turn the fish over.) Remove the skin completely and discard any of the brown meat. Generously baste fish again, grilling 3-4 minutes. Carefully flip back on the original side, basting generously and cooking an additional 3-6 minutes or until fish is opaque and flakes in large chunks or has an internal temperature of 140°.

Fish Seasoning Salt Preparation

In a small bowl, mix all ingredients until thoroughly combined.

Smoke Suggestions:

Apple, cherry, oak

Crunchy Basil Halibut |

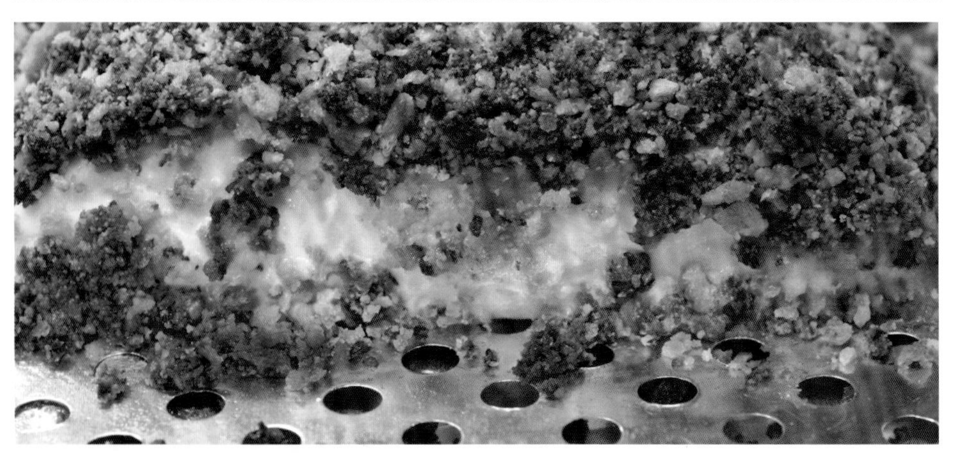

Ingredients

- 1 pound halibut
- 1/2 cup prepared basil pesto or (page 17)
- 12 Ritz-style crackers, crushed
- 3 tablespoons extra virgin olive oil

Cut halibut to desired serving sizes. In a small bowl, mix pesto, crushed crackers and oil until thoroughly combined. Place halibut on a greased fish grate or foil pan. Press mixture onto halibut pieces. Place on a preheated grill over indirect heat. Cook, covered until fish flakes in large chunks or reaches 140°. For a different flavor massage Herb Rub (page 144) into halibut and drizzle with olive oil 10 minutes prior to grilling.

Smoke Suggestions: Alder, apple, oak

Seared Asian Tuna

INGREDIENTS

- 1-2 pounds tuna, 1/2" steaks

JAPANESE MARINADE

- 3 tablespoons soy sauce
- 2 tablespoons wasabi powder
- 1 tablespoon chive or green onion, finely chopped
- Juice from 1/2 lemon
- 2 teaspoons rice vinegar
- 1 inch fresh ginger, minced
- Dash red pepper flakes, optional

In a small bowl mix marinade ingredients until thoroughly combined. Place fish steaks in a shallow pan. Pour marinade over steaks, turning steaks over to coat both sides. Marinate at least 30 minutes. Refrigerate if marinating longer. Place steaks on a well-greased, hot grill. Grill 2-4 minutes per side or until tuna reaches desired doneness. Do not overcook, tuna is best served rare to medium rare. Serve with Grilled Vegetable Salsa (page 144)

SMOKE SUGGESTIONS:
Mesquite, hickory, oak

Super-Fast Snapper

INGREDIENTS

- 4-6 red snapper fillets
- Juice of 1 lemon or lime
- Salt and lemon pepper to taste

METAL OR WOODEN SKEWERS
(soak skewers at least 1 hour in water)

Thread snapper fillets onto skewers. Squeeze lemon or lime over fillets. Salt and lemon pepper to taste. Place on a well-lubricated grill at medium-high heat. Cook 2-3 minutes per side. Turn using a spatula. Serve with Fresh Salsa (page 149)

SMOKE SUGGESTIONS:
Fruit woods, alder

Fish & Seafood
Grill It!

Mediterranean-Style Sausage

Ingredients

- 2 pounds ground turkey or pork
- 1/2 cup oat bran or crushed crackers
- 3 tablespoons olive oil
- 1 cup onion, minced
- 2 cloves garlic, minced
- 3 tablespoons fresh parsley, chopped
- Juice and zest from 1/2 lemon
- 1 egg, lightly beaten
- 1 tablespoon vinegar
- 1 1/2 teaspoons salt
- 1/2 teaspoon black pepper
- 1/4 teaspoon pumpkin pie spice
- 1/4 teaspoon cayenne pepper

In a medium bowl mix all ingredients just until combined. Refrigerate 15 minutes or until mixture is thick enough to form a patty or link. Shape into 6-8 patties or links. On a hot grill, cook sausage to desired doneness, at least 165°. Serve with Mustard Sauce (page 145) or Hummus (page 146).

World's Best Hot Dogs & Bratwurst

Ingredients

- 2 pounds hot dogs or bratwurst
- 3 cans or bottles beer

Cut bratwurst into 1"-2" pieces. Make shallow slits in a circular fashion down the length of each hot dog. Place hot dogs and/or bratwurst in a large stock pot. Add beer until hot dogs and/or bratwurst are covered. Cook at medium heat until hot dogs are plump, about 15-20 minutes. Place on medium-hot grill and cook until heated throughout. Hot dogs and bratwurst can be returned to a shallow beer bath on the grill for holding if needed. Serve with Sweet Onion Relish (page 69), Sauerkraut Relish (page 147) and/or Pickled Pepper Relish (page 149).

Italian Meatball Burgers |

NGREDIENTS

- 1/2 pound ground beef or turkey
- 1/2 pound chorizo sausage
- 1/4 cup pepperoni, chopped
- 2 cloves garlic, minced
- 2 tablespoons tomato paste
- 2 teaspoons Italian seasoning
- Provolone cheese
- Hoagie rolls, toasted

In a medium bowl combine all ingredients. Shape into 12-16 small patties (bigger than a meatball, smaller than a hamburger). On a hot grill, cook patties to desired doneness, at least 160° for beef, 165° for turkey. Place hot patties on a toasted hoagie roll and top with a slice of provolone cheese. Return to grill to melt cheese if desired. Use pizza sauce or mayonnaise and ketchup as condiments.

Turkey Burgers |

INGREDIENTS

- 1 pound turkey breast, ground
- 1/2 cup apples, grated
- 1/2 cup bread crumbs
- 1/4 cup onion, minced
- 1/4 cup dried cranberries, chopped, optional
- 2 tablespoons fresh parsley, finely chopped or 1 tablespoon dried
- 1 tablespoon fresh sage, finely chopped or 1/2 tablespoon dried
- 1/2 teaspoon salt
- 1/4 teaspoon allspice or cinnamon
- 1/4 teaspoon black pepper
- 2 eggs, lightly beaten

In a medium bowl mix all ingredients just until combined. Refrigerate 15 minutes or until mixture is thick enough to form a patty or link. Shape into 4-6 patties or links. On a hot grill, cook sausage to desired doneness, at least 165°.

Serve with Cranberry Chutney (page 125) or Peach Mango Chutney (page 82), if desired.

Smokey Maple Sausage |

INGREDIENTS

- 2 pounds ground pork
- 1 tablespoon maple flavoring
- 2 teaspoons red pepper flakes, optional
- 1 teaspoon poultry seasoning
- 1 teaspoon black pepper
- 1 teaspoon salt
- 1/2 teaspoon coriander
- 1/2 teaspoon liquid smoke, optional

In a medium bowl mix all ingredients just until combined. Refrigerate 15 minutes or until mixture is thick enough to form a patty or link. Shape into 4-6 patties or links. On a hot grill, cook sausage to desired doneness, at least 165°.

Hot Thighs with Spicy Sauce

Ingredients

- 2 pounds chicken thighs
  Sweet Chicken Rub (page 33)

Spicy Sauce

- 3 tablespoons ketchup
- 1 tablespoon hot sauce or sambal
- 1 teaspoon granulated garlic
- 1 teaspoon granulated onion
- 1 teaspoon white sugar
- 1 teaspoon cider vinegar
- 1/2 teaspoon red pepper flakes

In a large bowl, mix rub ingredients with chicken thighs. Let sit 20-30 minutes. Place thighs on a well- lubricated, preheated hot grill. Sear grill marks into thighs, turning frequently. Grill 15-25 minutes or until juices run clear. Place cooked chicken thighs in a large bowl and cover with Hot Wing Sauce or barbecue sauce of choice. Gently coat thighs with sauce, serve immediately.

Spicy Sauce Preparation

In a small bowl, mix all sauce ingredients until thoroughly combined.

Smoke Suggestions:

Pecan, fruit woods, Rugged Blend (page 8)

Grilled Chicken Breasts

Ngredients

- 4-6 chicken breasts, halved

Grilled Chicken Rub

- 1 tablespoon dried parsley, crushed
- 1 teaspoon garlic salt
- 1/2 teaspoon dried rosemary, crushed
- 1/2 teaspoon paprika
- 1/4 teaspoon black pepper
- Olive oil for drizzling

In a small bowl mix all rub ingredients until thoroughly combined. Massage rub into chicken breasts and let sit 10 minutes. Drizzle olive oil over breasts and place on a well-lubricated, preheated hot grill. Sear grill marks into chicken, turning frequently. Grill 10-15 minutes or until juices run clear. Do not overcook.

Serve with Crunchy Smoked Salsa (page 112) or Mango Salsa (page 147), if desired.

Tostada Patties

Ingredients

- 1 pound ground beef
- 1 15-ounce can pinto beans, drained
- 2 cloves garlic, minced
- 1 egg
- 1 tablespoon chili powder
- 1 tablespoon cumin
- 1 teaspoon salt
- 10-20 shakes hot pepper sauce

In a medium bowl, smash pinto beans with a fork. Add remaining ingredients and thoroughly combine. Make 4-6 patties for a tortilla shell or 10-15 patties for appetizers on a tortilla chip. On a hot grill, cook burgers to desired doneness, at least 160°. Serve on sour cream-topped tortilla with cheese, guacamole and salsa (see Index for a variety of salsa recipes).

Burger Basics

For best results, grind your own meat or purchase freshly ground meat. Beef with a fat content of 18% makes burgers juicier but if you're looking to use leaner meat, simply add an egg for better binding. Never overmix meat when making burgers or sausage as it can toughen and dry out the final product. When shaping burger and sausage patties, make the center a bit thinner than the edges for even cooking. Try to only turn burgers on the grill one time giving each side 3-6 minutes depending on thickness. Do not flatten patties with a spatula as this causes major moisture loss.

The recipes for burgers and sausage in this book are just starting points. The spice combinations and added ingredient possibilities are endless. Different ingredients can be added as a filling for burgers, such as cheddar cheese and diced green chilies or blue cheese and bacon. Also many things can be added to the patty mixture for different regional flavors like a Greek burger with sun-dried tomato bits, feta cheese and chopped kalamata olives. Try an "It's-All-Inside" burger by adding chopped pickle, ketchup, spicy mustard and minced caramelized onion to the mix.

When mixing any ground meat, always keep all ingredients as cool as possible and refrigerate if not cooking immediately. Burger and sausage patties tend to dry out quickly so if grilling for a crowd, keep a shallow pan on the grill filled with an inch of beef broth. Drop the burgers in the broth to keep simmering and stay juicy. Grilled onions can be added to this bath as they make a tasty burger topper.

SMOKE SUGGESTIONS: Almost any wood flavor will complement a burger. Experiment with individual woods or blends (page 8)

Ham & Swiss Burgers

In a medium bowl combine beef, Worcestershire sauce, wine, salt and pepper. Form 8 thin patties. Place slice of Swiss cheese on top of patty and top with another patty taking care to seal, completely enclosing the cheese. On a hot grill, cook burgers to desired doneness, at least 160°. Warm Canadian bacon and place atop burgers. Serve with Thousand Island dressing on a bun or use lettuce to make a wrap.

Ingredients

- 1 pound ground beef
- 2 tablespoons Worcestershire sauce
- 2 tablespoons red wine
- 1 teaspoon salt
- 1 teaspoon black pepper
- 4 slices Swiss cheese
- 12 slices Canadian bacon
- Thousand Island dressing
- Lettuce, optional

Flat Tuscan Chicken

INGREDIENTS

- 1 3-4-pound roasting chicken
- 1/3 cup extra virgin olive oil
- 5 cloves garlic, minced
- 3 sprigs fresh rosemary or 2 teaspoons dried
- 2 sprigs fresh thyme or 1 teaspoon dried
- Juice of 2 lemons
- Zest of 1/2 lemon
- Salt and pepper to taste

Clean chicken, rinse and pat dry. Cut the chicken partially through the breastbone and spread it open. Turn the chicken skin side up on a flat surface and press down to flatten. In a small bowl mix olive oil, garlic, herbs, lemon juice and zest until thoroughly combined. Loosen as much skin from the chicken as possible and rub the oil mixture into the meat of the chicken. Place skin back on top and spread more rub on top of the skin. Marinate the chicken in the refrigerator for at least 4 hours or overnight. Remove chicken from refrigerator and let sit at room temperature 20 minutes prior to grilling. Shake excess liquid off chicken, sprinkle with salt and pepper. Place chicken on a well-greased medium-hot grill over direct heat, skin side down. Place a foil-covered weight (bricks, rocks, cast-iron skillet full of rocks) over the top of the chicken. Close grill lid and cook 15 minutes or until skin is golden brown. Remove weights, turn chicken and return to indirect heat on the grill, replace weights. Cook an additional 20-25 minutes or until chicken is golden and juices run clear and internal temperature reaches 180°. Serve with lemon wedges and Pickled Pepper Relish (page 149) if desired.

SMOKE SUGGESTIONS:

Alder, pecan, West Coast Blend (page 8)

Curried Chicken Breast Packets

INGREDIENTS

- 2 pounds boneless, skinless chicken breasts
- 1 yellow onion, chopped
- 1 small head cauliflower, chopped
- 1 cup plain yogurt
- 4 cloves garlic, pureed
- 2 inches ginger, minced
- Juice and zest from 1 lime
- 2 teaspoons Garam Masala or curry powder
- 3/4 teaspoon salt
- 1/2 teaspoon turmeric
- 1/2 teaspoon black pepper
- 6 tablespoons butter

6-8 pieces of aluminum foil (12" x 12")

Cut chicken into bite-sized pieces. In a large bowl, mix all ingredients except butter. Divide chicken mixture evenly, placing in the center of each piece of aluminum foil. Top mixture with a pat of butter. Loosely wrap foil around chicken mixture, sealing packet at both ends. These packets can be prepared in advance and kept refrigerated. Add a few minutes to cooking time if putting on the grill directly from the refrigerator. Grill on medium heat 20-30 minutes or until chicken is done and vegetables are tender.

Pineapple Chicken for Four

Ingredients

- 4 spring chickens or cornish game hens
- 4 6-ounce cans pineapple juice

Sweet Chicken Rub

- 2 teaspoons brown sugar
- 1 teaspoon garlic powder
- 1 teaspoon sweet paprika
- 1 teaspoon celery salt
- 1/4 teaspoon white pepper

Follow directions for Beer Can Chicken. Reduce grill time to 45-60 minutes or until chicken is golden and juices run clear and internal temperature reaches 180°. This recipe easily adapts for one or two, just divide the rub and save it for later. Serve with Grilled Tomato Peach Salsa (page 23) if desired.

Sweet Chicken Rub:

In a small bowl mix all rub ingredients until thoroughly combined.

Smoke Suggestions:

Apple, cherry, Pacific Northwest Blend (page 8)

Sweet Asian Chicken

Ingredients

- 1 3-4-pound chicken
- 1 can Dr. Pepper (not diet)
- 2 tablespoons olive oil

Five-Spice Rub

- 2 tablespoons Chinese 5-spice
- 2 teaspoons salt
- 1 teaspoon granulated garlic
- 1 teaspoon black pepper

Follow directions for Beer Can Chicken. Serve with Sticky Sweet Sauce (page 123) or Cilantro Mint Sauce (page 148) if desired.

Five-Spice Rub Preparation

In a small bowl mix all rub ingredients until thoroughly combined.

Smoke Suggestions:

Fruit woods, pecan, Tropical Blend (page 8)

Original Beer Can Chicken

Rinse chicken and remove giblet packet and any excess fat. Pat dry and place on a large plate. Using half of the spice rub, massage spices into chicken, lifting skin wherever possible. Sprinkle some inside the bird. Drizzle olive oil over the outside of the chicken. Let sit 10-15 minutes. If not using a vertical roaster, cover the can with aluminum foil. Open the can of beer, discarding 1/3 of the liquid. Carefully pour remaining rub into the can of beer. If using a vertical roaster place the can inside the roaster or pour the liquid and rub into the roaster. To place the chicken on the can of beer or on the vertical roaster, hold the bird upright, wings on top. Lower the bird onto the can so the can fits into the cavity, use the legs to form a tripod. Place chicken on a hot grill over indirect heat. If not using a roaster, put a drip pan underneath the beer can. Cover grill and cook 70-90 minutes or until chicken is golden and juices run clear and internal temperature reaches 180°. Using heavy- duty oven mitts, remove chicken from grill and let sit 5-10 minutes. Using a narrow plastic spatula, loosen chicken from can or roaster and lift off. Cut chicken into quarters or halves and serve. Discard can and leftover juices.

Ingredients

- 1 3-4-pound chicken
- 1 can beer
- 2 tablespoons olive oil

Chicken Spice Rub

- 1 tablespoon chili powder
- 2 teaspoons dried cumin
- 2 teaspoons dried coriander
- 1 teaspoon salt
- 1/2 teaspoon dry mustard
- 1/2 teaspoon dried oregano
- 1/2 teaspoon black pepper
- 1/4 teaspoon cayenne pepper

Chicken Spice Rub Preparation

In a small bowl mix all rub ingredients until thoroughly combined.

Smoke Suggestions:

Cherry, alder, Cowboy Blend (page 8)

NOTE: Better Than Beer Can Chicken

Virtually any spice, herbs and type of liquid can be used to make this chicken. The technique is special because the flavor is cooked into the meat and the liquid bastes the chicken from the inside out. Chickens will never be dry and because they are roasted standing up, they lose much of their unwanted fat. Depending on grill size, multiple chickens can be cooked at one time. Chicken cooled and refrigerated makes wonderful sandwiches and salad topping. Chicken prepared this way can also be frozen after cooking to use in dishes calling for precooked chicken such as casseroles, enchiladas and lasagne.

For best results, and to avoid ingesting any toxins from the can, use a roaster designed for the "Beer-Can Chicken" method. They are available in many stores and on the Internet. Cans also may be covered in foil to avoid getting any paint on the chicken.

Thai Pork with Tropical Salsa

In a bowl or large sealable plastic bag, combine all marinade ingredients. Place chops in marinade, refrigerate at least 1 hour or up to 3 hours. Place chops on a well-lubricated, preheated hot grill. Sear grill marks into chops, 2-3 minutes. Repeat process on the other side. Grill to desired temperature; medium 160°; well-done 170°-180°. Serve with Tropical Salsa.

Tropical Salsa Preparation

In a medium bowl, gently mix all ingredients. Refrigerate at least 30 minutes before serving.

Smoke Suggestions:

Hickory, pecan, Tropical Blend (page 8)

Ingredients

- 6-8 pork chops or medallions

Thai Marinade

- 1/2 cup sherry
- 1/4 cup soy sauce
- 2 tablespoons toasted sesame oil
- 4 cloves garlic, minced
- 4 shallots, minced, optional
- Juice and zest from 1/2 lemon
- 1/2 teaspoon black pepper

Tropical Salsa

- 1 green banana, peeled and chopped
- 1 cup pineapple, finely chopped
- 1 mango, chopped
- 2 tablespoons fresh cilantro, chopped
- 2 teaspoons fresh ginger, minced
- 2 teaspoons Asian chili sauce
- 1/4 teaspoon salt

Pork Tenderloin with Pomegranate Glaze

Ingredients

- 1 2-pound pork tenderloin

Basic Pork Rub

- 1 teaspoon salt
- 1 teaspoon ground coriander
- 1 teaspoon garlic powder
- 1/2 teaspoon white pepper
- 1/2 teaspoon ground cumin
- 1/2 teaspoon granulated garlic

Pomegranate Glaze

- 1/4 cup orange juice
- 2 tablespoons pomegranate syrup or pomegranate molasses
- Zest of 1/2 orange or lemon
- 1 tablespoon olive oil
- 2 cloves garlic, pureed
- 1/2 tablespoon fresh ginger, minced
- 2 teaspoons sugar
- 1/4 teaspoon cayenne pepper
- Salt to taste

In a small bowl, mix all rub ingredients until thoroughly combined. Massage rub onto every surface of the tenderloin. Cover and refrigerate at least one hour or overnight. Remove tenderloin from refrigerator 30 minutes prior to grilling. Place tenderloin on a well-lubricated, preheated hot grill. Sear grill marks into every side of the tenderloin. Move pork to indirect heat and cook 20-30 minutes or until internal temperature reaches 160°. Turn frequently. Baste with pomegranate glaze during the last 10 minutes of grilling time. Allow tenderloin to rest 10-15 minutes before slicing thinly. Serve with additional pomegranate glaze.

Pomegranate Glaze Preparation

In a small saucepan, combine all glaze ingredients. Bring to a low boil and remove from heat.

Smoke Suggestions:

Maple, alder, hickory

Pork Chops with Apple Cinnamon Sauce

Ingredients

- 6-8 pork chops, 1” thick
- 2-4 apples
- 2 tablespoons canola oil
- Salt and pepper to taste

Apple Cinnamon Sauce

- 1/3 cup applesauce
- 1/4 cup ketchup
- 2 tablespoons cider vinegar
- 2 tablespoons brown sugar
- 2 tablespoons Worcestershire sauce
- 1 tablespoon canola oil
- 1/2 teaspoon granulated onion
- 1/4 teaspoon cinnamon

Let steaks sit at room temperature 20-30 minutes. Core apples and slice into 1/2” rings. Brush apple slices with canola oil and place on a well-lubricated, preheated hot grill. Grill until grill marks appear, turning only once. Set aside on a square of aluminum foil. Place chops on a well-lubricated, preheated hot grill. Sear grill marks into steaks, 3-4 minutes. Repeat process on the other side. Grill to desired temperature; medium 160°; well-done 170°-180°. Baste chops with Apple Cinnamon Sauce during the last 2 minutes of cooking. Serve chops with apple slices and additional Apple Cinnamon Sauce.

Apple Cinnamon Sauce Preparation

In a small saucepan, combine sauce ingredients. Simmer on medium-low heat, 30 minutes.

Smoke Suggestions:

Alder, fruit woods, Mid-America Blend (page 8)

Southwestern Tenderloin Chops

In a bowl or large sealable plastic bag, combine all marinade ingredients. Place chops in marinade, refrigerate at least 8 hours or overnight. Drain marinade and sauté vegetables on the stove or in a foil grill pan on the grill. Place chops on a well- lubricated, preheated hot grill. Sear grill marks into chops, 2-3 minutes. Repeat process on the other side. Grill to desired temperature; medium 160°; well-done 170°-180°. Serve chops topped with marinated, sautéed onion and pepper mixture.

Smoke Suggestions:
Hickory, fruit woods, Cowboy Blend (page 8)

Ingredients

- 2-pound pork tenderloin, sliced 3/4"

Southwestern Marinade

- 1 can beer
- 1 red onion, thinly sliced
- 1 jalapeño pepper, thinly sliced
- 1/2 cup lime juice
- 1/2 cup fresh cilantro, chopped
- 2 tablespoons olive oil
- 1 tablespoon lime zest
- 1/2 teaspoon salt
- 1/2 teaspoon black pepper
- 1/2 teaspoon red pepper flakes
- 1/2 teaspoon ground cumin

Grilled Sirloin Steak or Fillet Minion |

Ingredients

- 4-6 6-8-ounce steaks
- 2 cloves garlic
- Salt and pepper to taste
- 1 lemon, cut into wedges
- 1/2 cup fresh parsley, chopped

Let steaks sit at room temperature 20-30 minutes. Cut garlic cloves in half and rub all sides of the steaks. Discard garlic. Salt and pepper steaks to taste. Place steaks on a well-lubricated, preheated hot grill. Sear grill marks into steaks, 1-2 minutes. Repeat process on the other side. Grill to desired temperature; rare 140°; medium-rare 150°; medium 160°; well-done 170°. Remove from grill and squeeze lemon over steaks. Sprinkle with parsley and serve. For an Asian twist, marinate steaks for 30 minutes in Orange Ginger Marinade (page 149).

Smoke Suggestions: Mesquite, oak, Southern Blend (page 8)

Teriyaki Flank Steak |

Ingredients

- 1-2 pounds flank steak

Teriyaki Marinade

- 1/4 cup soy sauce
- 1/4 cup cream sherry
- 1/4 cup olive oil
- 3 tablespoons shallot or green onion, finely chopped
- 1 tablespoon brown sugar
- 1 inch ginger root, peeled and grated

In a bowl or large sealable plastic bag, combine all marinade ingredients. Rinse steak and lightly score in a diagonal pattern. Place flank steak in marinade, refrigerate at least 8 hours or overnight. When using marinade as a basting liquid, remove all meat from marinade and bring marinade to a rolling boil for 3 minutes in order to kill any bacteria. Place steak on a well- lubricated, preheated hot grill. Turn occasionally taking care not to pierce steak. Grill approximately 12-15 minutes or until steak reaches desired temperature. Baste often with cooked marinade. Drizzle the marinade on the steak to prevent any utensils from contaminating the cooked marinade. Cut steak in thin, diagonal slices and serve in remaining marinade. To keep meat warm and moist, a grill-proof dish can be placed on the grill with sliced steak simmering on low heat in cooked marinade.

Side Suggestion:

Serve with Rhubarb Ketchup (page 145) or Black Bean Salsa (page 116)

Smoke Suggestions:

Pecan, hickory, Cowboy Blend (page 8)

T-Bone Steaks with Herb Butter

Ingredients

- 4-6 8-10-ounce steaks
- Salt and pepper to taste

Herb Butter

- 1 cup fresh parsley, cilantro, sage and/or chives
- 2 cloves garlic, pureed
- 1 tablespoon lemon juice
- 4 tablespoons butter, softened
- 5-10 dashes hot pepper sauce, optional

Let steaks sit at room temperature 20-30 minutes. Salt and pepper steaks to taste. Place steaks on a well-lubricated, preheated hot grill. Sear grill marks into steaks, 3-4 minutes. Repeat process on the other side. Grill to desired temperature; rare 140°; medium-rare 150°; medium 160°; well-done 170°. Remove from grill and top each steak with a generous spoonful of herb butter. For a more intense flavor, rub steaks with Sweet & Hot Rub (page 144) 15 minutes prior to grilling.

Herb Butter Preparation

In a food processor or mini-chopper, blend all ingredients until thoroughly combined. Keep refrigerated until ready to use.

Smoke Suggestions:

Alder, pecan, fruit woods

Grilled Mustard Tri-Tip

Ingredients

- 3-4 pound tri-tip roast
- 1 cup yellow mustard
- 1 cup rock salt

Basic Beef Rub

- 2 teaspoons granulated garlic
- 1 teaspoon granulated onion
- 1 teaspoon brown sugar
- 1 teaspoon black pepper

In a small bowl, mix all rub ingredients until thoroughly combined. Massage rub onto every surface of the roast. Let roast sit at room temperature 20-30 minutes. Cover roast with mustard and pack rock salt onto the top of the roast. Place roast on a well-lubricated, preheated hot grill. Turn grill to low and grill over indirect heat approximately 3 hours or until internal temperature reaches 165°. Remove roast from grill and wrap with aluminum foil. Allow roast to rest 10-15 minutes before slicing thinly.

Smoke Suggestions:

Mesquite, hickory, Eastern Blend (page 8)

Grilled Tomato-Peach Salsa

Brush tomatoes, peaches and Aneheim chilies with olive oil. Place on a well-greased medium-hot grill, skin side down and cook until skin begins to blister. Turn once and grill until grill marks are made. Remove all items from the grill and place into a sealed plastic bag or container. When cool enough to handle, remove skin from tomatoes, peaches and chilies. Chop grilled ingredients and place in a medium bowl. Add additional ingredients and toss gently. Refrigerate until ready to serve.

Ingredients

- 3 large tomatoes, halved
- 2 peaches, pitted and halved
- 2 Aneheim chilies, seeded and halved
- 2 tablespoons onion, minced
- 1/2 cup fresh cilantro, chopped
- 1 tablespoon lemon or lime juice
- 2 tablespoons fresh mint, chopped
- 1 tablespoon rice or cider vinegar
- 1 tablespoon brown sugar
- 5-10 dashes red or green hot pepper sauce, optional
- Salt to taste

Olive oil for basting

Smoke Suggestions:

Maple, pecan, apple

Sweet Peppers with Honey Mustard Marinade

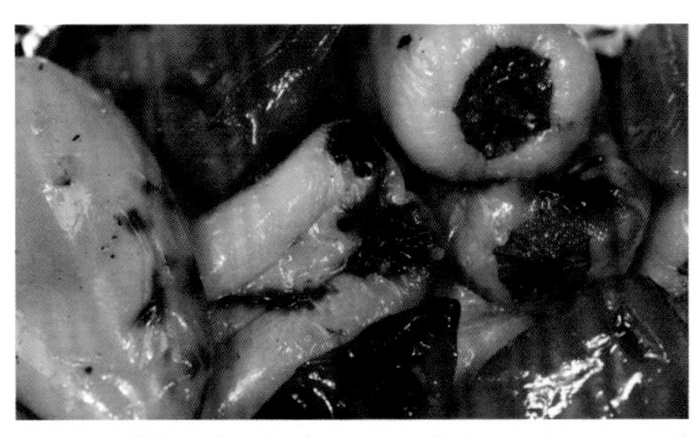

In a small bowl, whisk marinade ingredients until thoroughly combined. Place peppers in a sealable plastic bag and cover with marinade. Marinade at least 2 hours. Shake excess marinade off peppers and place on a medium-hot grill. Cook until grill marks appear 1-3 minutes, turn and repeat. Serve hot or cold.

Ingredients

- 1-2 pounds mini sweet peppers

Honey Mustard Marinade

- 1/2 cup extra virgin olive oil
- 1/4 cup honey mustard
- 1/4 cup cider vinegar
- 2 teaspoons granulated onion
- 4 cloves garlic, pureed
- 1 teaspoon salt

Smoke Suggestions:

Mesquite, pecan, hickory

Grilled Corn on the Cob |

INGREDIENTS
- 6 ears corn on the cob

SEASONED OIL
- 2 tablespoons olive oil
- 2 tablespoons melted butter
- 1 teaspoon salt
- 1/2 teaspoon white pepper
- 1/2 teaspoon smoked paprika

Peel husks and remove all silk from corn on the cob. In a small bowl mix all ingredients for seasoned oil. Brush corn with seasoned oil and place on well-oiled grill grates. Grill for 15 minutes, turning frequently until corn is lightly browned.

SMOKE SUGGESTIONS:
Mesquite, alder, maple, West Coast Blend (page 8)

Husk-On Corn on the Cob |

INGREDIENTS
- 6 ears corn on the cob

GARLIC BUTTER
- 1/4 cup butter, softened
- 1 clove garlic, pureed
- 1/2 teaspoon dried rosemary, crushed
- 1/4 teaspoon dried marjoram, crushed

Fold back the husks on each corn and remove the silk. Slather corn with garlic herb butter and fold husks back into place. Seal each cob in aluminum foil. Place on medium-hot grill and cook 15-25 minutes, turning frequently.

Tomato Cheese Pizzas

Topping

- 1/2 cup prepared pesto or spaghetti sauce
- 2 cups tomatoes, chopped and drained
- 4 tablespoons fresh basil, chopped, optional
- 2 tablespoons fresh parsley, chopped
- 1 1/2 cups mozzarella cheese
- 1/2 cup cheddar cheese
- Salt and pepper to taste

Smoke Suggestions:

Oak, fruit woods, West Coast Blend (page 8)

Crust

- 2 tablespoons olive oil
- 1 cup warm water
- 2 1/2 cups whole wheat pastry flour
- 1 tablespoon sugar
- 1 1/2 teaspoons rapid rise yeast
- 1 teaspoon salt

In a food processor or electric mixer, add dry ingredients and combine. Mix olive oil with water and slowly add to dry mixture. Mix ingredients until dough ball forms, adding more flour if needed. Pat dough ball with a thin coating of olive oil, cover and let rise until doubled, approximately 2 hours. Divide dough into four equal portions. Work dough to a 7" to 9" round. Place on a lightly floured surface. Be sure toppings are ready prior to placing the crusts on the grill. Heat grill to high heat. Place pizza crusts on a hot grill, over indirect heat. Cook until grill marks appear and crust browns lightly. Remove from grill and place on a lightly floured surface, browned side up. Spread pesto or sauce evenly over pizzas. Divide remaining toppings equally among all four pizzas. Place pizza back on the grill and cook with the lid down until crust is golden brown and cheese is melted.

Artichoke & Spinach Pizza

Ingredients

- 1 cup cottage or ricotta cheese
- 3 cloves garlic
- 2 tablespoons fresh parsley
- 1/4 teaspoon oregano
- 1/4 teaspoon white pepper
- 2 cups cooked spinach
- 1 cup mozzarella cheese
- 1/2 cup parmesan or romano cheese
- 1 14-ounce can marinated artichoke hearts

1 prepared pizza crust or split focaccia, cooked

In a food processor or mini-chopper, puree cottage or ricotta cheese, garlic, parsley, oregano and white pepper. Spread evenly over entire pizza crust. Top sauce layer with drained and pressed spinach, then shredded cheeses, and finish with marinated artichoke hearts. If the artichoke hearts are big, separate them into bite-sized pieces for better distribution. Place on a hot grill over indirect heat and grill until cheese is golden and bubbly and pizza is heated throughout.

Smoke Suggestions:

Oak, fruit woods, Pacific Northwest Blend (page 8)

Meat
Grill It!

Vegetables *Grill It!*

Salami-Wrapped Asparagus

INGREDIENTS

- 12-16 asparagus spears
- 12-16 slices salami
- 2 tablespoons Italian dressing

METAL OR WOODEN SKEWERS
(soak skewers at least 1 hour in water)

Trim asparagus to matching lengths. Wrap the lower end of each spear with a slice of salami. Push skewers through to secure salami, continue with 4-5 spears. Double skewer toward the top of the spear. Brush asparagus with Italian dressing. Place on medium-hot grill and cook 10 minutes, or to desired doneness.

SMOKE SUGGESTIONS:
Pecan, alder, Eastern Blend (page 8)

Curried Cauliflower

INGREDIENTS

- 1 head cauliflower, chopped
- 1/4 cup butter, melted
- 2 cloves garlic, pureed
- 1 teaspoon curry powder
- 1/2 teaspoon chili powder
- 1/2 teaspoon red pepper flakes, optional
- Salt and pepper to taste

In a large bowl whisk butter and remaining ingredients. Add cauliflower and lightly toss. Place on medium-hot grill and cook 12 minutes, or to desired doneness.

SMOKE SUGGESTIONS:
Pecan, oak, Cowboy Blend (page 8)

Onion Rounds

Smoke Suggestions:

Rugged Blend (page 8), oak, fruit woods

Ingredients

- 2 large sweet onions, sliced
- 1 tablespoon extra virgin olive oil
- 2 tablespoons melted butter
- Salt to taste

METAL OR WOODEN SKEWERS
(soak skewers at least 1 hour in water)

In a small bowl mix olive oil with butter. Slice onions 1/2" thick. Lay 2-4 onion slices on a flat surface. Using two skewers, stick through all onions, securing them together. Brush both sides of onions with the olive oil/butter and immediately place on a medium-hot grill. Salt to taste. Cook onions 7-10 minutes per side. Serve as a vegetable or a condiment for burgers, burritos or grilled sandwiches.

Ham & Spinach Stuffed Tomatoes

Ingredients

- 4-6 large tomatoes
- 2 tablespoons olive oil
- 1/2 cup onion, diced
- 2 cloves garlic, diced
- 2/3 cup ham, diced
- 3 cups fresh spinach
- 1/2 cup bread crumbs
- 3 tablespoons fresh parsley or 1 tablespoon dried
- Salt and pepper to taste
- 1/2 cup Monterey Jack cheese, grated
- 1/4 cup parmesan cheese, grated

Cut the top off each tomato and scoop out seeds and flesh, discard. In a medium skillet, heat olive oil on medium-high heat. Add onions and sauté until translucent. Add garlic, ham, spinach and parsley, sauté 1-2 more minutes. Salt and pepper to taste. Remove spinach mixture from heat and stir in cheeses. Fill tomatoes with spinach/cheese mixture. Grill at medium-high heat for 10-20 minutes or until tomatoes are cooked through. Once skins begin to show grill marks, move to a square of foil to finish cooking.

Smoke Suggestions:

Alder, maple, Eastern Blend (page 8)

Easy Potato Packets

INGREDIENTS

- 4 medium potatoes, cubed
- 1 sweet onion, chopped
- 4 slices bacon, chopped
- 1 tablespoon Dijon mustard
- 2 sprigs fresh-thyme or 1/2 teaspoon dried
- Salt and pepper to taste
- Nonstick cooking spray

4-6 pieces of aluminum foil (12" x 12")

Scrub potatoes and pat dry. Cut into desired-sized cubes. Lightly spray the middle area of each piece of aluminum foil. Evenly distribute potatoes, onions and bacon over squares of aluminum foil, keeping food in the middle. Dab each pile of potato mixture with a bit of Dijon mustard, sprinkle with thyme, salt and pepper. Loosely wrap foil around potato mixture, sealing packet at both ends. These packets can be prepared in advance and kept refrigerated. Add a few minutes to cooking time if putting on the grill directly from the refrigerator. Grill on medium heat 20-30 minutes or until potatoes are tender and bacon is cooked. Placed on indirect heat, these packets will stay warm and still taste great up to one hour.

Grilled Vegetables in Raspberry Vinaigrette

USE ANY COMBINATION OF THE FOLLOWING VEGETABLES

- 1 red onion, quartered
- 1 yellow onion, quartered
- 2 green peppers, seeded and quartered
- 2 red peppers, seeded and quartered
- 2 small zucchini, sliced lengthwise 1/2"
- 2 white eggplant, sliced lengthwise 1/2"
- 2 portabella mushrooms, sliced 1/2"
- 1/2 head cauliflower, sliced 1/2"
- 1/2 bunch asparagus, trimmed

RASPBERRY VINAIGRETTE

- 1/2 cup extra virgin olive oil
- 1/4 cup raspberry vinegar (or flavor of choice)
- 2 cloves garlic, pureed
- 1 tablespoon lemon juice
- 1 teaspoon sugar
- 1 teaspoon fresh thyme, optional
- 1 teaspoon salt
- 1/2 teaspoon white pepper

In a bowl or large sealable plastic bag, combine all marinade ingredients. Cut vegetables and add to the marinade. Toss lightly, let sit 30-40 minutes. Grill at medium-high heat. Turn after grill marks are made. Cook 8-10 minutes per side until vegetables reach desired tenderness. Baste with marinade while grilling if desired. Set aside on aluminum foil to keep warm if necessary.

SMOKE SUGGESTIONS:

Maple, apple, Pacific Northwest Blend (page 8)

Meat
Grill It!

Tomato Cheese Pizzas

Topping

- 1/2 cup prepared pesto or spaghetti sauce
- 2 cups tomatoes, chopped and drained
- 4 tablespoons fresh basil, chopped, optional
- 2 tablespoons fresh parsley, chopped
- 1 1/2 cups mozzarella cheese
- 1/2 cup cheddar cheese
- Salt and pepper to taste

Smoke Suggestions:

Oak, fruit woods, West Coast Blend (page 8)

Crust

- 2 tablespoons olive oil
- 1 cup warm water
- 2 1/2 cups whole wheat pastry flour
- 1 tablespoon sugar
- 1 1/2 teaspoons rapid rise yeast
- 1 teaspoon salt

In a food processor or electric mixer, add dry ingredients and combine. Mix olive oil with water and slowly add to dry mixture. Mix ingredients until dough ball forms, adding more flour if needed. Pat dough ball with a thin coating of olive oil, cover and let rise until doubled, approximately 2 hours. Divide dough into four equal portions. Work dough to a 7" to 9" round. Place on a lightly floured surface. Be sure toppings are ready prior to placing the crusts on the grill. Heat grill to high heat. Place pizza crusts on a hot grill, over indirect heat. Cook until grill marks appear and crust browns lightly. Remove from grill and place on a lightly floured surface, browned side up. Spread pesto or sauce evenly over pizzas. Divide remaining toppings equally among all four pizzas. Place pizza back on the grill and cook with the lid down until crust is golden brown and cheese is melted.

Artichoke & Spinach Pizza

Ingredients

- 1 cup cottage or ricotta cheese
- 3 cloves garlic
- 2 tablespoons fresh parsley
- 1/4 teaspoon oregano
- 1/4 teaspoon white pepper
- 2 cups cooked spinach
- 1 cup mozzarella cheese
- 1/2 cup parmesan or romano cheese
- 1 14-ounce can marinated artichoke hearts

1 prepared pizza crust or split focaccia, cooked

In a food processor or mini-chopper, puree cottage or ricotta cheese, garlic, parsley, oregano and white pepper. Spread evenly over entire pizza crust. Top sauce layer with drained and pressed spinach, then shredded cheeses, and finish with marinated artichoke hearts. If the artichoke hearts are big, separate them into bite-sized pieces for better distribution. Place on a hot grill over indirect heat and grill until cheese is golden and bubbly and pizza is heated throughout.

Smoke Suggestions:

Oak, fruit woods, Pacific Northwest Blend (page 8)

Rosemary Vegetable Skewers

USE ANY COMBINATION OF THE FOLLOWING VEGETABLES

- Onion
- Yellow squash
- Zucchini squash
- Red bell pepper
- Green bell pepper
- Yellow bell pepper
- Cherry tomatoes
- Mushrooms

ROSEMARY BALSAMIC MARINADE

- 1/2 cup olive oil
- 1/4 cup balsamic vinegar
- 2 teaspoons brown sugar
- 1 tablespoon garlic, pureed
- 1/2 teaspoon fresh or dried rosemary, chopped
- 1/2 teaspoon salt
- 1/2 teaspoon black pepper

ROSEMARY BRANCHES, METAL OR WOODEN SKEWERS

(soak branches/skewers at least 1 hour in water)

In a bowl or large sealable plastic bag, combine all marinade ingredients. Cut vegetables into bite-sized pieces and add to the marinade. Toss lightly, let sit 5 minutes. Thread on branches or skewers. Grill at medium-high heat. If using rosemary branches or wooden skewers, place a sheet of foil under the exposed wood to prevent them from burning. Cook 5-8 minutes per side until vegetables reach desired tenderness. Baste with marinade while grilling if desired. For a different flavor, marinate vegetables in White Wine Marinade (page 144).

SMOKE SUGGESTIONS:

Maple, alder, herbs, West Coast Blend (page 8)

Indonesian Satay |

Ingredients

- 1 pound boneless, skinless chicken

Indonesian Marinade

- 1/4 cup soy sauce
- 2 tablespoons creamy peanut butter
- 2 tablespoons shallots, minced
- 2 cloves garlic, minced
- 2 tablespoons fresh lime juice
- 1 tablespoon sugar
- 1 inch ginger, minced

Smoke Suggestions:

Fruit woods, alder, oak, coconut husks

Metal or Wooden Skewers

(soak skewers at least 1 hour in water)

In a medium bowl, mix all marinade ingredients until thoroughly combined. Cut boneless, skinless chicken into bite-sized cubes, set aside. Thread chicken pieces onto skewers and place in sauce, coating evenly. Let sit 15-20 minutes. Grill at medium-high heat. If using wooden skewers, place a sheet of foil under the exposed wood to prevent them from burning. Cook 5-7 minutes per side. Serve with peanut sauce. Beef can be substituted for chicken.

Peanut Sauce

- 3 tablespoons peanut butter
- 3 tablespoons coconut milk
- 1 tablespoon peanut oil
- 1 tablespoon lime juice
- 1 teaspoon sugar
- 1/2 teaspoon salt
- 1/4 cup fresh cilantro, finely chopped, optional

In a small bowl, whisk ingredients until thoroughly combined.

Appetizers
Grill It!

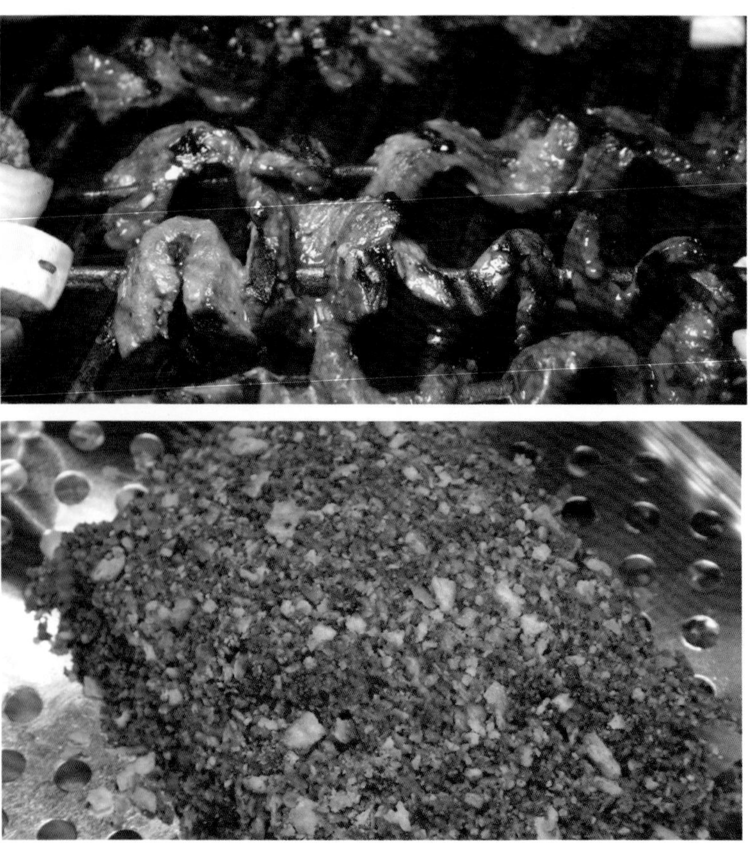

Washable, reusable and decorative, metal and cast-iron skewers enhance kebabs.

Disposable pans protect fish and keep grill grates clean.

spatula to turn, good for delicate foods like fish fillets and large items like pizza.

Large Platters: Plastic for putting raw food on the grill, glass for taking food off and serving.

Basting Brushes: Several styles to choose from, and what you use comes down to personal preference, but whatever you pick, be sure to always use a different brush for each marinade and make sure they are dishwasher safe for proper sanitation.

Wire Baskets: These come in so many different shapes and sizes, always make sure to lubricate well before adding foods.

Fish Grates: For delicate fish or fish with toppings, fish grates are a necessity.

Metal or Cast-Iron Skewers: No presoaking needed, these make a great presentation and help cook food from the inside out.

Wire Brush for Cleaning: Find out what works best for your grill grates and buy a few, keeping the grates clean is of utmost importance.

Foil: The duct tape of the grilling world, use foil for wrapping foods tightly to cook on the grill or loosely to steam-grill. Use as a drip pan, a holding area to protect food from direct heat, as a makeshift container or in a bind, roll-up a ball of foil and use to clean the grill grates. Most importantly, foil can be made into any shape and used as a house for smoker sawdust, chips and chunks when adding smoke flavor to the grill.

There are numerous options relating to all realms of grilling with more smoke flavor, and the more proficient you become, the more delectable each meal will be. In the end, you'll experience food flavors that go beyond what you ever thought possible.

Korean Kebabs

SMOKE SUGGESTIONS:
Mesquite, oak, hickory, fruit woods

INGREDIENTS
- 1-2 pounds beef tenderloin

KOREAN MARINADE
- 1/3 cup soy sauce
- 1/4 cup brown sugar
- 1/4 cup rice vinegar
- 2 tablespoons toasted sesame oil
- 3 green onions, minced
- 4 cloves garlic, minced
- 1/2 teaspoon black pepper

METAL OR WOODEN SKEWERS
(soak skewers at least 1 hour in water)

In a medium bowl, mix all marinade ingredients until thoroughly combined. Slice beef across the grain into 1/4" thick strips. Place meat in marinade and let sit 30 minutes. Grill at medium-high heat. Place a sheet of foil under the exposed skewers to prevent them from burning. Cook 5-7 minutes per side. Serve with Peanut Sauce (page 13). Chicken can be substituted for beef.

Lemon Grass Pork

SMOKE SUGGESTIONS:
Apple, cherry, pecan, Tropical Blend (page 8)

INGREDIENTS
- 1 pound pork tenderloin, cubed

LEMON GRASS MARINADE
- 1 stalk lemon grass, chopped or 1tablespoon lemon zest, minced
- 2 cloves garlic
- 3 tablespoons peanut or canola oil
- 1 tablespoon fish sauce
- 1 tablespoon brown sugar

4-6 STALKS LEMON GRASS, METAL OR WOODEN SKEWERS
(soak lemongrass/wood skewers at least 1 hour in water)

Using a food processor or mini chopper, puree marinade ingredients until smooth. If using the lemon grass stalks as skewers, poke a hole with a paring knife or skewer into pork cubes prior to threading. Thread cubes onto lemon grass stalks or skewers. Place in shallow pan and coat with marinade. Let sit 15-30 minutes. Grill at medium-high heat. Place a sheet of foil under the exposed skewers to prevent them from burning. Cook 6-7 minutes per side. Chicken can be substituted for pork.

Grilled Bread

INGREDIENTS

- 1 loaf artisan bread (French, sourdough, baguette, ciabatta, foccacia)
- 1 clove garlic

Cut bread into 1/2" slices. Brush both sides of the bread with olive oil. Grill bread at medium heat until toasty on both sides. Peel garlic, slice in half and rub both sides of the bread with the garlic clove. Bread can now be topped with desired topping and put back on the grill. Grill until topping is warm and serve immediately. Grilled bread can be prepared ahead and stored at room temperature in a sealed container.

SMOKE SUGGESTIONS:
Oak, apple, pecan

Toasted Bread

Any style of bread will work. Bread does not need to be pre-grilled before topping. Individual portions may be sliced or a loaf can be cut in half lengthwise and topped with toppings then placed on the grill over indirect heat. Grill until topping is warm throughout and cut to desired serving sizes.

SMOKE SUGGESTIONS:
Oak, apple, pecan

Toppings

Classic Bruschetta

INGREDIENTS

- 6 plum tomatoes, diced
- 1 cup fresh basil, chopped
- 1/4 cup purple onion, diced, optional
- 3 cloves garlic, pureed
- 2 tablespoons extra virgin olive oil
- 1/2 teaspoon black pepper
- Salt to taste
- Extra virgin olive oil for drizzling, optional

Dice plum tomatoes and place in a strainer. Let drain, discarding any liquid. In a medium bowl, combine tomatoes with remaining ingredients. Top grilled bread with mixture and return to a medium-hot grill. Warm and serve, drizzle with additional olive oil if desired.

Bruschetta can also be served atop cold grilled bread.

Toppings

Creamy Basil Pesto

INGREDIENTS

- 1 1/2 cups basil leaves
- 2 cloves garlic
- 1/4 cup toasted pine nuts
- 1/2 cup parmesan cheese, grated
- 2 tablespoons extra virgin olive oil
- Salt and pepper to taste
- 1 8-ounce package cream cheese, softened

In a food processor or mini-chopper, blend all ingredients except cream cheese. Place basil mixture in a small bowl and add softened cream cheese. Top grilled bread or bread to toast with mixture and return to a medium-hot grill. Grill until topping is heated throughout, serve immediately. This pesto is great warm as a pita or tortilla chip dip. For a traditional basil pesto or low-fat spread, omit cream cheese.

Sweet Red Pepper

INGREDIENTS

- 3 tablespoons olive oil
- 1 red bell pepper, thinly sliced
- 1 orange or yellow bell pepper, thinly sliced
- 2 cloves garlic, minced
- 1/4 teaspoon salt
- 1 tablespoon parsley, chopped

In a medium skillet on medium heat cook peppers and garlic in olive oil until soft and sweet, approximately 25 minutes. Take care not to brown the peppers. Add salt and parsley during the last 2 minutes of cooking time. Top bread immediately or cool and store in refrigerator for later use. Top grilled bread or bread to toast with mixture. Return bread to a medium-hot grill. Grill until topping is heated thoroughly, serve immediately. For a different presentation, this topping can be pureed (after cooking) and used as a pesto-type topping.

Sundried Tomato Mozzarella Bites

INGREDIENTS

- 1/2 cup sundried tomatoes packed in oil, chopped
- 1/2 cup mozzarella cheese, grated
- 1/2 cup black or green olives, chopped
- 2 tablespoons extra virgin olive oil for drizzling

Sprinkle all toppings on grilled bread or bread to toast. Drizzle with olive oil. Return bread to a medium-hot grill. Grill until topping is heated thoroughly and cheese is melted, serve immediately.

Olive Tapenade Wraps

INGREDIENTS

- 1 1/2 cups black or Kalamata olives
- 2 tablespoons capers
- 2 tablespoons lemon juice
- 2 tablespoons fresh parsley, chopped
- 2 tablespoons extra virgin olive oil
- 2 anchovy fillets, optional
- 1 clove garlic
- 1 teaspoon dry mustard
- 2-4 wraps or flatbread

In a food processor or mini-chopper, blend all ingredients. Take care not to over-mix as some texture in this spread is good. Spread wrap or flatbread with tapenade and place on a medium-hot grill. Grill until grill marks appear on bread and topping is heated. Remove from the grill, roll up and slice into bite-sized portions, serve immediately. This tapenade is great served cold on a burger bar or served as a cracker or veggie dip.

Chili Cheddar Quesadillas

INGREDIENTS

- 1 cup cheddar cheese
- 1/2 cup mayonnaise
- 1 4-ounce can diced green chilis
- 2 green onions, chopped
- 8 medium flour tortillas

In a small bowl, mix all ingredients. Top half of each tortilla with a thin layer of cheese mixture. Fold the other half over and place on a medium-hot grill. Grill until grill marks appear on tortilla and cheese is melted, serve immediately. For added heat, add a diced jalapeño pepper. Left-over grilled or smoked chicken in the quesadillas makes an easy entree.

Down South, in BBQ country, hickory tops the list. Other areas may tout pecan as the perfect smoking wood. One of our most amazing smoked-food experiences came in Fiji with an underground *"lovo"* flavored with mango branches and coconut husks. Another was in Hawaii with the amazing flavors of guava and kiawe wood.

While in Texas, I often laughed when our Texan friends scorned us for using anything but mesquite to flavor our foods, but after a week of eating food cooked over only mesquite fuel, we were just about ready to pack our bags and move south. It's all about personal preference.

When adding smoke to foods, I prefer using what personally appeals to my sense of smell. If the smoke coming from the grill smells sharp, or has a bitter tinge to it, I won't use it. Like adding wine to cooking, you should only use the kind you like.

An important guideline when focusing on smoke flavors is to keep marinades and spices to a minimum in order to get the full effect and be able to taste the wood flavor in your foods. Find out the smoke flavors you prefer, then spice up the recipes accordingly.

When working with chips, chunks or sawdust, it helps having a designated area in which to store different flavors of woods, using it much as you would a spice rack. The more you get into this form of cooking, the more diversified you'll want to become. And in this day and age of Internet commerce, almost anything can be shipped to your doorstep.

We tend to frequent sites that offer a wide variety of wood flavors as well as wood types, like sawdust, chips, chunks and planks. Be sure you are ordering from a reputable business. Make sure woods are from safe sources, free of chemicals, pesticides and other unwanted residues. Never add wood of unknown origin to your grill or smoker.

The Most Common Smoking Woods

ALDER: Common in the Pacific Northwest, gives off a delicate smokey flavor that is slightly sweet. Recommended for fish, poultry, pork and vegetables.

APPLE: Preferred for its mild, fruity flavor with a hint of sweetness. Recommended for all smoked foods. Great also as a blend with stronger woods such as hickory and mesquite.

CHERRY: Slightly sweet and fruity, this mellow wood is great for blending with stronger woods. Recommended most for poultry, this wood can be used with all foods.

HICKORY: The most common wood used for smoking, bold and sometimes peppery with a hint of sweetness. Recommended most for pork, chicken and beef, also flavors well with mesquite.

MESQUITE: Perfect for a short time on the grill, strong and tangy. Recommended most for beef, vegetables, pork and poultry, goes well with hickory.

PECAN: Common in the South, pecan is a versatile, mellow smoke flavor. Recommended for all smoked foods. Great also as a blend with stronger woods such as hickory and mesquite.

OAK: One of the most common fuels, oak has a subtle flavor that goes with a variety of foods and lends itself well to blending with stronger smoking woods. Recommended for all smoked foods.

Other Readily Available Flavors

APRICOT: A mild, sweet fruit wood. Recommended for pork and poultry.

BIRCH: Similar to the fruit woods. Recommended for pork and poultry.

LEMON: Stronger smoke flavor, citrus woods pair well with milder woods.

MAPLE: One of the most versatile smoking woods, mild and slightly sweet, flavors can vary in different regions. Recommended for vegetables and all other smoked foods.

NECTARINE & PEACH: Similar to pecan and the fruit woods. Recommended for pork, poultry and beef.

PEAR: Similar to apple, a mild, sweet fruit wood. Recommended for all smoked foods. Great also as a blend with stronger woods such as hickory and mesquite.

In Addition to Wood, Try:

- Corncobs
- Grapevines
- Hazelnut shells
- Coconut husks
- Dried seaweed
- Small amounts of dried or fresh herbs
- Pumpkin seeds in the shell

Of course, every recipe in this book can be prepared without the additional smoke flavors. They will all stand on their own as outstanding dishes. The recommendations of adding smoke simply boosts the recipes to another flavor dimension, one that many grilling fans will want to learn more about.

SMOKE SUGGESTIONS ARE GIVEN FOR ALMOST EVERY RECIPE. USE ONE OF THE SUGGESTED WOODS OR A COMBINATION THEREOF.

Soaking Liquids

Another grilling/smoking debate surfaces, and that is whether or not to soak your chips. After years of experimentation with different wood types and flavors, I believe it comes down to personal preference. There are people who prefer the heavier smoke that may come initially when some woods are soaked and others who find it makes more of a mess than it's worth. Some claim the liquid the chips are smoked in makes all the difference in the meal and some that say you can't detect any changes.

Just like the discussion over types of woods that can be used, I believe that if the cook has success with a certain method, it should not be debated. If the food is good, "the cook is always right!" Unless safe food-handling guidelines are not being met, differences in techniques and methods are a moot point, for it all comes down to personal likes and dislikes in the end product.

When experimenting I have found that woods soaked in wine or whiskey tend to hold a certain flavor, while adding fruit juices does add a touch of added sweetness to the smoke. Beer tends to add a yeasty twang. Even if it is simply adding to the aroma of the smoke, the effort may be worth it. Experiment, have fun, carry out taste tests and enjoy the experience for all it's worth.

Please Note: When grilling, it is always recommended to soak planks prior to cooking. When oven-planking, soaking is recommended but not necessary. Always soak wraps prior to oven or grill use.

Cooking Methods And Temperature Guidelines

HIGH HEAT/QUICK COOK

Be sure to use an instant-read thermometer for meats & fish.

Beef: Rare 140°; medium-rare 150°; medium 160°; well-done 170°

Poultry: White meat 170°; dark meat 180°

Pork: Medium 160°; well-done 170°

Fish: 140°

Keep in mind that food continues to cook even after it is removed from the heat source. It's often wise to pull foods 5° early, leaving the thermometer in to gauge when the food reaches its final temperature.

Low Heat/Slow Cook

Thermometers are not necessarily needed when slow cooking, as internal temperatures will go beyond minimal cook temperatures. They are, however, helpful if striving for a specific technique such as a desired "pulling" temperature or if wanting to reach a target temperature if holding foods for an extended period of time. It's important, though, not to allow slow-cooked foods to dip below 160° without refrigeration. Reheated foods need to reach 160° for food safety, as well.

With so many great choices on the market, thermometers are a "must-have" for grilling.

Grill It!

with more smoke flavor

"SMOKE-GRILLED." These words bring mouthwatering images to mind. Juicy cuts of meat, crunchy, seasonal vegetables and rustic breads top my list of grilled foods. While lounging on the patio, sharing meals with friends and family, is a summer tradition, at our house we grill year-round.

In our food-minded family, we are always on the lookout for simple, flavorful food combinations to make the most of our eating experiences. With many herbs, spices and flavorful ingredients readily available, it's easy to use more than salt and pepper to enhance foods. Using a grill and introducing smoke adds an additional layer of flavor to foods. Equipped with several types of grills and numerous boxes and bags of smoking woods, we have taken everyday foods to a new level.

Grilled food is great on its own, but adding smoke catapults the flavor to a new dimension. Cooking on a grill means so much more than hot dogs and hamburgers. All parts of a meal can be cooked on the grill, from appetizers to veggies, main entrees to desserts. A sample menu may include kebabs and pizza appetizers, a traditional tri-tip thinly sliced with grilled vegetables, topped off with chocolate bananas for dessert.

Having the opportunity to take food preparation outside is a welcome break for the dedicated kitchen cook. When grilling, meals are easier prepared ahead of time, saving meats for the last minute. Additionally, entertaining is pleasant with everyone around the grill, versus congregating in the kitchen. Grilling provides a wholesome, inviting atmosphere, whether it's a group of adults mingling outside with kids and pets frolicking in the backyard, or if it's time spent alone or with a loved one taking in a sunset with the smell of fine food drifting by.

ADDING SMOKE FLAVOR

Although opinions vary on how much smoke can really penetrate a food that is cooked quickly at high grilling temperatures, there is no mistaking that a good *"smoke"* adds an amazing aroma and a special taste to foods. Those T-bones that are cooked in minutes, obviously will not be developing a smoke ring, but they will have an essence about them that cannot be given with anything but smoke.When grilling, many people are not just quickly grilling a few steaks. There may be appetizers, vegetables and even desserts being prepared. If the grill is going to be on for a while, why not add a few smoke packets and get peoples' mouths watering in anticipation of a great meal. It is worth the extra effort to get the smoke rolling any time the grill gets fired up.

With so many ways to add smoke flavor to grilled foods, the flavor combinations and possibilities are endless.

Easy-to-create smoke packets keep sawdust, chips and chunks close to the heat but away from the flame, with easy cleanup.

Flavor combinations are a great way to create individual signature tastes.

Chips come in many sizes and shapes, what you choose comes down to personal preference.

Disposable aluminum containers make great "smoke boxes."

When adding smoke to the grill, sawdust, chips and small chunks need a high heat to begin to smoke. If using charcoal, the wood can be added directly to the coals. If using gas, the wood must be placed in a smoker box (either on the grill or an accessory), or in some type of foil pouch or container and placed as close to the heat source as possible. The key is to get the smoke rolling while the grill is preheating. By the time the smoke is going, the grill is hot.

Chip-Blending Recipes For The Grill:

Enough for one smoke packet and any foods cooked under 30 minutes.

Cowboy Blend: 2 tablespoons mesquite, 1 tablespoon pecan.

Southern Blend: 2 tablespoons hickory, 1 tablespoon pecan.

Eastern Blend: 1 tablespoon each of maple, oak and cherry.

Pacific Northwest Blend: 1 tablespoon each of alder, apple and maple.

West Coast Blend: 1 tablespoon each of apple, cherry and peach.

Tropical Blend: 2 tablespoons oak, 1 tablespoon lemon or orange.

Rugged Blend: 2 tablespoons each of hickory and mesquite.

Mid-America Blend: 2 tablespoons hickory, 1 tablespoon oak or maple.

Grilling Basics

Although grilling is one of the most common ways to cook food throughout the world, the styles of grills are endless. Our family has enjoyed tasty grilled food from converted fifty-gallon drums in Beijing to tiny charcoal brazier curbside vendors in Bali to food from a grill at the county fair that was the size of our kitchen island. The styles and innovations of grills are many, and growing every year.

While someone may favor their Traeger pellet grill for smoke-grilling large cuts of meats, someone else may cling to their hibachi for Korean-style kebabs. My dad would never give up his convenient high-tech gas grill with a built-in thermometer, and I have a friend who frowns on anyone that doesn't start every meal with their charcoal chimney in hand.

Because I enjoy cooking foods with the idea of infusing them with smoke flavors, I have tried numerous types of grills. Truth be told, I enjoy each and every one of them for many reasons. But for most people, to fill the patio with every style of grill is not only aesthetically unpleasant, but it is just not convenient and can be costly.

Grills don't always follow the motto of, *"You get what you pay for."* We have enjoyed some outstanding grilled food on a $15.00 grill from the local drugstore. The important thing was that the cook in charge of the $15.00 grill knew what their grill could do.

The single most important aspect when grilling food is that you must know your grill. Know what it is made to do—be it just grilling, grilling and smoking, or even baking foods at a regulated temperature. You may already have a grill and know what it can do, you know where the hot spots are and how to troubleshoot any problems. But if you have a new grill, or have switched to a different type of grill, get to know it. Read all of the manufacturer's literature that is included with your purchase, and go to their website and check out their tips and recipe suggestions. Even finding a forum that others have contributed to can be quite helpful when starting out with a new grill. Learn what other people do, what tricks they may have, and you will be ahead of the game from the start.

When using a new grill, purchase cheaper cuts of meat; don't go for a leg of lamb or an expensive tenderloin. Try some chicken legs and pork chops first. Experiment with many types of meat from ground beef, thin steaks and chops, to thicker cuts like tri-tip and turkey breasts. Try several types of fish as well. Go easy on the marinades and rubs, initially, to learn the flavors your grill will produce. Then start adding smoke, eventually progressing to marinades and various smoke flavor combinations.

Unless you have a great deal of experience cooking and grilling, invest in an instant-read thermometer. This device takes the guess work out of cooking and reduces the risk of over-grilled, dried-out food. Thermometers are especially helpful with poultry, thick cuts of meat and fish, as well as any stuffed foods. The confidence that food is cooked to a safe temperature adds a lot to any grilling situation, and greatly accentuates the full flavor of the food.

Gas, versus charcoal, is more convenient for many people for various reasons and today almost any style of grill is available for gas, be it propane or natural. Current statistics confirm that the majority of Americans grill over gas.

If choosing to use charcoal, go with a high-quality hardwood, lump charcoal and a charcoal chimney starter. Always give ample time when heating the coals and plan ahead—usually coals need to burn 30 minutes before they are ready to cook on. Avoid using lighter fluid.

Some heated debates exist over cooking with gas versus charcoal versus wood fuel, but again it all comes down to personal preference and convenience. There are some foods you can detect a difference in when comparing gas to charcoal, but what makes a big difference is adding smoke in the form of sawdust, chips, chunks and even planks. Bottom line, any type of grill that has a cover can bathe food in smoke, whereby adding multiple and unique wood flavors.

Grilling Heats

Direct

As you get to know your grill, you'll soon discover it has hot spots, places where heat is distributed more intensely. Cooking over direct heat means placing foods that are to be quickly cooked over a direct heat source. This does not mean placing foods over an open flame. There are no foods that benefit from direct flames unless you prefer your marshmallows black. There are many foods that benefit from a good, hot searing but you want the sear to be on the food and caused by the hot grates, not from burning, fat-fueled flames that may cause strong, undesirable flavors. Searing both sides of the food and then either moving it to a cooler location or simply turning down the grill temperature is one of the most reliable grilling techniques.

Indirect

Foods that do not need a sear, such as a roasted chicken or veggies in a foil pouch, benefit most from indirect heat. This is the area of your grill that puts out less-intense heat than the direct- heat locations. Visually monitoring your food and having a thermometer on-hand will help you learn where the best locations are on your grill for cooking over indirect and direct heat.

Covered

The most common grills have covers, but everyone should understand the purpose of the cover. Throwing some food on the grill, lowering the cover and setting a timer can be disastrous. Just because the grill can be covered does not mean that the food will cook properly without attention.

But if you're desiring smoke flavors to be infused into food, there is no other way than to lower the cover and *"bathe"* food in the smoke. Again, this is where instant-read thermometers will come in handy as there are foods that can be covered and left for a certain amount of time as long as there is an alert to tell you the food has reached its desired temperature. Sometimes it may be just enough time to grab the salads out of the refrigerator, other times the entire table can be set before the main course is completed.

Uncovered & Indoor Grills

Every recipe in this book will work on any form of grill, and each was personally tested on foods without additional smoke flavors. If grilling on an open grill or an indoor grill, simply follow the manufacturer's instructions and make adjustments as necessary, especially if cooking foods that require lower cooking temperatures and longer cooking times.

Grilling Equipment

Shopping for grilling equipment can become addicting and quickly spin out of control. There are many wonderful gadgets on the market, and most with sensible applications. I've tried just about everything from flavor-infused skewers to casserole pans crafted from wood. Though many devices sit in the cupboard, waiting to be used, there are certain tools I can't do without. For organizational purposes, it's a good idea to keep everything in a specific location so when it's time to grill, you're ready to roll. Below are some of the more important items I rely upon on a steady basis:

Tongs: Several sizes, longer for direct-heat grilling, shorter for small items.

Large Spatulas: As oiled as a grill may start out, many foods need the extra help of a

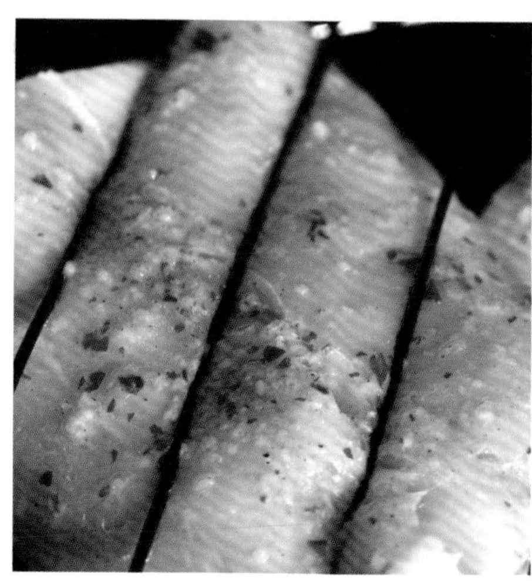

When grilling delicate fish, these baskets assure the fish will not stick to the grill grates.

To keep wooden skewers from burning, protect with a strip of foil.

Baskets come in many sizes and most often non-stick surfaces.

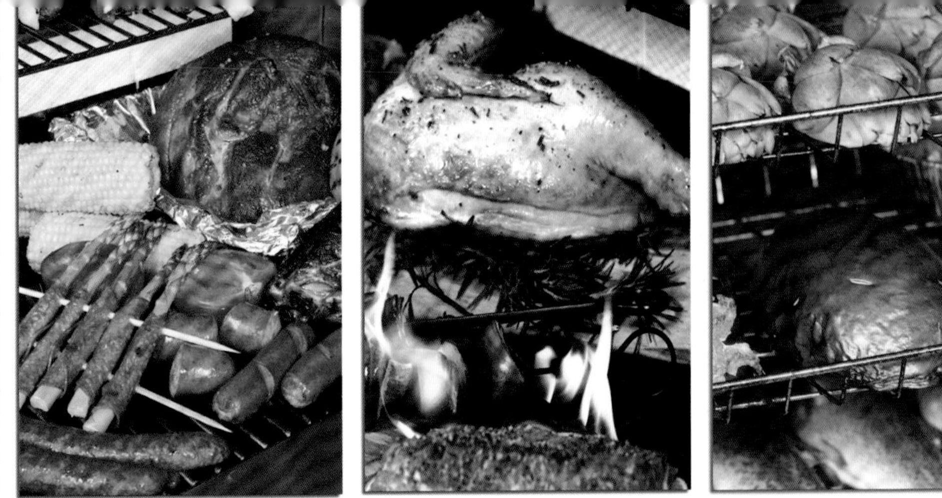

Introduction

The world's interest in cooking food with smoke flavoring is at an all-time, modern-day high. In America, for instance, smoked meats constitute one of the fastest-growing forms of snack food. It was such enthusiasm that spurred the creation of this comprehensive book, whereby capturing the most effective, applicable approaches to preparing foods with more smoke flavor.

Be it on a grill, plank or in a smoker, the act of cooking food with smoke flavoring is simple. In each recipe found within these pages, the goal is to impart easy-to-attain ingredients, with delicious smoke flavor in a practical fashion. Whether smoking meats, seafood, vegetables or appetizers, this book will show how to do just that, in a variety of ways.

Not only are the recipes in this book original, but they underwent extensive testing to reach their final point. However, keep in mind that when cooking with smoke flavor, perfection lies in the taste of the beholder. While one smoke flavor may be admired by one person, it may be considered too strong by another. Thus the need to approach each recipe with an open mind, and a willingness to modify it for the next go around.

If, for example, the hickory wood used was too sharp, try another flavor. At the same time, if the food was bathed in heavy smoke for extended periods whereby overpowering the spices, make necessary adjustments for the next time you attempt the recipe.

Cooking with wood flavorings, no matter which method you choose, is a continual learning curve. Several variables factor into why a food may turn out perfectly to your liking, or not. In either case, note what was done, both right and wrong. Only by practicing patience can the full rewards of cooking with smoke be realized. I've been cooking in this way for most of my life, and am still learning; that's what makes cooking so enjoyable and rewarding.

Creating such a comprehensive, information-packed book was a great pleasure, and I hope you enjoy it half as much as I did putting it together-and as our family and friends did taste-testing every single recipe.

Life goes too fast, don't let the good things pass you by. Good cooking, and God Bless.

Smoke Flavors

Almost as numerous as the spices one can add to food, smoke flavors are many and the added layer of flavor is sure to make every grilling experience that much sweeter. Regardless of where you may be in the world, there is no perfect smoking wood, but there are many good ones.

In the Pacific Northwest the preferred woods tend to be alder and fruit woods, and of course the famous cedar planks. My grandfather never let anything in his smokehouse but vine maple and oak, while my husband's family primarily utilized apple and alder when smoking their salmon.

Contents

Grill It!

Plank It!

Smoke It!

Dedication

To the boys in my life,
Thank you for your love.

Spiral bound ISBN-13: 978-1-57188-416-9
Spiral bound UPC: 0-81127-00250-4
Book Design: Esther Poleo Design
Photography: Tiffany Haugen
Printed in Hong Kong

Published in 2007 by
Frank Amato Publications, Inc.
PO Box 82112 • Portland, Oregon 97282
(503) 653-8108 • www.amatobooks.com

Grill It! Plank It! Wrap It! Smoke It!

Tiffany Haugen